NUMBER

Flora Jennings is a fir
in bookselling and te
combines part-time wo
and lives in London.

To Clare
Much love
Flora x

FLORA JENNINGS

Number One London

HarperCollins*Publishers*

The characters and events in this book are entirely fictional.
No reference to any person, living or dead,
is intended or should be inferred.

HarperCollins*Publishers*
77–85 Fulham Palace Road,
Hammersmith, London w6 8jb

Published by HarperCollins*Publishers* 1999
1 3 5 7 9 8 6 4 2

The Author asserts the moral right to
be identified as the author of this work

A catalogue record for this book is
available from the British Library

ISBN 0 00 651193 7

Set in Sabon by
Rowland Phototypesetting Ltd,
Bury St Edmunds, Suffolk

Printed and bound in Great Britain by
Caledonian International Book Manufacturing Ltd, Glasgow

CHAPTER ONE

✳

Fear wakes me.

Nerves mobilised in my calves. It's today already. Twenty to seven and the room's full of sunshine. Monday morning. Panic. I haven't had time to prepare. It's all happened in such a rush. Hide back under the duvet. Oh, this is ridiculous, and I know I'm being a pathetic scaredy-cat student, but it's my first day at a job in the real world and I'm too nervous to get out of bed.

Don't get me wrong: of course I want the job. I want the job big time. It's a dream job. Boring Philip, my older brother, minder, and manager of an esteemed stationery shop, told me about it only last Thursday, and I've been high on adrenaline ever since. When he rang, though, I was glued to the TV, watching a documentary about sleaze in high places. It was particularly irritating to have to stab the mute button.

'Nancy?'

'Philip. Hello. Again.'

Only call number ninety-nine so far. Ever since I've been in London (ten days) Philip has been ringing non-stop to check up on me. I know he doesn't really give a damn, and it's just that my mouse of a mother has commanded him to keep a close eye on her baby girl while she wanders around looking for trouble in the big smoke, but you'd think I had some kind of death wish the way they treat me.

'Everything OK, Nancy?'

'I survived the night.'

'Don't be rude. Listen. I may have some good news.'

What the fuck is it now? I mean, he took me to the zoo last Sunday, and I'm nineteen years old. With the brain power of a broom, though, that's what you're thinking? Not quite all there? No. Sorry. I'm an undergraduate reading History at university. I've just finished my first year, it's the summer holidays and I've come up to London to share a friend's flat. I don't do drugs or drink to excess and I don't yet walk the streets. Nice girl with a nice life. No flies on me.

I just happen to come from a very dull Surrey family who have a problem with genuine ambition.

'Now, I may have found you a job, Nancy. It's not too exciting, but –'

Don't tell me, Philip. Shelf-stacker in the shop. Or maybe even a till girl. If I'm lucky. Will I get to wear a tabard? My dear big brother (a responsible and mature thirty-five) works in the City. So to speak. His shop, just down the road from Liverpool Street station, is one of a big chain, and it was a proud day for him last year when he was promoted from the measly square footage he had been grimly patrolling in Wimbledon for years. Since then his already insufferably parental tones have gone up a few notches.

'– are you listening? I bumped into this woman I used to know yesterday.'

Woman? Bumping? Steady on, Philip.

'She used to live in Wimbledon, and came in the shop a lot, extremely nice in fact; we got on very well –'

I know that tone. Extremely nice means she was upper class and he licked her arse, scuttled round gathering everything she wanted, offered to order what wasn't in stock, and then produced a satin cushion for her to lay the platinum Amex card on. Dribbling the while. I've seen him at work.

'And we had a bit of a chat –'

2

Oh, get a frigging move on, Philip. She patronised you for a minute and a half. You're boring me.

'– about this company she now runs. A television production company.'

Oh.

All of a sudden, I'm listening. Hard.

'The thing is, their receptionist just walked out. They need a temp to start on Monday.'

So. Yes. It's me. The new receptionist. Television company. Foot in the door. Job of a lifetime. Films. Soho. England's Hollywood. A world I've pranced in fantasy ever since they read out my letter on *Blue Peter*. One day, some way, I would work in television. Any old job would do. Be a part of it somehow. Say no more.

I've refined my career plans since then, though. Now I want to read the news. National, I mean. A reporter first – I suppose it'll be holes in the road in Rutland for a year or so – then abroad, Baluchistan correspondent or whatever. Our voice delivering the truth from the back of beyond. After a few such years of Holiday Inn breakfasts I intend to hop back home and work myself up into that nine-in-the-evening hot seat for which every pinstripe in the country folds aside their fingered copy of *The Times* and adjourns to the television. The voice of authority. I always used to have to be quiet during the news. Mum would be clearing the table and if Philip was there he'd tell me to shut up. If he wasn't, my fascist of a father would say it instead. One day, and it had better be before he grows too blind to recognise his own daughter, I, Nancy Miller, will be reporting live from the inferno, shells whizzing behind me, flak jacket on. My views on the development of the present conflict will be sought by the desk in London and should the line crackle and my words get broken up, they'll wait for me to come through. Occasionally, on spotty days, I toy with the option of remaining behind the camera, where unusually quickly I'll get a name for being in the right place at the right time and, all coy, will have to welcome the esteem of gnarled old pros; but such lapses of self-confidence seldom last, and I always return to the image of myself wearing that suit, with that hairdo, at that desk, received pronunciation crisp even in the face of Welsh place names, professional exterior never once ruffled by scenes of suffering which some viewers may find upsetting.

Anyway. Philip strung out the conversation, refusing to give up the details in a hurry. He wanted thanks. Or, at the least, a spot of enthusiasm; while I was sitting there with the receiver rammed against my ear and my thoughts in turmoil.

Though jubilant at the prospect of the job, wasn't it so typical that I should have to be grateful to Philip? You see, the pattern always is, he tells me what he has to say, and I get it told to me, and the idea is that then I go, thank you, big brother. And, because things get nasty when I don't, I do usually comply. Reluctantly. Eventually; but I always try to make him beg.

'Go on.'

'So I mentioned you, Nancy. You're staying in London. You want a career in TV. You need experience. It's perfect.'

It is. Just a thought, mind: I'm supposed to be going to Greece for a fortnight at the end of August, with my college housemates. It's a plan I've not yet mentioned to Philip, or my worrying mother, but the job won't last till then, surely?

'And, you could start on Monday. I said you were completely available all summer. Although, I suppose it will only go on until they hire someone permanently.'

Silence. Don't want to put him off. Best not to mention the holiday plans now.

'Obviously, to grease the wheels, I said you'd do it for free.'

4

'Philip, hold on a minute. I'm not working unpaid for anyone.'

Liar. I'd have done the job for cold potatoes; but he always rises to my bait.

'Nancy, please don't start. I don't think you quite realise just how difficult –'

Here we go.

' – it is to get a chance like this. You may think you can just walk in there, wow them with your academic results, but you couldn't be more wrong. Thousands, literally, thousands of young people like you apply to these TV places every week, offering to make the tea and buy the biscuits for no wage, desperate to get a foot in the door, just in the hope that one day they'll be noticed.' Philip is creaming his jeans. 'CVs are shredded on a daily basis, trust me.'

How does he know? You'd have thought he was head of MGM.

'Now. Have you got a pen? Here's their number. Write it down before we go any further. Speak politely. It's your phone voice they want, after all. And don't lie about anything. You know it never helps. And don't assume you'll get the job, because I'm sure they'll be seeing lots of other people. Ring them first thing in the morning. OK?'

'OK. Thanks, Philip.'

And that's all you're getting, boy.

'You're welcome. Oh, and, Nancy?'

'Yeah?'

'Don't mention money.'

So I did. Ring them, I mean, not mention money, and the boss, a brusque-sounding woman, offered me the job straight away without even an interview. I stuttered my acceptance. She also mentioned a salary, riches to me, so I graciously accepted that too. On a trial basis, she said, but didn't mention a time limit. There was no indication that they might be looking for a more permanent person.

So there, Philip! That was easy.

There's only the two of us in my family. He didn't get in to college. When I was small I used to wonder who the strange man was who kept coming to our house. You eventually get flashes of insight, though, or have them forced upon you: a friend of mine at school, a monster called Marcia, once explained, within the hearing of several other people, that I was plainly 'a mistake'.

'It's obvious, isn't it? There's fifteen years between you. Your mum had you when she was forty. Now, she wouldn't have planned to get pregnant at that age, would she? It's dangerous, and you might have been mental. So, either you're a mistake, or, even worse, your dad is the milkman. You're lucky you weren't aborted.'

Now the alarm goes off. Seven o'clock. Even though I have been watching the minute hand edge its way to the hour, the noise still shocks me. I slap down the button and blink. Screw it. I must get up. Everything will be fine. It's my career and I'd be robbed if they took it from me now.

Philip is right, though I will never admit it to him. This is my foot in the door. That all-important first job. Contacts: everybody says this is the way to get in to TV. It couldn't have been easier. You see, so far, plans for my future have all been in the head. I've not actually sent out any CVs to prospective employers yet, nor filled in a single application form for courses or training programmes. A couple of my friends at college started that kind of thing as soon as they arrived. Never too early in this day and age, they constantly advise, but I kind of reckoned that I'd join the film club and do a bit of journalism for the college newspaper first and then get round to all that picky stuff in my final year. Now this little baby has landed in my lap, though, I can't help feeling smug. Why sweat over things if luck gets you there quicker?

I have been staying with my friend Sarah in her aunt's plush flat near Gloucester Road underground station.

6

Sarah's a large Sloane Ranger with a velvet Alice band in her hair. She's doing History with me at college. Her aunt, at the last minute, asked her to flat-sit while she 'summered' in the Caribbean from June till October. That's the kind of money we are talking about. Sarah asked me if I'd like to join her, rent free, until next term if I wanted; so I hummed and haa-ed and weighed up the pros and cons, then accepted graciously and moved in an indecent couple of days later.

I lean down to the parquet floor and pick up the crumpled piece of paper on which I've written all the details. The address is in Greek Street. Apparently this is the very heart of Soho itself. Terror in my stomach. The building will be a towering glass palace, set back from the road, transparent lift gliding up and down the outside corner. Countless floors of staff will be visible, urgently huddled over computers that stretch back in rows to the horizon like you see behind the sports news reader on a Saturday afternoon. The director will have an airy office with a panoramic view of the Thames and nervous hirelings will cower in front of her vast desk while she makes or breaks them on her swivel chair. I am particularly impressed it's a she: tall and achieving, with flame-red tresses, my boss will be late thirties, firm but fair, charisma incarnate. The place for me: a forward-looking atmosphere. No doubt I'll be parked behind a vast sloping switchboard bubbling with lights as the calls come in. Oh God. How will I deal with them all at once? Will they teach me how to do it? Or do they think I've done this before? Will I manage?

More to the point, what to wear? Last night I tried on every combination of every item available, was satisfied with none, threw the whole lot on the floor, picked everything up, tweaked off the fluff, folded them, after a fashion, and finally decided to check out the weather before I came to a decision. I also washed my hair, and slept with it wet, so now I'd better check for bed-head in the bathroom mirror. No, it's OK, only a hint of that cleaving of the Red Sea effect which a comb reinforced daily through my childhood. I used to have a shoulder-length bob, side parting, so the first thing I did on reaching college was to get it all cut off. Now it's shortish, with an easy-going fringe and no need for controlling paraphernalia. Colour: sandy brown. Intended effect: laid back; don't want it to be thought that undue effort is being put into hair. Calculated gamine. I take a good look at myself.

How do police in films say 'white girl'? 'Female Caucasian.' That's me. Eyes: blue-grey. Nose: all right; wouldn't have surgery even if I was from California. Ears: standard size, pierced once in the left and twice in the right (lobe, not cartilage). Teeth, all there; cheekbones, slightly freckled; eyebrows, somewhere between chestnut and blonde. Strawberry roan. I was blonde when I was a baby, hamster-cheeked and smiling, no doubt repulsive to all but my mother, the usual thing. Nothing special. Skin: pale, though not unhealthy. Bit of a flat chest, I fear, but Marcia did once assure me it wouldn't 'completely ruin my chances'. Weight: no bag of bones, I do have 'something to hold on to' (dear Marcia), but it's not a thing I worry about. Height: five foot seven. Not bad legs, longish even. Arms and hands my least favourite bit: I want to have those bony limbs that come out of sleeveless shirts with impunity, and wrists round which a watchstrap will oh-so-intellectually hang, and fingers with knobbly knuckles over which rings will easily slide and expensively collect; but I don't. Still, that won't show on screen.

I have ranged several times through the aunt's extensive and expensive wardrobe choices to see if she has some nippy outfit I can slither into, and be thus transformed into a business person, but even if I had fitted them (she is one of those petite women for whom all the best things are designed), they are far too old for me. The woman must

8

be at least forty-five. Sarah has offered me the run of her clothes, but the skirts are big round the hips and the shoulders too wide, so that's out. My own collection is fine for college, but it has never needed to cater for the workplace. On Saturday afternoon I laboured up and down Oxford Street, but couldn't afford anything I liked. Fleeing from the sweaty crowds at closing time, empty-handed and in a bad mood, I resigned myself to making do with my only suit. This is a black and white hound's-tooth number which I wore for my interview to get into college. Although it is a bit heavy, and in this weather I'll definitely be boiling, isn't it more important to be smart than comfortable on day one? First impressions remain with people. Then I can see how everyone else is dressed and adapt accordingly. It'll have to be the suit. And underneath? Oh God.

The truth is, I've never done anything like this before. The college interview was the smartest I've ever been. I've lived all my life in a Surrey town, seldom coming up to London, and I'm at university on the South Coast. How am I going to compare with those polished office women, power-dressing like you see in the glossies? Scratch the page and the perfume lodges under your fingernails. If I go out with my friends, intentional scruffiness could describe our dress code (well, apart from Sarah's). It's funny: when you're young, you assume that adulthood will one day knock at the door and there you will be, ready attired by some magical make-over session. One day I would go to work in London and the ideal outfit would grow on me organically, that's what I always thought. But now the job is today and such a miracle has not taken place.

Under the suit? My white long-sleeved T-shirt at last wins the contest. It does feature an evil hole starting at the right armpit and heading off across my back, but I secure the two edges with a safety pin, and, if the jacket stays on, no one need ever know. Oh, please, weather, get colder. I have opened the curtains now and, of course, out there is a beautiful day. On the legs? I can't have bare skin with this suit, it'll look ridiculous. Also my legs are too white. So, tights, black. Shoes? These I can borrow off Sarah; *nice* flat loafers with a chain across the front, very respectable, not middle-aged at all.

At eight thirty exactly I shut the flat door behind me and head for the underground, as dressed and brushed and washed and lotioned and painted as possible. I have given myself an hour to get from Gloucester Road to Leicester Square on the Piccadilly Line, and thus find myself back in the light of day only thirteen minutes after leaving it. I didn't realise it was such a speedy route. Shall I go home again? No, what for? After buying a newspaper from a stall by the station exit and walking up the road a bit, I enter a coffee bar whose chrome frontage gleams ahead of me. One cappuccino and a disappointing croissant filled with a slimy cheese glob later, which attaches dough flakes to my lipstick, and necessitates a hurried check-up in the ladies, I can delay no longer. Roller coasters are crashing against my stomach walls, and I am possessed of a low fear.

CHAPTER TWO

The next half-hour is truly surreal. At twenty past nine I am definitely in Greek Street, and in front of what claims to be the right number. It's a tall building painted matt black, squashed thin by its neighbours, with a dusty metal door on which 'Fuck you all!' has been freshly fingered in the grime. Surely this can't be right; but there's a rectangular panel screwed into the wall with buttons next to several company names, and 'Toolis Television (UK)' is, without a doubt, written in Biro capital letters on a peeling white sticker by the top one. They only have a single floor? Oh well. I look round, dig into my bag, dart the hairbrush at where my parting will be thinking I haven't noticed its resurgence, inhale stoutly, and press the buzzer. Nothing happens. The door stays shut. I press again, and lean for a few seconds, but still nothing. It's twenty-nine minutes past now. I mustn't be late. Beneath the list of names there is a single larger unmarked button, so I give this a try, and immediately the door *ddzz-es* smartly, belching forward a couple of inches. I haul it to me and step over the threshold.

I'm in the dark. Inside is even blacker than outside, partly because it is painted black, and partly because the only natural light comes from the open door. When it shuts behind me I am left with the flickering of a yellow tube on the ceiling. Is this modern London décor? The down-a-coalmine look? A withered old man, looking just this side of death in the gloom, is sitting inside a sentry booth of reception reading a tabloid newspaper. Drawn face, greyish skin tinged blue by some surely terminal condition, he breathes with a wheezy rattle. I turn away. We are in a narrow hallway, and the only picture on the wall is a clip frame from which a mouldy Fire Emergency Procedure poster lurches out of one loose corner, dated ten years ago in just-readable ink. There's a smell of cigarette smoke, but I can't tell where it's coming from.

'Erm, I'm going to Toolis TV.'

'Right-oh, love, all the way up. There's a lift, or else you can climb upstairs with those nice legs of yours.'

Tightening all my sphincters, I neglect to thank him. He lifts and folds his paper, revealing page three, and I flee towards the stairs in a rush, jumping up two steps at a time until I have turned the corner. Even though I slow down after my initial escape from the death's-head moth on the desk, sweat is sealing the T-shirt to my skin by the time I reach the top floor. I'm gasping. It's nine thirty-three. There is a dark doorway ahead, a shiny plastic plaque on it with a design of the globe in white on black and 'Toolis Television (UK)' strapped horizontally over it, and yet another buzzer button on the wall. I push this, then lean down, both to catch my breath and to hoist up my tights, whose crotch, I now notice, is spanned taut across at mid-thigh level. Yanking them upwards a bit too sharply, I watch, stupid, as four ladders waste no time in shooting down to my knees. Shit.

'While you're down there . . .'

What? The door has opened silently and I straighten up in alarm to face a man whose features, on that first viewing, I can only describe as the opposite of sculpted. His face wobbles and his eyes blink as he takes me in. I am not sure if that is a smile or not. I'm not sure I like it.

'Hello.'

'Oh, hello. I'm Nancy, your new receptionist.'

With ladders in her tights.

'Hi! I'm Alastair.'

Deep voice; and I am offered a palm that is reassuringly dry. Yet, though his greeting is cheerful enough, he doesn't look so fresh; almost as if he has spent the night here. Medium height, in his late twenties, I guess, he wears new-ish jeans (is that a crease ironed down the front?) and a tartan shirt open at the neck from which a growth of dark chest hair sprouts. The hair on his head is receding fast and has been cut very short to disguise the fact, while his jaw, on which I can almost hear the stubble growing, is doing its best to compensate. Blue-black bristles advance as far north as his cheekbones, on a halloween pumpkin face: yellowish, with brown eyes and a big mouth from which the smell of last night's drinking heads straight up my nose. Overall, not attractive.

'Come on in. No one else has made it yet. They wander along at about ten or eleven, lazy bastards. All right for some, eh?'

When did he last wander out, more to the point?

'What? Oh, yes.'

'Would you like a coffee?'

'Sure. Thanks.'

'Right-oh.'

So, here I am. I lower my bag to the floor and look around. Oh. Hardly the multistorey palace of my dreams. I am in the corner of a small stuffy room, longer than it is wide, that reminds me of a classroom. Alastair has disappeared through a door leading off to my right. Big windows run along the length of one wall, but, as in a classroom, they are too high to look out of. Several wooden desks are no doubt meaningfully arranged. Two of these catch my attention. The first stands at the back of the room, front to the wall and chair behind it, facing me. It is a big old proper polished dark brown desk, heaped high with books and papers, and, because it is standing on some kind of elevated platform, like a teacher's desk, it commands a superior outlook across all it surveys. Directly in its line of vision opposite, positioned so that whoever sits there will be under the scrutiny of the teacher, is another desk on my right. This one is long but low, with only a few items ordered neatly upon it, and an impressive red leather tall-backed chair waiting behind. Between these two, half a dozen other desks are placed at varying angles in the middle of the room; computers stand on three of them, and files and letters and magazines and coffee mugs wait untidy all around. This is no empire of glass.

'Milk and sugar?' Alastair's egg head.

'Both, please.'

Now he is reversing precariously out of the door with a cup in each hand.

'Here you are.'

It's one of those Styrofoam things that fat New York police wave round the corpses of mutilated prostitutes. Alastair has filled it only just above the halfway level, and it's much darker than I like. The first hasty sip burns the end of my tongue, but, despite being thus robbed of most of my taste buds, I can still tell it's a vile cup of coffee.

'Thanks.'

'That's OK. This is where you'll be, by the way.'

Waving his arm unsteadily at the front desk, Alastair knocks the lonely pot plant standing there. We both watch it jump out of its plastic container, dry earth particles clinging in fear to the roots, and bounce onto the floor.

'Your predecessor. She wasn't big on watering.'

'What happened to her?'

'Oh, God knows. Went cuckoo. Upped and off last week, back to Mars or wherever she was from. Didn't really explain what the problem was, though. Maybe a visa or work permit thing? Mind you, she always was a bit odd.'

Smiling, a wide tooth-filled grimace, the tension in his mouth stretches an unidentified white residue gripping to the corner of his lips. He is stamping soil into the liver-coloured hairy carpet tiles.

'It'll never show.'

The phone on my desk starts to ring. I look at it. He looks at me and it. I look at him. He picks it up.

'Greg. Where the hell are you? Hang on. Terrible, actually. And yourself?'

Placing down the receiver Alastair retires to another extension where, after swinging his legs onto the desk, he continues the conversation. I pick up my goblet of venom and go to investigate the other room. It's a tiny kitchen occupied so comprehensively with industrial cleaning equipment that less than a square yard is available in which to tread. A percolator is marooned in a pool of water on the sideboard by the sink. I pour away my coffee, but it can't drain because a slimy skein of tissue paper is blocking the plug hole. A microwave oven, its door bearing the evidence of many a baked potato explosion, rests four stumpy feet in a puddle on the easy-wipe surface. Chipped and dirty china mugs with company names on mooch about, while disposable cups are floating on their sides. A box of sugar lumps is being infiltrated from below by brown water. I notice a fawn and chocolate kettle and see that the end of its flex is also partly submerged, so I give it a shake and a pointless dab with a crusty old towel before plugging the connection back in. God, health and safety standards are round about our ankles here! A dry growl issues from the kettle, so I halt the process and attempt to add some water, whereupon the tap blasts forth such a high-speed jet that only about a tenth enters the kettle, leaving the rest to drench most of the front of my jacket. Which I can't take off, because my T-shirt has a hole in. Shit. It's nine forty-four. I haven't been here fifteen minutes.

Back in the main office Alastair is off the phone. His head is now in his hands. From here I can see the baldness is extensive. Maybe he is older than I thought. He looks up. The grey beneath his eyes contrasts with the green pallor of his cheeks. He's giving me an odd look. I fold my arms across the jacket.

'What a night I had. Girls, girls, girls. Can't live with 'em, can't live without 'em. You're not in the market for a new boyfriend, are you? I'm clean.'

Bloody hell! Dream on, slaphead. And cut the tragic Don Juan routine. I suppose he fancies himself a fast mover. Ever heard of foreplay, Alastair? Imagine snogging those slack lips. Saliva all over the shop.

'No thanks.'

'Just let me know.'

I promise, and settle down at my new workplace. Great chair; more like a throne. It whirls to left or right if I only slightly lean in either direction. I'll have to be careful I don't end up spinning round and round all day in an indecipherable blur. Alastair is watching me with something between a leer and a grin, so I work hard to avoid his eye. Hasn't he got anything better to do? He must fancy me. I can do without this. He's so blatant, it's embarrassing. I inspect the desk.

Squatting, like a dopey toad, plum in the centre, is a fat little tear-off calendar, bearing a motto for every day of the year. The top page shows Friday, 12 July, so I rip off the weekend to reveal today's words of wisdom: *Remember that the waste-paper basket is your truest friend*. I'll bear that in mind. A vertically tubed pen holder sprouts a bushel of new Biros, lids still on, as well as sharpened pencils, while a telephone message book is positioned anally parallel to the edge of the desk. The shiny black phone, far from being the awesome console with which I had battled in my worst-case scenarios, is only slightly larger than a normal one. It does feature a measle rash of alien buttons above the normal digits, which do look a bit complicated, but overall I think I can relax about this aspect of the job. One of the measles lights up red. Alastair has the receiver from his desk gripped between a shoulder and an ear, and he is now dialling, painfully slowly, stabbing number after number as he reads them off the back of a tube ticket.

I don't want to reveal that I'm listening, so I get up for a walkabout. My chair bounces as I leave it, swinging round of its own accord.

'Juliet? It's Alastair. We met last night in that bar? You remember?'

She plainly can't. I think I'll make another coffee in the windowless kitchen. While I'm waiting I check out the two mean little lavatory doors opposite me, barricaded behind a looped trachea of Hoover piping: one has a scratched metallic cutout of James Dean glued on, the other Marilyn Monroe. I peer into the latter: minute, the door missing the off-kilter seat by less than an inch, it has no window either. Isn't that illegal? Diarrhoea will be a problem.

Taking my coffee, milky with half a sugar, I escape into the light of the office. Alastair, amazingly, still seems to have Juliet on the line. Immediately to my right, base level with my crotch and rising to chin level, is a metal mesh case divided into open-fronted message compartments. A named label is attached to each of these. Top row, from left: Accounts; Reception; Miscellaneous. Aha, I am Reception now. Will anyone write to me? Second row: Lesley Sharpe, Production Manager; middle one empty; then, Alastair Kent, Research. Not in charge, then? He acts like he owns the place. Bottom row: Heather Toolis, Managing Director, Director/Producer. She was the woman who offered me the job. Next, an empty one, then, Stella Fitzpatrick, Executive Development Director. She's Philip's friend who mentioned it in the first place. None of the boxes has anything in it apart from Stella Fitzpatrick's. This is full to the top with letters, a stuffing-leaking parcel and a many-paged fax.

Turning away, I travel down the window side of the room. Beneath the high sills a continuous length of iron shelving runs along the wall. Painted matt Nazi grey, and in places bent out of shape either by its current burden or some previous abuse, this detail is particularly reminiscent of a classroom. Maybe the whole place was a school once, and where I stand the science lab, hence the acid-scarred and child-proof metal fittings, damage resistance the top priority. Strained and bulging lever-arch file cases, all colours, identified in felt pen by such incomprehensible titles as *Intensive Care Patients – Expenses*, *Terminal Friends – Finance and Budget*, and *The Dead – Release Forms* are rammed in all the way along. I can see I am going to have to learn this TV jargon. On the top row there's a collection of several hundred different-sized video tapes, and, of these, the largest one's label catches my attention: *Death – the Master*.

What shall I do now? Is anyone else ever going to turn up? Alastair is still talking to Juliet. She must be desperate. Not so desperate as to let him spend the night, though. I bet he did sleep here. The phone starts to ring. Oh, no. Oh, help. I'll have to answer it. The big desk at the back is now nearest to me, so I lean over.

'Hello?'

'Oh, hello, is that Toolis TV?' A high-pitched Scottish voice.

'Yes.'

'Could I speak to Billie, the lady on reception, please?'

'Yes, I mean no, you can't, she left.'

'She left? I only spoke to her last week.'

'Well, she's gone.'

'Oh, that is inconvenient. Tell me, is anyone standing in for her, do you know? Sorry, may I ask who I'm speaking to?'

'It's Nancy. I'm on reception now.'

'Are you now? What a lovely name. My granny's name. I was only round at hers yesterday saying how much I liked it! So, that'll make you the Stationery Monitor, won't it?'

18

It would?

'I don't know about that. I think you'd better ring later.'

'No, no. It'll be you. For sure. Don't worry, though. Listen, Nancy, oh dear! Let me introduce myself. It's Derek, Derek Sinclair from –' what sounds like – 'Select-A-Pencil. We're *the* premium stationery outfit in the Southeast. Billie booked me in today to preview my full autumn range, at, let me see, midday. Now, I'm going to be a bit late, in fact it will be more like two, so I'll see you then, OK?'

Is this a question? Should I say yes? Could I say no? I'm not sure I'm up to previewing anyone's autumn range on day one. As I stall, my attention is handily diverted by Alastair, who has put down the phone and fast approaches. Taking a step up to the wooden platform, he is dangerously near.

'She blew me out! We'd been getting on so well. I can't believe it. Said she was going away for a while. Do you think she's telling the truth? There's nothing wrong with me, is there? Tell me honestly. You're not repelled by me, are you?' He's speaking slowly, slurred like a broken recorder. Moving closer. 'I know how to satisfy a woman –'

'Get away from me!' I push his shoulder hard.

Derek squeaks inside the receiver. 'What was that, Nancy? Shall I take it as a yes?'

Alastair's body doesn't resist my hand at all. I can see his energy sap.

'Sorry, Derek?'

'This afternoon, two o'clock, I'll see you then?'

Alastair isn't trying to save himself. Time creeps to a standstill as he begins to topple backwards off the step. In simultaneous disbelief and with an entirely incongruous remnant of good manners, I avert my eyes to the clock on the wall above him. Five past ten. Back to Alastair, who still isn't stopping himself. If anything, his body is relaxing in mid-air.

'Oh, my God. Yes. fine. Bye.'

Clattering the phone down, I can't move. All I can do is watch in horror. There's grace in his movement as Alastair collapses onto the floor, ever so stylishly, in that considerate slow-motion manner that dispensable Germans or diminutive Vietcong do so beautifully in war films. Meeting the carpet tiles tenderly, his head rolls, eyes shut, in my direction.

Holy fuck! Is the man dead? He can't be. He might be. I've killed someone? Already? Not on my first day. Please. It's not possible. Alone in here with a dead body. Emergency services, paramedics zipping up the body bag, police taking notes, cups of tea, statement, arrest, more tea, confession under pressure. Toolis TV will be strung round with yellow tape and my career will be up in smoke. Life imprisonment, and by that, young lady, I mean life. Such injustice in a man's world: sexually harassed, I did it in self-defence, my lord. I will be a feminist martyr.

Oh, stop it. He can't be dead. I see no seepage of blood from his matted hair (not enough hair), nor tell-tale runnel tipping from one deceased nostril. Moving closer, I crouch down. No sign of life. Eyes closed. Has he cracked his skull or something? Oh, this is not happening. This is not what I had in mind. Bloody man! Bloody fifth-rate little place! What am I supposed to do? I don't want to have to give him the kiss of life. I don't know how to. I cannot go near those lips. Oh, help. I can't let him die. Or maybe I can? Or is that criminal negligence? They'd find out. You did nothing? What, absolutely nothing? I don't have time to think about this. I have to act fast, or it'll be too late. What do I do? Pinch the nose? Oh, why didn't I take First Aid at school instead of elocution?

Very, very reluctantly, I kneel by Alastair's face. The carpet bristles scrunch beneath my knees. In very close. I can count the hairs piercing the pastel-green slime in his nostrils. Those lips are mere centimetres away. There's nothing for it. Swearing that if we were alone on a desert island I'd leave him to his self-inflicted fate, I take hold of Alastair's nose with my left index finger and thumb, then move in my mouth. Immediately my grip slips on the grease from his pores, a thumbnail slices his cheek, and I start back as shock catapults his mouth open – black fillings in all the molars – to release a noxious gas ball burp of nothing more life-threatening than the fumes of wine in the morning.

Alastair blinks.

'Nancy! You're a bit fresh, aren't you?'

This *cannot* be happening to me. Arrested, I'm still leaning over him, mouth slack with revulsion, and we just about hear the sound of keys being forced into the door.

'Oh fuck,' says Alastair, feeling his cheek, grimacing at the blood on his fingers, and reaching for a desk leg with which to pull himself up. 'It's Toolis.'

Heather Toolis? My new boss? Where? Alastair and I struggle up in a discreet hurry. Shit. What will she think of me, already on the floor with the researcher? Fucking typical. Could the day possibly have started more badly? Alastair slides sideways into the nearest seat. I stand, brushing my suit, and prepare for the worst. Where is the woman?

Alastair breaks the silence. 'Morning, Heather.'

A sharp movement down by the message box. I lower my line of vision. Now, when I spoke to her on the phone, this woman had a tall voice. Well dressed. Big hair. Meaning business. A mover. A shaker. A definite career maker.

No such person eyes me now.

'You must be Nanette.'

'Nancy.'

'I see you two have introduced yourselves. Good morning, Alastair.'

Heather Toolis. Small. No, tiny. A molecule of humanity. Not quite a midget, but the next level up. I don't think she can be much over four foot. In one hand she is adjusting a pair of plain black-framed NHS glasses so as to get my proper measure, while in the other she grasps the fax to Stella Fitzpatrick. She has tiny little pale hands, not young any more, with unvarnished child-size fingernails cut short. I have never seen such a tidy woman. She has demonic hair; pitch-black, or as black as Anglo-Saxons can get it without chemical assistance, it's cut in one of those perfect bobs that fall so neatly they more resemble crash helmets than a hairstyle. A tidy face with scrunched little features. The line of her mouth in an arch curved downwards. Wearing a navy collarless, buttonless, creaseless jacket over a no-necked and shiny midnight-blue blouse, I reckon she must be weasel-thin underneath. The knee-length confines of her dark tubular skirt eject spindly legs in navy gauze tights and the diminutive feet at the end of them are shod in black tap dancing shoes. A compact little Parisian pug dog.

'Right then, Nanette. Sit down. Time for a few office rules.'

She doesn't hang around. I pull the nearest chair towards me.

'No, no, no. Sit at reception, by the phone. You'll be no use to us away from it, I can tell you!'

Toolis lifts the seat that I vacate and marches it next to mine. It's bigger than she is. Now she is far too close to me, and I don't like it. I can smell her shampoo. Medicated? There's no dandruff on that blue scalp. She swoops upon a Biro and begins to pen bullet spots on a piece of paper from the bin.

'All the negatives first. No outgoing personal calls, and I mean never. The OPC, a dirty word round here. As for an IPC, incoming, well, if someone calls you, get them off the line immediately. In fact, I would be grateful if you didn't hand out your number here to anybody. We are an extremely busy company and must not damage our considerable reputation through an inability to maintain a first-rate reception service. Is that clear?'

'Yes. Of course.'

What did the last receptionist do to this company? Run her own mail-order business?

'Next. Sniffing. Weeping. Uncontrolled sobbing. If you want to fight with your parents or split up with your boyfriend or have a nervous breakdown could you please, oh please, do it at home? Not during office hours? On my money? Please?'

A strangled tone, but she needn't worry. There'll be no tears on the telephone with me.

'Of course.'

'Also. Eating at the desk. Reading magazines at the desk. Putting on make-up at the desk. Brushing your hair at the desk. Filing your nails at the desk. Items of personal medication on the desk. These are now entirely forbidden. No smoking in the office at all. And last, but by no means least, slamming the photocopier lid. As of today that is a sackable offence. That photocopier is an expensive machine and if we treat it well it'll last for many more years!'

She shouts out this last sentence. Alastair's head jolts upright from a snooze and, wearily, he stands up.

'Erm, Heather?'

The phone rings. Damn.

Toolis waves an indifferent claw in Alastair's direction and nods expectantly at me. Oh, no. Not straight in at the deep end. Please no.

'Hello?'

Toolis rolls her eyes to the ceiling.

'Nan! Hi!'

It's flatmate Sarah. Bugger. Probably wasting her mobile battery in some King's Road shoe shop. She must be got rid of. This is, after all, an IPC. I lower my voice, even though Toolis is less than a foot away.

'Oh, hi. Listen, Sarah –'

'You'll never guess who just called. Loverboy. He wants to stay tonight. I said that was OK, but I gave him your number at work. How's it going, by the way?'

Toolis is tapping her fingers on the desk.

'Look, I can't talk now.'

'Oh, tricky moment, sorry. I'll let you go, you high-powered media tart you.'

'Bye.'

I cut her off.

'Sorry, that was my flatmate. I had to give her the number, really.'

'Well. Even if that hadn't been your first and, I sincerely hope, last personal call of the day, your handling of it was quite wrong. Quite wrong. I'll tell you why in a moment.'

'Heather?'

Alastair is trying again. I am sweating.

'Yes, Alastair?'

'Erm, I was thinking, it might be an idea to put in a day's reading at home, erm, you know. I need to really concentrate on all this, erm, background material.'

I have never seen anyone take such a literally dim view of a suggestion as Toolis does now. She adjusts her glasses at him as she replies: 'Very well then. We'll have a breakfast meeting here tomorrow, at eight, and you can update me.'

Alastair must be amused, for he smiles, insincerely wide, gappy teeth on show, and only just gets his hand to his mouth in time to catch another burp. How disgusting. I can't look. Heather ignores him.

'Right. Let's get on. There are two – how shall I call them? – untouchables at Toolis Television. We never, ever want to see them cross this doorstep again. Understand? The first is a grimy little outfit called Miss Moppy Cleaners, who I am due to meet in the small claims court in six weeks' time. The other is a lying sales rep from one of

those office stationery companies, Choose My Ruler or
something – what's he called now?'

The waves are sloshing in my stomach again. I know
what his name will be: but I wait for her to speak.

'Derek somebody, I think.'

I knew it. He's coming in this afternoon. How can I stop
him?

'Now, what next? Concentrate, please. You must always
let the phone ring at least twice – we don't want to seem
desperate – but never more than four times, as that says
incompetence, and incompetence is not something I ever
want said here!'

Calm down, ducky.

'We have a company greeting. If there's another thing I
never want to hear in this office, it's "Hello". Think about
it. You ring a company and someone says "Hello". How
do you know that you've got the right number, that you've
not called a private home, that you've not got some semi-
conscious drug addict out of bed? And if, which is rare, a
commissioning editor rings in person –'

What's a commissioning editor?

'– and hears that miserable word, what will they think?
Oh, a couple of mistakes like that, and you can lose us a
commission. I'm not joking.'

Don't worry, Toolis. I'm not laughing.

'So. Follow after me: Good morning, Toolis Television
(not TV, mind you, that's too downmarket); so, Good
morning, Toolis Television UK, Nanette speaking, how
may I help you?'

She's almost singing. Am I hearing right? What a ridiculous bloody mouthful! I'll never remember it. Does she
want me to practise right now? I'll sound like a shop girl!
Alastair will laugh at me. He's wearily loading documents
the width of at least three phone directories into a plastic
bag. Perhaps he's too hungover to listen. If only the phone

would actually ring, then I can say it all for real and it won't feel so stupid.

It rings. How bizarre. Toolis looks excitedly at me.

'Right then. Company greeting, remember?'

Funny thing is, I don't. I've forgotten even what the company is called. Old habits die hard and out it comes: 'Hello?'

Toolis gasps.

'Oh God, sorry, erm, Nancy here, who's that?'

Toolis covers her eyes.

'Is that Toolis Television?'

Officer tones, sound as a bell. Someone important. It's a commissioning editor. I know it. That's it, then. I haven't even made it to mid-morning.

'Yes, yes, yes, it is.'

Fool. I should have told him it was a wrong number. My every word till now has shrieked incompetence.

'Splendid. And you're new, are you?'

'Yes, sorry, I am.'

'For goodness' sake, don't apologise. Welcome to the company. It's Jerome here, Dr Jerome, and I'm the company physician, so let me tell you a bit about myself, a few personal details. Do you want to know what really gets me going, or hots me up, should I say, first thing in the morning?'

Eh?

'I'm sorry?'

'You must help me along. Put your hand inside your shirt, slowly at first, that's right, under the bra strap, if you wear one?'

My hand is already moving upwards before I click. Jesus. I cut him off dead. Toolis puts her head in her hands.

'Who was that?' Alastair is by the desk now, and has seen my expression.

'Some weird doctor. Jerome?'

Alastair is delighted. 'Aaah! He's not called for weeks!

What did the old pervert ask you to do? Tell me. Go on, shock us all.'

He's drooling. Toolis sighs pertly, but I get the impression she doesn't mind.

'Alastair, please. Nanette is busy. See you in the morning at eight sharp.'

My hopes for even a thimble of sympathy from Toolis are quite misplaced; she's clearly relieved it was only a dirty old man. Her lecture hurries straight on after Alastair's exit.

'That call illustrated the importance of my next point. What does this say?' She is pointing to a well-worn word written by one of the phone buttons.

'Hold.'

'Exactly. You will soon realise that the hold button is the most vital tool in your job. A receptionist without her hold button is naked.'

I've already been undressed over the phone. Am I now to be stripped?

'If, if you had proceeded as I had asked you to, and found out who that man wished to speak to, you could have avoided any trouble. Got his name, and put him on hold. And left him there for ever if you wanted. That way, we decide what to do with him and not vice versa. It's all about control. You're in charge.'

Right. Very likely.

There is no time to reflect before the next command is upon me. I am to supply Caller with any of a wide range of replies. If, after that compulsory period in the limbo of Hold, communication is to be permitted, then a simple but friendly 'Putting you through' will suffice. If Caller is not to be allowed such access, then, according to the degree of reluctance to speak to Caller, and, clearly, with honesty not an option, I am to choose from a variety of filthy dirty lies: 'I'm afraid all lines to that floor are currently engaged'; or, 'You won't believe it, but she only yesterday left for a fortnight in Papua New Guinea'; or, a rare treat not to be used lightly, 'I am sorry, but she's in a meeting till the end of time.'

'And last, Nanette, but so very much not least, the biggest of them all.' Toolis pauses for effect.

My name is not bloody Nanette!

'What do you think we are trying to sell here?'

Eh? You've got me there, short-arse. I shake my head. Toolis tuts, darts an exasperated look full in my eyes, and launching herself towards me, grips the edge of the desk with tiny knuckles taut.

'Success! Isn't it? It's an atmosphere that you are selling, yes? Yes. So, I want bubbly. As before, you ring a company. They tell you who they are, but they say it so drearily, their lack of interest is so obvious, that you wish to have nothing to do with them. I would be appalled, quite appalled, to have that happen here.'

Oh, would you now? Toolis' orders are rattling to left and right like rounds from a machine gun. Sound vibrant and happening. Callers must have a picture in their minds' eyes of a buzzing and productive office, peopled by hip, industrious, talented individuals. Who are not, however, too run off their feet to help them. The caller must always come first, like the customer in a shop; must be my absolute priority though the lifeblood drains from me. Their worries, my worries. They are my bread and butter.

'You see, what we seem to be, Nanette, that's what we are to them. How are they going to know any better?'

So, such is the world of work. Play-acting. At some point during my training I am conscious of a new person bursting into the room. Though my attention is on loan to Toolis I do get a brief impression: a long-haired brunette in brown jeans, hauling a couple of metal equipment cases, plus a bloom of carrier bags and a rucksack looking so heavy it could be filled with bricks. Training for the SAS, perhaps? She huffs and puffs her way to a desk and then, instead of taking a rest once she has set down her cargo, immediately starts to undo the rucksack. No greeting is issued to either of us, but Toolis speaks.

'Good morning, Lesley. How did it all go?'

From the back of her head, bent over the unpacking: 'Well, we finished at six this morning and I headed straight here, but the traffic was unbelievable, and then Ken wanted to be dropped off at Luton, and I had to avoid the North Circular because it brought back Ron's memories of the crash, so it's taken me this long to get here, and I don't know how I'm still awake, I haven't been home since Thursday.'

Lesley? The Production Manager? Whatever that is.

'Well, take a morning off next month when it all calms down.'

'Thanks, Heather, but I won't have the time. Don't worry about it.'

The phone rings. Toolis gives me a nervous but, sort of, encouraging look.

I put my heart into the job and trill a welcome: '*Good* morning, Toolis Television UK, Nancy speaking, how may I help *you*?'

'Christ, are you for real? What happened to Billie? I was getting used to her suicidal tones. Still, no time to waste. Is Lesley there?'

'Yes, hang on.'

'No, no, just tell her it's Dave, and if she doesn't get that camera here by yesterday I'll have to charge her. Bye now.'

I give the message to Lesley's mane. She whimpers and a loud sneeze erupts, initiating a train of such explosions. After blowing her nose with a muffled snort she pushes away the hair that has fallen over her face, and in so doing I notice she leaves a strand of snot coiled on the crown of her head. Only seconds later she has shuffled across the room like a refugee, metal cases bending her spine forward

29

into an arch, and the door has slammed behind her. Toolis jumps down from her chair.

'Honestly. She makes such heavy weather of everything. Anyway. I'll leave you to answer the phone now. You get the hang of it, don't you?'

Nothing happens for about twenty minutes. Toolis trots off to the big desk at the back. All I can see is the top of her head. The phone stays quiet. This is not what I would call a busy switchboard. Lesley returns, minus the cases, and smelling of cigarettes. Maybe there'll be some action now; but all she does is pick up the phone straight away and, in between more sneezing, describes to several different companies how their product or hire equipment or personnel have conspired to make filming at the weekend go about as badly as is physically possible. Refund demands are shooting thick and fast and I am wondering whether I should let her know that I am Nancy, by the way, when she looks up – well, manoeuvres that hair sideways – and actually speaks to me.

'What's your name?'

'Nancy.'

'Make me a tea then, Nancy. No milk or sugar. And a black coffee for Heather.'

It's getting hot. I'm sticking to the chair. Having to keep this jacket on is quite some trial. Phone not ringing. The saga of Derek the stationery man comes back to me with an unpleasant jolt. Can I ring to put him off? Do I have his number? No. Is there a Yellow Pages round here? No. Billie must have had an address book. I've not rifled in the desk drawers yet. In I go. The right-hand one is full of stationery: serious marker pens with indelible ink, some over an inch wide, arrayed in a row like bodies after a disaster. Back-up supplies of vital reception-ware are ordered neatly: two elastic-banded bundles of virgin pencils; stainless-steel staples, one box; a compass, spike in my direction; also a calculator and three transparent rulers. The metallic smell of sharpenings, of school. No address book. I try the other drawer. An empty paracetamol bottle and a flattened box of plasters containing, let me see, only those odd-shaped ones for inconvenient toe wounds. Aha; there are books in here, at the back, spines upward. Yes, an address book. I pull it out, and the volume next to it flops sideways: *An A–Z of Women's Health*. Billie's? No, Hendon Library's. Its binding is cracked and the page falls open on P for Pregnancy, slightly greasy pages showing a diagram of the womb expanding through Figs 1–9. Was Billie pregnant? Did the patter of tiny feet hasten her departure? No wonder answering the phone in a happening way wasn't her first priority.

Phone rings. Sounds louder than usual. Oh no, two lights are flashing. I assume Lesley or Toolis will get one line if I answer the other. In this I am quite wrong: both their heads are bowed low, and neither makes any move. Clearly they *would* like me to drown in the deep end. Here we go then.

'Good morning, Toolis Television UK, Nancy speaking, how may I help you?'

'Oh, hello, dear, I was given your number by the operator –' it's an old lady's voice – 'and I thought I'd give you a call, just for a chat really – well, no, I mean it is about your films, so, yes –'

Line two is still blurting furiously.

'– now, a friend of mine, she lives in Cornwall actually, near Truro it is, do you know the area?'

Oh, hurry up, woman. I mustn't be rude, though. She is my bread and butter.

'No. Never been.'

'Anyway, she sent me a video of one of your programmes –'

'I'm sorry, can I put you on hold one second?'

'Oh yes, dear. I've got all day.'

So I'd noticed. On hold she goes. Now for line two.

'Hello, Toolis Television?'

Shit. Hello. The forbidden word.

'Lesley, please. It's Laetitia.'

She sounds tough. I tell Lesley.

'Urgh! Get rid of her. She's from programme finance. I can't possibly speak to her. I'm on the other line. No, I'm out. Oh, anything. I'll get back to her later. Oh, make something up.'

What? And who should I refer Grandma to? Oh, screw her. Laetitia first.

'Erm, hello again, I'm afraid Lesley's not available at the moment. She's, erm, out, I mean away, this whole week.'

Lesley's expression says I could not have answered worse.

'What's that, love? The video, yes, well, she sent it to me over a year ago, I must say, but I've always been meaning to call, because –'

Bugger it, wrong line. Will the crone be able to tell if I put her on hold again? I'll risk it.

'Laetitia?'

'I'm still here.'

'Right. Erm, Lesley's popped out for a few minutes.'

'Well, when Lesley has popped back in again, could you tell her that I cannot possibly approve these expenses she's put in without more details? She'll know what I'm talking about. Got that? Thanks.'

I report the good news.

'Which expenses are they, Lesley?' Toolis asks.

'Oh, Stella's. From the smackheads in the Gorbals. She gave them £500 cash for their travel to London and wonders why they didn't answer the phone when she rang back for receipts.'

'Oh, my God. That woman will ruin me.'

'Don't worry. Nancy can call them.'

Oh, yeah? Do her dirty work? This Lesley seems like

trouble. I look away and hurriedly rescue the old lady. She's not missed me, that much is clear. I interrupt her mid-narrative.

'. . . so I was wondering whether my story would be of any interest to you? For the next series? Don't you think it sounds perfect? Obviously, I am massively scarred, and I think that would film well, and also, of course, there's the fatalities. Ideal, really? Don't you think?'

Whatever is she talking about? What atrocity has occurred while I have been away? Or is it only lunatics that ring up Toolis Television? I take her number anyway, and her name, Dolly Dryhope, and write it in the book just in case.

One o'clock approaches. I want lunch. Will Toolis expect me to remain sealed to my chair all day? Unpeeling my humid backside from the seat, I rustle about obtrusively, bracing myself to ask permission to leave. This is just like school.

'Er, Heather, do I get time off for lunch?'

'As long as the phone remains covered. It is never to be left unmanned. It is absolutely paramount that we do not lose any calls. Lesley, are you in for lunch?'

'No. I have an appointment. Very soon.'

Lying cow. The witch is almost giggling.

'Well, I have to go out myself for a couple of hours –'

Toolis will be away till three? Then there is a God. I can get Derek in and out before her return. I smile, relaxing for the first time today.

'– so, Lesley, can you wait ten minutes and cover the phone while Nanette gets some lunch?'

'I suppose so.'

Yes! Toolis instructs me to look sharp, and call the cleaners when I get back, since, as well as a generally dishevelled air about the place, she has noticed what seems to be dog waste trodden into the carpet by my desk. Oh, anything for you, boss. I romp off and down the stairs to

33

hunt down a supermarket and buy some food plus a new pair of tights in a mood of hyped-up exhaustion. Apart from exams, of course, I never knew that a few hours could be so stressful.

CHAPTER THREE

✳

Lesley is jumping down the stairs as I forge back up them. The hurtling overbagged apparition does her best to cripple me, but I paper myself to the wall just in time.

'Lesley! I don't have a key to get in the office.'

'It's open.'

Gone. When I get there I see she has lodged a box of something heavy in front of the door, so I leave it ajar to let some air into the place. How nice. Nobody here. I check under the desks to make sure Toolis isn't lurking, and then strip out of the jacket. Much, much better. Shoes off. Tights as well; straight in the garbage with them. Next I lay out my purchases: tuna sandwiches, toffee yoghurt, slice of chocolate cake from a French bakery, orange juice. It cost a fortune. I retrieve the women's health book from the drawer and open it at the start: A for Abortion. Oh, not over lunch. Pushing the volume aside I read my paper instead.

Time for the yoghurt, and I don't have a spoon. Presuming there must be one in the kitchen, I pad off barefoot to have a look. The door closes behind me. Two forks and a corkscrew plus an unopened packet of chopsticks in the drawer under the sink. They must have a spoon. Just one. In the fridge? Nothing immediately apparent. A hierarchy of geriatric milk cartons is lined inside the door. I inspect them all. The older specimens are worse than rank: their contents have turned into green free-floating bodies. Repelled, I slosh it all into the sink, but I've forgotten that the plug hole is blocked by tissue paper, so am left to watch the formation and inhale the smell of a shape-shifting dairy mountain. What has been revealed, though, briefly jutting out? Do I see a spoon handle? Or will it belong to another fork? I'm not putting my fingers in that glob; but how else to find out? No, the suspense is too much. Tearing open the chopsticks, I use one to stab away the offending stoppage.

Is that the phone ringing? Yes? No? No. Silence. My ploy is working. The mountain shrinks. I turn on the tap, carefully, the horrible mass quickly vanishes, and there is my treasure: a big taramasalata-stained serving spoon stranded like flotsam at low tide. I knew there'd be one somewhere. After washing it I kick the door open and, humming loudly, return to my post.

Well, holy fuck.

A film star is sitting at the desk. Your basic hero blueprint, but with softer edges. A poor man's Paul Newman, shot through sunshine gauze. Staring, dazzled, my eyes screw up at the sudden brightness in the room. I have no shoes or tights on, there is a rip across my back that will show if I turn around, I am holding a spoon high in the air, and my mouth is hanging open. He's reading the health book, which has fallen open on Pregnancy again. I can't remember when I last blushed, but I'm doing so now.

The man looks up from the book and straight at me. Kind eyes in an interesting face. How embarrassing. Does he think I'm pregnant? Or want to be? I can't move, so smile awkwardly instead, and he does also. Oh, lovely smile.

'Sorry about this, but the door was open. I thought the place was abandoned.'

Lovely voice too. Professional, sort of Radio 4, but not at all snotty. Cheery. Laid back.

'No, it's just me here.'

'Right. I came to see Lesley.'

Lesley's boyfriend? He can't be. I don't like her. He

36

probably is, though. Maybe she does things no man can refuse.

'She's just gone out for lunch.'

'Oh, right.' He looks at his watch. 'I don't think I can wait. I'll try again sometime. It's Aidan, by the way.'

I have trod forward and held out my hand before reflecting that it might be a bit of a gauche thing to do. He takes it without hesitation or surprise, though, and we shake firmly.

'I'm Nancy. Nancy Miller. The new receptionist. Today's my first day.'

He nods in acknowledgement. 'Well then, Nancy –' he called me by my name! – 'I've got a confession to make.'

Oh, spit it out. Don't be shy.

'The phone rang just now, and I'm very sorry, I didn't take the name or number; but this man said he'd be late to see you today, nearer three than two, was it? I think it was. Has that ruined things for you?'

Eh? What? Am I staring too obviously? Oh. That would be Derek. I don't mind too much about him any more. Whenever he turns up. The prospect of his walking smack into Toolis, which I know now is destined to happen, no longer holds such horror for me.

'No, it's OK. He's a salesman that apparently Toolis – I mean Heather – can't stand for some reason, and she never wants to see him again. And he called this morning before I knew this and –'

'So I've screwed it up for you. You could have stopped him. Please forgive me. What can I do to make amends?'

Just a few possibilities spring to mind and I laugh for the first time today. Chuck Lesley, to start with.

'Don't worry. It doesn't matter.'

'You sure? Well, sorry again. I'd better be off.'

Oh, don't go. He gets up and heads for the door. The chair is now dented and warm on my bare thighs. He takes one look back.

37

'See you then, Nancy.'

I very much hope so.

'Bye, Aidan.'

Did that really happen? Any of that? Eyeing the slice of cake, I'm not sure I want it any more. Was he really here? What did he look like? I was so astonished by the general impression that I didn't check the details too closely. A living breathing leading man. The rare sort you very, very occasionally notice in the queue at the bank or something, and suddenly your overdraft situation turns curiously dramatic. Not very tall; hair, dark brown but lighter on top, short back and sides, bit of a forelock at the front; and certainly handsome. Age? Definitely the older man. Not geriatric, though nearer forty than twenty-five. Eyes? I can't remember. What colour, I mean, not whether he had any. Skin, a drained-away tan, as though it had been under tropical heat a few months back. Body? Well, leanish trunk, presumably muscled. Clothes? There had been a general navy-blue effect, but not crisp or well defined. I think it was a suit, but a kind of soft one, floppy edges, nice to stroke. Dark shirt of some colour, can't remember, and maybe a tie as well. As for the shoes, I must have looked, but I can't picture them right now. Black leather, I suppose. What a classic. And he's nice. Such a man cannot be going out with Lesley.

He's gone. Ten to two. Lesley will be back soon. Derek will turn up. Followed by Toolis. Though why on earth did Billie make an appointment with Derek if he is such an enemy of Toolis Television? Did she go mad? Was she extracted from here in a strait-jacket? Oh, I'm tired. I feel weird. I can't face the afternoon. Roll on hometime. Another coffee, I think.

In the event, the rest of day one speeds by. The miracle of the man at my desk has conferred a blessing on proceedings. The phone keeps quiet until Derek calls at two twenty-five to say he's chock-a-block in traffic. I happily envision his car snug in the middle of a jam stretching from one shimmering horizon to the other, and give him every permission to peel off at the next exit and head back home. He sounds fawningly grateful and I promise to reschedule the appointment once I've had a look at his new catalogue plus a complimentary token of Select-A-Pencil's esteem which he will pop into the post. I consider asking for an unmarked envelope but refrain, since I'll be chucking it anyway. Feeling goodwill to all men I stretch my legs round the room and even risk a snoop at Fortress Toolis. Heather's desk surrounds the sitter on three sides, leaving only the rear vulnerable to attack. It is fronted by a barricade of tiny drawers which explains why only the top of her head is visible from where I sit. A neat little office chair stands behind, black circle of a seat raised to the highest possible elevation, and by its side, much lower, a Dalek footstool like you see in bookshops. Does she need that to climb up? I shouldn't laugh.

In crashes Lesley.

'What's so funny?'

'Nothing.'

I swivel and fix my gaze onto a cork board which hangs low on the back wall. Pinned upon this, so that no one piece of paper overlaps another, is a collection of, I look closer, graphs of audience viewing figures. They show the top twenty TV programmes over last summer. A yellow highlighter pen is striped, at varying high positions on all of them, across the italicised title *I Watched My Loved Ones Pass Away (Toolis)*. I remember that series. It was a real nail-biter about people having fatal accidents at home: exploding kettles, asps in the broom cupboard, garden forks with minds of their own. Did this lot make it? It must be the programme that the old woman called about. Oh no, did I say I'd get back to her? Well, tough. She can wait. Above the board are several clip frames. They show hugely enlarged newspaper print quotations: '*Toolis,*

filming as ever with a telling eye for human pain'; and
'*A controversial subject yet again handled with tact and
sensitivity by Toolis*'; and, magnified about fifty times,
'*Toolis have certainly landed a monster here*'.

A bark from Lesley. 'Any messages for me?'

Oh, a flood of apologies for faulty equipment has been
pouring in. Shall I mention that Aidan came by?

'No.'

'Are you sure?'

'Yes.'

She swings a lumpy handbag onto her desk and unzips
it in a panic. If there's anything breakable in there it'll be
smashed. Several used paper tissue balls roll out and she
darts upon one, gripping it to her nose just in time to catch
a shockingly loud sneeze. After these hurries a landslide of
medication: nasal spray, at least five different silver foil pill
blisters, white vitamin bottles, an inhaler or two. Silence.
Then, one second later, a wire pronged brush matted with
a thousand of her Rapunzel hairs clatters out as well. I'll
try and be friendly.

'Pollen count high?'

'What do you think?'

She's wiping angrily. I force myself to have another go.

'So, do you have hay fever or asthma?'

She gambles on a reply before another sneeze is upon
her. 'Both.'

Leaving Lesley to her slimy fate I return to my desk. I
don't want to be caught straying when Toolis returns.

This is boring. The phone isn't exactly humming. Back to
the health book, I suppose. Pressing down some uncharted
pages about the hot-wiring of varicose veins, I hear the tap
of titchy heels. Where is she?

'Messages, Nanette?'

It hails from my right. I didn't notice her pass.

'There aren't any.'

'What's this then?' Toolis has assaulted the phone mes-

40

sage book and is reading out loud. 'Dolly Dryhope? Who's she? What does she want?'

I explain what little I understood from our conversation.

'Oh, ignore all those calls. That series is finished. Although, actually, maybe not. We might do another. One day. Ring back and get her to write it all down. Number of deaths, et cetera. And send any pictures, if she had the presence of mind to take any. Especially colour. Post her a profile of the company for now. In a used envelope. And a second-class stamp, of course.'

'Where do I get a profile?'

'Oh, print it off the computer. Lesley will show you.'

Easier said than done. All I can see are her weeping willow locks. All I can hear is a miserable semi-sob.

'Lesley?'

Hair showered backwards.

'What?'

She is sticking a spray pump up her nose.

'I need, erm, a company profile.'

She directs a finger from the available hand at a computer behind me, so I take a look at the screen in question. It's dully dark like a dusty television. Panic. I don't even know how to switch it on. I'm going to have to ask for help. Damn.

'Erm, can you show me how –'

'Oh for God's sake! As if I wasn't busy enough!'

She gets up, though, at least, no doubt wishing I was some gleaming computer-literate secretary who could silently process her instructions. Right now I wish I was a gleaming computer-literate secretary, because I'm not going to learn much from Lesley here. She makes such a kerfuffle about the affront that I hang back and don't see how she turns the machine on or finds her way about or anything. All I can gather is a certain amount of frosty mouse-work.

'There.'

'Thanks very much.'

Writing's on the screen, but how do I get it to print out? I can't ask her again. I mustn't panic. A box appears. 'Now printing' it says, then vanishes. Thank the Lord. A crunchy chugging commences from somewhere near Toolis, so off I go to play hunt the printer. I find it lurking dangerously near her gaze on top of a file cabinet by the window, but she takes no notice of me as I lift two warm sheets from its thin wide mouth.

'Don't send the original. Make copies on the cheap paper.'

'Oh. OK.'

Quite a cluster of machinery in this corner. No doubt Toolis wants to keep an eye on who's doing what, so there'll be no photocopying whole library books from my reading list while she's around. A television and video accompany a dumpy photocopier on a low table top. This must be the item whose lid is never to be slammed. I must not slam that lid.

It seems a simple enough model. I'm used to tank-sized copiers in the library at college. Press the green light. Whirr. Buzz. Clack. Nothing. A threatening orange squiggle lights up on the control panel. Toolis picks up the phone and dials out. Lesley's head seems lower than usual.

Forty-five minutes later, after the photocopier has destroyed a few dozen sheets of paper, and thus utterly foiled Toolis' economy moves, I return to my desk sweating, with the only passably acceptable copy of the document that I have managed to obtain. The nature of the paper itself seems to have been altered by its journey through the machine: brittle now, it's liable to snap like burnt toast at any moment. The pages are wrinkled in concertina folds, bands of toner run across in an interesting zebra pattern, and some lines of print appear to be flatter than others; but I have not, repeat not, even once, slammed that lid. Dolly will have to make do.

TOOLIS TELEVISION (UK)

Heather Toolis established her pioneering film company nine years ago with the express aim of producing high-quality low-budget popular television for the caring viewer. Success was waiting just round the corner in the shape of *I Watched My Loved Ones Pass Away*, a heart-rending ninety-parter which revealed anew television's power to bring us so much closer to the victims of those fatal domestic accidents to which we are all prone. The series achieved regular viewing figures of over fifteen million, and was followed hot on its heels by the probing and soon to be award-winning series *Go For It!*, a moving testimony to the courage of seven terminally ill friends who decided to take a positive approach to their situation and, with round-the-clock assistance from hand-held video cameras, asked the viewers to accompany them to their early graves. *We Never Got To Say Goodbye* is a thirty-part workshop programme featuring the parents of juvenile suicides who to this day do not know why their children chose to leave them. It is to be broadcast this winter, well after the watershed, and will include scenes that are quite brutal in their frankness. Television has never before reached so close to mankind's throbbing heart.

Great. So. Here I am. Blood and death and despair. Slasher movies. Snuff. Voyeurism. Victims. It isn't the news, or investigative documentary, or political commentary. This is no centre of influence broadcasting the truth to a waiting nation. I am very far from the heart of the matter here.

I know what Philip would say, though. Think of the CV. It's good experience, Nancy. Get off your high horse and be grateful. What did you expect? Did you really think the world was waiting, breathless, for your contribution?

Yes. I suppose, somehow, I did.

'What do you think, then, Nanette?'

43

Toolis. Has she been watching me?

'Oh. Fascinating. Really interesting.'

'Do you honestly think so?'

Didn't she? I mean, they produced the stuff.

'Yes. Of course. Don't you?'

She pauses before answering. 'No. It's cynical, well, dross really. But we're selling something here. People watch it. It makes money. If you want to work in television, don't make the mistake of thinking this business is about anything else.'

Oh. Is it not? I want to go home.

No, I don't. Presumably, since he never called, I have Loverboy to go home to. Eric. Eric is, I suppose, my boyfriend. I have rather hoped this summer will be a breather from our relationship. Oh no, maybe it'll be nice to see him. He's all right in small doses – like, very small: more than a few hours of conversation and we're struggling. He's been away for three weeks' orienteering in France, and will, I hope, have got a tan at least. I haven't ever asked him in detail what orienteering is, but I think it takes place outdoors, and involves physical exercise. Eric has a sporty young body, and I use him for sex. Well, we use each other.

I don't want sex with him tonight, though. He'll be all over me. Eric's like an irritating terrier: the further you throw him a stick, the keener he returns. Oh, well. I can handle him. At four thirty Toolis leaves and I slouch back in my chair. Relief, no less than a reprieve from death row. Lesley sends me out to catch the post, with what feels like a breeze block in a Jiffy bag, and I fit in a spot of window-shopping in Oxford Street before returning to the office.

'You took your time, didn't you?'

Why is she so horrible?

'I got lost.'

Silence. Do I have to stay here until she finishes? I fidget until five to six.

'You might as well go. I won't be out of here for a few hours yet.'

Wonderful. Release. Freedom. Who could have guessed it would feel so good? I grab my bag and jump down the stairs two at a time before Lesley changes her mind and orders me back to photocopy the phone book.

CHAPTER FOUR

✳

'Nance! Hi-er!'

Eric deflowered me last Christmas. I put down my bag. He's leaning forward on the sofa, rolling a joint. Eric takes being a student very seriously. Not quite able to get up because of the apparatus on his knees, he compensates by grinning and wiggling his bottom from side to side like a puppy.

'Sarah let me in. She's having a bath.'

I suppose I should go over and kiss him somewhere on his anatomy, but don't. He can suffer a while. I check him out: not looking bad. Though his mother's from Stockholm, Eric's lived all his life in Portsmouth. That hair has gone even blonder at the front, in the bit that falls over his eyes, which does increase the Nordic charm, and he is decently bronzed by the French sun. This is good news. I have a look at the back of his neck, after pulling up the window. He's had his hair cut recently – they've done a nice tapering shave – and is wearing a red grandpa shirt with khaki shorts. Nice legs. Mind you, things always appear acceptable with Eric.

Unfortunately, his massive manly desert boots have already been taken off and parked at the edge of the sofa.

'Oh, please put them back on, Eric.'

'Nance, I've only just got here!'

'I know, but they smell.'

'Well, I'll air them. Come here, Nance, relax and give me a kiss.'

He has made the joint and now looks up at me. I feel weirdly, jerkily shy and stupid. I am going to have to walk across the room and bend down to him or make some other such ungainly movement. I stay still. So he picks himself up and moves over and, muscled nineteen-year-old arms round me, his thin lips hover like a bee near my face. I don't move in, but I don't move away either, and we kiss each other as best you can in such circumstances. What am I doing with him?

'Have you missed me?'

'Sort of.'

'Oh, Nance, don't be so coy.'

Aaagh! Such arrogance. How dare he? How did a worm like him get to be so cocky? I'm only experimenting with him anyway. He should be so lucky. It's been nice without him.

'My name is Nancy. Now, I want a drink.'

Like me, he's a first year. Unlike me, doing Maths. This seems to be a self-contained subject requiring no mention in his social life. We met at a party, one of Sarah's in fact, when Eric came through the door with his better-looking friend Howard. Because Howard was a trifle aloof, I pursued the strategy of chatting exuberantly to Eric in order to keep his friend in the vicinity; and so, through every fault of my own, therefore, Howard was later found entwined with another woman in the arctic garden. I had to make do with Eric, but I wasn't so drunk that I couldn't quite rationally decide to have sex with him when he asked me back to his room. This business had to be got over with.

Up till then, sex had been for other people. I wasn't saving myself for marriage or anything like that, but somehow circumstances had never been quite right. Sixth form was littered with the debris of romantic snarl-ups where I had literally crashed into other people's relationships. There was this occasion when Marcia, already mentioned, had a new boyfriend her mother didn't much approve of, and so she asked if she could meet him one afternoon at my house when no one else was there. I couldn't say no, because I couldn't ever say no to Marcia, but misgivings buzzed round my head like a cloud of gnats. Marcia said she just wanted to chat with him, but since she'd lost her virginity at fourteen I took that with a pinch of salt. Anyway, a couple of hours after I'd left the house to wander dumbly round the park, I returned to make sure they had gone, as agreed. All was quiet, so I ambled up to my room where, to my horror, I found them both sitting up, naked in my bed, sharing a cigarette. (Marcia didn't smoke. Her mother put her on the pill on that condition.) The covers were on the floor, so I had no choice but to stare, and obviously the boyfriend's shrunken dick was going to be the immediate object of my gaze. Marcia leapt up, grabbed my duvet to cover herself, and started to shout: 'Just fuck off, Nancy, you nosy cow, just fuck off for two minutes, can you?'

Our friendship was never quite the same after this, and I started going round with a different group of girls, intellectuals who thought Marcia was a slag. One of these had a gorgeous boyfriend, and they had been going steady for two years, but nevertheless I somehow managed to convince myself that he secretly fancied me more than he did her. At his eighteenth birthday party I got unspeakably drunk and made a pass at him on the landing while we were both waiting for the loo. I tried to kiss him, but he moved his head and I ended up smearing pearly pink lipstick on his ear. I can still remember word for word what he said as he rubbed it off, surprised and angry: 'What the fuck are you playing at, Nancy? What kind of a friend do you think you are? Get your own boyfriend.'

So I'd crept away in shame and mentally put the whole grimy business on hold until college, where I was sure the quality of male would be inestimably higher than at home anyway. Imagine my surprise when I discovered that the general standard there was even lower! They were so young and moronic. I was expected to have one of these for a boyfriend? Jesus. Not that it seemed to prevent anyone else getting on with the job. Everyone was having it away: the already-married-aged-eighteens who had long been great friends with each other's parents; the ones who put 'Do Not Disturb' signs on their doors but might as well have added the rider 'I'm-having-sex-and-I-want-you-all-to-know-it'; and those who were never ever there because they were sowing their wild oats away from college and who would only appear looking frazzled and prematurely aged at classes.

I suppose the mature breeze of compromise had finally blown over me by the time I met Eric, though a less generous verdict might have suggested desperation. No, the main thing was that although the situation left some things to be desired, I had been in control. I chose to sleep with Eric. Medium height, quite slim, two arms and two legs, decent haircut, beardless, few spots, an acceptable face, no obvious deformities. He would do. Now I look back, I reckon he was thinking something like that about me too. Pleasure was not on the agenda for either of us that night.

'Would you like to have sex?' he whispered, very politely, subtle as hell, leaning by me in the darkened hall, beer bottle in hand; and I said, 'OK, why not?' as though he'd offered me a stuffed olive, or asked me to be his partner in a chemistry experiment. We headed for his college room.

He'd not made the bed before going out and a thin duvet was draped over the chair. After the darkness of the party, where the lights had been off all evening, I was cruelly brought back to earth by watching Eric tidy up in the glare of the electric light. The drink was wearing off. I could smell feet, so walked over to the window and opened it. I was to make that short but vital journey several times in the ensuing months. The freezing cold night air rushed in.

We'd never manage anything at this rate, I can remember thinking, but I was going to get it done, I was. So I told Eric I was off to buy more beer. Blundering downstairs I went to find a shop that was open. Eric's room is in a college residential building on the other side of town from where I share a terraced house with two friends, but on the road outside his hall there's a bus stop. One of the passing night buses would take me home. To shag or not to shag? But the thought of waking up a virgin still was too terrifying. I crossed the road and hunted down the beer.

When I came back to the room I caught Eric washing his feet in the basin, thank God. He'd taken off his jeans, so I took a good look at the legs. They boded quite well for the rest of the body: nice shape, thinnish, good ankles, hairy up to a point. Help, this is terrifying, I thought – we've got to get all those clothes off. What will be revealed? I hoped it was all there. Already I could discern a hint of brown Y-fronts under the hanging shirt. Dark chocolate with white edging, his legs very pale where they came out. Time for more beer. I handed him a can and started one myself, then sat back on his bed.

'Can we turn this light off, Eric? Have you got a lamp?'

'Er, yes, here.'

He switched one on that was standing by the bed. Then, turning off the main light, he subsided into an armchair. Much, much better. Darkness fell upon his room: upon the posters of feverish gothic guitarists; upon the fat maths textbooks' wide spines, falling out backwards from the mean bookshelves; upon his tall dark wardrobe in which I'd spied a tumbling trove of underwear; and upon the one orange and one mocha towel hanging from the rail beneath his basin, no doubt bought new for him by his mother for life away from home.

I had done so much research for this moment, but it was very odd. The countless books I had investigated had not spoken of the problems that I now encountered: total body paralysis, chills, sweat, a sudden inability to talk. And contraception? The power to speak of anything at all, let alone mention that subject, had long since left me. I was not on the pill, I did not have an IUD inside me, I had certainly not inserted a diaphragm. A packet of three condoms had been lurking in my bag for the previous eighteen months, waiting, with me, just in case, for their use; but somehow, as it sat on the floor near the window where I had left it, my bag seemed such a distance away.

To my lasting gratitude and simultaneous chagrin, the moment was saved by Eric. I've probably stayed with him because of it. He got up and came over to the bed. Putting the beer can on the small cupboard by it, he laid himself down next to me.

'Do you want to get in?'

'Erm, yes.'

What a good idea. Far lower visibility there.

'You'll have to get undressed first.'

'So will you.'

Damn, just not drunk enough. So, I faced up to it; time to be brave. I was wearing a green sweatshirt and some nasty black jeans, I think. The sweatshirt came off in one over-the-head swoop. I stood up and had to wrench down the jeans after undoing the zip.

Eric was wearing a proper do-up-at-the-front shirt. In his haste or fear or both he tried to pull it up over his head like I had, but he hadn't undone the button at his neck, and it got stuck over his nose so that he couldn't see for a moment. I took the chance both to retreat speedily under the bedcovers and take a good look at his chest. His arms were in the air, drawing his muscles up with them and showing him to best advantage: strawberry-blond armpit hair, half going northward, half heading south; pale skin stretched over the ribcage; a certain presence, no more, of blond hair, around the nipples, meeting between them, and heading down to the navel, over the flat stomach and on down in a thin line growing darker and darker. The Y-fronts were still on.

Any minute now they'll have to come off and I shall become familiar with the hot contents of Eric's drawers, I thought, filled with false bravado. He lowered his arms again and looked embarrassed. I looked for my beer. He undid the top button and took off his shirt. Then he stopped.

'I must go for a piss.'

I waited to be his. He returned less than a minute later and got straight into bed. I wanted to go to the loo as well but didn't dare do anything so decisive. At the time, of course, I didn't know that Eric was as nervous as I was, and so I tried to maintain an atmosphere of average familiarity with all this palaver.

He turned round to switch off the lamp and then leant back towards me.

'Let me take your bra off.'

I proffered my back to him and he undid the clip with surprising efficiency, but when I faced him again in the darkness he sounded scared.

'Touch me.'

Where? His knees? I put my finger on those warm Y-fronts.

'Wait.'

He arched up his back and pulled them down over his feet, hurling them out onto the floor. Then I put my hand back and for the first time in my life touched a boy's dick. Hot and hard but very soft-skinned. Quite a moment.

'Would you, er, stroke it?'

I ran my index finger up and down. An interesting twitch when I touched the tip. I did it again and this time, you could say, it lurched a bit. What a weird thing, I reflected, that they all hide one of these in here. A small very different other world.

Eric lay on his back while I did this to him. He grunted a bit, and gasped on and off, then pushed up his groin slightly repulsively. At this I shook myself and thought: what am I doing here, nearly naked in bed with a naked man I've known less than four hours? Doing this? But I assured myself this was what adults got up to, like it or not, and it had to be done.

'Shall we have sex?' he'd asked. He hadn't touched me, and I was quite relieved. Let's keep this simple.

'Will you put on a condom, Eric?'

I was proud of myself.

'Yes, I was going to. I've got some here.'

He turned the lamp back on and out of the drawer in the bedside cupboard he took a similar packet to the one in my bag. We had so much in common. Tearing open the wrapping he took one out and tried to rip off the cover. His hands were shaking and unassured. Then I knew he'd never done this before. Somehow, unfairly, I felt so superior.

He sat on the edge of the bed so I couldn't see what he was doing. The first attempt failed. From where I was, since closely inspecting his efforts wouldn't have helped, I think he got it on some of the way, but inside out; so he peeled it off and opened another. I suppose he got this one on somehow, but the process by then must have quite devastated his erection, for his shoulders sagged and he said 'Oh, fuck' at least twice. Then he turned off the lamp and clambered back towards me.

'Can you get your, er, knickers off?'

He plainly didn't want to risk doing that for me, so I obliged, hurling them in a different direction to the one in which he'd sent his. Then he placed himself on all fours over me, and lowered his body to touch mine. I felt his manly part brush against me, withering in its rubber prison, and he tried to stab it against me. It lacked thrust. He tried again. Nothing doing. This was hopeless. We hadn't even kissed yet. Eric rolled sideways off me and choked a little. Was he crying?

'I'm sorry. I've – I've not done this before.'

He was past caring whether I knew or not now. I felt sorry for him.

'That's all right. It doesn't matter. Honestly.'

It did matter, though. I had wanted someone to deal with this for me, swiftly and efficiently like animals kill each other in nature documentaries. No mess, no fuss. I needed it sorted and it wasn't.

God, I felt stupid lying there, repelled by it all, as though someone I knew was going to walk in and turn on the light and say, 'Nancy! What *do* you look like?' It must have been pretty late by then. I felt ill. I put my arm around Eric because I thought I should, and amazingly, I now realise, we stayed like that; not separating or turning away from each other until we were both asleep.

Failed, failed, failed. I was woken by a taut bladder at around six in the morning. I had been dreaming that I was emptying it in a bucket, naked, in front of my family, and that I had just had sex with Eric, only somehow we'd done it without touching each other's bodies, and I was a virgin no more, and this was all quite normal. My head was pounding with hangover and strange-bedness and not enough sleep. Breath like a dragon's escaped from my mouth. I had to get out of the bed over Eric and find my sweatshirt in the dark. When I had escaped from his room and left it to hunt down the bathroom I planned my escape, only needing to retrieve my scattered garments before slipping out. Eric seemed to be a deep sleeper. I could melt from his life as suddenly as I had materialised into it, and he from mine. I didn't envision him stopping me. I would be better prepared for the ordeal with someone else.

On my return I pushed the door open ever so quietly and began the hunt for my clothes. The quest went well and I had collected a little heap on the floor when I realised my bra was somewhere in the bed, I had no idea where. Eric was mainly concealed by duvet and I presumed the bra was too, so I leant over him and lifted it up. There was the first indication of morning light coming through the window and by it I could see that one arm of my straying upholstery was looped around a fine erection nudging Eric's ironing-board stomach. Bugger. Could I abandon the bra? It was my favourite and would have to be rescued now while Eric slept if I was to get away with never speaking to him again. I had no option but to place one hand on the strap. With the other, I lifted Eric's mildly resisting dick; but, the job done, I foolishly let it thwack softly back against him. He moved. And opened one eye.

Damn.

'Nancy? Could we try again?'

I had assumed the situation was entirely lost, and was only hoping he'd not have seen enough of me in the dim light ever to recognise me again. Was this a chance of salvage? I nodded – Eric could just see me – so he leant over for his third and last condom, which, I noted, he rolled on with impressive calmness. He must have been mentally practising all night. The gloomy dawn had mercy on him. I lay down. He turned towards me and without much further ado young Eric sorted us both in an accurate and devastating plunge. I gasped. It hurt. But it was done.

I think I left his room about an hour later, having pretended to sleep a bit. We'd not exchanged numbers or addresses, and I'd intended to avoid where he lived, lying low. Eric tracked me down two weeks later, however. Well, we walked past each other in a pub, and he greeted me with apparent pleasure, bought me a pint and introduced me to the friends he was drinking with. He was plainly happy to see me, as though our encounter had been the most romantic of occasions; or maybe he wanted to rewrite the horrible truth of our union by hastily improving upon it. We got drunk again and went back to his airless room and had another go at sex. It was better this time, and we even managed a spot of foreplay, and I thought, well, you can be my pot-boiler of love.

Since then we started seeing each other about once a week, mainly meeting at night and me departing in the morning. I suppose we've stuck with this dispassionate arrangement until now, rather than give it up as a bad job, for the crude but usual reason that we both feel better about ourselves this way. I would rather go out with Eric than no one at all, that's my shoddy motivation, and I presume it's his too. Beyond the fact that we are both at the same university at the same time, though, we don't have much in common. Eric reads fantasy novels and is obsessed with the *Alien* films and knows how nuclear weapons work and the number of six-foot men placed end to end you'd need to go round the equator: in short, he's handy in a pub quiz. He always knows the technically correct answer to everything, and always says so. Unfortunately this can be a problem. He doesn't know when to keep his mouth shut, so comes across as a bit of a know-all. I suppose, essentially, it's the paradoxical mixture of geekiness with arrogance that offends. Sarah summed up Eric horribly accurately after she'd first met him. I'd treacherously implied that it was OK if she was brutally honest, since he wasn't exactly the love of my life, and so she was.

'Nan, let me put it this way. There's a simple test for men. They either pass or fail. Do they, or do they not, have RP?'

'What?'

'RP. It stands for "Restaurant Presence". You're out having a meal. Can the man you are with attract the waiter's attention in twenty seconds or less?'

Oh God. I'd known the answer straight off. Since then the failed RP test has crystallised all my reservations about Eric. It does me no credit, I know, but there you go. Let's face it, I don't even much like Eric, let alone love him. He irritates me with his assumptions, and as for what I'd feel if he got run over and killed, I honestly don't know how upset I'd be. He seems proud of me, mind, and introduces me as his girlfriend whenever he gets the chance, and I was even displayed to his parents one weekend when they came to visit. I admit he's been to ours, and met mine, but all this really achieves is to make me mildly ashamed of myself.

I take a good long look at my boyfriend as he sits there on the sofa. That's what he is. A boy. Maybe we should call it a day. It's not fair to string him along. We're not at college now. I need a proper man, more like that one that strayed into the office today. Making a snap decision I resolve not to hang about any longer. Eric will have to go. Tonight.

CHAPTER FIVE

*

Sarah and I are keeping a list of the bottles we'll need to replace from the drinks cabinet. I lord over the range and proprietorially swing a decanter of whisky, the gracious hostess, yanking out its golf-ball head.

'What would you like?'

Eric doesn't answer, just looks around.

'I say, this flat's a bit of a palace, isn't it, Nance? We look a bit out of place here, don't we?'

'Speak for yourself, scum.'

He's right, of course. The flat *is* thoroughly unreal, from start to finish. Sarah grew up in London with more money about the place, and takes it all for granted, but me, well, I revel in every high-cost inch.

My parents have always lived in the same house. At the end of a cul-de-sac and less than half a mile from our thriving town centre, it is, in brochure speak, a detached four-bed family home of considerable character set in its own grounds with garaging for two cars. Sheltered from road frontage by a mature beech hedge and chain-link fence the property comprises the handsome oak porch entrance leading to a hallway with a distinctly old-world feel ... and so on. In truth, it's a gawky off-white pebble-dashed edifice erected in the fifties which suffers from a severe charm bypass. It's quite big (too big for us) and, with a garden that supports enough rhododendron bushes in its acid soil to hide behind for a drag on a cigarette (even now my parents don't know I smoke), the overall feel is one of dankness. Inside and out. Dank, dank, dank. Not that the walls are dripping, it's just an atmosphere. The opposite of cosy. The furniture seems to rattle around. I don't know, maybe you can't help nursing an ungrateful hatred for your roots. Perhaps you need this crushing process. Maybe it's like the seeds of certain plants that have to pass through the intestines of an antelope before they can germinate, miles away from their birthplace. Maybe it's just Surrey, and the neutrality of the commuter belt. When I think of my parents' house I see a grey sky and mist rising above wet tissues on damp station tracks. Maybe it's just me; but I want out, and I'm getting out.

I used to view people who left our road as special beings, blessed to be moving on. Those tall vans full of furniture and canvas drapes always said adventure to me, and possibilities, and the potential for transformation. They still do. I used to dream that my family would move, anywhere; in fact, they nearly did, when I was fifteen, but the sale fell through and we stayed put. Seriously disappointed, I remember actually kicking my bedroom door for a furious ten minutes. My father, Thatcher's child, is the manager of one of the banks in our high street. He'd got a pay rise or something, and wanted to impress my mother with a massive newly built house on a luxury estate further out of town. It had a poncy classical-pillared doorframe that was already cracking off the brick, and the rooms smelt of glue and you could tell the lawn had just been unrolled. I think my mother was secretly pleased when everyone lost interest. Actually, I don't know if my dad really liked the prospective new place much either, but that wasn't the point. He liked its price tag. My father's got a big chip on his shoulder. Maybe this whole roots business is hereditary: his father ran a corner shop, years ago, but went bankrupt and turned to drink and is now, in his eighties, waiting in vain in a depressing old folks' home for his son to visit.

The Grim Reaper will get there first, if you ask me, but I'm not hanging around to find out.

'I bet you like the bathroom here best, Nance.'

'What? Sorry, I was miles away.'

Eric is looking straight at me. 'The bathroom. Are you ever out of it?'

'Oh. Ha-ha.' Giggle. 'No, I'm not.'

How embarrassing. He is referring to the fact that I tend to retreat into the bath for at least an hour and a half after spending the night with him. Washing him off me, he accuses. Damn, he always has to be right; and yes, here, in this palace, I do spend most of my time in the bathroom. A high gilt-edged mirror above the basin, coupled with a swivel-headed lamp, now makes squeezing the blackheads on my nose a pastime to which I can devote many minutes before sluicing myself down in the huge and memorable bath. I lie there for hours. There's such intense pleasure to be gained from things like the marbled soap in the shell-shaped dish on tiny legs, the fat raspberry-coloured towels embraced by golden rings on the walls, the force of the hot water pelting out of the shower heads and draining away tidily without spraying all over the floor. I have never been so clean.

The kitchen's crowning glory is its prize-winning fridge. When we arrived this had been left filled by the aunt with such expensive items that I had assumed they weren't for us to touch: but Sarah assured me we could take our pick. It's one of those tall American cream-coloured, rounded-at-the-edges ones, into which you could step on a hot day, if you took out the racks; nothing mean or cheap about it.

I don't think the aunt can cook. The carrier bags folded under the sink, with ribbons of receipts left in them, reveal her to be a highly favoured customer of several extortionate nearby delicatessens where you can pay over two pounds for a bag of crisps; and, yes, I've checked, she has. Wild boar and redcurrant flavour. In fact, the contents of the fridge resemble a typical cold display from any such shop: goose liver pâté next to Ardennes ham and Stilton cheese and Tewkesbury mustard.

There's only one bedroom in the flat and that of course went to Sarah. I don't go into it too often, as Sarah sometimes has her boyfriend, Nick, to stay for the night, and I feel a certain reluctance to invade the unventilated privacy of the room; but she leaves the door open in the day and you can't help but see the white sheet from the unmade four-poster bed drape itself artistically over the edge and onto the floor. There's a beautiful antique dressing table in there, on which stand bottles and flasks of scents and lotions and moisturisers and such apparent necessities as 'clarifying cream' and 'reinforcing exfoliator' and even a 'petrifying liposome face-mask'. We've borrowed them all.

I sleep on the sofa in the living room, but this is by no means the inferior option. Such a vast sofa I have never seen before: nine foot long and five foot wide, with massive flopping navy-blue cushions, it is so much more comfortable than my bed at college or at home that I am not in the slightest bit jealous of Sarah's four-poster.

The flat is at the top of one of those whopping unthinkably expensive white houses in a street off Gloucester Road, part of a block forming a square around tidy private communal gardens. Georgian? Early Victorian? Don't ask me. A proper smart bronze lift takes you most of the way up, leaving one small flight of stairs to climb before you come to our door. Far grander than anywhere I have ever stayed, and way beyond anything I ever hoped to inhabit, I have thus been transplanted into dreamland. As in even the meanest hotel, there is a holiday air to the place.

'I'll have a gin and tonic, darling.'

'Oh, Eric. You still here? I think we can run to that, Tarquin.'

While mixing his drink I wonder what Sarah's up to

tonight. I know I have to do the dirty deed soon, but I hope Eric and I aren't left alone together just yet. We'll either have to go out, which will cost money, or stay in and watch TV, which will be sofa-based and lead too quickly to other things. Eric is plainly going to be frisky after his spell away. He won't be happy with just a video. When shall I say it? Will he have to stay the night?

A steamy atmosphere has entered the room: Sarah must be out of the bathroom. Indeed: she marches in looking like a shampoo advert, swathed in a large white towelling dressing gown and with her fair hair twisted upwards and beturbaned in one of the aunt's vast towels.

'Hi.'

She sinks into the sofa next to Eric. The gown falls open and he turns to look down her hot wet sun-bed-tanned deep cleavage. Little shit. Sarah turns to me.

'Nan, Philip called. Checking how your first day went. I said you'd ring him.'

'Oh, right.'

'Pour me a drink, will you? Thanks. So, what are you two up to tonight then?'

This is ridiculous. All of us pretending to be our parents. So in control.

'Well, what are you doing, Sarah? We could all go out if you like.'

'Sorry. Tonight –' she pulls the robe shut – 'tonight, I'm afraid, I'm going out to dinner with Nick's parents to celebrate his finishing finals. After that we'll go back to their house and stay over there. So, you two –' she gives me a wicked glance – 'will have the place to yourselves.'

Eric's happy. 'Great – I mean, I'm sure you'll have a great time.'

I say I'm not sure what we'll be doing. Up bounds Eric to say that he, for one, knows what he wants: he hasn't had a square meal for days and he's going to treat me to dinner. I say OK. It'll kill a few hours.

Sarah's getting up to go and dress.

'Nan! I forgot to ask. What *was* your first day like?'

'Oh, erm, it's an odd place. Nothing like I expected. It's tiny, and this repulsive man passed out on the floor, and there's this woman boss who's really weird . . .'

'Well, you can bore me in detail tomorrow, but the main question is – and you'll have to forgive me, Eric – but is there any available talent?'

'God no. Well, there was only this one man, and he was unconscious and not fanciable at all; mind you –'

'Yes?'

She's such a shark, sensing a pinprick of blood from miles away in the ocean! Eric doesn't notice.

'Oh, nothing.'

'Tell me!'

'Nothing, honestly.'

'I do not believe you, Nan, but I'll worm it all out tomorrow. Now I must change.'

My friendship with Sarah has proved a moot point at college. She is Miss Gleaming Thoroughbred Filly with her own car and ready-filled bank account. My family's comfortable enough, but my father's mean as sin and votes Tory and thinks that helping me financially will turn me whining and dependent. He grew up in a flat above his father's shop, him and his brother, several hundred years ago by the sound of things. Well, he was born in 1934. Their mother, my grandmother, worked as a housekeeper for the local doctor, and, as my dad constantly recalls, worked herself into an early grave. I am so sick of my dad's background, mainly because he's made Philip and me and my mum suffer for it. No wife of his is going to work and no child of his is going to have to fight for an education; so, my mother once had to beg to be allowed to do a part-time crap secretarial job, she told me, just to stave off total nervous collapse, and Philip and I were

63

forced to work our butts off at expensive private schools. They sent Philip to board at a place half an hour's drive away from home, where he was homesick and bullied and pushed too hard but wasn't quite bright enough to get into college. I refused to board and was packed off to the nearest private day-school, a superior girls-only establishment that turned out to have a cool attitude to women getting careers and whipped most of the sixth form into university whether they liked it or not.

Sure, it was money well spent, but now I'm a student I needn't think it came from a bottomless pit. Oh, dear me, no. My dad coughs up what he has to for my maintenance, but as for the rest I can apply for loans and do a job like everybody else. So, in effect, I might as well be on the breadline. Well, not that bad. I've done bar jobs and wait-ressing like everyone else. Most of us have money prob-lems. I suppose it's now traditional for students to be forced to have an excessive interest in the subject, so in this con-text you can understand why Sarah sticks out. It was only a month ago that I moved into a house outside college for my second year with a couple of genuinely penniless friends. Our new home is a shithole behind the football ground, damp even when we first saw it at the end of May, but com-petition was tough and it was all we could get. Yet when Sarah first came round she gave it the once-over and said: 'If you all hate it so much, why don't you just move?'

I hadn't dared look at the others. They only know Sarah through me. I suppose they only know each other through me, actually. I made friends with Grace in my first week; she is an attractively extrovert figure who trampled through all that initial weirdness and told me her life story the first time we met in the college bar. Her father is a Pakistani lawyer working for an inner city law firm in Manchester and her mother, who's white, is a teacher in a comprehen-sive. There's three brothers and not a penny to spare. It all sounded so relentlessly PC I could barely dare to admit my origins, but Grace then laughed loudly and shrieked that she was so bored with the whole thing she wanted to get rich quick in the City and then blow out at twenty-six.

Rebecca I like for opposite reasons. She is one of the calmest people I have ever met, never making any sudden movements and only talking quietly in a flat West Country monotone; although, if you listen closely, you realise she is making outrageously offensive statements most of the time. Her life ahead is mapped out. Security is the main priority. She will be an accountant. Her mother, unmarried, had her when she was seventeen and Rebecca has never met her father. They live in Bristol and mother, who works in an estate agents, comes on the train to see her every third weekend. Both are pear-shaped blondes and very freckled, so people constantly mistake them for sisters.

To be honest, I think the difference between Grace and Rebecca hangs like a threat between them. They're slightly scared of each other's strengths and therefore need me to hold them together. What happened was that both of them asked me to share a house on separate occasions during the same week. Arriving at a decision being way beyond me, I forced the issue by announcing my dilemma to both of them at once. They had little choice but to share me, so we pooled our meagre resources and moved into the musty pit halfway through June.

Then, into this delicate situation, jangles many-bangled Sarah. Her father had bought a house for her, with central heating, and she shares it with three hefty rugger-playing men, one of whom is Nick. Sarah's funny; she just doesn't see the complications of life without money. She can't begin to imagine it, and this always cheers me up. Anything's possible with her. I've never seen her in a bad mood. So when she asked me to come with her to London, only a fortnight after we'd moved in, I knew I'd have to betray my housemates. I furtively sub-let my room to an Italian summer student for a month, a glamorous woman from

Milan who stank of scent and to whom I charged more than my share of the rent so as to ease the overdraft. Since I left in a hurry, before either she or the others complained unduly, I hope they're getting on with each other and that her English isn't improving fast enough for her to realise she's being ripped off.

'How about an Indian?'

'What?'

Eric is speaking *at* me.

'I said, Nancy, how about an Indian? Meal?'

'Oh, right. Yeah, sure, OK.'

Twenty minutes later, and entering the first place we find, we order far too much and speak little. Afterwards, we go to the pub round the corner from the flat. Eric forked out for the food, so I head to the bar and look back. Sitting at a little table by the window, he's been watching me, and catches my eye and smiles. Damn, he'll be encouraged by that. Eric's all right; but he isn't for me.

Who, then, would have been? My mother would gasp, almost tearful, in clothes shops: 'Oh, what *do* you want, Nancy? Please decide soon.'

'I'll know it when I see it.'

I always knew it when I had, too, though such items, invariably, cost far more than I ever intended to pay. I did want Eric, at first; not for himself, but for what he could do for me. I suppose we only get what we deserve. I pay for the lagers and walk them back to our table.

'You look really nice tonight, Nance.'

Eric leans his head as close to mine as he can. Oh, bugger off. It's taken you long enough to come up with something as imaginative as that, boy. And if you call me Nance again . . .

'I'm really pleased to see you, you know.'

Here we go. Eric on tender sweet nothings overdrive. Why do I feel absolutely numb?

66

'I know you are, Eric. I am too, I really am.'

'Honestly, Nance? You know, even though we started this without knowing each other, I'm really glad we met. I think – I think I more than just like you, you know?'

Oh, no. What's he saying? I fear I do know. Please don't have the nerve, Eric.

'I thought about you so much, well, all the time, in France, and I realised I'm getting used to seeing you and things, and, well –' here he lowers his head even further – 'the sex is pretty good, isn't it? Could we do more things together, do you think? I mean, do you think this might last, a bit, you know?'

Damn. Making me do some talking. Is he asking for a decision here? Not something I thought would ever be called for. Does he want me to say, Stay For Ever or, Go For Good? Or does he want the truth, which I shall willingly give him, translated, which is, it doesn't matter too much either way whether you're around for now or not? Though – and this bit I can't give him – I'm on my way up, Eric, and you're not coming too.

'Look, Eric, I don't really know whether I can say that now. Can't we just go along as we are? We're doing all right, aren't we?'

'Well, Nance, no, I don't really think we are. It feels like something's missing. I don't really know where I stand with you. Sometimes I think you don't care at all, and then you say something really sweet, so I know that you do, a lot; and then I think it's all going better and better when all of a sudden you can be such a cow, and ignore me or something or talk as though I'm not there. I mean, when we first, er,' whispering, 'made love, properly, I thought that was something quite special, you know? I know men aren't supposed to feel like that, but, I did. I found myself thinking this isn't just anybody. This girl is nice, I thought. You seemed so honest about what you wanted, and you wanted me.'

Typical. Know-all. He's got it wrong, a hundred per

cent. It's a hot evening, and the room is full of people shouting. Our table is beside a group standing up and bawling their heads off right next to us.

'Eric, I'm not saying this to avoid answering, but can we finish this conversation at home? I don't want people to listen here.'

'Yeah, OK, sorry.'

He's mortified. The drink continues desultorily. What am I going to say to him? Let's have another.

Eventually we walk back.

'Nance? Did you say there was a garden behind the flat? Can we go in it?'

Good idea. Delaying the moment of truth. Oh, this is terrible. Suddenly oppressed by a poison of self-hatred flowing all through me, I remember every moment of physical closeness with Eric, and am repelled by them all. Surely it isn't supposed to be like this? Standing in the darkness with the key in the lock of the garden gate, I'm surprised how none of it has been any good.

'What's wrong? Is it stuck?'

'No! No! Just, just, leave me alone!'

I push the gate forward and run through onto the lawn. Tall dark sycamores stand guard, rustling; and I am crying without being able to stop myself, though I'm not going to have him see that. Crouching down onto the warm grass I roll onto my side and hide my face in my hands. Disgraceful behaviour, but I don't care.

Of course he can both see and hear.

'Nance! What's wrong?' He lies down beside me. 'It's PMT, isn't it? I know your cycle. That's it, isn't it?'

Right. He has to go.

'Look, Eric, just fuck right off! I don't want to see you any more, I don't want you to stay tonight, I don't want to talk to you ever again. I want this – relationship – to finish for ever, right now. I only ever slept with you because Howard got off with somebody else!'

He switches from moving his face and sympathising, to keeping it still and, quite interesting to see it in him, turning angry. I've gone too far now. I can't clamber out of this. And I don't want to.

'Oh fine, Nanc-y. Fine. You can just sign off, you can just order me to go away, now, off, anywhere – just out of your sight. I'm just one of your mistakes. I do my best for you and you constantly put me down, treat me like an, an appendage; and then when you're bored, no, when I actually have the cheek to ask where I stand, to ask for a bit of honesty, oh no, you can't have that, can you? Putting you on the spot isn't allowed, is it? Well, you know what you can do?'

I can't look at him and don't answer. The turf smells lovely, warm earth and grass and worm-breath.

'You know what you can do, Nanc-y?'

'I don't fucking care what you want me to do.'

'Well, I'm going to tell you anyway. You can go back to your fucking History degree, and you can continue to despise Maths students for not being too interesting, and you can condescend to sleep with them when it suits you just to make you feel grown-up and clever, but if I were you, I'd be grateful that anyone would touch you, you ugly bitch. And while you're at it, I'd do something about your sexual technique, just in case any blind desperate dosser needs comfort, one day, because right now, Nanc-y, you don't have one.'

Jesus. I'm impressed. He's not said so much in all our conversations put together. Nasty. And funny peculiar. I feel so distant from him. He's gone to sit on a garden bench at the edge of the grass, head in his hands, miles and miles away, gone.

Another watershed reached. Another marker on the road to adulthood. Chucked my first boyfriend. I'm afraid it just didn't work out. I suppose we didn't have that much in common. No, but you did the decent thing once it was obvious it wasn't working. You're right. I did. Pity. Yes, but these things happen. And you're still so young. So much ahead of you. You mustn't blame yourself. All right then, I won't.

'I'll need to go and get my stuff.'

'OK.'

We walk up in silence to the flat, silent in the lift. This is so odd. Forty minutes ago we'd found things to say. Eric's sports bag is slumped on the floor by the sofa. He goes straight over, picking it up with one hand and hurling it over his shoulder. So clinically clean and tidy. I yawn. He looks at me and heads for the door.

'Goodbye.' He is furious.

'Bye, Eric.'

The door slams. Where he thinks he'll go, I don't know. The sofa is mine again. I lie full stretch along its glorious length and hunt for the television's remote control, digging under the cushions where it always gets lost. Finding it at once, I start to doze in front of a scratchy black-and-white film about shooting lions in Africa in the twenties.

The persistent ringing of the door-buzzer wakes me and I swing to from sleep, dribbling. What time is it? My teeth need a brush. Should I answer? Has Sarah left her keys behind? I struggle to the intercom.

'Yes?'

'It's Eric. I'm going to have to stay the night.'

How does he make it into a command like that? He should be begging. I press the 'open' button, then leave the door on the latch. Blundering to the bathroom to clean my teeth, I have a look in the mirror. He's right. I do look shocking. I am ugly. My hair is hooked in ratty swoops. Dried channels of grey tears trail down my cheeks to converge on my neck. Puffy. Bloated.

Eric's boots on the carpet outside. I hastily paste and get

frothing. No one looks great doing their teeth, but it'll bypass the need for talking.

'I'll just go on the sofa.'

Oh, no. It's *my* sofa.

Too late, though. He throws himself down and switches off the TV. I was watching that. Who does he think he is? My ex now, that's who. I was going to banish him to Sarah's bed, but this'll have to do; so I sleep on the four-poster that night, past caring, too tired to mind the chilled alien smell of Sarah and Nick and her long gold hairs on the crumpled pillows.

CHAPTER SIX

※

Despite the strange bed, I sleep surprisingly deeply and am woken again by the sun around half-past seven. It zooms hotly onto my eyes. Just as well, since setting the alarm clock was hardly a major concern last night. Dehydrated, my head starts to throb. Day two looms.

Eric's gone, the sofa left barely dented. No note or anything. I start to feel guilty as memories return from last night, surges measured from a drip. Mind you, the prospect of the day ahead's not much better. Pug woman and the rude sneezer. It's already hot. No tights today. Jeans? Perhaps it's a bit too soon to slide that far downmarket. Lesley was wearing jeans, though, wasn't she? And Alastair too? Maybe, but somehow they were smart jeans, and that's not an image I can muster. Summer dress and sandals? Surely. How is my face now? To the bathroom to check. Better: deflated, calmed. I get a grip. Headache: pain-killed. Hair: re-fluffed. Face: exfoliated, clarified, moisturised. Lipstick: a hint tastefully applied. I set off at five to nine.

Greek Street is hot, and smells are rising from the piss-filled channels at the edge of the tarmac. Hillocks of restaurant refuse from last night's dinners are stacked on the pavement, cabbage leaves and mozzarella packets falling out of rat-ripped binbags, and the matt black building in which resides Toolis Television towers upwards in a Gotham City kind of a way. Nine twenty-seven.

Lesley is not here but Toolis and Alastair are already

huddled at the back of the room when I fall into it. Literally: I trip on the corner of a doormat, which I'm sure wasn't there yesterday, and burn my wrists on the carpet. Damn: Soho grime is trodden into that floor. All I can see are desk and chair legs. I suppose they saw me? Oh, yes: a scud missile of a greeting explodes somewhere above my head.

'Good morning, Nanette!'

'Oh, hi.'

This floor is quite clean, actually.

'Not "Hi". Never "Hi". Good morning, please!'

I am not going to say good morning to this woman. She can fuck right off. Then again, maybe I should. Otherwise my career may suffer. Depression descends. I stand up.

'Good morning.'

'That's better. Today you will be doing research.'

Oh. Research. So soon? She must think I have potential.

'That sounds interesting.'

'Excellent! Coffee first. Black, no sugar.'

The kitchen is sinisterly clean. Surface wiped. Plug unblocked. Sink reeking of bleach. Aha. The cleaners. They must have been. Didn't I forget to call them yesterday? Oh, well. They turned up anyway, and, with a bit of luck, Toolis won't mention it now.

I might even have an interesting time today, lolling on the phone asking questions, and being paid to do so. Easy-peasy. What will the subject of my research be? This certainly is a step forward. It's only my second day.

Coffees in hand, I approach Toolis and ask what she has in mind. Alastair is snatching at a custard doughnut and has sugar on his lips. It's falling onto the desk. Toolis is shepherding the grains round with one little hand, fencing them in and driving her collection into a heap as fast as Alastair showers down more. Why does she put up with this slob? I haven't made him coffee because he already has a large hot chocolate.

73

'Oh, right. Well. I've got this idea for a little series, say eight or ten half-hours, about, well, in which we cover the subject of health taboos head-on. Now, the taboos I'm talking about here are those which, because of their intimate nature, are likely to remain taboos, unless they are confronted openly and frankly in a public forum, et cetera, et cetera. Which will be the series. Now the subjects I have in mind are not life-threateners like AIDS or drugs or mental illness or anything like that, but rather those chronic debilitating problems, invisible to the outside world, but which can cause serious distress to the sufferer; and which the sufferer, because of the social taboo, or stigma, attached to the condition, cannot mention or ask to be taken into consideration, for instance, at work. How this affects their family, love-life, career. Both men and women. The hidden dramas of our daily lives. How about *Suffering in Silence*? Or *My Hidden Calvary*? I envision a maybe not large, but faithful audience. Two, three million, up? Ten thirty, eleven in the evening maybe? Well after the watershed.'

What is she talking about? Toolis, peering at the ceiling, has strayed into selling mode. She'd better explain.

'Right, I see. Did you have any particular problems in mind?'

'Well, yes. We could perhaps have a more serious one, then one less so, in each programme: say, genital herpes and cold sores; cystitis – now that is a biggie – and incontinence, well that is too, really; thrush – the sufferers run to millions; genital warts, and so on. But you get the main idea, don't you – it's a problem, and we can't talk about it. Also, a huge amount of money is being made for relieving these things – how about *The Invisible Industry*?'

Oh. Oh, no. Now I get her; and I don't want anything to do with this. Alastair catches my eye and grimaces, letting fall a chewed gob of dough onto his Filofax. He puts it back in his mouth.

'There's two stages we're going to have to work on – deciding on the topics, and finding out the statistics for all of them, then getting sufferers to talk about the problem. We'll need to call surgeries and STD clinics for information, and that's where you come in. Don't say where you're from or what we want the data for. It's none of their business. Ask for the press office. How does that sound?'

Terrible. Where shall I say I am from? I can't lie to these people. Can I get out of it? Oh for God's sake, woman, I upbraid myself, it's not coal-mining. You're hardly in a sweat shop. She's just testing you. This is television. You want this. Don't lose sight of your greater goals. Hordes of aspirants would indeed slaughter their grandmothers for such a chance. I smile blandly.

'Fine, right, yes, I'll have a go.'

'Excellent. I'll leave you to it. Right now, though, Alastair and myself are in a meeting. OK? Don't put through any calls unless they're urgent, you know, commissioning editors, accident and emergency departments, police . . .'

I don't want to do this.

I know I'm being pathetic, but I don't want to do this. I don't know how to do this. What exactly does she want me to do? What does she want to find out? Don't I get told how to do it? Where do I start? They both have their backs to me now. I daren't ask her, daren't say this is all a dreadful mistake, daren't confess I want to be a ballerina after all.

I was so tough with Eric. I sorted out all that business by myself. I've always sorted out everything by myself. But now I'm going to cry, alone at the party and I want to go home. The prospect of speaking to anyone in this state is poor. There is that span of dead time before you start to cry. All goes silent and still. You will cry, you cannot stop it. It is similar to the throttling spasm of the throat that comes the second before you are sick. You will vomit.

75

Perhaps these moments are unsettling because they announce something so rare: an absolute knowledge of what is to come.

'Nanette! Green bin bags?'

What? My eyes are swelling. Hand in front of the nose. Getting harder to speak. 'Ye-es?'

'These bags. I thought we'd agreed they'd never be seen again in this office?'

What *is* she talking about? Does she not believe in explaining anything? Must I always be left to estimate the workings of her tiny mind? I suppose I am staring, very stupidly, tensing my whole face; so I turn to look away, up and out of the window.

'Yesterday, I asked you to call the cleaners, didn't I? Nanette?'

Fuck. I don't need this. I nod. It's already mixed with a sniff.

'Well, you called the wrong company! You called those cowboys Miss Moppy, didn't you?'

Do I admit that I forgot? Which is worse, to forget to obey an order, or to obey it wrong? It's an academic question anyway: I am physically incapable of telling the truth to her now.

'I didn't know which ones they were! These were in the address thing. Just under "cleaners".'

They'd better be. I hope she hasn't checked recently.

'I told you. Billie and I spent the best part of the last three months trying to sack Miss Moppy! Getting out of the contract we had with them took that long! They didn't think that gross incompetence when they did bother to turn up coupled with a near nil attendance rate were adequate grounds for "reasonable dissatisfaction" with their service! And then, at the beginning of last week, they finally agreed to refund a month's advance – *advance*! – payment and never to darken this doorstep again!'

I am chilled into immobility. Maybe she can even stop

76

the inevitable? The tears hold back. She is so angry. How has this happened?

'And then you ask them back. They must have been surprised! That woman Phyllis will be laughing herself silly! They've not sent that refund yet! You must call the other company in there – what's their name? Yes, call them and find out what happened – did they turn up, I mean. And why didn't they clean over the weekend anyway? That's what I want to know. It's no good if they're even worse than the old lot. I cannot believe this.'

I can't either. Are the wheels of all industry run on such fuel? I have to escape. Toolis turns back to Alastair, who has the decency at least to pretend to be reading. Into the kitchen. More coffee. Kill some time.

The phone rings. No. Not now. Fuck bubbly. I give my answer the funeral parlour feel, but it sounds euphoric compared to this caller's drone.

'Billie, please.' Not a trace of humanity.

'She doesn't work here any more, so perhaps I can help you?'

I'm gazing up at the window in order to eke out what little control I have left. This woman better have good news or I will cry this time. I can't look at Toolis.

'Yes, well I hope so. It's Margaret from Completely Clean –'

It'll be bad news.

'– and I don't know if you know anything about this, but last night, around eleven, my employee turned up, whereupon she was met by another outfit in the process of cleaning and –' it sounds like a crime report – 'this lot were none too polite, to put it mildly. None of which was very considerate to your poor young lady still at work there.'

Lesley? Hasn't she heard of workers' rights?

'Now I did understand you were having trouble terminating their contract but this has now happened more than

77

a few times so we at Completely feel it's getting beyond a joke, and much as we hate to turn down any prospective clients, there are exceptions to this rule, of course, as I'm sure no doubt you will understand.'

'Oh, please don't take it that way. It's all my fault, I'm new here. Please come back, it won't happen again, I only started yesterday, it's just a bit of confusion.'

Which it is. I really am utterly confused. Why did the Moppy people turn up at all if Toolis is taking them to court? What is going on here?

'Well, obviously there's an awful lot of confusion at your company, Miss, er, who'm I speaking to?'

'It's Nancy.'

'Right. Well, Nancy, I have to say this isn't the only problem. You see, you wouldn't have had to call anyone out yesterday if we'd been allowed to do our job early on Monday morning.'

'I'm sorry?'

'Again our team goes to your office as and when we're supposed to, only this time we're met by a person who, my employee tells me, made an inappropriate move towards her in no uncertain terms. And, not to put too fine a point on it, this man was drunk.'

Alastair! Has he no shame?

'Well, Margaret, I don't know anything about that particular incident as it happens, but I can quite understand your concern, and I shall do my best to sort it out at this end.'

I'm getting quite professional at this, though I say it myself. Maybe a career in customer services would be more me?

'Well, that is the very minimum response we would expect, but if we are to continue with this contract, I will need some form of guaranteed assurance that . . .'

Oh, just fuck off. Do you think I give a damn? What do I say to her now? Wheeling round, receiver clenched to my hot ear, I tense the phone wire stretched between my two fists.

Oh, my God.

That man is back. Aidan. Sitting at an empty desk reading a newspaper and idly scratching his hair. My heart leaps, shocking me, and I go red. When did he come in? The voice squeaking out of the receiver fades away, her volume strangely lowered, and I hear myself promising that I will personally make sure this kind of thing never happens again. How, I don't know. Rottweilers on patrol from dusk till dawn? The cleaning hours? I am so way past caring. At last she retreats, pacified, and I put down the phone, exhausted. Was he watching?

'Well done, Nancy.'

He was; and he remembers my name! I look up and smile.

'Thanks.'

It's a bit of a shock to have someone be nice, I must say. He does have a lovely face. I study it. So, that's what it's like. I remember now. He looks worried. Imagine soothing that furrowed brow.

'Aidan!' The shout rents the air. 'How's it going?' Alastair is striding towards him, now pumping his hand. I'm staring.

Toolis catches my eye. The VD clinics. I have to call them. And those other cleaners. While Aidan's in earshot? This *is* fun.

'Fine, Alastair, fine. How are you? I've come to see Lesley.'

As if on cue, the phone rings, and Lesley, minus any form of greeting, rasps from afar: 'Is Aidan there?'

I suggest that she take something for that throat, then pack her on hold where she belongs and tell Aidan the call is for him. He takes the receiver from my hand and leans in front of me on the desk. I am *this* close.

I can read the figures on his watch. It's huge. Khaki green

with metallic effects. Knobs all round the outer rim. One of those chunky digital deep-sea diving ones that connects you to NASA and things like that. I'm impressed. I can count the hairs squashed beneath its strap. Glints of gold. The hand itself, kind of squarish, box-shaped, effective, like it's used to doing things, delivering the goods on a daily basis. I have no choice but to listen to his conversation.

'Oh really, that's a shame. Don't worry though . . . No, no, that's OK. No, I'm afraid tomorrow and Thursday are no good for me. What about Friday? . . . Yes? In the morning? All right. Eleven? Here? Let me write this down.'

He glances round with an urgent pen-and-paper-hunting look. I push both towards him and he nods at me. You're welcome. All in a day's work. He says goodbye to Lesley and puts the phone down.

'Thanks, Nancy.'

I'm glued to the seat here. I do like this calling by name business. Aidan resumes his conversation with Alastair. He doesn't seem in any rush to go. I open the yellow pages for Central London and look up some clap clinics. I do not, repeat not, wish to be doing this. Not now. Not ever. And especially not with this man Aidan here: but I have no choice. The bullet must be bitten.

'Good morning, Summer Vale Clinic.'

'Hello, could I speak to your press office, please?'

'We don't have a press office, may I ask what is this concerning?' A sharp clipped female voice.

'Er, well, yes, er, it's statistics. I'm looking for figures about the people and the problems that you treat.'

'May I ask who is calling please? Are you from the media?'

'Er, no, it's Nancy Miller from, er, well yes, I suppose so, it's a TV company, and I'm doing some research into these things for a possible programme, so I want some information really.' Quite professional, I think.

'Which TV company, please?'

'Er, Toolis Television UK, we make documentaries.' *We*. That sounds good.

'And what would this programme be about in particular?'

I lower my voice. How hideously embarrassing. 'Oh, erm, it's about, erm, well, problems that people have that they don't want to talk about. They keep them secret because they're ashamed – not the really, really serious ones – I mean, things like er, herpes, that isn't going to kill you but will affect your daily life, you know? I mean, that must apply to everything you deal with?'

This is all over the place.

'Not necessarily. By and large that might be true, though. If I understand you right. But what do you want to know exactly?'

Good question.

'Well, we're interested in the figures of a typical place like yours and also, if possible, we wondered if any of your patients might be willing to talk to us, or whether you could give us some names or something? We want to have interviews with some sufferers –' I inject some baby softness here – 'so as to make it all real.'

'Are you joking? Total confidentiality is vital for this kind of establishment. Most people come here and give false names, and we don't ask for any address. And I seriously doubt whether any of our clients, even if we could get in touch with them, would have any desire to talk about their experiences.'

And I would support them one hundred per cent in that, I must say; but then the woman relents. Maybe a mother herself. I obviously sound desperate.

'I could fax you our leaflet, though, which does include some of the kind of figures you might want. Do you have a fax number?'

Of course. I take what feels like many minutes to find

it and then put down the receiver in a shivery sweat.

'No, no, no, no, no!'

Toolis on the warpath, heels a-click. What's her problem? I did all right by the end, didn't I? Rather a successful initial foray into the science of information retrieval, even, though I may have infringed her orders slightly.

'I don't think you could have done that worse! Are you going to tell me what you did wrong, before I do?'

'Sorry?'

Aidan looks up. Alastair too. I don't know where to look.

'Oh, really! Just look back at what you did. You told everything to whoever it was you were speaking to, everything! Now you simply cannot do that! As a company, we are only as good as our ideas! That's what we sell! We can't go around telling people what they are! They are valuable! And what did you get in return, I wonder? Did she tell you anything?' Her hair hat jerks back and forth. That control is ruffled.

'Erm, well . . .'

'Speak up now!'

She doesn't care that the others are listening. Will I be able to speak? If I speak, I'll cry. I so much want to say that it's not fair, that you can't do this, that it isn't my fault; but when you most need to be lucid, that's when your voice leaves you. Toolis waits. My eyes have filled with tears.

'Heather, can I have a word outside?'

Aidan?

'Oh, not now. Can't you see I'm talking to Nanette?'

'I know, but I think we'd better speak right now. Outside the office.'

I look up. She appears nonplussed, but doesn't have much choice except to oblige. Out she briskly trots, tutting.

Alastair has watched this all in silence, following the

movements with his whole head as if at a tennis match. Now he pulls a bemused face.

'What on earth is going on? Raised voices? In our little office? Hey, what's wrong?'

For at last I am weeping. Which rule have I broken now? Hysteria, but not unmixed, as they say, with glee. Aidan stood up for me. This is all way too much. I wave away Alastair, for what help is the coward now? He backs off, redundant.

Aidan doesn't reappear. Toolis comes back alone a while later. She gives me a very odd look. What has he said to her?

'Right, Nanette.'

Oh God, please help me. Leave me alone, Toolis, please, I'm tired of you. She seems distracted, though.

'What did the clinic you rang say?'

Wearily: 'That they don't have the names and other details of people because they're assumed names most of the time and they're faxing me their information leaflet.'

'Oh yes, I'd forgotten that. They would be anonymous, wouldn't they? Damn!'

Has she forgotten her fury?

'We must think of another way.'

The office stays calm for a while, hung with that respectful restraint always exhibited after an emotional outburst. I am so embarrassed for revealing such a lack of self-possession. Why couldn't I just have said I didn't want to make these calls? Why couldn't I admit that I never rang the cleaners? Why can't I speak when I need to?

'I know! Nanette! Adverts!'

Does she never shut up?

'What?'

'We'll put adverts in the papers. You know, you must have seen the ones I mean? *Have you attempted suicide? Were you bullied at school? Do you loathe your neighbours? If so, serious documentary TV company would like*

83

to talk to you ... We can do one for the taboos idea – I'll write it now.'

A reprieve?

'Do you think it'll work?'

'God yes. People are desperate to appear on TV for any reason. They'll be glad they've got something wrong with them. Probably make it up!'

I look round the room in despair. Still an hour to go before lunch and the day is boiling hot. Pushing a chair into position beneath one of the windows, I climb up onto it. Now I am level with the glass I can see out of my prison. What an astounding view of the city! Our building must be higher than it looks, for countless roofs are now beneath me. They bake in the sun and are descended upon by warm-feathered itchy pigeons. On some of them figures are sun-bathing, crouched on cushions to avoid burning their toes on the lead. Far below to the right I can see activity on Greek Street, to my left the back of the next street. While upwards there soars away the vast blue sky, beneath me is the darkness of the tar and the pits of dirty shadows and the gleam on a black motorbike's petrol tank. People speed along.

'Nanette? Come and read this.'

Toolis is standing below me, her head about level with my calves, a piece of paper waving in her hand. Will she never leave me be?

'Here it is. What do you think? We'll put it in the papers right away. *Suffering in silence? Thrush? Cystitis? Herpes? Have you now or have you ever had one of those problems that you just can't mention? Is your home and working life ruined by any of a number of taboo complaints like these? Respected TV company wants to talk to you for documentary programme. Please call Nanette, or fax her with your story.* I thought you'd like to handle the calls, wouldn't you? You could ring some papers today?'

What a great privilege! I don't think. She is smiling,

looking at me straight in the eyes. Butter would melt nowhere near her. I have already had more than enough of this woman.

'Sure.'

'Excellent. Now. You must call Miss Moppy and make it perfectly clear to them, once more, that we wish them never to set foot in this office again, that we fully expect a refund as previously agreed, minus the price of one day's service, and that if they fall at all short of this within the next seven days then we will go considerably further than merely messing about in the small claims court. There is absolutely no way that they are going to avoid paying me my money. Do you get that? Call now so I can listen.'

Sadist.

I spend the rest of the day on the phone, starting with Miss Jane Moppy herself. She turns out to be a charming woman who explains that she, too, was amazed when Billie called her early last week to say that all was forgiven and could they run up a new contract to start afresh the following week? How odd. This mystery deepens. Billie had plainly lost all touch with reality in the final days. What's more, Miss Moppy adds, they also have a letter signed by Stella Fitzpatrick to that effect. Really? She can fax it back through, if I like. I accept the offer and with one hand over the receiver explain all to Toolis.

'Stella! Stella signed a letter to them? What has happened to that woman lately? She must be losing her mind!'

Intrigued, I ask Toolis whether she'd like to continue the conversation now, since she knows more about the situation than I do, but she declines the offer and orders me to deal with it. I take my heart in my hands and tell the woman that Billie has been hospitalised for depression since then and that whatever she may have promised is now invalid.

'I see. Back to my lawyers then. They'll be in touch.'

Toolis fumes. What's the problem with Stella Fitzpatrick, I wonder? And why isn't she here? I daren't ask right now, though. No doubt all will be revealed in the fullness of time.

CHAPTER SEVEN

✳

Wednesday and Thursday pass with me hunched embarrassed over the phone, either placing the dread advert on classified pages up and down the country, or muttering with complete strangers from more clinics about sexually transmitted diseases. Lesley must have got home at some point and washed her hair because she turns up on Wednesday with it looking as though a few thousand volts have passed through recently. Clamping the frizzled mass down with her hands every forty seconds or so, an operation so futile that I suggest she tie it back somehow, she emits an incredulous snort and puts on the foulest expression I have ever seen on man or beast.

'I don't tie my hair back.'

Clearly she believes it to be her greatest asset. I say sorry, I just thought it might look nice. She doesn't forgive easily, though, and makes an extra special effort to include me in things. After lunch she asks me to take the corner of her vegetarian sandwich back to the shop, along with the microscopic shard of suspected prawn shell that she has found in it, a task I perform with little grace; and, on my return, with full refund I may add, she hooks her finger at me and hisses that there is a stain on the bowl in the ladies and could I either remove it myself or get the cleaners to come round immediately? This little job I neglect to perform at all. Last thing on Thursday I record a message on the answer phone encouraging callers who have read our advert to share their harrowing experiences after the beep. I'm praying there are no takers.

Later that evening at the flat I am wondering what to wear tomorrow. Aidan is coming to see Lesley at eleven. The phone rings.

'Hello, Nance.' Eric, sounding constipated. I've barely thought about him since Monday night.

'Oh. Hello. Where are you?'

'Back in my impoverished student accommodation, scrimping and saving so as to be able to eat and keep this rotting roof over my head, while you live and work in unparalleled luxury.'

Sarky little shit. Getting chucked *has* improved his word power.

'Well, funny, but I've just had toast and a boiled egg for dinner and I can't afford to go out.' Such a lie.

'Oh, fridge empty already?'

'No. Just exercising a bit of restraint.'

It's hard to know what to say. Keep it frivolous.

'Are you all right, Nance? You know, I am a bit worried about you.'

How dare he be?

'Why?'

'Well, you weren't being exactly normal the other night.'

Oh, thanks. He is beginning to remind me of Philip. Such a man, so stupid, so fucking superior!

'Maybe I was tired of being "exactly normal".'

'Oh.'

He doesn't know what I am talking about. I can't really blame him.

'So did you mean everything you said then?'

What did I say?

'Yes.'

'Oh, Nance, I thought if I left you to cool down a couple

88

of days you'd get over it. So you've not changed your mind?'

'No. Sorry, Eric. I really am.'

'Oh, bullshit!'

He's snivelling now. Does he really mind? Surely he didn't actually like me? I was pretty horrible to him; but then maybe he's never had anything better. But then I've never had anything better. I feel cold as a little stone.

'Sorry, Eric.'

'Yes. So am I. I'd better go then.'

Pause.

'Bye then, Nance.'

'Bye, Eric, take care.'

What a killer, that 'take care'. I am such a bitch. The line goes dead. Why did I ever stay with him? There were other men I liked the look of, the mere sight of whom had the power to shift my guts more than Eric ever could, so why didn't I pounce on them? Fear, I suppose: they were birds in the bush whereas Eric was securely in the hand (forgive the metaphor) and though I might like the look of them, their liking me was a whole other question. Too much risk. Eric wasn't going anywhere. What guilt I've ever felt about using him has always been pitched in a losing battle with pragmatism.

As I'm approaching the drinks cabinet the phone rings again.

'Nancy babe!'

It's Grace, abandoned flatmate one. Now I do feel guilty. We've not spoken since I came here.

'What are you up to, babe?'

'I've got a TV job! Oh, and I've split up with Eric.'

'I know. I ran into him in the bar, drowning his sorrows. He didn't know whether to ring you or not, so I told him he should.'

'Oh, thanks. I've just spoken to him.'

'And?'

'And nothing. It's finished.'

'Oh.' Silence; but she knew we weren't that serious. 'Well, I'm sorry. But you're not too upset, are you? Oh God, that's a bit blunt, isn't it? Me and my big mouth. Still, babe, you'll need a holiday now, won't you? Greek men and all that? I can't wait to hit the beach.'

Shit. Here we go.

'Oh yes, right. Listen, I don't know how long this job is for, mind, but I don't think it'll last till then.'

'Oh, you're not going to duck out, are you, babe? No, sorry, I know you won't. I trust you. Tell me about the job, though. It sounds very glam.'

I proceed to describe it. She's undoubtedly impressed, but I water down her enthusiasm: 'Oh, it's not very exciting really. I just answer the phone. In fact, it's pretty boring. I'll probably walk out in a couple of weeks anyway.'

'You sure? I'm sorry, I know this sounds selfish, but I can't go away with just Rebecca. I love her, honestly, but you know she's not the sun, sea, and sand type. It'll be a complete disaster if you don't come.'

We've been planning this for a while, but haven't booked anything yet because Grace has a theory about eleventh-hour bucket-shop bargains.

'Don't worry. I'll be there.'

'Well, find out about your job. It's not too urgent yet but I suppose we'd better not leave it till the very last minute. Shall I ring tomorrow night?'

'Er, no. I'll ring you, when I know.'

'Don't forget. God, babe, I must say, I can't wait. I'm sick of watching Luisa pull every night.'

'Who?'

'Luisa. Don't you remember? You let your room to her.'

The summer student. 'Oh, her. How are you all getting on? Everything's OK, isn't it?'

'Oh, she's doing fine. She's way too good-looking, mind. I promise you, there's a different man here most nights.'

'What, in my room? I didn't include that in our agreement.'

'Well, babe, sorry, but talk about spunk up the walls.'

'Grace! You're not serious?'

'I am. Rebecca and me aren't getting any sleep. I can't wait to get away just for a rest.'

Great. We natter some more. She says goodbye and I put down the phone. Hmm.

Friday dawns grey. Wardrobe reassessment. Aidan's coming in today. It could turn hot later. Or chillier. Jeans? Can I get away with them now? Plus classic (non-ripped) long-sleeved T-shirt? Casual tone to herald the approaching weekend? Why not? I think so. In front of the mirror I look thinnish, if not quite hauntingly enigmatic.

Bang on nine thirty I find only Lesley at the office, raking those gorgeous locks. She arrived at least three coffee mugs ago. A small mirror stands on the desk in front of her, along with various pieces of make-up. Between her lips a tortoiseshell hair clip is preventing her from saying hello, had the will been there. A hair clip? Is she going to take up my suggestion? I'm flattered. Bugger that, though – is she after Aidan? She has to be. Or, and I must be realistic, since he keeps dropping by the office for no apparent reason, he's probably after her. I wait for one of the clip's spiky teeth to stab her mouth. No such luck. She removes it and anchors a swoosh of gleaming tresses away from her eyes onto the back of her head. Now I see why she doesn't tie her hair back. The carefully manufactured tendril effect of her fringe which normally curls apparently carefree about both temples now fails to cover a stressful mountain range of spots on her forehead. The red beginnings of a boil are also evident on her chin. A lone gleam of sunlight slithers over her greasy skin and illuminates where she has surely dipped her face in a bucket of fierce orange foundation. This angry film meets her hair at the temples and widow's peak and disappears behind the ears, then descends to follow her jaw-line. Here it stops sharp, revealing a neck that is pale, unshiny, dull. You'll need to redo all that by eleven, my girl.

'There's about a thousand messages on the answer machine for you from that advert. Some of them are disgusting. I couldn't carry on. Can you go through them all in case there's some for me or anyone else as well in there?'

I haven't even put my bag down yet. Not offering her a coffee but making myself one, then pottering around needlessly for over an hour, I eventually settle down to the messages. They've not taken long to come in.

'Hello, this is a message for Nancy and I'm calling about the advert in today's Herald. *My name is Sue and I'm from Solihull and I think I could rightly say I have had my life ruined by incontinence. I have tried every product available but to be frank there is no way you can hide the evidence of it completely . . . I would be grateful to talk about this, Nancy, and would be happy to be interviewed and my number is –'*

Oh, lovely.

'Hi, I saw your advert in the Mail *and I'd like to say, oh sorry, my name is Morwena Richards from Newport, Gwent, and, yes, well, I have suffered from thrush, intermittently, throughout my life, since I was twelve I think and my mum and dad gave me a new bike for my birthday, I can remember it exactly, as it happens, it was slightly too big for me, I mean the seat was too high, and I thought it was so grown up so I wouldn't let them lower it for me, so when I rode it I think it chafed, you know, and I got it that way? My doctor said this was quite likely, but that was recently you see, I didn't dare mention it at the time, I was only a kid and I thought I was pregnant first through some kind of miracle, we were a church-going family, you know . . .'*

Morwena is going to use up the tape at this rate. I sneak a look at Lesley. No flicker of amusement on that painted face.

'. . . so I never mentioned it to anyone for years and kept trying to find out cures all cloak and dagger like and tried to read up about it in the library but I didn't even tell my best friend because I thought she'd think I'd done something I shouldn't have, you know?'

The phone is ringing. I switch off Morwena.

'Nanette? It's Heather. Listen. I'm not going to be in today. Alastair and I are going out on a bit of a recce in town all day. Is Lesley in?'

'Yes.'

'Any messages?'

'Lots about the advert, I'm going through them all.'

'I told you so. Get their names and numbers and details. Then you can call them all next week. Now, no time for chat, I'm in a rush.'

Gone. I reactivate Morwena. Strangely, she's run out of steam:

'Anyway, I better not go on too much now or I'll use up all your tape on the machine, but it'd be lovely if you could call back sometime for a chat as I'd be happy to discuss my problem further. OK, bye now.'

Pause on tape. Click. Cough. Quietly spoken man.

'OK then, [cough] my name's Geoffrey and I'm not sure if this is the kind of thing you mean in your advert but anyway here goes: my, er, organ's too small. And the testicles are invisible – so my love life's nonexistent. It has ruined my life. I've never before said about it to anyone. Actually, hang on, this probably isn't the kind of thing you wanted to hear about, was it?'

Click.

'Geoffrey! Come back!'

I am bending towards the machine so as to hear properly.

'And who, may I ask, is Geoffrey?'

A familiar voice above me. Aidan. Early. My heart begins to pound. I can feel my temperature rise. All these things. I reply quietly so Lesley can't hear.

'Geoffrey's, erm, bits are too small. He answered our advert, well, it's Heather's, but I have to speak to them.'

Aidan laughs, crow's-feet appearing. Same lovely sight, same horny suit effect, though more greyish than navy this time, same smile. Here he is again and I am relieved, as though the time he spends out of my sight is an enemy to be vanquished. God, what's taken over me? I am talking to this man like I know him, who he is and what he does: but I don't. Not a thing. Such ignorance is no barrier to our communication, though, since I assume he knows what I am talking about. Have we started to play games with each other? If so, very good.

'Oh, poor Geoffrey. So, you're going to get them to come to you now, are you?'

He remembers Tuesday.

'Yes. Oh, listen, thanks for whatever it was you said, or did, to Heather the other day. She laid off me afterwards.'

'What? Oh, that's OK.'

I go all shy. 'Well, thanks.'

'My pleasure. Now, where is the very lovely Lesley?'

We both look around. Yes, where *is* the Lesley? Practising advanced winsomeness in the loo? At that moment she bursts out of the kitchen door and pitches me a frankly aggressive glance. Her hair is now cruelly stretched into a ponytail, making her look like an alien, slitty eyes yanked backwards.

'Here I am, Aidan! Thanks for coming in earlier. I just couldn't put off a client.'

Client? Honestly, what is she talking about?

'That's all right. Where shall we sit?'

'Oh, here.'

She pats a seat, almost simpering. Slut. He takes off his jacket and hangs it on the back of the chair, then rolls

94

up his shirt sleeves. The vista of his forearms does not disappoint. I attempt to keep my ogling discreet. They sit down together and start discussing something. I gather it's about money, but I can't understand much else. Lesley is so animated. A different person. No sneezing.

It's lovely to see Aidan. That face again. Not because it's handsome, although it is – no, it's, oh, I don't know, it's the way he smiles and laughs and looks worried. He looks sympathetic. Worth spending time with. You wouldn't die of boredom. You wouldn't have to pinch yourself before you could be bothered to converse with him.

I turn the answer phone back on and swivel up the volume.

'*Good evening, it's Tom Abbott here and no, I don't want to share my harrowing story, thanks very much. I'd rather urgently like to speak to Heather Toolis. I'm not in the office, I'm afraid, on Friday but you can get me on my mobile. Thanks very much.*'

Aidan looks up. Lesley's ears are flapping.

'Was that Tom Abbott? Yes? You must get hold of Heather, you know. He's a commissioning editor.'

'She said she was out on a "recce" with Alastair. How can I get hold of her?'

'Ring her mobile.'

'Do you know the number?'

'Nancy! Can't you see I'm busy? Look in the address file.'

I look. I find. I dial. A digital female tells me that the cellphone I am calling has been switched off. I'm to please try later. Oh well, I've done my best.

'No answer?'

'It's been turned off.'

'Leave a message on her home number.'

Good thinking: but it just rings and rings. I try again and it is answered, this time.

'Hello?' A hoarse cancerous growl like some harpy off *EastEnders*.

'Is Heather Toolis there?'

'Hello? Who's that? Hello?'

It must be a wrong number. I give up.

'Nothing doing, I'm afraid.' I voice my regret out loud. I can't help but look at Aidan, and, oh, how embarrassing, he's staring with a concentrated expression. I smile at him, and look away in a hurry, but Lesley catches me, and sends her own competitive beam in his direction. We're both putting on a performance for the man. I chuckle to no one in particular. This sets Lesley off again.

'Look, it does matter, all right? You must get in touch with her.' Then she trills girlishly: 'Sorry about that, Aidan. I won't waste any more of your time.'

Aidan has remained quiet throughout this exchange. Now he speaks: 'That's all right, Lesley. Not your fault.' Then, slowly, looking her full in the face and focusing on the boil, he continues: 'Hold on a minute. Is that a tomato pip stuck to your chin?'

Her jaw actually drops, my heart goes *Ka-Boom!* – and it's love.

I can't look at either of them. This is all too much. Did Aidan really say that to Lesley? My hero! I slump back into the chair. Time to listen to more tales of genital woe from people only too willing to discuss the tyranny of their private parts to me. As the gruesome testaments spew from the machine I lean on my elbow staring into space, barely concentrating. A strident male voice shakes me from my musing.

'This is James Stuart from Edinburgh and I won't leave my number because something tells me you won't be calling anyway. This is a message for "Nancy" though I suppose that's just a fake name, is it? I read your advert in my newspaper today, and to be honest I'm only calling to express my feelings about programmes such as these which

quite blatantly exploit the suffering of people foolish enough to trust you with accounts of their problems. I am tired of watching trash like this appear on my television screen . . .'

I sneak a look at Lesley and Aidan. Surely their meeting isn't more interesting than this?

'. . . and I am depressed by the thought of how much money goes towards making it, and, Nancy, if you have any choice in the matter at all, I suggest you seriously reconsider the direction of your career. Thank you.'

Excellent! This is all so odd. Why are these people either confiding to me problems far too personal to mention to their closest relatives, or berating me for suggesting the idea?

'Ridiculous man,' says Lesley.

'Maybe he had a point?' I suggest.

'Maybe he did?' says Aidan.

Lesley fizzes noticeably. Not much later, she gets to her feet.

'Right then, Aidan, I'm afraid I'm going to have to leave you to it. I'm so sorry.'

She's irritated. Had to cut her flirting short. He's cool, though.

'Oh, don't worry about me, honestly. And don't rush back. I'm happy going through all this myself.'

Lesley has no choice now but to leave. She should have cancelled her 'client'. Make your bed and you have to lie on it, viper, I rejoice. I have him all to myself now, and, at last, I'm going to have some fun in this rat-hole.

How very nice. No one else to interrupt. I take my time, gazing at his head bowed over the paperwork, and don't speak until a respectable few seconds have elapsed.

'So, what are you doing here?'

'Oh, Lesley's been sorting me out.'

All's now becoming clear, I don't think. I daren't ask

anything more ambitious than this, however. I've gone all shy.

'I see.'

He chats on, though, friendly enough: 'Are you hungry? Shall I go and get you a sandwich? I could do with one myself.'

'Do you mind if I go? I'll get you something if you like, it's just I have to go to the chemist's.'

Oh, *why* did I say that? Even mentioning the chemist's is tantamount to saying I have a body and – heaven forbid – a boyfriend.

'Oh, yes, sure, erm, ham, cheese and pickle, please. No mustard, though. What if the phone rings?'

'You answer it with a lively, happening, and bubbly air. I'm sure you'll cope beautifully.'

Leaving him to it I romp out to stagger up and down the aisles of a nearby chemist's. I'm drunk with smugness and everything seems in a mist. Stop. Slow, my beating heart. There's no rush. Aidan isn't going anywhere. He's waiting for me to bring him his lunch. So. What am I looking for? Sandwiches. And where am I now? Dental Care. Ah, yes. We've finished Auntie's nutritious and grossly expensive chive and coriander toothpaste, so I pick up some home brand for under a pound and head for the sandwiches.

Now I am faced by a chilly escarpment bedraped with those transparent cold-containing plastic strips through which your warm hands dart at the chosen victim. The assignment: ham, cheese and pickle (no mustard). Oh, nothing's quite right. What is the nearest combination on offer? Grated Cheddar with Country Pickle. Ham Salad with Mustard Mayonnaise. A three pack for hicks (corn sheaf on the packet) of Cheese and Crunchy Pickle, Honey-Cure Ham with English Mustard, Egg and Cress with Horseradish Mayonnaise. Maybe the perfect combination is to be found in the Lo-Calorie section. I have to hook my elbows into a crush of matchsticky-armed females to survey what remains in this obviously popular area. The ranks have been savaged by starving vicious dieters. Tuna and cucumber clearly a favourite. Prawn and Dijon mustard not so hot. Ham and pickle a possibility. Of course none are buttered, and cheese is nowhere to be seen.

Hopeless. I buy a Gruyère and grape effort for myself, full fat, plus the toothpaste. Then, heading for a sandwich bar, I wait in the queue a good twenty minutes before it's my turn, but don't begrudge a second. Aidan's request will be made to order. A grossly overweight Italian man constructs it, smearing on the butter and laying four cheese slices and two thick pieces of ham on top.

'And pickle, please.'

On are spooned the wet lumps. Down goes the top half of the bap. Fat death-white fingers wrap it in Cellophane and twirl it into a brown paper bag. I pull out my purse. Paying for my fancy man's lunch.

'That will be four pounds fifty, love.'

What? You fat bastard! I loathe Soho.

I have begun to use the lift now, since I noticed Lesley sticks to the stairs. When I asked her why, she said the lift had got jammed with her in it once, for four hours, and consequently they lost their deposit on a film editing suite. She had to be cut out by firemen. I think I laughed, which didn't help. Now, after messing up my hair in front of its greasy-fingerprinted mirror, in what I hope is an intriguingly carefree manner, I stride into the office.

Oh, no. Who is this? Aidan is talking to some man, their backs turned. I walk over to have a look. Tall and sallow-skinned, dressed in a tracksuit. Aidan is laughing. They turn towards me.

'Nancy, meet Ben, who does the accounts.'

Ben extends a hand. 'Hello, how do you do?' Eastern European accent.

'Hello. I'd have got you some lunch if I'd known you were here.'

He holds up both palms in mock horror. 'No, no! I'm on a diet.'

'Oh.'

I hand the roll to Aidan.

'Wonderful, Nancy, a proper lunch, not some stupid sandwich with fruit in! What do I owe you?'

For some reason I lie: 'Oh, about a pound, I think.'

'You sure? That's cheap for round here.'

I blush, and turn sharp back to my desk. I have to be cool. Is he looking at me weirdly?

'There were a couple of calls. Yes, here, I wrote them down: Mrs, erm, Wilford from Milford Haven, she went on about sores up her backside for a while until I said the best thing was to smear caustic soda up there; then a Mr Smith from East Lothian discussed his almost total lack of rectal control until I told him he had the wrong number.'

I laugh and go even redder. Is Aidan flirting with me? He can't be!

The afternoon is pure bliss, for a while. After checking out the seventeen remaining messages on the answer phone – more gruesome confessions – I lean back in my chair and decide to do absolutely nothing. Few people call. A deeply satisfying Friday languor spreads over the proceedings. Aidan reads his stuff while Ben taps away at a calculator. This is breeding yards of coiled white paper that trail down into a little hill on the floor. Aidan catches my eye a couple of times. He has a way of smiling directly at me, which is simultaneously disturbing and thrilling, as though he is looking right into my head and asking it a question which, need you ask, I am anxious to answer in the affirmative as soon as possible.

Too soon, though, it's all over. He tidies up and moves to leave. I am devastated at the prospect. I don't want him to go. I don't want to be left alone without him. What is happening to me?

'Bye, Nancy.'

'Bye, Aidan.'

'See you.'

He smiles, then closes his mouth purposefully, and walks away. The door shuts. I itch to run after him. The spell evaporates. The office is dreary. A desk is a desk.

My desolation doesn't last long. After about forty-five minutes the phone rings, and although Toolis isn't here, I perfect a textbook greeting.

'Oh, well done. That was professional. It's Aidan.'

'Oh, hi.' Thumping of the heart. I am dead shy now, more so than when he was in the room; and blushing again, as though he can see.

'Er, I was wondering, did I leave my jacket there?'

'Oh, what does it look like?'

'Well, it's my suit jacket. I might have left it on the back of the chair by Lesley's desk.'

There it hangs.

'You just might have.' A hint of the hussy, no more.

'Oh, great. It's got all my cards in. I'll come round and get it.'

A stroke of luck? Or did he leave it there on purpose? Come on, you don't walk out of a place without your jacket. He fancies me. I know it. My God. An older man. Imagine taking that shirt off. What is underneath? Mentally, I undo him button by button. Of all out-of-the-question things, just how out of the question would that be? I gulp, and take a risk.

'Or, I could bring it to you, Aidan, er, later, I mean when I've finished here, unless you need it this minute.'

Shameless, shameless.

'Oh, Nancy, that would be kind, but I couldn't ask you to do that. I'm probably right out of your way.'

'Where are you ringing from?' The thought of meeting

Aidan on neutral ground outside work is the most exciting prospect I've ever faced.

'Well, I'm in Gower Street now, but I could head back towards you. I suppose we could meet halfway, if you like. I'll tell you what, how about a drink, if you're not too busy?'

What? Did he say that? I would have cancelled God himself for this.

'No, no, that's OK, that would be nice, a quick drink. Where shall we meet?'

What made me put in the 'quick'?

'Oh, I know somewhere. Lesley took me there once. I think it's called Bar Desdemona, in Wardour Street. Up near Oxford Street on the right.'

'All right, I'll see you there. About six o'clock? Yes? Bye.'

Unbelievable.

This speed of events is stunning. I have spent my life asleep compared to this. Am I to spend only a week in my new job before being scooped up by a man whose glory I have never seen the like of before? It's unsettling. Perhaps it's all too quick, even for London. Maybe he's a mass murderer? My God, how can I be so naïve? He must think I am just too easy for words. I have fallen into his trap. No, jumped. Simple provincial girl, desperate for adventure, experience, passion; decaying body found headless in the Fens, sexually assaulted, no leads. And I have thrown myself at him, asking for trouble. Nancy, I admonish myself, calm down. If you're worried, don't go. As if. Or ring Sarah then, and tell her where you're going.

I call the flat. Sarah isn't there. The phone rings on and on. I wonder where it is? Muffled by the duvet on her bed? Is she ignoring it? Or just plain out? Damn. Surely he's not a murderer? A rapist? What should I do?

The phone rings. In a quandary I answer: 'Hello?'

'Nanette! It's Heather. I'm in a call box, so don't waste

my time with small talk. Now, what's happened to answering like I told you? It may be Friday afternoon but that's no excuse for laziness! Right? Any messages for us?'

'No.'

'Put me through to Lesley.'

'She went out at lunch time and hasn't come back.'

'You are joking! When you think how much I pay that woman!'

Beep-beep-beep. The money runs out. Cheapskate, she can't even run to a phone card. High-powered business executive my eye. Anyway, where is Lesley? It's five o'clock. I don't know how to lock up if she doesn't come back, and I can't hang around waiting for her. My hot date looms. With a murderer. Ring Sarah. She isn't home. Then I'll just have to keep my wits about me. Maybe, of course, there is the possibility that he isn't a murderer. Maybe he is a nice man. Maybe he just likes me. What the hell? Live dangerously. No, don't. Ring Sarah.

Engaged. A-ha-ha, the old slapper is back, after four nights on the trot away from the flat. She and Nick are at it all the time. I want to be like them, young and in love. Maybe I'm on the verge of exactly that.

The phone goes again, and I look at it for three rings. Toolis again? Or Aidan, having changed his mind? Can't make it after all. Age difference too horrendous? A couple more rings. Ben looks up, wondering why I'm not answering it. I've forgotten he's here.

'Hello, I mean, good –'

'Nancy, it's your mum. You sound professional.'

I sound like an idiot; but it's a relief to hear her. She has a sweet quiet voice with a kind of wiry core.

'Tell me, is it all right to call you at work? It's not too busy? You won't be fired or anything?'

'No! It's fine.'

My mother's funny. There's much about her I love, but too often she exhibits some of the worst traits of womanhood. I get so angry with her. She's weak. My father is not. She always lets him have his say. He treats her horribly sometimes. Talks past her as though she is dead space, and she lets him.

They married fairly early on in his meteoric rise from the gutter. Both in their early twenties, he had a junior clerk position at the bank and she was a lawyer's daughter. They met at a dance. I still wonder how they got it together, but I suppose he had a sense of humour then, or at least some sort of badboy charm. After parental disquiet on both sides and a short engagement she found herself alienated from her family and married to a budding domestic dictator. Well, that's how I read the family myth. It's pretty complicated, and I think they do love each other, albeit in a mismatched kind of a way. They've stayed together, at least. That must mean something. Anyway, all of nine swift months after the wedding day bouncy baby Philip arrived to complete their happiness and then little me came along, a bit late in the day, fifteen years later. Their ewe lamb; the apple of my mother's eye; the only thing she's allowed to fuss over, and I have the cheek to have a brain and want to leave home.

Now she starts trying to find out what I am doing in general, and who I am doing it with in particular; and I endeavour to tell her nothing, both in general and particular, as kindly as possible. I must confess, though, that after a minute or three of this I am also, ever so slightly, trying to get her off the line, because to me she spells responsibility, and caution, and not going for drinks with strange men, and that is not what I want to think about right now.

Fortunately the other line goes. She can hear it. We wind up in an indecent hurry and I promise to ring her soon.

'Nan? It's Sarah. I haven't spoken to you for *yonks*.'

Bollocks. Typical Sloane exaggeration.

'Listen, thank God you rang.'

'Why? And why are you talking so quietly?'

'I have a date tonight.'

'What! Oh my God. Who with? Anyone I know?'

'No, it's –' voice sunk to a furtive whisper – 'it's a man from here.'

'What? Already? You're such a dark horse, Nan! Eric's not been gone ten minutes!'

'Oh shut up. But, listen, I have to tell you in case this one's a murderer and I disappear. So I'll tell you his name and where we're going, all right? Are you listening?'

'Like a hawk, Nan. Like a hawk.'

Whispering ever more quietly I get the information across only seconds before Ben walks over to raise his jacket off the coat rack.

'You have to tell me everything, Nan. What's he like?'

'Later, all right? Everything later.'

'Well, I'm not going to be here tonight, so it'll have to be tomorrow; but I'll leave the place tidy for your later pleasure.'

'Oh, I don't think that'll be necessary.'

The receiver still attached to my ear, I wave Ben good night. Sarah gets off the line. Where is Lesley? Five forty-five already. I don't have keys. I don't want to be late. I *can't* be late. That woman is not going to make me late. Fuck her; I've got to go now. If I just turn everything off, to be safe, and slam the door locked behind me, surely that will be all right? I don't actually care if it isn't, to be honest; so I sprint round switching off lights, kettle, photocopier, printer, Lesley's computer, shut the windows, put the answer phone on and, yes, that's it. All done. I put on some make-up and reverently place Aidan's jacket into the carrier bag from the chemist's. Right. Here we go. Collecting myself, I know I'll need my wits about me. Tonight I have to sparkle.

Crunch. Door shut. I'm out of here. No going back. In the lift now, and with a spasm of gripping dread, I remember Tom Abbott's message for Toolis. I never told her; but the panic passes in a moment. Too bad; I have more important things to think about now.

CHAPTER EIGHT

*

You know when you want time to stop and preserve an occasion for ever so you can go back and live it again? Or return, rather, to before it has even happened, to when it is about to take place; but what actually occurs is that you start to forget straight away until eventually you're not even sure what did happen? You forget what you did talk about? What someone's face is actually like? It's my worst fear: so I caution my memory to work extra hard tonight. I want no trouble recalling such momentous happenings as these.

Thus, maybe, roughly, sort of, it goes like this: I step into the street. Little slam of the outside door. There's been a shower of rain. Clouds threaten more. It's unusually dark for a summer evening. The streets of Soho are wet. This wash makes their usual disgustingness slightly less horrible. Not that I'd care if they are swimming in sick this evening, forcing me to walk through other people's dinners down the road, tomato strands of mucus on my toes. I am going to have a drink with Aidan and I don't care. It's Friday night and I stopped caring at five forty-five. Fuck Toolis and fuck her commission and fuck Lesley and her fucking hair. They can go fuck themselves. What a nasty girl: out to get what I want. Past the tables on the pavement, gay men tapping cappuccinos in Old Compton Street, then the fumes of a coffee-bean shop, and a pub front open onto the street, drinkers' rumps reversing outwards, short girls looking up to tall men, theatrically holding cigarettes, nodding yes – yes – yes, absolutely, to the men's every statement, none of which they can hear. Heels in the channels of dark grey water running along the edge of the street, I jump in and out of these crowds and puddles, my lunch time path to the sandwich shop transformed into a grey-skied thundersome trail, through the darkened jungle and down to a moonlit drinking pool.

One window before the Bar Desdemona I take a look at myself. It's only six o'clock but the sky is electrically charged beautiful blue, and my reflection is itself dark against such a backdrop. Hair wisping about. Rangy, almost gaunt? An egg cup of rain from the gutter above splashes onto my nose as I lean forward, hands on my denim knees, approving of what I see.

'Are you going to admire yourself *all* night?'

Damn! Aidan is watching me, but not laughing or anything. He's only just got here, slunk up out of the darkness, wet on his shirt shoulders.

I straighten up.

'No, I've finished now.'

I walk in ahead of him, pulse pumping, feeling vulnerable that he can see me from behind. Eric would always touch me, repulsively gently, on either my waist or shoulder when he followed me through a door, as though he owned me. I'd often wished for a knife with which to whip round and stab him, but it wouldn't have looked good in court. Aidan keeps his hands off.

The bar is filling fast so I dive at one of the few empty tables left. Aidan manoeuvres himself into it after me. I pull his jacket out of the bag, lay it on the bench between us, and stand up again. I'd better get the first round in so he doesn't think I'm scrounging.

'Do you want a drink, Aidan?'

'No, no, I must get them. You brought my jacket. What would you like?'

'Erm –' What to order? What do you have in wine bars?

'Wine OK?'

'All right.'

'I think beer is allowed too.'

'Maybe beer then, if you'd like some.'

He must like beer, along with the cheese, ham and pickle sandwiches.

'Beer it is.'

I watch Aidan walk to the bar. Among the fashionable young backs and fronts of the men ordering drinks and the women sitting down unhooking handbag straps off their shoulders he pushes a lonely path, then returns empty-handed.

'They're bringing it over.'

'Right.'

'So, did the rest of the afternoon go all right? Ever get hold of Heather?'

'What?'

'Oh, I thought you had to give her that message?'

The message from Tom Abbott. My God. He remembers such a tiny detail from my little day? Pleasant astonishment does not begin to describe the sensation.

'My God! You're right. The commissioning editor! No, I completely forgot. Toolis rang in for messages and I told her there weren't any. Why can't I get it right with her?'

'Don't worry, he's probably just some jumped-up two-bit short-arsed idiot who likes getting people to kowtow to him. Probably beats his wife.'

'And tortures the cat.'

'Oh, definitely. I should forget it.'

Pause while the beer is put on our table, and a bowl of oily black olives. Aidan leans back with arms folded.

'So, how did you get the job? Do you know someone at Toolis TV?'

'Yes. I mean, no. I mean, yes, my brother does. Stella Something. The other director. She's not there at the moment, so I've never met her. Philip, that's my brother, is a friend of hers. Apparently she's "extremely nice", that's what he said, so, knowing him, it probably means she's a snotty cow.'

'Oh.'

Aidan seems well confused now.

'Sorry. You don't know what I'm on about. Anyway, I'm hopeful. Stella has to be better than Toolis. I mean, Heather.'

'Are we to understand that you don't like working for her?'

'We are. Mind you, I can see she's a bit pathetic. That doesn't let her off the hook, though. You kind of think it's worse when losers are cruel, than when winners are, don't you?'

'Who do you think are winners? I mean, what makes her a loser?'

'Oh, well, the usual things – mad, ugly –'

Damn. Romantic spell pricked. I have just revealed myself to be shallow.

'Right. You get straight to the point, don't you, Nancy?'

'I don't know. Do I?' Oh, so innocent.

'I think so. More than the rest of these media arseholes in here.'

That seems a bit harsh. I wonder why he said it? Maybe I can change the subject and do some information gathering.

'Why are you hanging around in Soho if you hate it, then?'

'You make me sound like a dirty old man.'

I've gone too far.

'Oh, sorry.'

'That's OK, you have every right to be curious about –'

He stops, so I carry on for him: ' – some strange man who keeps turning up inexplicably and then asks you out for a drink after being nice to you for no apparent reason a couple of times when your boss is picking on you.'

I push my mouth into the froth on top of the beer, giving myself a moustache, and glance at him sideways.

He stares for a few seconds too long before speaking: 'That's an improvement.'

'Why, thank you.' I'd better not pry any more.

Aidan defends himself, however: 'I had to see Lesley, but she's never there.'

'You don't have to explain. Lesley likes you, doesn't she?'

'Does she?'

'Yes. She is electrified by your presence.'

He is embarrassed now. 'Well, she's a very lovely lady, and I could do a lot worse.'

'You do realise, don't you, that she's a *Come Dancing* champion, and that Alastair is her partner, and they wear tight backless body suits, and practise on the roof?'

A smile cracks up his face. Hah.

'No, I didn't.'

He stares at me now, which is both wholly disconcerting and far too good to be true. My groin throbs, I hope not visibly. It's not done that too often before.

He leans into his jacket inside pocket (no, I haven't spied in any of them, though I was tempted) and asks: 'Do you mind if I have a cigarette?'

A-hah.

'No, go ahead.'

What will he smoke? I bet it will be one of those vicious foreign brands for those who place looks before lungs every time. Wrong, as it happens; he gets out a Rizla packet and a plastic envelope of tobacco. I can see I am now going to be turned on forever by the finger actions required to make a roll-up; not something Eric's amateur joint manufacturing ever achieved. I bury my nose in the tobacco. Aaarh. Beyond sublime.

I am dying to ask Aidan about his love life, and what has featured in it, but I can't possibly bring up that subject. It would certainly give the game away as to what is going on in my head; also I barely know the man. Maybe I fear a dead wife or some such horror, recently laid in grave, some rare beauty whose innocent features will never be ravaged by the onslaught of time. His face would crumple, the mouth wobble, eyes stare unseeing into the distance, and the evening be ruined. Leukaemia, probably, an agonisingly drawn-out death, the end no doubt a merciful release. I wonder how long they'd known about it before she'd died, how long they'd had together before he lost her? He eyes me disconcertedly.

'Don't look so miserable. Have I said something? Do you not approve of smoking?'

'What? Oh no, no, that's fine. I'm fine, please, I love smoking.'

'I'm not asking you to love it, Nancy. It is, after all, a number one killer. I only smoke these to help me cut down. I used to have the proper ones, thirty a day at least. Do you smoke?'

'Erm, a bit. I mean at parties and in the pub, you know. I can take it or leave it really, I'm that cool.'

'I bet you're one of those parasites who has never paid for a packet in your life, just sponged off other people. My –'

'I'm not! I pay for my own. I don't think I inhale properly, though, as I have never even slightly felt, like, I *have* to have a cigarette, you know?'

'Aah, to be in such a state of innocence! What wouldn't I give?'

I bite an olive. Too late I realise I have chewed straight through a chunk of garlic, snogging potential thus reduced to nil.

He picks one up too. 'I love these. The garlic's a killer, though. Just as well I won't be kissing anyone tonight.'

Then a mischievous sideways glance. The olive goes into his mouth.

'Yes, shame you're so hideous, you wizened old wreck.'

He chokes. I laugh.

Raising his hands in the air he surrenders: 'I suppose I asked for that.' Then he refills both our beers. 'So, Nancy, do you think you'll stick the job?'

Cooling things down, I suspect. Disappointment.

'Oh, I think so. It will be good for the CV and my eventual career.'

'Oh yes, and what's that going to be?'

'I want to be a TV news reporter, and maybe read the news one day.'

'Why?'

'Oh, bloody hell, what a question!'

'Well, other people will ask you, so it's best to be prepared, isn't it?'

'OK, you're right, well, I want to be a TV reporter because . . .'

Now I feel really stupid. No one has ever actually put me on the spot on this subject; but, still, something is pushing me towards telling the truth to this man.

'Well, because I want to, you know, get to the heart of the matter, and be where it's at, and succeed, in the world of men, and facts, and politics, and power, and –' here my voice lowers to a squeak – 'piss off my father.'

'Excellent! Explain.'

Aidan is resting his chin on one palm and has a concentrated expression. He's looking at me but, to be honest, I'm not sure his eyes are focused. Maybe I just happen to be in his line of vision? Maybe I'm boring him?

'Oh, no, sorry. I didn't mean that. I don't know really. It doesn't matter.'

God, I am being such an idiot. What am I doing? Why should this man give a fuck? Common sense warns he probably doesn't.

'Oh, come on. It does matter. Honestly. I'm interested.'

'You're not. Why should you be?'

He raises both hands in the air, fingers stretched out, and smiles his beautiful smile.

'Nancy, I am! Why do you want to piss off your father? Talk to me.'

'OK. Where to start? Oh God, this is impossible!'

'Try.'

'OK. My father is a hard man. Pulled himself up by his bootstrings and we are never allowed to forget it. He's a bank manager. I've one brother, Philip, who is much older than me. He's a manager with a stationery shop chain. There's only him and me. Apparently, my mum told me, my father pushed Philip, ever since he was little, after school, with extra homework every night, and only ever gave him encyclopaedias and dictionaries and things for birthday and Christmas presents. Then they dispatched him to a boarding school, but he still had to work in the holidays! It was a waste of time, though, and Philip failed to get into college. He was born to be a shopkeeper. I know my dad is disappointed in him.'

'Go on.'

'OK. Anyway, until I was about eight or nine I was invisible, a little girl in dresses with bows in my hair. I suppose I was the pointless afterthought of a daughter who only had to look nice and probably be, I don't know, a secretary or something. I think in my dad's mind that was the only decent job a women could have. He pretty much ignored me. I have a dim memory of telling terrible lies all the time. Well, they all tell me I did. Soon everything changed, though.'

I sneak a look at Aidan to gauge his attention level. He catches me and smiles.

'Carry on.'

'OK. At one Sunday lunch when I was nine, I think, or ten, so I suppose Philip was about twenty-five, i.e., old enough to know a lot better, I can remember it really clearly, we had trifle for pudding, and there was one spoonful left. Philip wanted it and I wanted it. My mum wouldn't have spoken even if she did want it; she doesn't know she's allowed to ask for what she wants. In fact, I don't think I know what it sounds like, her asking for what she wants. It really pisses me off! Sorry. Anyway, yes, my father would decide, so he said, presuming this would kick me out of the running. "Whoever can tell me the correct answer to this question will get the trifle." Philip was wetting himself. My dad always randomly quizzes him, even now. Philip quite often gets it wrong. Anyway, back to the story, so my dad then said: "Right. Whose dead body sits in a glass case in University College in London? Philip?" Philip put his head to one side, because he didn't know, and he began to panic, but I couldn't believe my luck: a programme had just been on TV about the place. Probably my father had seen it without realising I was in the room. I shot up my hand, since I'd forgotten I wasn't at school, and as my father turned, surprised, to look down at me, I squealed out: "Jeremy Bentham!" Everyone was astonished, especially me. I don't know, I suppose I felt like I had declared war on men, nothing less, and had won the first skirmish by beating them on their terms. It felt great. I became a feminist that day. It was my finest hour; although if I'd kept my mouth shut it would have saved me hours of homework in the long run, because my dad then put me through his hot-house programme. I was pumped with facts, but I didn't really mind, though. I had a direction now.'

Aidan guffaws. 'Excellent! You'll go far. Then when you've got there you can retire and do what you really want. Mind you, you could always achieve your goals without appearing on TV, couldn't you?'

'Yes, but my father wouldn't have to watch me then. He's got to see.'

'Hmm. What a can of worms.'

'Oh, it's probably just a phase I'm going through.'

I drink my beer, shut myself up. I can't keep talking about me, me, me. What shall I ask him?

He hangs on in there, though: 'What subject are you doing at college again?'

'I've not told you the first time, have I?'

'That is true. So, for the first time, what is your chosen subject, Miss Nancy?'

'Icelandic Drama, the Gnostic Gospels and Home Economics with a View to Catering.'

'Fibber.'

'History.'

'Ah. The hard stuff. Nothing fancy. No waffling for Nancy here. Do you like it? Why did you choose it? In a short paragraph, please.'

'Oh, I've always found it easy, I suppose, therefore I enjoy it, or maybe it's the other way round. I don't know – I've got a good memory, I like reading, you know, the way people behave the same down the centuries; we never change, we're very predictable, despite technology, we never learn.'

How nice it is to be talking to him. How nice of him to ask.

'Also –'

'Yes, Miss Nancy?'

'– well, also, how it could all be wrong, you know?'

'How?'

'Well, in terms of who wrote the stuff always, and where they got their facts from, and what they considered worth recording. I mean, it's all about kings and what they did and who they killed and who killed them and on and on and blah blah blah so that now, your man on the street thinks that's what history is about, that's why there's all this fuss about the royal family, merely because they're descended from a long line of killers. I mean, it just happened to be power which was the story worth remembering. Not to mention –'

'Yes?'

Aidan's tone is humorously wary, just this side of taking the piss; but I can't stop spewing. Something about him makes me more earnest.

'– not to mention women.'

'What about them?'

'Well, exactly. Where are they in the unrolling of the centuries? What do we hear of them? Just think of all those untold stories. Untold, because they weren't considered fit to be told. That's what really fascinates me, the stuff which isn't in the books. The invisible narrators, the ones who probably saw everything, but who weren't ever asked for their opinion.' On I drone. I really should let him get a word in edgeways.

'Right.'

'That's sort of why I want to find out what really happened, get to the real story, ask the right questions of the right people, not just the obvious ones, because I get the feeling that "History" as we know it is nowhere near the real story.'

'I see, splendid. The good old pursuit of truth.'

'Suppose so.'

I blush. He's laughing at me. I wince. What do I sound like, showing off, trying to be clever? Stupid little student, he probably thinks. Have I ruined everything? I'd better check.

'Sorry, I was ranting.'

'Don't be silly. It's fine. Makes a nice change.'

We stare silently at the others in the room for a while. Aidan appears to be thinking. I try to appear to be thinking. We really must talk about him soon.

Music fills the room. Opera, pouring out of speakers high above the bar, played loud enough to be audible over the shouting of the drinkers below. Singers roaring of *liebe* at each other, cascading sound tipping down onto us all. For a few minutes, it seems, it renders the room and everyone there into things of beauty. Then, just like that, the volume drops and talking once more dominates.

Our beer is finished. Aidan shakes his head as if waking from sleep.

'Well, what shall we do? Do you want to get something to eat?'

Oh, my God, yes please. Has he been shy about asking me? A grown man? I melt, and accept with a judder of my chin. The evening is definitely moving on to another stage now. But softly, I warn myself, go carefully. Don't assume anything. Aidan is moving his head from side to side in tune with the still just audible music. Oh, do not end this evening.

'Do you know what it is,' he asks, 'the music?'

'No, do you?'

'Mozart. The *Seraglio*.'

I say nothing. I know nothing about classical music, and my thoughts go beyond speech. I am just so happy to be here, Aidan, now, talking with you.

We edge out of the bar. I look back to see that a hysteria of women in Lycra has already descended on our table. The crowd ejects us and we might never have been there. My head is befuddled. I have to concentrate to walk straight. Aidan leads the way. I'm not watching where we are going, I'm too busy relishing the fact that I am walking down the street with him, that he is by my side and he is with me. I love these streets tonight, I love the people in them; I harbour no mean thoughts to any soul anywhere.

We stop outside a small Italian restaurant, one of those which, if you are a student, you glance at and then always pass because the prices of the starters are more than you had in mind for the whole meal.

'Let's go in here, Nancy, and I'll treat you.'

I can't complain. This drink is quite definitely turning

into a date. We bend down through the doorway. Inside it's low-ceilinged, dark and cluttered. When we are seated, breadsticks in front of us, I feel I can hesitate no longer.

'So, Aidan, tell me what you do?'

'Oh, can we order first?'

'All right.'

I am holding in front of me a large rigid menu, wondering just how expensive a choice I can, in all decency, make. The most expensive, the veal, might be a bit cheeky, but the cheapest, pasta with spinach, is too martyrish. I do want to try the veal, anyway: I've never had it before.

'I presume you're a vegetarian, Nancy? If not vegan?'

'Why?'

'I thought all students were?'

Bastard. Right, the veal, I don't care how short its life was. No limp escapist pasta for me. I pull a face.

'I'm sorry, Nancy. I can't help teasing you.'

I remain silent, but inwardly rejoice. Wonderful life! If that's not a come-on, I don't know what is. Mind you, caution; maybe I don't know what one is.

'If you're ready you'd like to order now, huh?' A balding many-fanged waiter stands poised with Biro and pad at the ready. He looks depressed, obviously grumpy, but I don't care. Nobody can upset me tonight. Aidan crosses his eyes and I snort out loud, then point at the relevant area on the menu so as not to have to reveal my atrocious Italian pronunciation.

'And for you, sir?'

'Oh, nothing extravagant, just the soup followed by, er, yes, the tortellini, please.'

I sink my head low. I can't look at him.

'And to drink?'

'Oh, what would you like, Nancy? Wine? Or more beer?'

Oh, tap water, or the dew from under the eaves if you have it.

'Er, beer, please.'

Cheaper I suppose; and I have no desire to sober up on mineral water yet.

'Sure? I think I'll have some wine.'

'Oh, OK, yes, that'll be nice, er, white wine.' I am a mouse now.

Aidan orders a bottle and the waiter moves off; but then, with a sudden movement, and before the man has gone very far, he leans round and calls him back. Talk about Restaurant Presence.

'I'm sorry about this, but can I change my order? I don't know what came over me. I'd like the prosciutto –' perfectly pronounced – 'followed by the steak.' Oh, what a jester. 'After all, I am celebrating.'

I fold my arms in front of me. 'What are you celebrating, Aidan?'

He appears tired and serious all of a sudden. 'You. You make me laugh. You get my jokes. And I'm sorry I teased you.'

I have grown used to life being ordinary, mundane, unremarkable. The high points of my early childhood were pretty standard ones: exams passed, presents given, birthdays and Christmases reached at last. Through my teens I learnt that, by and large, life is more full of what you don't get, results that don't surprise you, prizes you don't win, boys who don't notice you. So I set off for college resolute in my determination not to let this horrid reality hamper me, to devote my energies to making the possible happen and not to mourn the non-appearance of the miraculous. Now the grey clouds of everyday have drawn back while I wasn't looking to let down a ray of pure gold. I don't know what to do about it.

'So, Nancy, tell me some more about yourself.'

'Well, we've done family, and college, and ambitions, so what else is there?'

'You tell me.'

Can he mean boyfriends? Does he want to know about

that? Is he too shy to come out with it direct? I'm not sure what he means. No, I think I'll play the dark horse, just in case; my miserable pretence of a relationship with Eric, and lack of any others more meaningful, will not sound impressive.

'Nothing I can think of. Now it's your turn.'

'What for?'

'The third degree. First of all, what do you do for a living, if you are employed, that is?'

'Oh, you don't want to know about me.'

'I do. Go on, what are you?'

'Guess.'

'OK. Let me think for a minute.'

Bloody hell. I'll never guess. What roles do film stars always play? Policemen, secret agents, pilots, astronauts, men who are good with dogs and children. No, no, no. I must work this out logically and, by a process of elimination, worm my way to the truth. What do I know about Aidan? He keeps coming in to see Lesley about something, but doesn't seem to be associated with the place. Yet, they all seem to know him. Has he assisted them with some research? And are they paying him? Is he an outside expert on something? That's quite likely. Yes. Now what subjects do they cover? What programmes have they made? Those things about people dying. A lot about death, as far as I can remember. Who deals in death? Doctors. Yes! He must be a doctor. That figures. And he smokes. Doctors are always the worst. Maybe a surgeon? I pause to relish the vision of Aidan in blue surgical gear, chest revealed by the V-neck, then think further. What sort of a doctor? Some sort of specialist? A specialist on death? Wasn't there a programme about people dying? What would they most likely be dying of? Cancer? Surely. A cancer specialist. What are they called?

'I've got it.'

Ah, the triumph of reason. I'm jubilant that I've worked

it out. I just know I'm right. I'm good at this. Aidan has his eyes down, rolling a cigarette. The food's not yet arrived.

'Go on then. What am I?'

'An oncologist.'

He stops rolling the tobacco. Looks stunned at the ceiling. Bursts into laughter. I must be right. What a triumph. I laugh too. I am the woman for him. I'll bear him sons.

'Where,' he wipes his eyes, 'did you get that idea from?'

'Am I right?'

'No!'

Oh.

He laughs even more. I explain my logic.

'Well, good in theory, I suppose. Just wrong, that's all. Have another guess.'

'No. Just put me out of my misery.'

'OK. You'll be disappointed now.'

'Just say!'

'I'm a TV producer. Of a current affairs series. You might have heard of it.'

Oh. Oh fuck. He can't be. I don't believe this. He can't be. Maybe he's joking?

'You're not really?'

'I'm sorry, but I am.'

'Really? You really are?'

'Afraid so.'

'What's the programme called?'

He names a brilliant series of investigative reports that I always try to watch. My dad hates it because it invariably uncovers the clay feet of the sort of people he respects, such as, well, mainly in fact, the Conservative government. Don't these lefty journos understand what makes the world go round? Why are they so surprised that life is only about money? He's got no soul, my father; but I think it's an excellent programme, and just the sort of thing I'd like to get into one day. Now, however, my humiliation is complete. I could die. All that claptrap I spouted earlier and here's an old pro. The real thing. So typical.

It's weird. I don't know what tone to take. Aidan's been so flirty, but maybe I ought to be more respectful now? It's an evil thought, but I couldn't have run into anyone better able to kick-start my career. Maybe he could get me into a really good job! Yet I think I've been deceived, somehow, and patronised; in fact, he's as good as lied to me. Genuinely angry, I sit up and fold my arms defensively.

'You bastard! Why didn't you say?'

'You didn't ask till now.'

That's true. I was going on and on about myself. 'True.'

He smiles.

'I forgive you.'

'Thanks.'

And at last I get to grill him.

'So, are you a commissioning editor then? A jumped-up two-bit short-arsed idiot?'

Gone too far again? No. He can take a joke.

'Ha-ha. No. Commissioning editors work for broadcasters. I'm hoping to be one in the not-too-distant future, though. Right now I work for a large production company. We make the series for the broadcaster.'

'Oh, right.' I'm not sure I grasp the difference, but who cares?

'God, don't sound so disappointed.'

'I'm not disappointed!' Let's change the subject. 'Tell me about your family, Aidan. The early years. All that. First, where are you from?'

'Me?'

'No, the waiter. Who do you think I mean?'

'OK, OK. Well . . .' He looks away. Quiet for a while. Turns back. 'I was born in Africa. My parents were both, erm, doctors for an aid agency. Only child. We moved all over the place, travelled from conflict to conflict. I went everywhere with them. It was a wonderful upbringing. Very happy, though I grew up young, and had my eyes opened to genuine human suffering pretty early on. They're still out there, but I don't get to see them much.'

'Really? My God, that's unusual. Go on. What next?'

'I came over here to go to university. My first job was as a local radio journalist, up north, then TV, then I came to London to work for the BBC, as a TV reporter. Next I left them and worked as a freelance foreign news correspondent for –' he's counting on his fingers – 'well, several years, and then, yes, well, I've been in my present job for five years.'

I'm impressed. I wonder how old he is? I don't think I'll ask yet, though, as this is quite interesting enough for the moment; and thank God we don't have to talk about cancer.

It's like Christmas come early. This is the greatest time of my life. My veal arrives. That baby calf did not die in vain. Within a fortnight of my arrival in London I am having a more than romantic candlelit dinner with a very big cheese. The job's not quite what I had in mind, but what the hell? I can conquer the world. I must be getting drunk. We order another bottle of wine. Aidan tells me about his adventures. He has been to almost every country on earth. He is at home with corruption, war, pestilence, famine. He feels most relaxed abroad, in fact, he's never really happy here. No one ever properly comprehends the horror. Even now, he's not sure he can manage a desk job for too many more years. All he ends up talking about is budgets and censorship and litigation, clipping the gruesome truth for spoilt Western eyes. I suggest it's good to have someone with a conscience, isn't it, in his job? He can be of more use here, surely, where the broadcasting decisions are made? It must make a difference? He agrees, but says his feet still itch. Maybe he'll be up and away one day soon, back to the wilderness. With someone who understands the pressures. Oh, but I do, don't go without me, I almost shout out loud.

After the veal, a slab of three-coloured ice-cream which tastes like wallpaper glue. Probably is, in fact, made from the calf's mother. My heart's going *ker-boom, ker-boom, ker-boom boom boom boom*. I'm getting what I want. A winner, a winner, a winner! Maybe I'm going to have a heart attack and end the evening in intensive care. The date with a difference. So I'd better get in my main question, then, before I'm carted off in an ambulance.

'So, Aidan,' I slur, 'why?'

'Why?'

'Yes, why? Why this career?'

He thinks a minute. 'News? Trying to tell it like it is? Well, you've put me on the spot now, haven't you?'

'Sorry. You don't have to answer.'

'No, it's OK. Fair enough. I suppose, really, it's because the one thing I cannot stand is hypocrisy. Bullshit. Cover-ups. The abuse of power. Lying to the little man. Injustice. That's what it's always about. I suppose it is a moral thing in the end.'

He looks straight in my eyes and then quickly away as though embarrassed by such honesty. Then, muttering almost: 'You know something, Nancy, we're pretty much alike. In pursuit of the truth, you and me both.'

My hero.

Aidan gets the bill at quarter to eleven (I discreetly look at his watch) and writes out a credit card slip to pay. I can't read his handwriting upside down, but the name on the card is Aidan Rivers. Oh, very nice. Nancy Rivers. Nancy Miller-Rivers. Nancy Rivers-Miller. The amount: £63.29. Jesus. No one has ever spent that much on me before.

We leave the restaurant. The night is fast slipping away. He'll probably want to go home now. No, I know, sure as eggs are eggs, that he will want to go home now. So I'll say thank you and goodbye and try to walk steadily until he is out of sight. I'd better do it now, or else there'll be that tricky moment, and he'll get in there first.

I hold out my hand.

'Thank you very much, Aidan. That was fun, but I must be off now. Good night.'

It hurts like hell, but I'm proud of myself.

CHAPTER NINE

✳

'Oh, Nancy. Really?'

Does Aidan seem disappointed?

'Do you have to go? You sure you don't want another drink somewhere?' Did he say that? 'Since it's Friday night and still quite early?'

Ha-ha. Got him! I now know sure as eggs are eggs that he doesn't want to go home after all.

'Oh, all right.'

I incorporate a hint of surprise in my answer, as though not leaving now is an interesting option that simply hasn't crossed my mind.

'Do you know anywhere, Nancy?'

'How would I know anywhere?'

'Oh, sorry. Well, let's go and look around, shall we?'

Aidan takes my hand. Oh my God, this is all too much. Rockets explode. Thunderbolts shoot across the sky. His palm is dry in mine, and relaxed. He's no wet-handed student. I tighten my grasp, and he turns to look at me. This is getting serious. The urge to kiss him is hardly controllable.

'Are you having a nice time, Nancy?'

'Not bad, Aidan, not at all bad.'

I try to keep a straight face but end up laughing. The street in front of me and all who walk upon it are shimmering in and out of focus.

'Pleased to hear it.'

'I think I need to sit down, though. I need some water.'

If I am sick now I will never speak to my gut again. I command it: become the stomach of a hardened drinker!

'Are you going to throw up on me?' He doesn't sound unduly dismayed.

'No. I'm not that drunk. I just – need – to sit down. With you.' This added in a moment of carefree abandon. What am I doing?

'Don't worry. You've got me.'

Did he really say that? Marvels are flowing thick and fast tonight. I've got him, I've got him, I've got him.

The dizziness passes. I feel better. Passers-by resemble passers-by again, not fleeting cackling ghouls. We set off down the street. It's nearly last orders, so we look for a bar that isn't too full. A bit hopeful: they are all packed, crowds humming on the street in the muggy evening. The night is steaming up. Oh my God, is that Alastair leaning on a car bonnet and waving a beer bottle at some woman? I turn away and drag Aidan onwards.

'I'm not forcing myself through them to pay a fortune for some designer lager,' he says.

'You sound like my dad! I suppose in your day beer cost tuppence ha'penny a bottle.'

'I'm not that old. It's just those morons wouldn't know real life if it hit them in the face.'

I would. It often does. But why is he so bitter? Or is he just drunk? We continue our search, tramping the warm sticky tarmac. I yawn. Garlic vapour rolls out.

'You're ready for bed, aren't you, Nancy? I'll have to let you get home soon instead of boring you here.'

Oh, no. Trying to run away now after all? It's the garlic breath. I must keep cool. Seduce the man.

'That's true. I mean, I think, on consideration, that this has been one of, if not *the*, most boring nights of my life. Yes, actually, perhaps the most dull. I look forward to sinking deep into my sofa at the flat. Do you know, it's larger than any single bed I've ever slept in.'

'Really, Nancy? What about the double ones?'

'Oh, well, where to start? Just the UK, for now? Otherwise we'll be here all night.'

'Fine by me.'

Time to gamble.

'Aidan? Do you want to come back to my flat tonight? No one's going to be there.'

'Oh, Nancy.'

He sounds sad, almost. My heart stops. All is lost. I've made a terrible mistake. That isn't what the evening was about at all. He thought I was a nice girl. He was only being a knight in shining armour to a poor beleaguered maid. If he's given any other impression, well, sorry, but –

'If you are sure you'd like me to, I'd love to.'

Thank you, God. Bold as brass, I have inveigled Aidan into my lair. Help.

'I'd like you to.'

'Right.'

He sounds relieved. I am relieved. Now I can relax; but panic returns. Is this all too quick? Have I actually asked a serial killer into my home?

'You're not a serial killer, are you?'

'That I'm not.'

He laughs, almost entirely to himself. Is it a killer's laugh? Oh, this whole business is exhausting! How is a girl ever to find a mate? You can't ask for a reference.

'Let's forget about the drink and get a cab now, Nancy, what do you think?'

Fine by me. Is he looking a bit more pensive, though, than is healthy at such a time? Second thoughts? Is it best to ask him?

'If you're having second thoughts about going home with some strange woman, that's quite all right, you know. I'd understand.'

'What? Oh no, I don't think you're strange at all.'

I give up. Be grateful, girl, for what the Good Lord is handing you, for no immediately apparent reason, on a plate.

No taxis to be seen. I babble at Aidan as we walk along. He seems to be listening, or as well as you can in a noisy street, anyway. He nods almost innocently at whatever details I describe, and whenever I stop, thinking it only decent to let him speak, he prompts me again. The disconcerting thing is that I keep finding myself giving him the uncensored version, but whether from inebriation alone, or from a faith that I ought to reveal my true feelings, I am not sure. I tell him things I haven't revealed to anyone before. He is such a sympathetic listener. At the same time, performing like an actress, I embellish the descriptions and make things funny that have nothing funny in them.

'So, have you got a boyfriend then, Nancy? I'd better find this out now, I suppose.'

Curiously, I have still managed to omit the Eric affair from my ramblings. Now I give a brief summary of the situation, leaving out both my cold-blooded motives for going out with him in the first place, though, and for then ending it; but stressing the finality of the latter decision. Am I exaggerating or underplaying my lack of experience? I am having to balance a pretence that I am more in control of this than I really am with a hard-to-explain urge to cut the crap and tell him everything. But I just about manage to hold my tongue, and paint Eric as the man I have been with the longest and the most recently, rather than the only man I have ever been out with. When I try to ask Aidan a similar question, however, my tongue just will not oblige. I cannot say the words. Nor is he forthcoming on the subject. I am convinced of a lurking unspeakable tragedy, his silence a mute request for mercy; and so I spare him.

A black taxi pulls to a stop beside us. I give the orders and we tip in. Head swimming, I must record everything on to my memory as it happens to me: but my brain seems to have shut down. I am in shock, voices are shouting in my burning ears: Nancy, this is epic! Life will never be the same again! So live it! Enjoy it! The here and now is here at last!

The cab has very high lean-and-snog-in-the-darkness potential which I am anxious to exploit without delay, given that it's only a short journey to Gloucester Road. Off we sail into the night. How shall I sit? A trifle separate, hands crossed over the knees? As far away as possible from him, glued to the opposite window and looking away? On one of the two special little seats, fold-out beds for your pet toad, which pull down and then slam straight back the minute you get off them? Or right in there, hooked under his arm, cheek to shoulder, body language as positive as it comes? Complications, choices, decisions.

'Nancy, come here.' Aidan puts his arm along the back of the seat and nods towards his flank somewhere. 'That is, if you want to.'

Need I a second bidding? Do ducks like ponds? It's to be simple after all. I am well drunk enough to have forgotten shyness, so I bounce over along the shiny leather. Then comes the kiss. At bloody last. Down he leans. Is the driver watching in his mirror? I check. The man seems to have his eye on the road. I glance out of the window: we are pelting down Piccadilly, I think. Face him, Nancy: enjoy. So I lean up. And in. And, ah, oh, heaven. He smells so nice. Aftershave? No, just warm scratchy face.

The kiss: nice firm lips, not wet or aimless or limp, tongue in but not forceful, interesting, no faffing about, the kiss of a man who knows how to kiss, who wants to be kissing the mouth he is kissing. Aaarh. My heart's pounding is levelling out now. This is for sure a foot in the door. I pull back my face and look at his. He blinks slowly, eyelids shut tightly and then released.

'Well, Nancy, thank you very much.'

'Sure, yes, er, do come again soon, please.'

Smirk. I sit back and stare ahead of me. Cars whiz past on the road outside. Hyde Park Corner. What will happen at home?

The taxi swerves too sharply. Aidan grabs my arm to stop me from shooting onto the floor. The vehicle moves smoothly again but I stay in his arms. Now the streets we're driving along are to be hallowed for ever by the fact that I can see them from this carriage in which my dreams have come true. I will walk up them later and think, we drove down here, along here, round here, down here. By then the taxi will be parked miles away in front of the house of the driver who has driven us tonight, somewhere the grumpy waiter who served us will get on with his life, and neither of them will know their faces are extraordinary to me. It's a funny feeling, to be in exactly the situation you want to be in, to be doing exactly what and with whom you would do if asked by some benevolent wish-granter to describe your wildest fantasy. My request would not include anything more than what I have been given so far this evening.

We purr down Knightsbridge. Harrods is lit up, like I imagine Manhattan looks at night: banks of light shooting up and away to my left, and still going on up when I push back my head towards the stars. I shift to the edge of the seat and over to the window opposite Aidan, and practise looking out so that I can't see him, concentrating for a second, and thinking of the grimmest reasons why I might be in that cab driving down that road, alone, and then I turn back, and there he's sitting, looking confusedly at me, and quite plainly without a clue as to what is going on in my head; and me laughing at the joke, and doing it again.

'Nancy, I think the driver wants to know your address.'

'What, him too?'

'Very funny.'

Are we nearly there? The X-hour looms. We have started to sail among tall creamy squares, between low sports cars and bullet-proof diplomat saloons and high-floored roomy Jeeps parked on both sides of the road. I recognise that food shop. My heart is thudding. Shall I tell the man to just keep on driving? Spin out the dream?

'This'll do.'

I get out on the driver's side and pay him, plus tip, a small contribution to the evening, but perhaps the most valid: ferrying my quarry home. As we stand there in front of the huge pillared doorway, while I fiddle for my keys, I imagine that this is all mine, that I am returning to my own address, that my vast vehicle is parked only inches away, that upstairs waits my flat, my clothes in the drawers, my photos on the bedside table, my vast disposable income evident at every turn.

'Good God, Nancy, you've made it in the world, haven't you?'

'Well, Aidan, nothing less than many years of hard work have brought me to where I am today. To quote my dad.'

We're in. A light switches on automatically. Even more impressive than the doorway itself is the vast hall, a warm blood-red-carpeted affair. A six-foot-high mirror hangs from the wall on the right, over an unused fireplace which is mainly hidden by a large heavy cupboard. On top of this rests a big copper oval tray on which the caretaker puts everybody's post. Above, on the mantelpiece, sits an extraordinary polished dark wooden porcupine from whose carved-out back sprouts a thicket of spiky dried plants. An entirely useless hallway kind of article.

'Way-ell, please welcome to ma lil' home.'

I throw my arms up and out sideways. They hang in the air rather stupidly for a second.

Aidan moves forward and lifts me onto the top of the cupboard with no apparent difficulty. What does he think he's doing? God, he's strong. Then the light clicks off and the hallway is plunged into total darkness. What now? I resist feebly.

'Just keep still for two minutes, woman.'

He's undoing the buttons on my jeans. I shriek in mock panic.

'Aidan, what are you doing?

I can feel him but not see. Thoughts of serial killing fly from my head.

'What if someone comes in? Let's just go upstairs.'

'I can't wait, sorry.'

Am I to get any breather in this relationship? He moves round to the end of the cupboard so that I am on my back with my knees up and he is facing me, not that I can detect his expression in the darkness. It's all very gynaecological to start with.

'OK, knickers off.'

He sounds bored almost. Dull job, someone's got to do it. I start giggling.

'You dirty bastard! What kind of a girl do you think I am?'

'Come along, Miss Nancy, get a move on and then we'll all be in bed by midnight.'

Aidan pulls the jeans legs back, and my underwear too, so that both are round my ankles binding them together. I feel a cool gust of wind on my naked skin. We can't do this here. Caution nags – someone might appear at any time – but I don't want to put him off his stride. Thank God I had a bath this morning.

'That's a bit nippy.'

He pulls me forward and lifts my legs, still joined at the ankle. This is ridiculous.

'Do I get to play any part in this?'

'Yes. Enjoy it.'

Aidan lifts my legs over his head so that they trap him in a yoke and then bends forward to put his face on, erm, how shall I put it, my love-gusset? Odd feeling, much as you'd expect it to feel, to start with. Interesting, not entirely disgusting. I don't think Eric knew you could do this. It gets nicer. This is outrageous! It's all too much. Ah, the simple pleasures of life, cheap and easy and they can all be done in the comfort of your own home, or a friend's aunt's hallway, whichever is nearer at the time. Aidan gets down to it; I relax. Questions more urgent than whether we might be disturbed now address me. My eyes grow used to the darkness and I can make out the porcupine above me. It has an appalled look on its wooden face. I lean back and my head lands on the letter-tray, which squeaks on the cupboard surface and is pushed backwards. It's not alone: I squeak on the cupboard surface and am pushed backwards.

Aidan surfaces to breathe for a moment.

Arching backwards in the dark I close my eyes and think through the groin. Funny how it's all so instinctive. I mean, I could be a wildebeest in this mechanical process born of the flesh. I can't see Aidan, only feel what he is doing to me. What follows, pretty soon, without properly consulting what I always thought was me, is shocking. Entirely unexpected. I've never had an orgasm before. I suppose that's what this is. Not much I can do about it. Beginning with, well, small beginnings, and then continuing, uninter-rupted, and getting more, well, delicious, and then, there I am, pushing up against the underside of the mantelpiece, gasping and moaning and shouting and pincering Aidan's head between my thrashing thighs. A momentous porcu-pine-and-spiky-plant-wobbling event. Light floods my eyes. My God, is the vision affected too?

'Whatever is all this noise?'

Oh, fucking hell. Who's turned the light on? Blink. I can see now. It's the caretaker's ancient mother who lives in the downstairs flat. She is very, very old and, I hope, completely blind, for she peers at us like a vole with tiny glasses on. Wearing a blue nightie, and velvet slippers, and hair in curlers, her eyes are scrunched up against the glare.

My head is lolling to one side, tongue hanging out. Aidan

135

can't easily get from under me. Slowly he lifts my legs and reverses out, pulling me forward and tugging up my clothes.

'Splinter. This poor unfortunate woman sat on a splinter. I got it out at last.'

The nerve. We stagger into the lift. I am weak with hysteria, shivering in the descent from ecstasy. On the top floor Aidan carries me out, asking which is my door, and lifts me over the threshold after I have given him the key. As soon as the door slams behind us he asks where is the sofa? As he lowers me onto it I pull at his belt buckle. Get that undone, get that zip down – I can feel his erection pushing at the trousers. He finishes the job for me and I pull them down over his bottom and then his dick falls forward through the gap in his boxer shorts and I put it into my mouth – it seems like a good idea – pulling the cheeks of his hot backside towards me. What a whopper. Actually it isn't, just standard I suppose, but bigger than Eric's. I never did this to Eric, mind.

Aidan has a dreamy expression on his face as he falls back into the sublime cushions.

'Aah, Nancy, what a great time I'm having. Do you have any condoms?'

'I certainly do.'

Astonishing. Another modern man facing up to this modern moment. We sink into the heavenly depths of the sofa and grind ourselves to mincemeat.

CHAPTER TEN

❋

Monday already. I'm at my desk. The grimy dawn of a new week. I ignored the alarm clock and woke at nine, so got here late and sweating. Mentally, I'm still in bed.

Blessed relief. Only Alastair's in, tapping his watch and pulling a face.

'What time do you call this?'

'Shut up.'

He holds no horror for me now. Coffee ritual time. I open the mail. How nice: a battery-powered revolving clock with pencil hands from Derek, which would be so perfect for the desk, but I'd better take it home in case Toolis recognises its origin. *Select-A-Pencil* is, after all, written on the base. It'll enhance the flat décor no end. The answer phone light is flashing. Fuck. The dread advert came out again on Saturday, so there are sure to be more tragedies for me to dredge through. I brace myself.

'What did you get up to this weekend, then, Nancy? Any hot sexual encounters?'

Funny you should say that, Alastair.

'No. You?'

'Yes, as it happens. Well, not, strictly speaking, hot. More lukewarm.'

What a thought: having sex with Alastair and actually being conscious at the time! I am not going to ask for details.

137

'Don't you want to hear about it?'

'Actually, no. I have a job to do.'

I switch the answer phone on and start to note down all the names, numbers and dilemmas contained therein, humming the while: I love my job, I just love it, love it, love it. An ex-nun from Gillingham begins droning on about something foul in a soporific confessional tone, so I close my eyes to remember.

Did Friday night really happen?

I opened my eyes with a stinking headache and near-exploding bladder far too early on Saturday morning. Pound, pound, pound. Hot, blotchy, hardly Miss World. Aidan, fortunately, was still asleep. I stepped off the sofa with a great deal of care and tiptoed across the wooden floor on my way to the bathroom. Once I got there, and went to the loo and did my teeth super conscientiously and washed my face, I climbed into one of the aunt's towelling robes, and sat on the edge of the bath to ponder upon my good fortune. Had any weekend ever started so well? Frankly, no. It wasn't even eight in the morning. I went on sitting. If I stayed in there for ever, I thought, then he would never go away, and the day would never end. Finally, though, I had to go and check on the real thing, and I ran into Aidan, naked and heading for the bathroom himself. I remember thinking he'd leave the seat up, and I determined not to lower it again until Sarah returned to witness my triumph. Then I got back under the duvet, still in the robe, and waited for Aidan, feeling deeply smug that I was covered up while he would have to approach me with nothing on.

'Don't stare, Nancy. I've gone all shy.' He placed both hands, ineffectively, over his crotch.

'Stop playing with yourself, Aidan, and get in here.'

He did as he was told, bringing his face right up close to mine.

'Oh, you're so clean, Nancy.'

'I know.'

'Don't smell my breath, or you'll never agree to see me again.'

'What makes you think that I'd want to anyway?'

'Oh, the nerve of the girl! Don't you remember you agreed to marry me last night?'

'Bollocks!'

'Come here, Nancy. And let's get this, what is it? – judo costume? – off you.'

This being easier said than done, a few seconds passed before I was unrolled, but then Aidan had me in his arms and I laid one leg over his thigh and even now I can feel how hot his skin was.

When I woke for the second time that morning, head still drumming, I was able to make him out in the curtained light, sitting on one of the armchairs, bending down and doing his laces up. Trousers on, but not yet his shirt. He hadn't noticed I was awake. The hairs on his chest seemed a lot darker because of the crunch of his body. His arms were stretched down to pull the laces tight, and I noticed that his abdomen, folded in loosened ridges, had lost the tension of a young man's. Jerking the duvet off the floor and wrapping it round me, still afraid he might think I was pretty plain in daylight, I asked him if he was going already?

I had wanted to get up first and have a bath, so that I could be lying there even more washed and fragrant than earlier and available for yet another bout of simple passion when he woke. After that, woozily drained, clothes just thrown on, we could have gone out for breakfast in a dreamy, wandering-the-streets-of-Paris-in-a-hatchback-advert kind of way. Sipping hot chocolate we would tease croissants out of their twists at a street café and look deep into each other's eyes and shut out the world.

He said he had to go somewhere for work, or something, and I said, what, on a Saturday, and he replied that stories don't only get made on weekdays between nine and five; but he said it regretfully, and when he was ready to go, he came over to me, and crouched down to my level, and reached into one pocket for something, and into the other pocket for something else, and then touched me on the cheek, and asked me what my phone number was, and wrote it on a Rizla paper.

It half killed me to say goodbye, but we kissed, and I stayed wrapped up on the sofa all the while, and acted cool until the door had shut behind him. Then, paracetamol, quickly, and I ran a deep bath, since I stank of sex, I remember noting proudly.

The hangover proved not to be one of that very worst kind when you swear never to drink again if God will take away the pain now. You sell your family in such moments. I stared at the tiled wall above my bath, and wondered why I felt so profoundly satisfied. Why did another human being make so much difference? Why the urgency to achieve such transparent goals? What did one piece of flesh matter to another? That Aidan had been with me, why did I care? What did it matter that it was him? What was better about him than Eric? Was it because I could talk to him? I couldn't really talk to Eric. With Eric I had been alone.

Phone ringing. I'm in the office. Back to the real world.

'Yeah, hello, is Heather Toolis there?' Not a voice to be messed with.

'No, I'm sorry, she's not made it to the office yet, but is no doubt on her way.'

'Yeah, OK, give her a message. Get her to call me as soon as possible, it's Tom Abbott here.'

That commissioning editor. Mr Instantly Forgettable.

'Of course, Mr Abbott, right away.'

I trill up in the air like a skylark. I can hear the lift reaching our floor. It'll be Toolis, so I can give her the message warm from the oven. Sitting up straight, I continue to assault the post.

Sarah had a party at the flat on Saturday night, to which, with some concern for the well-being of the furnishings, she had invited only about fifteen or twenty of her 'closest' friends. I'd seen some of them around at college, but the rest she knew from school. I wonder how many 'closest' friends I have? Maybe three, on a good day?

I chain-smoked, and drank a lot, and yawned in people's faces, despite having been asleep all day. The closest friends probably thought I was rude. Sarah had set me up with a potential date, David (she realised her plan was obsolete now, but introduced us anyway), and he wasn't too bad, although she'd described him as having 'wavy brown hair' and in fact it was tightly curled blond like a poodle's. He was obsessed with sport. I wasn't interested but flirted confidently, catching Sarah's accusing eye a couple of times, and returning blank innocent looks at her. Swilling beers and dragging on a cigarette with what seemed to be especially adult nonchalance, I generously asked David to tell me all about white-river rafting, and didn't hear a word of his answer. I was shawled in smugness. My man was way out of these boys' league.

The door's being pushed open now. Wake up. Toolis? No. Instead of Toolis a beautiful woman walks into the office. What on earth's someone like her doing in a place like this? Must be lost. But no, she seems to know what's what. Lowering a pair of briefcases with a heavy leather thunk by the message box, she turns towards me, shaking hand proffered.

'Hello. You must be Philip's sister. It's Nancy, isn't it? I'm Stella.'

Oh. That's who you are. A thin, squeaky voice, very upper class, though not quite the Queen: *nice*, but also, nice.

'Oh, hello.'

We meet at last. She has a very long appearance. Tall, that's why, wearing dark silky drapey clothes which drop unhindered from shoulders to knees. Expensive. Good legs and a really nice pair of shoes. Dark bobbed hair (loose, wavy, no fringe, nothing like Toolis'), pale face, grey bags under big blue eyes, barely noticeable freckles on her cheekbones like those paper-thin flakes of husk in your Ready Brek, doesn't look too well, perhaps the skull too apparent. Sort of tragic-actress look you get in made-for-TV dramas, lots of smoky goodbyes at railway stations on the eve of the Second World War. Hand held out to shake, dry and a little cold, veins showing grey mauve. Top drawer. A blue blood. An aristocrat.

'You don't look anything like Philip, if I remember right.'

'No, I'm a foster child. My real parents didn't want me.'

A bemused pause. 'Really?'

'No, of course not. Sorry, it was just a joke.'

'Oh. Right.'

What on earth made me say that? Typical: far too familiar, far too soon. I've probably blown it with everyone in the place now. Alastair saves me, I must admit.

'Don't listen to that lunatic, Stella. She's on another planet.'

'Alastair. How's it all going?'

She moves over to chat with him.

Sunday dawned about lunch time, a grey day. Sarah and Nick were still asleep and an unidentified man lay on the living-room floor, his trunk sprouting from a sleeping bag, smoking and watching *Little House on the Prairie* with the volume on low. Charles Ingalls was kneeling by the deathbed of a bearded old woodsman. The weekend was ebbing away. I needed to do some reading. Aidan would ring today. Or send flowers maybe. Was he the type? Probably not – I hoped not – though, in fact, it might be nice, as nobody had ever sent me flowers – well, except for Eric on Valentine's Day. He'd brought round some yellow roses, and put them on my bed without me noticing, and I'd sat on them, and pierced my thigh with a thorn, and screamed at him. Somehow, flowers from Eric were worse than no flowers. Anyway, florists were shut on Sundays, weren't they? So that was out. The edge of panic I'd felt when saying goodbye to Aidan returned, a strange feeling which seemed to be able to do things to me that I didn't know could be done. It made me powerless and I didn't like it. Why hadn't I got his phone number? I could be calling him. I had a look in the phone book and found a few Riverses and considered ringing all the As. Then I brought myself up short. He'd be ex-directory with a job like his. And anyway, I wasn't that desperate. He'd ring me.

Stella is by my desk again, smiling.

'How did you find last week? I'm so sorry you were thrown in at the deep end. Was Heather nice to you?'

Should I tell her the truth?

'Yes, fine.'

'Really?'

'Yes.'

'You're tactful. She normally eats receptionists for breakfast, and then spits them out at lunch. But it's all bluff.'

I smile guiltily but say nothing.

'Now, you're a student, aren't you? Tell me, you are available until you go back to college, aren't you? That is right, isn't it? I think that's what Philip said.'

Oh, shit. The holiday. I was supposed to ask.

'Well, I thought you'd be looking to get a permanent person?'

'No, no, not if you like the job, and it's going OK. That's all right, isn't it? Tell me if you can't for any reason. I mean, the truth is –' and here she leans towards me as though confiding a secret – 'the truth is, if it does go well, the job could be yours as a permanent position.'

Eh? I must be looking bemused.

'What I mean is, you could drop college and stay on if you wanted, but obviously I doubt you would. A degree is so important. And what am I doing, rushing so far ahead already? Don't think about it now, though. Just bear it in mind. It's not impossible. But the main thing is, you can definitely do the next couple of months, yes?'

Bye-bye holiday.

'Yes. Sure. Thanks.'

'Wonderful. You're a star.'

Stella moves away from my desk. Well. What about that? She's known me for less than five minutes! Nothing for weeks, then ten buses at once and you have to choose. I'm in a right old state now. A permanent job, for ever? No need for CVs? Contacts from now on? No more exams? What a thought. I'm stunned. But, damn it, I've a more immediate decision to make. The holiday. I just said 'yes' to Stella. Just like that. No scruples about Grace and Rebecca. What kind of a friend am I? Couldn't I have explained my commitment? Well, I could have, and I could disappear for two weeks bang in the middle of the summer, just when Toolis TV wants me. And I could come back and find they've given my job to somebody else. And Aidan could think I'm not interested. And I could lie on a Greek beach, sand gritting to the suntan oil, comparing the local talent to what I know is available back in London, and, my God, I'd be in a sulk. They wouldn't want me there. No, no contest. My decision is made. Fuck: I don't look forward to telling Grace the bad news. Though she's got a generous heart, I'm not sure its bounty is unlimited. This is a real pain, because I was dying to ring and brag to her about Aidan, but had held back because I knew she'd ask about the holiday. Now I've got an answer for her, but she won't want to hear it.

144

'Nanette! No slouching!'

Dear Toolis, once more amongst us. Just for the briefest second, when she sees Stella, it looks on her crotchety face like she's choking on a slug.

'Stella! You're back. We must talk.'

'Heather! Sure. Let's go out for breakfast. Executive meeting. I think petty cash'll run to that.'

'Very well. Now, let me see, messages. Nanette! Any messages? Or post?'

I ungraciously slide a few envelopes across the desk and one shoots over the edge and onto the floor.

'Oh, sorry.'

Toolis eyes me, then bends down to retrieve it. The shimmery jacket of her charcoal suit is pulled upwards, taut and straining over the tiny shoulders, and her shirt is pulled out of the skinny skirt waist revealing a dead-white muscled midriff. When she stands up again she shudders herself back into shape. She's caught me staring. I watch her, like a cat keeps an eye on the dog so as to be aware at all times where its enemy is.

'Is there really nothing else for me? And no one has called?'

'Nothing.'

I am mesmerised. Does she think I eat her post?

'Right. Stella? Ready? Alastair? We must speak later. And where's Lesley? Still not here?'

Toolis scuttles out. Stella follows, glancing back at me and smiling. Thank God, a nice person in this place. By the time they've probably reached the street, I remember Tom Abbott's message. Oh, fuck. Not again. I haven't even written it down.

Aidan didn't ring yesterday, but his aura is still with me. He's probably leaving it for a decent couple of days so as not to appear too keen. How sweet. Where is he now? I wonder. I must say, though, it does give an added *frisson* to the job: my heart misses a beat every time the phone rings.

The girlies return a bit too soon for my liking, as I'd hoped for at least an hour's peace, and at last I get to tell Toolis about the message.

'Really? Tom Abbott? Are you *sure*, Nanette?'

'Yes, definitely.'

'Right.'

She smartly pulls together her jacket lapels and draws up a chair beside me. Stella sorts herself out in the background, settling at the empty desk beyond Lesley's and pulling things out of her cases in a haphazard fashion. I get the feeling she's nervous, for some reason. Maybe Toolis just bollocked her about the cleaners fiasco?

'OK, Nanette. You must get Tom Abbott on the line for me. You've got his direct line, haven't you?'

'Of course.'

Have I? There are several numbers scrawled on the pad in front of me. One of them is encircled by a constellation of pencil stars. Is it Tom Abbott's? What if it belongs to some sufferer of something? Where does the man work? Anyway, lazy cow Toolis – why can't she ring him herself?

'Now, Nanette, this will be a good lesson for you. The reason I am asking you to ring is so that Mr Abbott is as impressed as he can be by our obvious professionalism. You are to be my secretary. If I was to ring in person, he'd think: oh, she can't afford a secretary. What a loser. I'm not investing in her. He has never been here, you see.'

Lucky man.

'He doesn't know that there aren't several hundred people working here, does he? He has to be convinced, by your voice, that there are. Your voice has to say to him, confidence, reliability, success, high viewing figures, profit, profit, commission, second series, profit, profit, profit, more profit.'

My voice has never said any of these things before.

'So, I want you to say the following to whoever answers: "I have Heather Toolis on the line for Tom Abbott." OK?

And remember: bubbly. Wait one second while I get ready.'

Stella catches my eye. Toolis retires, pincers a sheet of economy paper from the photocopier tray and climbs up to the chair at her desk.

'I'm ready, Nanette.'

Here we go. I dial, but with my heart in my mouth. This had better be his number.

A voice bleats at me: 'Hell-o-o-o.'

What? Sounds like a drug addict dragged out of bed. Fuck, fuck, fuck. It must be the wrong number. Still, I'd better ask for the man just so it sounds right.

'Oh, hello.' Fuck. 'Could I speak to Tom Abbott, please?'

'Who's speaking?'

'Well, I'm calling from Toolis Television UK, and I've got Heather Toolis on the line for him.'

'Oh, can't she phone him herself?'

Maybe it is the right number? I'm impressed. This junkie's keeping her end up quite well. She is so laid back.

'What? Erm, sorry, erm, well, yes, but she asked me to do it.'

'Oh, some people!'

A human being?

'Actually, his line's engaged, so could you, or her, he-hee, call back in five minutes?'

Why certainly. I make my goodbyes and put the phone down.

'What's wrong? What were you talking about? Is he there?' Toolis is elevated on her little forearms. Furious French pug dog.

'Yes, but he's on the phone. The woman who answered wondered why you didn't call him yourself?'

I shouldn't have mentioned it, I just haven't yet learnt discretion; but also I am showing off to Stella, who I can tell is listening. I feel she's my ally in some way.

'Why I didn't call him myself? How ridiculous! I'm a busy woman. Cheeky little girl! Probably some sarcastic graduate! They all think they're too good for the job! Now, can you try him again immediately? I don't want him going out.'

'Isn't it too soon? He's probably still on the phone.'

'Nanette! It is not your job to question my opinion, it is your job to do as you are asked.'

I go red. Stella is embarrassed. Alastair is smirking. I call back, and am put through to, surprise, surprise, Miss Sarky Graduate Media Junkie herself.

'His line's still engaged. I think you left it one and a half minutes at the most.'

'I know. Sorry. I'll probably speak to you shortly.'

'Yes, I expect so, but in no less than a good three and a half minutes, please. Bye for now.'

She's a droll old coot.

I report the good news triumphantly: 'Still engaged, I'm afraid.'

'Well, keep trying, and get hold of me the minute you get through! This is terribly important!'

She's shouting. Stella and Alastair both seem hard at work.

When a poor seven minutes have passed, I find new friend Sarky is definitely smug.

'You're not going to believe this, but he's gone out for about twenty minutes. Do you want to call back then, or shall I call you?'

Oh, this is thrilling. What a fab way to earn a living.

'Oh, I don't know.'

The potential for these two missing each other all day is looking quite healthy. I give up all pretence of reception etiquette.

'Oh damn, oh, sorry, well, could you call when he's back? That's probably safest.'

We agree this is a mature way to solve our problem. Communication, co-operation, compromise. Damage limitation. Always the best thing. I update Toolis.

'Oh, for God's sake!'

She sulks. A sort of calm, for now. Oh, Aidan, give me a call. Don't show me heaven and then leave me to fester in hell!

Stella walks past me on the way to the kitchen. She smiles encouragingly, and whispers: 'You're doing very well, believe it or not. Billie would have been in tears by now.'

Great, poor stupid Billie. It's all right for Stella, she's not a minion who can be shouted at. She's rich and successful and no doubt has everything she wants. It's easy to be gracious when it's not your hide being whacked. No, that's not fair, I know. Stella's been kind to me so far. Aidan, Aidan, call me.

The phone. A mail-order clothes company.

'It's for you, Heather.'

I had such high hopes for the summer. Now I'm sitting in a dingy room listening to a deranged woman ordering her nightwear wholesale. It's only Monday. Stella reappears to ask if I want anything to drink. God, does anything ever happen here beyond the consumption of hot beverages?

'Yes, tea, strong, lots of white, no sugar, please.'

Ring me, Aidan.

'Tea – strong – white – no sugar. Right. Now, how do you take coffee, so I'll know?'

For fuck's sake. She's *too* nice.

'The same.'

'Right. I'll remember.'

You do that, honey. Phone ringing. Oh, let it ring. *Ring ring*. Stella's head round the door. I grab the receiver.

Stella whispering: 'Oh, sorry, Nancy, I thought you had your hands full.'

Very likely. I wish.

Male voice. Nobody I know. 'Could I speak to Heather Toolis, please?'

'Her line's engaged, I'm afraid.' Because she's a busy woman, don't you know?

'Oh Christ, this is ridiculous. Well, can you get her to call Tom Abbott urgently?'

'Oh, hold on, can you wait one second?'

'Yeah.'

I put the graceless oaf on hold and wave at Toolis, but she's not looking. I can just hear her complaining to some poor sucker from the mail-order firm about her flesh being cut at the waist. Aidan would laugh. I have to move over and click my thumbs rudely under her eyes and hiss: 'Heather! Tom Abbott's on the phone!'

She waves at me to go away, strained, as though there's interference on the line.

Right, that's it. I inform Tom Abbott that Heather Toolis is unable to speak to him right then.

'Well, get her to call me immediately so we can stop messing about. And in person, please.'

Phone smashes down. Not a happy man. I am sick of this, getting all the crap from both sides. What do they think I am? Some robot with no brain or feelings? Fuelled on tea and coffee? Aidan, fucking ring me! Time to vote with my feet. I head for the door. Toolis puts down the receiver.

'Nanette! Where are you going?'

'Out. I need a bit of fresh air.' Don't ask me anything else woman, for God's sake.

'No, you're not. Who was that on the phone?'

Stella's shaking hand judders a cup onto my desk, but I'm beyond tea now. I tell it to Toolis straight.

'It was Tom Abbott, and I told you, but you didn't listen, and now he's in a very bad mood, and would like you to ring him straight away, in person, all right?'

Toolis' jaw drops. Stella looks pleasantly shocked. Alistair grins openly. I slam the door behind me.

It's only eleven forty-five. The sun is shining, and it's

hot. I stomp into a bar and order a Coke. Hoisting myself onto a high stool I stare out of the window. My pulse is pumping, my forehead on fire. Shit! Where did all that come from? What is the matter with me? I don't understand myself sometimes. That was my meal ticket I've just thrown away. Well, it's down the drain now. I almost managed five and a half days. My Coke is delivered in a small glass, and tastes watery. Half the bottle, and that diluted. What a rip-off. Is all London a rip-off?

I think of my mother, and miss her, a rare event. What kind of a life has she had? At the beck and call of a mean man who takes her for granted, a dull life in a dull house with a dull garden in a dull street in a dull town. That secretarial job she had was before I was born, but after I came along my dad never let her go back. I wish she'd fought him sometimes. It's good for you, a spot of adrenaline. What would she tell me to do now? Go back and apologise, without question: but no way. Not yet.

Oh, fuck.

It can't be true. I've left my bag behind. I have to go back to the office now. No. I can't. I must. I can't. I have to. Toolis won't actually attack me. I get down and head slowly back, feeling sick. Surely I'll be sacked?

When I reach the door I brace myself before turning the handle. As usual, I'm sweating. Oh, for God's sake, Nancy. What can she do? She's only a pathetic female. And Stella is in there, she'll help you. Here goes.

'Nanette! Quickly!'

What now? Does she ever do things quietly? I stumble through the door and am confused by the vision in front of me. It is by no means self-explanatory. Toolis is sitting on her desk, short legs crossed and toes stabbing the air, while Stella is beside her looking oddly beatific. Alastair is on the phone at my desk.

Toolis barks: 'We're celebrating! Take a couple of pounds from petty cash and go and buy some biscuits!'

'How about a bottle of wine, maybe?' adds Stella drily.

Am I forgiven?

'Can I ask why?'

'Tom Abbott has commissioned a pilot for my women's programme!'

Madman.

The afternoon, thank God, passes by in an almost alcoholic haze. Lesley never turns up. Neither Toolis nor Stella say anything about my outburst, Stella departing after lunch and Toolis closing the office early at five. Bemused, I get home with a throbbing head and, unbelievably, my job intact. I hurry up to the flat. Aidan is sure to have left a message.

CHAPTER ELEVEN

✳

Four messages for Sarah, one for me. From Philip. I don't return his call, nor ring Grace about the holiday, nor touch a heap of books I have to make a start on. Did Stella really offer me a permanent position? Quite an opportunity. Even so, it *would* be crazy to ditch the degree. Oh, that's too much to think about right now. Parking myself in front of the TV all evening, I never stray far from the phone. When Sarah gets in around ten thirty she's asking the million-dollar question almost before she's properly through the door.

'So, has he rung?'

'I'm sorry?'

'Nan! Don't pretend you didn't hear! Has your "New Love Interest" called you?' She is talking especially slowly, putting her keys back in her bag. 'Or should I say your "Potential New Boyfriend", or even, at the very least, your "Most Recent Shag"? That man you –'

'No, he bloody hasn't!'

'I'm sorry. Sorry. He did take your number, didn't he?' I don't answer.

'Although, if you'd got his, like any self-respecting old slag, then we needn't have any of this. But then I suppose you wouldn't have dared ring him and then –'

'Shut up.'

'Mind you, I only have your word for it that he exists anyway.'

'Sarah, trust me, I couldn't have invented Aidan.'

*　　*　　*

Tuesday is chaotic at work. They all turn up eventually, falling over each other and complaining about everything and shouting down the phone. When I walk in the door Lesley and Toolis are huddled by Lesley's desk and Lesley, without any preamble, asks me if I turned off her computer on Friday night. Because, if so, I have managed to lose her entire prospective budget for the women's programme. Oh. Did I? I fled in such a hurry that night, for reasons I'm not going to share with this lot, so I suppose I must have.

'I can't remember. If you'd left it on I may have. Did you not save it? I probably presumed you weren't coming back from your long lunch.'

That should shut her up. Toolis sniffs; but Lesley rallies to her own defence.

'I was not having lunch. I didn't even get lunch on Friday. I was checking out those studios in the Isle of Man, you know, Heather, the ones that cost a tenth of prices round here?'

Even Toolis is impressed. 'You went to the Isle of Man on Friday? How? What time did you get back?'

'Sunday lunch time. By car. In fact, on the way, I broke down outside Birmingham – a flat, can you believe it – and the rescue people told me our company cover had elapsed. I gave them hell, I can tell you, but it was no good. I had to change it myself.'

I envisage Lesley alone on the hard shoulder, lorries thundering past and sending that hair flying into her face. A hot dusty day. Perfect allergy weather. I smile. I can't help it. Alastair does too, but his desk is behind hers, so Lesley can't see him. Lesley slides a sideways glance in my direction but says nothing, so I presume the subject's closed, one nil to me. She must hate my guts.

Stella swans in at about eleven thirty, looking pale but pricey in a crumpled rose-pink linen suit. Toolis very obviously checks her watch while Stella's shuffling through the post. Then Stella offers to make me a coffee, which I accept.

She remembers how I said I liked it, places a cup in front of me, and then gets a paperback out of her briefcase and wonders if I could be a sweetie and photocopy a chapter of it? The book's called *Drug Dependence and Social Deprivation* and the chapter in question is headed *The Underclass*. Thirty-nine pages. I shudder. The photocopier will never stand for this.

Stella must be able to read my mind. 'If that old fossil conks out then take the book down the road to the nearest copy place.'

Thank God; but, not so fast. Toolis is defending her baby.

'The copier is not an old fossil and it won't conk out. It just needs to be treated properly. Please don't waste petty cash on that, Nanette.'

Who do I please? Is one of them more senior than the other? What is their relationship? I thought Toolis ran the place, but Stella does have a tone which presumes obedience. She looks at me.

'Well, I need this doing in a hurry, so if there is any problem, please let me know, OK, Nancy?'

A friendly smile: it speaks collaboration to me. She'll see me right.

'OK, Stella.'

I approach the fossil.

'Nanette! Could you rather urgently call around a few places to get some quotes for these?'

Toolis is waving some sheets of paper at me. Stella lifts her head. I like Stella, but I'm scared of Toolis. Although, Stella asked first, and nicely. I must be firm.

'After I've done this, all right?'

That was easy enough. I turn my back on both of them and watch, in astonished gratitude, as the previously recalcitrant photocopier does its job like an angel.

The day carries on in the same vein, with Stella and Toolis demanding my time and attention merely to ensure that the other can't have it. Stella, it seems, actually does very little. I catch her writing out the contents of an old address book into a new one, and painting Tippex onto her mistakes, then she phones a nursery in Norfolk to order some extremely expensive rose bushes (I have to find the number for her), and calls a jeweller's to see if her watch is ready. Each time she asks my help with any of these minute tasks, Toolis' body tightens and, as if automatically, she gets me to do something practical. Lesley then joins in and darts endless requests at me which are too insignificant to refuse legitimately, but take up far more time than they should because I don't know how to deal with them efficiently. The pair are working out how much their new series will cost to make, and their special trick is to throw questions at me one by one, and to demand the answer within seconds of asking the question, so that I am forced to call all the same equipment hire places and facilities houses and editing suites again and again, and to interrogate, with my main eye on economy needless to say, several patient weary people in a vocabulary which I don't understand and with whom I am incapable of conversing when they do their best to answer.

At lunch time I am handed a sandwich list as long as your arm and bristling with all their nutritional peculiarities. Alastair's request is the most ridiculous – reconstituted soya duck on buckwheat bread – and I am about to put my foot down, but he says sorry, only joking, and heads out for a burger. I am sent to a particular vegetarian deli for Lesley's alfalfa sesame melt, which she says is a little north of Oxford Street, but I eventually discover it closer to King's Cross, and yet, when I finally deliver it to her hungry hands, she once more manages to find a chip of prawn shell in the penultimate mouthful. By the time I trail back with the fishy evidence in a brown paper bag the place has, of course, closed for the day, so I chuck the debris in a bin and dawdle awhile, staring at some footless pigeons in Russell Square for half an hour just to get my revenge. I feel like I'm playing truant. Hugging my knees on a warm bench, I recall every inch of Aidan. Why hasn't he called? Has he lost my number? It's quite possible, since it was only written on a Rizla paper. Why not ring the office then? Well, that's understandable; what if – very unlikely, but not entirely impossible – what if Lesley picks up the phone? He won't want anyone knowing about us yet. Maybe he thinks a week or so is a decent time to leave it? I mean, it only happened four days ago. Maybe he's shy, and doesn't want to presume anything? Or he's treating me mean and keeping me keen? That's what you do. Just how abnormal is the poor man's silence? Or am I just a slag? Where is he now? Will I recognise his voice if he does call? Did I dream him up?

That evening, he doesn't call, and Sarah tells me that whether I like it or not, it was a one-night stand. I don't like it.

Wednesday looks as if it'll be more of the same. Toolis starts the day by enquiring how I'm doing with the taboo problems people, so I tell her the calls are drying up now, and snigger to myself, if only their subject matter was. She tells me I am to get together with Alastair to co-ordinate the in-depth research conversations. He grins from the phone, one more furtive follow-up call to his previous evening's social efforts no doubt, and adds a leery wink. The prospect is hideous, but I am saved for the time being by Stella. She notices my less-than-enthused expression, or I think she does, anyway, because at this very moment she chirrups out, to no one in particular, or the room in general: 'I know! A party!'

The timing is perfect. Lesley resembles a sailing ship buffeted by storm waves of paper sheets on her desk. She has lost something, and is hunting in vain in the white crests around her. As she pushes one aside, another takes its place. She gives up and, in despair, leans backwards, placing her hands to her face and sneezing, the loudest sneeze in Christendom, projectile glob no doubt clinging to her palms. No one moves. Alastair places a hand over the receiver. Toolis is holding a plastic letter-opening dagger, which she has instructed me to use on the post in future, so that we can recycle more envelopes, and as the sneeze reaches its climax, she presses its harmless blade to her wrist in a theatrical gesture of suicide.

'I'm sorry, Stella. I didn't quite catch that.'

Stella trills away: 'A party, Heather. Don't you think it's a good idea? We've never had a party before, we've got a new commission, it would be a great idea to bring all our friends and clients and contacts together! Don't you think? While the weather's good?'

Toolis' eyes are popping. She is visibly counting the cost already. Stella's idea of a party will no doubt involve sparkling wine at the very least, but if Toolis doesn't like it, why doesn't she say so? She clearly resents Stella's every waking moment but, though she grouches, she never does enough to piss her off entirely. I don't get these two.

'Come on! Let's decide a date in a few weeks' time, and I'll do an invitation, then Nancy can get them printed and send them all out. It's time Toolis TV saw some fun.'

'Very well. If you say so.'

While Stella is designing the invitation she gets me to collate all their contacts' details onto the computer so that we can print off labels. Thank God for such an out-of-harm's-way task, I must say. Along with answering the phone, it saves me both from Lesley and Toolis, and also puts off my meeting with Alastair to decide the fate of the callers with the personal problems. Spinning out my task for as long as I can, I daydream, and the latter half of the morning idles by almost pleasantly. He'll ring tonight.

By one o'clock I have reached the letter E, and am allowed to have a proper lunch break because Alastair has

generously offered to 'do my bit and man the phones'.
Stella and I go downstairs together. She is leaving already.
Friday is only two days away. Good things happen at weekends. Aidan will ring and everything in the garden will be
lovely. Right will prevail.

Stella says goodbye and heads up Greek Street, another
flawlessly elegant outfit rustling in the warm midday
breeze. She says she is off to a lunch meeting. Dust specks
fizz in sunbeams, and office windows on the upper storeys
are open wide all along the street. I am in an extravagant
mood, so decide to have lunch in a distinctly media bar,
treating myself to an hour's peace. I fork out a king's
ransom for smoked chicken on focaccia bread and a glass
of apple juice, and stare out of the open window, and
squint at the great British public battling on by.

Two o'clock comes too soon, as always, and I idle back.
My vision is so assaulted by the darkness of the stairs that
I am only just rebalanced by the time I open our door, all
hot. Toolis advances immediately, a determined look on
her face. What have I done wrong now? I'm tired all of a
sudden.

'Nanette! I've been looking at what you are doing, and –'

'Yes?'

'Well, it's just that you're doing it alphabetically, yes,
straight from the Rolodex?'

'Er, yes. Is that wrong?'

'No, well, yes. I'd like you to do it differently. You see,
if you do it alphabetically you're going to take all day,
aren't you, at this rate? I mean you're only on E now. And
I really don't want you wasting any more time on this
wretched party than you need to. Stella has lost this company quite enough money lately. Whatever she says, we
don't want to ask most of these people. I mean, would
you want to share a canapé with Miss Moppy Cleaners
herself?'

'Er –'

Is Toolis making a joke? Alastair, still sprawled at my desk, chips in here that it's more than a canapé he'd like to share with Miss Moppy Cleaners, and Toolis, instead of ignoring it or rebuking him as I expect, opens her tiny mouth to reveal tiny microscopic teeth and shudders her face up and down with a breathy chuckle. Is this, for her, a loss of control? I never cease to be amazed by the woman. She must be the only creature on the planet to find Alastair anything other than repellent. I blink; and the vision has gone. She is Toolis again.

'So, Nanette, I'll go through the Rolodex, marking with different colours the people we want to come. Red can be vitals, blue can be next best, and green can be scraping-the-barrels. If they're not marked then we certainly won't be inviting them. While I'm doing that you can begin putting in all the definites, starting with everyone you've met so far. And their partners, if they've got one, obviously.'

'OK.'

Who first? I look around. Alastair can be last, that's for sure.

'Lesley?'

'Yes?'

'Could I have the correct spelling of your full name and address, and also that of your partner, if you've got one, obviously?'

It's worth it. I have never seen anyone look so horrified. I've really gone too far this time. My victim and I stare at each other. I hold my breath.

'L-E-S-L-E-Y S-H-A-R-P-E, 5, HALLIWELL TERRACE, spelt H-A-L-L-I-W-E-L-L, LONDON NE27. And my boyfriend's name is James Parker –' then, after a pause, and her gaze does not waver – 'and he's at the same address.'

Oh! Cohabitation. Goal to her.

'Thank you very much.'

I smile gratefully, tapping in the information. Alastair approaches.

'Nancy, can I let you know who my partner will be nearer the time? You know, these things do change so quickly, I find.'

'Could you wait your turn, please? Thank you. Now. Heather?'

Will there be a Mr Toolis?

'I won't be needing an invitation, Nanette, since I shall no doubt have to host the thing.'

'All right. What about Stella, then? Does she have a partner?'

I hate that word, it's so clinical.

'Of course.' Lesley fills me in. 'She's married. Her husband was here last week, remember? Aidan Rivers.'

CHAPTER TWELVE

❋

Aha. Well, that sorts that out. Like when you open those exam results and you think it'll be so embarrassing when you get an A with distinction because your best friend only got C, and she's sitting next to you right now, and then the mean little slip of paper in your sweating hands has the nerve to say D. Because you did no work and thought you were clever enough not to have to. Only worse, only so much worse. A terrible dull dead shaming sensation.

I feel sick. The sun is in my eyes. My limbs are chilled and I stay completely still, apparent indifference my sole escape from Lesley's utter triumph. She must not see that anything is wrong. I begin to type the horrible revelation into the computer; but it's impossible to press the letters.

Lesley must have sensed something.

'Anything else I can help you with? Just ask.'

The afternoon drags, heavy as lead, to its conclusion. I speak barely at all. Eventually it is time to go home. Now I know that Aidan's phone call, which innocent little me wanted so badly, will never come. How stupid I've been! Sarah's doubts were right after all. Strangely, I don't care about losing face, I just want to cry on her shoulder. For now I can't face being alone. Oddly, I don't hate Aidan for a second. Why not? I've had my best thing taken away from me, and I just want it back, unchanged, no charges will be pressed.

The flat is empty. I pour myself a big drink, Southern Comfort with Coke and ice. I don't know why I bother with such a theatrical gesture when nobody else is there. Perhaps it's the most natural thing to do: I always pretend there's an audience watching my movements. It numbs the pain and puts off the moment when you admit you're by yourself and have to face the indifferent truth. Pretend you're in a film, that the focus is on your face, that you have a duty to the viewers, that you are not alone. Oh, be quiet. What's in this stuff? By the time Sarah appears I am on my third glass of the mixture; like syrupy cough medicine it is slithering down my throat.

'Nan? What's brought this on?'

I must look weird.

'Guess what?'

'Aidan's married?'

'How do you know?'

'I don't. I'm joking. He isn't, is he?'

I nod gravely. I can't say the word. She sits down suddenly, horror breaking out across her face.

'He isn't? My God! How did you find out? I hope it was him that told you?'

'No, of course not. I've not spoken to him. But, Sarah, guess who he's married to? That's the worst bit.'

'Who?'

'Stella, of all people. Stella, one of my bosses at work, the nice one!'

'Oh, no! The bastard! Oh, I'm so sorry, Nan. That's, that's really – terrible.'

It's all too much. I start to sob loudly. My temples are thrumming and I've been shouting, I realise. I catch a look of panic on Sarah's face: she's got a night of counselling to look forward to now.

She copes with it brilliantly, I have to say. She's turning into a good friend. By the time I pass out four hours later, face down on the duvet, we have drunk a great deal and she has convinced me, she hopes, to forget all about Aidan and to look on the whole thing as one of life's little tricks that you can either let get to you or else cast aside as unimportant. The latter, she assures me, though it seems impossible now, is the more adult response. In fact, she reckons, I've had a lucky escape: married men are *always* trouble. I am to call in sick tomorrow as well and then, very soon, I will be over him. It is, apparently, the only way.

Next morning at seven thirty the alarm wrenches me, sweating and feeling predictably awful, from a dream set in the age of the dinosaurs. While hiding under a palm tree to escape the vast towering threat of a tyrannosaurus rex, which was chasing me personally, I stumbled on to a heap of huge eggs, all except one of which were hatched and empty. The last one had a rip in its vast side (the egg was about four foot tall), out of which protruded, in stabbing movements every minute or so, a sharp claw. I was crouched about five yards away and unable to move. The rip widened and then a huge eye met mine, filling me with fear. I recognised that eye. Seconds later the whole shell cracked open and out rolled Toolis, dark clothing glossy with yolky mucus, fists clenched, helmet on, a ready-made assassin. At first I thought she might ignore me, but no such luck. Now her mouth was level with my terrified face.

'Nanette,' she said, in her normal voice, but scalding fumes of eggy hatred were blasting out of her jaws, and she spat a projectile glob which frothed like sherbet when it hit the ground. 'We all know about you and Aidan, but you mean nothing to him. He loves Stella, Stella, Stella, his wife, his wife, his wife, Stella.'

The repeated name was a bell echoing through the forest. Getting louder with each ring it catapulted me awake: 'Stella, Stella, Stella, STELLA.'

The clock alarm. Time to get up. Oh God.

The prospect of work is oppressive, an awful hovering

ghoul; hateful and alien and frightening. I never want to set eyes on the inside of that office again, never want to see any of their faces for the rest of my life. It feels as if they all knew but ganged up on me and didn't say. Shall I resign? Right now it is tempting. Maybe I will.

No! Hold on. Don't be so extreme. Why should I? I need that job. I want that job. I have a right to that job. Calm down. Think about this. All right. Why not just ring in sick both days until the weekend and then go back on Monday? OK. Today, certainly. I can't face seeing Stella today. Desolate, I want to cry, but, hot and dry-skulled, can't even manage that. At twenty-five to ten I call the office and speak to Toolis herself, telling her I have what I think is a spot of summer flu, that I will not be able to make it today, and have my doubts about tomorrow.

'Oh, no. What a bore. Just what we didn't need. OK. Goodbye.'

And good riddance to you. Now what? Sarah pampers me. She tries very hard and buys croissants and chocolate ice cream and makes milkshakes and collects the ingredients for a cake. We get as far as mixing them and then eat the whole lot raw, an action which forces me to realise that I have a long way to go before true maturity is mine. The weather remains hot, but sluggish, and threatening thunder; and though no cooler by the open window, I perch there anyway on the sill, in a T-shirt and dressing gown, licking a fork and watching the traffic far below. By lunch time I feel sick and bored. I'm still not dressed. Sarah leaves after the midday Australian soaps have finished. Feeling miserable is hard work, I must say: it permits no levity to release the tension. And, needless to say, Aidan doesn't ring. He'll know that I know, by now – he must do – that Stella is his wife. Wife. Bastard. All last night and today Sarah has been trying to make me angry, to recognise that I have been wronged. She's done a good job, and my main frustration now is that I cannot get at Aidan to shout at him, to demand an explanation for such shite behaviour, to avenge my insulted self-esteem. I give Auntie's varnished wainscoting an angry kick, but a bit too hard, and stub my toe, and fall back onto the sofa in real pain. Fuckwit! Damn him! The things I'd like to call that man now! This is the worst bit: I can't get to talk to Aidan, regardless of what I would say.

The ringing of the phone wakes me from a bleary nap. Four o'clock already? It'll be Aidan. Oh, please, please, please.

'Hello?'

'Nancy?' A woman's voice, one I don't immediately recognise. Slightly breathless.

'Yes?'

'Nancy, it's me, Stella. Are you OK?'

It's her! How cruel is this life? Stunned, I cannot answer.

'Nancy? Are you still there? How are you feeling?'

Can this be true? *She* is asking me how I'm feeling?

'Oh. Fine. I mean, a bit better, thanks.'

'Good, good. I thought I'd ring and see how you are. I'm a bit worried about you. I mean, you seemed all right yesterday. Mind you, I wasn't there in the afternoon; maybe you were struck low then. I suppose it's one of those bugs that descend with no warning, is it?'

Huh. You could say.

'Suppose so.'

'You poor thing, Nancy. Oh, I do feel for you.'

Oh, fuck off, woman. I hardly know you, I certainly have nothing to say to you, and I slept with your husband.

'I'll be OK.'

'Well, don't come in tomorrow if you're still poorly. We're fine here. I mean, we can answer the phone for ourselves, for goodness sake! But I thought, if you're better, or even if you don't come in to work, whether you'd like to come round to dinner at ours tomorrow night? Actually, why not bring Philip too? I could come and pick you up in the car if you don't make it in.'

What? 'Ours'? To see 'them'? Aidan and her? With Philip? It is the very last thing on earth I wish to do.

Thinking fast: 'Well, that's kind of you, but I don't know how I'll be feeling by then, so, can I let you know? Also, Philip is away at the moment.'

'Really? On holiday? Where's he gone?'

Shit. Lies are never simple. Where would Philip go on holiday if he ever took one? Hastings?

'Oh, some sweaty beach.'

'I see. It's all right for some, isn't it? Still, you could come by yourself. But sure, of course, if you're ill, I'll understand. If tomorrow's no good, though, maybe we could make it next week sometime?'

Bloody hell! Where is this onslaught coming from?

'Yes, sure, maybe. Listen, I can't really think straight now, and to be honest the thought of dinner makes me feel ill, so can we talk tomorrow?'

Just get off the phone and go away, please. I know you're being friendly, but not now.

'Oh, sorry, Nancy, I'm tiring you out. I must let you go. Just take it easy, though, all right? Don't do anything strenuous, OK?'

What, like fuck your husband?

'Of course not.'

'Bye, now.'

At last. I put down the receiver in a cold sweat. Yesterday's unwelcome discovery seemed, a few minutes ago, and however painfully, to make things drastically simple. I'd never speak to Aidan again and, once I could face going back to the job, I'd keep as well clear from Stella as possible. Now I'm not so sure. It might not be so clear cut. With an extremely hot cup of tea I plot in the armchair. Aidan sat on this. Of course I can't go to dinner at their house; but then she'll just ask me again. I can only avoid that completely by abandoning both the job and London, now, in a hurry. But no way. Just because she is there? No! I want the job. Damn this! What to do? Stella is the spanner in the works, not only because she exists, but because she's one of those overfriendly people who won't leave you alone. It's all getting horribly tangled. I've woken to a nightmare.

Sarah rings to say she's gone round to Nick's, and have there been any developments? I assure her so, telling her about Stella's call, and she sounds suitably impressed by the growing complication of it all.

'You're not going to go, though, are you, Nan?'

Does she think I've lost my mind?

'God, no. You must be joking. I'll just call in sick and hopefully she won't ask again.'

'Right. Good idea. You could have done without this, couldn't you?'

'You don't say.'

'I wonder what hubby thinks about it? Do you think she's mentioned you to him yet?'

'How do I know? Why should she have? Though, put it this way, it's a bit more likely than him mentioning me to her, don't you think?'

'Oh, just a little. Listen, though, I've got to go now, but you'll be OK, won't you? I'll be back sometime in the morning, so we can dissect this further then. But, for now, take just a shred of advice?'

'What?'

'Try and forget it. Laugh it off. What's one shag between here and eternity?'

'You're right. I must get a life.'

'That's the spirit.'

Another empty evening. I have no intention, let alone ability, to get a life. Maybe I'll ring Eric, scream abuse, and then slam the phone down. Or look up Lesley in the phone book and do the same.

Or, ring Grace.

I should ring Grace. I have to tell her about the job and the holiday, but what do I say? She'll know I'm upset, and I'll probably burst into tears or something, and then she'll make me say why; but I can't tell her about Aidan, now that he's married. On that night when we'd first met she also told me that she'd fallen in love with her English teacher in sixth form, and they did get it together, but he was married, and strung her along for nearly a year, I think, until she got pregnant and he realised he loved his wife. Grace had an abortion and doesn't believe in romance any more. So, that's out. I know exactly what she'd say. Walk away. Do not even *think* of getting involved. Come back immediately and we'll all go on holiday.

I suppose I could do. It's the sensible thing. Walk away.

No, no, no. No way. Don't be such a drama queen. I have a job to go to. Sorry, Grace. Anyway, she'll ring me, if I don't look out. I turn on the answer phone in a hurry, then collapse back onto the sofa.

So, Aidan, you're married, are you? Jesus! My poisoned day has driven me to hatred and I think of Stella and her flawless taste and her no doubt limitless credit status and I wonder what sort of things she cooks. What is their kitchen like? Yesterday morning I had fantasised about Aidan wandering around some bachelor flat somewhere, gorgeous and alone. Nausea. Stella asked me on Tuesday if I'd mind popping out to pick up some shopping for her from a Soho delicatessen, pressing a fifty-pound note into my hand, and I'd returned with a carrier stuffed with Italian cheeses and salami wrapped in greaseproof paper and a loaf of bread so hard you could use it for a doorstop. In their kitchen no doubt there'll be gallons of extra virgin olive oil and jars full of sun-dried tomatoes and sheep's cheese cooling on marble larder shelves that have never known baked beans. Maybe Aidan creeps out every day for Cheddar and pickle sandwiches. A rush of affection for him joins forces with a spasm of exhaustion to clamp on my temples with a pair of forceps. I lean over and switch the answer phone off again, then, slowly, stiffly, start to cry. I don't want this. Weeping creakily until I bring on a headache and have to fall asleep to get rid of it, my last thought is how ridiculous this all is.

Eleven hours of sleep later I am physically and mentally restored. I have a plan. Friday already. The end of week two. I shall get up and dress with confidence and go to work. There I will graciously accept Stella's invitation to dinner and then, if the chance arises, I will treat myself to mutter something spiky to Lesley. This evening I will accompany Stella back to her marital home where, either, a) I shall find Aidan, her husband and the man with whom I had rampant sex only a week ago; or, b) I shall not find Aidan (as above) but will be able to undertake extensive practical research on the subject of Aidan Rivers in his natural habitat. A thorough snoop will reveal so much.

I'm sorry. I can't resist it. I'm hooked into this story now. I want answers, and I'm prepared to grub for them. He made the perfectly adult decision to have sex with me and she invited me to eat in their home in a thoroughly mature way and if they have problems informing each other of their decisions that is their problem and not mine. Is it my fault they have asked me into their lives? Has any of this been my fault? Hardly. No, for the time being I won't even attempt to reason any further than this. I need the results of tonight's experiment first. So what? – to all of it. I'm cool. By taking such action instead of brooding at home I will restore the confidence lost in this romantic setback, and rejoin once more the track to my future. Lastly, I will not be informing Sarah of this decision until after the event.

The day goes roughly as planned. I manage to maintain an overall bonhomie and sense of purpose. Seeing Stella again in the light of her being Aidan's wife is a sensation I have tried to prepare myself for, and one for which she has also unwittingly primed the ground by her phone call yesterday, so it ends up being a strangely objective experience despite the irony of her genuine greeting. I don't feel guilt or anything like that, rather more a sense of distance between the two of us which is vital for my own wellbeing. She asks about dinner again, and is pleased when I accept.

'That's excellent! Wonderful! So, is there anything you can't eat?'

What a joke. You'd be putting the arsenic into the food, dear, if you knew what kind of serpent you were having round.

'Well, I'm not too keen on hot curries, or anything too hot for that matter.'

Is a hot curry exactly what she has in mind? Her expression stiffens for a fraction of a second before relaxing into a generous smile.

'OK. Don't worry, nothing hot. Give me another suggestion?'

'How about something Italian? That would be nice. Perhaps a pasta effort, drizzled in olive oil, garnished with plump tomatoes dried in the Calabrian sun, the tangy crumblings of an Apennine cheese lending a whiff of mountain air to the dish?'

(And then you won't have to get in anything specially, I nearly add, but stop just in time.) Oh, have I gone too far again? She's giving me an odd look, and then bursts out laughing.

'You're mad, Nancy. You *are* on another planet. I don't know where you're coming from.'

Nor where I'm going, either. This is a much healthier pace with which to run things. Stay cool, hang loose, admit nothing. This is more like me, the old killer Nancy back. I nearly lost myself there, for a while, and all for a man. I am almost content. Aidan Rivers, eh? Married! A TV producer! Nancy! What would people say? Well, my family would disapprove, obviously, and Eric would despise me, that goes without saying, and Grace would read her past onto my future and wag a warning finger; but Rebecca would be impressed, housemate number two. Obviously, I haven't dared ring because of the brewing holiday show-down, but I wish I could tell her everything. She doesn't have a boyfriend, and I'm not sure she ever has. Come to think about it, I have no idea what her past contains. She's very discreet, and kind of commands respect, so you daren't ask her for details. Maybe she's never slept with anyone – that's what I rather suspect. I wouldn't be surprised. I think she quite liked Eric, in fact, because sometimes, if I'm honest, I could see he got on better with her than he ever did with me. She's great, though; if I told her about Aidan she'd give me real audience money's worth. Nancy, you are bad! A married man! Aidan Rivers! Stella's hus-band! And, my God, what would anyone say here in the office if they knew? I recall Lesley's girlish flirting with Aidan, and, frankly, I feel superior. Then the day when Aidan saved me from the wrath of Toolis, and the moment itself when he asked me for the drink; and I sit there brood-ing on all the things he's done like a bird warms her eggs, and quite restore the core to myself. These things have all happened, and very recently: a man, though married, has, for some reason, sought human contact with a person not his wife. So? Married men do that all the time. Yes: but now it's Aidan and now it's me. It happened once and could happen again, and while I harbour not a single evil thought of Stella personally, I love myself more, and look-ing after me will occupy my time from now on.

At five o'clock Stella asks me if I'm ready to go. Will Toolis mind if I leave now? She's not there to notice, though, and the others can lock up, surely? I get my things together. Alastair tells me to have a good one and even Lesley manages to wish me a nice weekend, through near-rigid lips. The chimpanzee's grimace with which I return her compliment tells her that I will, Lesley, trust me on that. I think Stella notes my insincerity, for she catches my eye, and smiles, as if to say, I know you hate her. Then I remember my joke with Aidan about Lesley and the ballroom dancing, and I laugh out loud, and Stella laughs too, thinking we are laughing at the same thing. Fool! What a romp: out of the frying-pan and into the fire.

Stella drove in, so we walk to get the car. I follow slightly behind, carrying one of her leather cases and jauntily getting in a spot of window-shopping, evilly calling out whenever I see something that I like. I don't know why I'm doing this; but I'm not, by now, and here, in any mood to question my motives. All I know is that this behaviour is a defence which has come to me when I need it, and I'm grateful. The car is a wonderful dark green BMW with shaded windows. As I sink into its generous upholstery and it noses smoothly into the street, Stella leans forward at the wheel.

'Stick in a tape, Nancy. There's a whole load in the dash there.'

I rustle among them. Mainly classical, with some jazz and rock and typical eighties stuff like the Stones and Talking Heads and the Smiths, there are also homemade recordings with faded pencil labels. As they clatter about and a few plastic covers fall off, I notice Mozart's *Seraglio*, excerpts. Well, here we go. It'll be all like this tonight. I put it into the tape machine to check it's the same as the opera we'd heard in the bar together. Actually, part of me hopes it isn't, because hearing it with Stella will compromise the original experience: but I can't help it. I need to know. This is strictly a fact-finding mission.

The opening notes mean nothing to me. Stella gushes, though.

'Aah. Very good choice. You must have musical taste after my own heart.'

I turn up the volume so that we don't have to talk, and lean back, and listen while we drive slowly through central London and head north. I have learnt their address off by heart now: 12 Dragon Park Gardens, London E9. I have checked in the A-Z where this is – somewhere in wildest Hackney. I've never been to Hackney. There! It is, of course, the same music, and now the very same bit that Aidan and I listened to is playing. No, I'm not this detached. Bending forward, I eject the tape. Stella, though keeping her eyes on the road, is obviously not happy.

'Why did you do that, Nancy? I was having a musical reverie.'

I bet you were. Well, so was I. Maybe this won't be such a painless experiment, after all. What am I doing so close to this woman? Am I mad? My answer is nasty: 'Oh, it's just a bit much at this time of day, that's all.'

I'm not going to imply I don't like it, and have her think me ignorant. Stella goes quiet, reproached and dog-like, and then I do feel guilty.

'Sorry, I'll put it back on if you like.'

'Oh, no, no, you're right, let's have something else. How about the Smiths?'

Yes, fine, anything but Mozart. So I put on a Smiths album and straight away we're hurtled mid-song into some cheery sentiment about a car crash. Hah! I laugh. What if Aidan comes home to discover our chewed-up bodies have had to be cut out of the BMW, so mangled they can't tell which is which? That might teach him caution.

Stella's saying something. I lower the volume.

'Sorry?'

'I was just wondering whether the job was useful to you, Nancy, overall?'

'Oh, right. Yes. Of course it is. It's excellent experience. I mean, do you think this is true, that such a big part of a job is just getting on with the other people there and proving you can work in a team?'

I'll be sending Philip his royalties for this.

'Oh, *ab*solutely, without a doubt. I mean, Heather has an unfortunate manner, I know, but she's pretty solid underneath, and Lesley's quite sweet really, and you get on with Alastair OK, don't you? It's quite fun sometimes, isn't it?'

Are we talking about the same place? I fear our experiences are poles apart.

'Yes, sure, and, listen, thanks for mentioning the job to Philip, you know? I mean, I'm virtually a total stranger to you.'

Oh, ho-ho-ho. Aren't I polite?

'Don't be silly. It's a pleasure.'

And isn't she a little gem?

'I'm just glad we had something for you so soon after he rang.'

'What did you say?'

'After Philip called me.'

'Sorry? I don't understand.'

'When he called me to ask if I knew of any TV gofer jobs, you know? About three weeks ago? I was amazed he'd tracked down my number. I hadn't spoken to him for years. It was such a long shot. I mean, no offence, but I don't know him well at all. I just used to go into his shop a lot and must have said I worked in TV. But I was really impressed. I mean, I wish I had a brother who would look out for me like that.'

'Right. Yes. It was good of him.'

Well, I never. Philip made up all that business about bumping into her? He went to all that effort to help me? I don't know what to think. Oh, I bet my mum asked him to find me a job. Still, better ring him soon and say I'm all right.

'Nearly there now, Nancy.'

'Where are we? I've never been to this bit of London before.' Except in my dreams.

'Well, we've just passed through Islington. It's got some of the most beautiful streets in London, I think. Look at that road there, for instance. Isn't it lovely?'

'Have you always lived here?'

'In Hackney? God, no. I was born and bred in Notting Hill. My mother sees this as a major fall from grace. She thinks Hackney is common, frankly.'

'Oh, right.'

'Aidan loves it, though. Sorry, he's my husband.'

Really? Apology not accepted.

'He wanted to have a big garden, if possible, so he could be reminded of the great outdoors, and you just can't get that sort of thing in central London any more, unless you're multimillionaires. Actually, I've learnt to love the garden and I spend more time in it than he does now. Oh, here we are.'

The car turns into a gravelled driveway overhung by the delicate leaves of some drooping light-green tree. The day, which has been overcast till mid-afternoon and then rainy, has cleared at last, and the evening sunshine is reflecting off every wet plant and leaf. It all has that fresh and clean beauty of nature look, untouched by human hand. From the street you can only see a dark-brick wall, about six foot high, above which grows some climbing plant in a hedge so dense it prevents a view of the garden. The entrance is formed where the wall ends on the right, and a five-bar wooden gate, white paint flaking off it, is open, pushed inwards until stopped by the edge of the lawn. We pass through and Stella switches the engine off in front of the door. The drive curves to the left and a little downhill so that the house is invisible from the gate. You have to go and look for it. There. It's low, made of dark brown brick like the garden wall, and the porch – white painted metal with a woven, pink-rose-enmeshed canopy – juts outwards onto the edge of the driveway. Stylish white shuttered windows on either side of the front door, and on the first-floor level above. The grey-tiled roof slopes unthreateningly; chimneys at each end. I am reminded of a black and white photo I saw once of Charles Darwin's house, I think it was, at the end of his life: so I suppose that dates it round the end of the last century, or the early part of this one. The lawn, its velvet emerald grasses unmown and gazing downwards in waterlogged clumps, extends from the edge of the drive up to the shadowed foot of the wall where the hedge holds sway. Stepping out of the car I go and stand on the grass to stretch my legs and get my feet wet and wash away Soho. A complete turn around confirms what I originally suspected: nothing indicates you are in London, or in any city at all. It's the perfect front garden, blossoming healthy flowers. Could be anywhere in England. Maybe this is its strongest resemblance to a scene from a hundred years ago.

Stella is watching me. Is Aidan here? In the house? I'm nervous. Can she tell? Despite all the outraged resolution with which Sarah managed to fuel me, I so much want to see Aidan again. Of course I do. I miss him. What if he does appear and I rush into his arms? Maybe I should just ask her outright if he's in? What would be weird about that? The windows show no signs of life, though, and there's no other car here. They must be a two-car family, on their money. Oh, please be home, Aidan.

'Come inside, Nancy, and I'll show you round.'

Stella puts a key into the front door lock. He can't be in if the door is locked. Hope drains through my feet and seeps into the gravel, and I follow Stella, glumly, into the house.

'This is the hall, leading to the drawing room on the left, and the dining room here on the right.'

Oh, how lovely. Stella speeds on through and turns into what I discover is the kitchen by the time I catch up with her. She's collapsed into a wooden chair with varnished arms and a high back, the sort of thing you see in a museum of country artefacts.

'God. I need a drink. I expect you do too. Could you bear to do the honours?'

So, I am to be her personal assistant even here? Still, I can have a good look in every drawer of every cupboard.

'Of course, what do you want?'

'Oh, gin for me. It's in the dining room, on the left as you go in, and the glasses are underneath, and there's tonic and ice and a lemon in the fridge here. Have whatever you like yourself.'

She is exhausted. From doing what? The driving has obviously taken it out of her. Maybe she has ME? Is Aidan staunchly standing by a spouse too weak to perform her wifely duties?

I set off. The hallway is dark and low-ceilinged with lots of expensively framed pictures and clocks and mirrors encrusted onto the walls like barnacles. In the dining room everything is old – I mean antique: dark-stained wood furniture and portraits with gloomy backgrounds and cutlery on a sideboard with mottled black-turquoise blooms on the metal. Two windows look onto the front garden, but their view is obscured by heavy draped curtains as well as the shutters on the outside. I have an urge to smash aside these obstructions and let the light of day come rushing in. There's a falseness about the décor: you'd have thought Stella's family ought to have lived here for centuries, and that she evolved from the earth under the floorboards. Yet it isn't quite genuine. What's wrong? Too tidy? Not dusty enough? Not lived in? None of it indicates Aidan. His presence is missing. But what am I doing here, so out of place? It's like part of the room has been roped off from tourists, and I have trespassed on the wrong side of the rope. A heightened sensation, hovering somewhere between thrill and nausea, has been with me since we left the office. I feel like I'm having an out-of-body experience: watching myself while I do something I shouldn't.

I pour us both a gin and return to the kitchen. This is a much lighter room, a big window facing out the back towards the now setting sun. Again, it's sinisterly tidy, especially for a kitchen. Stella is clanking about with pans and things.

'Oh, thanks. Here's the tonic. I need this. Now, do you like chicken, because I could roast this little one, it wouldn't take too long, or is that not summery enough? Maybe chops and salad? Do you have any views on the subject?'

'Oh, I like both, but maybe the chicken, if you don't mind?'

That'll take longer to cook and maybe Aidan will be back by then. A phone begins to ring somewhere, not in here, and Stella goes to answer it. I can hear her say 'Oh, hi', in the way you might to someone close, so I creep up to the edge of the door and listen.

'OK.' Pause. 'Oh, no, I didn't.' Pause. 'Yes. All right. Bye.'

She reappears. I am looking out the window by now. A glass conservatory stands directly in front of half of it, so that on the right side of the kitchen the sunshine is muted, while on the left it is pure. Was that Aidan on the phone?

'What a lovely garden you've got, Stella.'

'Isn't it?'

I have a devil in me. Don't tell me he can't come. 'So, what time does your husband get home?'

'I'm sorry?'

'Your husband? Aidan?'

'Oh. Right. Actually, he can't make it tonight. No.'

I knew it. So his voice was in the next room, speeding down the phone line only feet from me. Was it really the same man? It makes me shiver. Am I disappointed or relieved that he won't be turning up? I do want to see him, but not with Stella, and not here. Oh, what am I kidding myself for anyway? It was a one-night stand, a married man playing away from home. He won't get in touch again.

'It's a shame. I wanted you to meet him. He works in TV, you know, current affairs, so you could have had a good chat about it all.'

Yes, well, I do need to spend a few minutes with your husband, you've got a point there. If only to give him a good kick. I want to hear him scream. I kicked Philip in the bollocks once, when I was small. I had no idea of the effect it would have, and he howled in pain before crunching to the floor. It certainly hurts them. Still. Shall I lead Stella off the subject, or get her to tell me more about Aidan?

'Does he often work late?'

'Yes. He works very hard. I suppose it's fair enough – I mean, you wouldn't do it if you're a nine-to-five person.'

'It must be tough on you?' How could I?

'Well, yes, I don't see much of him at all some weeks. And he's abroad a lot for film festivals and research trips and things. But, you know, I'm very happy.' She sounds so fake. 'I've got my work and the garden and everything else.'

Oh yeah, such as? Tsk, the idle rich. Stella waves her hands in a vague gesture of industry and giggles feebly by way of explanation. Maybe she doesn't mind too much that she sees so little of him? Don't hunt for chinks, Nancy, one part of me warns. Another part ignores it.

'How long have you been married?' Meaning, how long did you have in mind to stay married?

'Erm, it's nearly ten years now. Yes.'

'God, that's a long time.'

'Is it?'

'Oh, I think so. So, when did you meet?'

Is this a completely bizarre question? Surely not. It is the sort of thing you ask, isn't it, even when you don't have an ulterior motive? I hope she doesn't mind. I've only known her since Monday. Stella is now washing her hands in the sink, and turns round, holding them out in front of her, water dripping onto the earthenware-tiled floor.

'Oh, you don't want to know all that boring stuff?'

Is she blushing? Oh, please no, coy and in love. Plainly dying to tell me all that boring stuff really. No pain, no gain, though. I am stoical, and wait for her to speak.

'Well . . .'

She takes a cloth off a peg on the side of a large dresser – it has a picture of a big red heart on it, the towel, I mean – and dries her hands, between every finger and even under the wedding ring.

'Well, we met through work, I suppose.'

Now she's opening the fridge door and taking out a chicken and peeling off its plastic coat. I sit myself down opposite the dead bird's chilly bottom. Nice room, of course, full of fine furniture like the others, sort of old-style Provençal, all wholesome stuff like the floor and the table and dresser and wooden draining board and cups hanging off hooks and dark wallpaper. That must be the secret of making it look ancient, dark green wallpaper with tiny yellow and purple flowers on it, so that the big silver fish-baking tin on top of the dresser lurks in a darkness like the depths of the sea. She has to have shares in Habitat.

'Go on.'

'Oh, what's to say? I was working at the BBC then, and one day I met Aidan and it was love at first sight, I suppose.'

She laughs shyly. I'd laugh if I didn't want to throw up. Stella is bending over the chicken to pull out its cold bloody bag of giblets. Her dark bob hangs coolly down over her face, moving in one swathe when she tilts her head.

'Pretty sickening, eh?' She cackles hysterically, picking out a blackened and plainly much-used roasting tin from some cupboard. It's not that funny, dear. 'Then, you know, it followed on from there. The usual thing. We got married a couple of years later, and bought this place, and lived happily ever after really. Boring, but true.'

Beat that, Nancy. Beat that, little girl. I look round the kitchen and take in all the evidence of a happy home, the accumulation of meaningful trifles which the couple have gathered: a large patterned plate in the middle of the table containing several tiny bits and pieces, each intrinsically saying nothing, but all there for some reason: an acorn, a lid from a toothpaste tube, a shell, a bit of paper with a phone number on (not mine), a wristwatch with a broken strap, a cork from a champagne bottle. You can't deny such trivia its power. It is pointless to fight against such permanence. I am overwhelmed, by a kind of grief, I suppose: the meeting of a small mountain stream with a god-almighty thundering river that cannot help but consume its lesser rival. She got to him first. I can't beat this. The younger child, the victim of time, you don't ever catch up.

'How about you, though, Nancy? Do you have a boy-friend?'

Wince. I'm stung; but must rally.

'Not at the moment, no. Only just got shot of the last one.'

'Oh, I'm sorry. Say no more.'

Isn't she considerate?

'It's OK. I'm over him. I've had it with men for a while. Too much like hard work! I can take them or leave them. Tell me more about yourself, though. About your family. And your husband's.'

'Oh, God no, it'll send you to sleep!'

She has her hand inside the chicken, forcing a whole onion into its long-stilled pulmonary cavity. I try again.

'No, no, it's all valuable scene-setting. Unless you think I'm being nosy? Oh, am I? Sorry. I always do this. Forget it. I always go too far. It's just I'm too interested in people. I won't pry any more.'

'Don't be silly, Nancy! It's OK. It's fine. Nobody usually cares enough to find out about anyone else, that's all.'

Oh, I hate this! Aidan slept with me! He did. He betrayed Stella, this happy wifey woman. I didn't make that up. It did happen, it did! – that voice answers back, shrieking shrilly as it gets carried along in the fearful torrent, fighting the force, not going under. It did happen. I don't understand. Something must be wrong with a marriage if one member, however briefly, wants out, gets out.

So what if there is, though? Where is he now, then, Nancy, your man? How many times has he called you in the last week? How many times will he ever call you again? So, he slept with you. He never will again. Give up, get out, leave this house, you're not welcome here.

'This is fun, isn't it, Nancy? I haven't had a good gossip for ages. I'm so glad you could make it.'

Stella is changing the level of the oven rack, kitchen gloves on, putting the chicken in.

Yes, yes, ducky. I'm tired. I shouldn't be here. Have I gone mad? I might as well enjoy the meal and then go, and not hurt this kind and slightly sad woman. So I smile politely, and grit my teeth; but there's no escape from Stella's hospitality yet.

'Right. Let's go into the other room while this is on, and I'll get you another drink. OK?'

'Sure.'

I follow her into the dark living room. She heads to the window and pulls back the shutters. Moving towards the nearest armchair, I lift off a sleeveless jacket laid across it.

'Jesus! What the hell's this?'

I can hardly move the thing. Stella looks back in surprise, no doubt shocked by my language.

'Sorry, Stella.'

'Oh, that's Aidan's flak jacket. I know, it weighs a ton. I broke my toe on the wretched thing once. Sit here instead.'

Flak jacket? God, men in uniforms. Holding our glasses we settle opposite each other. Silence. What in heaven's name to talk about?

I crunch into the fast-forming ice.

'Is that you?' A big portrait of a little girl, hanging above the mantelpiece.

'Yes.'

Stella smiles. Standing up, I walk over to get a closer look. Aged about eight, the child is wearing a long white dress with a blue sash and a navy hairband over long brushed hair, and she's sitting on a red velvet cushion with golden tassels. It's like a picture of a Victorian child; I almost expect a date from the nineteenth century to be painted in the corner.

'Isn't it lovely? I remember sitting for it. Pure hell. Six weeks, on and off. I was so glad when it was finished.'

'You've got lots of pictures here, haven't you?'

'Yes. They used to be my father's. He was an art dealer, and gathered quite a collection over the years. Most of them are still at my mother's, though. He died seventeen years ago.'

'I'm sorry.'

'Oh, well, he was getting on.'

'Do you have any brothers or sisters?'

'No. Just me. My parents got married quite late in life. Spoilt me rotten. I had a wonderful time.'

'So, how old were you when he died?'

'Just nineteen. About your age. I'd just started college, actually.'

'What did you do?'

'History of Art, up in Scotland.'

'Oh, right.'

'My mother was completely devastated at my father's death. She's turned the house in Notting Hill into a kind of shrine to his memory – changed nothing.'

'What about you? After college?'

'Oh, I got a job at the BBC, straight after, in fact. An arts programme. I loved it.'

Oh, isn't it all so easy for some people? Next, you met

Aidan and fell in love and got married and we'll fast forward that bit if you don't mind.

'What is it that you, er, do now at the company?' Meaning, in what death-like struggle are you and Toolis knotted?

'Oh, well, I'm a director, you know? Me and Heather. So, well, I keep an eye on things, oversee it all. I've a few projects of my own, too, that I follow in particular. In fact, erm, just to fill you in a bit, that's a bit of a sensitive subject with Heather at the minute.' She hesitates.

Oh, don't stop! 'Really? Why?'

'Well, I've had some bad luck with getting commissions lately, and right now I'm taking more from the company purse than I'm putting back in, if you see what I mean. That's the problem with this business – you have to spend money on developing ideas in order to make them credible, but there's no guarantee you'll ever see it again. Get it wrong too often and you go under. Heather's a bit paranoid about the subject. You may have noticed –' here she giggles and looks at the floor – 'that it's all been blood and gore TV till now at Toolis?'

Does she want an answer? 'Well . . .'

'Don't say it. Sensational voyeurism. Circus for the masses. But unfortunately we do have to make money, and that stuff does get commissioned. It pays our wages. And makes it possible for me to try to restore the balance with a touch of, well, integrity, I suppose. There has to be more to life than money, doesn't there? Proper documentaries that might make a difference, you know? I'm trying to get a commission for a story about some heroin addicts up in Scotland at the moment. But you know that.'

'Yes. I see. But it's good about that women's programme pilot, then, isn't it? That's not blood and gore. You must be pleased?'

'Oh. Yes. Of course.'

'Might they go on and commission a whole series? If

they like it? That would be good, wouldn't it? Is that the idea?'

'Yes. That's the idea.'

She answers distractedly, appearing to have lost interest. Maybe because the programme is one of Heather's successes? They're so competitive. Let's talk about Heather, then.

'So how do you know Heather, since, you seem so, well, different?'

'Oh, erm, I can't remember where we met actually! More wine?'

'Thanks. Has she lived in England long?'

'I'm sorry? Who?'

'Heather? She's French, isn't she?'

'What are you talking about? Heather's not French!'

'Oh. I thought she was French. She looks like . . .'

She looks like one of the Duchess of Windsor's Parisian pug dogs. She calls me Nanette. I just assumed she was French. Really, this isn't good enough. When will I learn to keep my eyes open and my mouth shut? On this occasion, though, it's too late, and the confidence of my claim trails away in the face of Stella laughing her head off.

'Heather! French! You are a fool, Nancy!'

'Well, how am I supposed to know?'

'Oh, forgive me, I'm sorry for laughing. But Heather! French!' She wipes her eyes after the guffaws subside. 'You do make me laugh. Heather's an East End girl. More English than I am. Done very well for herself. Whatever made you think she was French, though? With a name like Heather?'

'Oh, I don't know.'

'You are mad, Nancy. But don't get me wrong, nice madness. Anyway, what are your career plans?' She's still smirking.

'Well, I was planning to get my degree first, but I want to be a TV journalist.'

'Well, then, you're right, you probably should get the degree. The offer of the job still stands, though, if you change your mind. But you really should talk to Aidan some time about current affairs.'

Choke. A half-lump of ice goes down whole. Careful now. Ask her something.

'Tell me, though, Stella, would you recommend a career in television, overall? Would you live your life again, with hindsight?'

Oh! She looks at me sharply. I've hit something.

'Can I get back to you on that one?'

What have I said? 'Sure.'

'Sorry, I didn't mean to be mysterious. Now, would I do it again? Well, it's given me a great living, and it's an amazing thing, of course, incredible technology, getting better all the time. And with news, well, obviously, that would be a super life, lots of travel and adventures. You'd be good at it, Nancy, because you have to be interested in other people. I expect you'd worm out the truth! Sure, it's been great. Anyway, how can you know what other choices might have been better than the ones you made?'

She giggles. I get the feeling she's not really talking about her job here. What does she have to regret? Why the doubt? A TV producer! It can't be the job. Her private life? The state of her marriage? But she's been behaving like a love-sick teenager all night. She seems to think her marriage is doing all right, although I dare say time might tell on that one. So, what else is there? She's got the man, she's got the job, she's got the house. Aha. There's that certain cuddly something missing.

She wants a baby. Of course. It's obvious. They all get desperate at that age. She's thirty-six; I've worked that out. Not too late, surely? Maybe Aidan doesn't want children? Or she doesn't? Or they both want them, but for some reason she can't? They keep trying with IVF, but nothing doing? It's costing a fortune? That could be it. Her secret gnawing sorrow. Uterine malfunction? Hereditary disease carried through the females? Messy abortion when she was sixteen? Her life saved in the nick of time, but she'll never be a mother? Or, it's him! Firing blanks! Is my ex-hero small but imperfectly formed? It has to be something like that. Shall I ask? Do I dare to enquire about their family planning policy? I can't. I mustn't. I feel like I'm lying in bed between them now, not daring to look to left or right. Strangely, I'm cheerful. Oh, what the hell?

'Are you hoping to have children, Stella?'

'What!'

She jerks forward and tips a healthy slosh of wine into her lap. Hah! It's obviously a contentious point. So, I was right. My faith in logical deduction is quite restored.

'Oh, damn!'

'Don't move. I'll get a cloth.' I jump up. She waves me down.

'No, it's OK. Listen, do you want to have a look at our wedding photos?'

Oh, great. That was a *very* unsubtle change of subject. I suppose I asked for it, though. The very, very last thing I want to see is their wedding album. Still, I'll get to see Aidan, and I suppose I can mentally airbrush her from all the shots. I can't exactly decline her kind offer.

'Sure.'

I feel sick. So far I've had no reminder of what Aidan actually looks like. She sits herself down next to me on the sofa so that our thighs are touching, so cosy, and opens up Volume One (of two). I brace myself. I do want to look at them really, but alone, and with a pair of scissors. Here they come.

The wedding dress is viciously cool, and Stella looks great. It's kind of more like a suit than a flowing white job. Creamy silk tailored jacket over a knee-length dress. Tasteful bouquet. So expensive. Drop-dead gorgeous, I think you call it. I am just plain jealous now. How could he not fancy her? Next, she's standing on some steps, one satin toe pointed stylishly in front of the other. Flowers all over the place, amid the harsh sunlight of a cold bright day. Is it winter time? I am struck too dumb to ask. Where's Aidan? I turn the page. Here he is. The happy couple, the deed done; I breathe a sharp breath inwards but say nothing. He's looking so young and beautiful and combed and polished I want to cry. It's as if a spear has been thrown from an earlier time, to seek out my heart and mine alone, and when I see that Aidan looks *happy* in the picture, then I feel the cold blade.

After the photo viewing (more and more of the same, each one hurting less and less, or me being increasingly numbed) we go for a tour of the back garden. As at the front, there's no way of telling you're in London, but with one major exception: the winking tower of Canary Wharf over the tree-tops. Stella says it ruins the view. I suppose she's joking. I smile to myself that she could think a major architectural landmark is the only eyesore on her horizon. She doesn't know what I'm laughing at. The back garden slopes downhill and is surrounded by the high wall behind some trees. There's more unmown lawn and stone paths and a rocky pond and a little house in the corner and a plot of vegetables at the bottom, with rhubarb and leeks and cabbages filled with rain on stalks as tall as children. She cuts off one wet head for supper and goes indoors.

I am following, but turn to the right into a room I've not looked in yet. Though I can't see very well, I can tell it's someone's study. Two of the walls are lined with books, while a desk-top runs around the others. A computer sits on this, and to the right of its finger-stained keyboard sits a heavy ashtray full of twisted old roll-up butts. A blind on the window drops three-quarters down, darkening the room, and the air smells of chill human skin. I just stand there. I have no desire to switch on the light. Right here and now, at his desk in his house, I am so close to Aidan, but Aidan is nowhere near.

We eat our meal in the kitchen, but before it's ready, I have to go to the loo. Stella directs me upstairs to the bathroom, and I head slowly to what I fear will be the worst place of all: worse than the bedroom even, I reckon, though I have no intention of going in *there*. It's the domestic married things that get done in bathrooms, I imagine; toe-nail clipping, shaving, baths with the door open. I go in and pull a cord for the light. The room's a low-ceilinged affair with a small window looking out the back. I stand at the basin and stare at myself in the mirror. This reports nothing except the reflection of their bathroom and my face in the same frame. A wooden shelf is fitted at chest level in front of it. Standing on this are bottles of her scent, and a greasy pot of cocoa-butter skin cream, and a china mug with toothbrushes and paste and a bristle-scattered metal-handled razor sticking out.

I sit on the edge of the bath and grip the side to stop me falling backwards. He probably stepped out of it this morning, grabbing a towel and drying his hot wet crotch with special care. God Almighty, Nancy, stop it. Steady. Stop doing this to yourself. Get out of this house immediately. Imagine Aidan turning up to find me there, being cooked a hot dinner by his wife. Like a child. Not funny. In a million years. Not entertaining for anyone in this pathetic nearly-drama. The audience would file out. The irony would chill. Grow up, Nancy. I stand, and as I move forward, a bar of soap sitting by the taps slips into the bath. I lean in to pick it up and a dark pubic hair comes off it onto my hand. I freeze. Maybe it's his. Maybe it's hers. Fuck her! I slam my palm sideways to dislodge it suddenly, but the hair stays and the back of my hand rams into the tap's vicious mouth and is cut open. So with my other hand I turn on the water, and it runs the hair and my blood together and they swirl away round and round and down the dark plughole to who knows where beyond.

Padding down the carpeted stairs. I shouldn't be here. Trespasser. All quiet. Stella waits. The proverbial grandfather clock is ticking in the proverbial hallway and I think, really, Stella, this isn't you. You're too young. Are we all in the wrong place at the wrong time? I certainly am right now. Approaching the kitchen doorway, and before she sees me, I catch Stella, chin leaning on one palm, the other hand clenching a pencil and stabbing it into the table. I make a noise. She stops as though doing something wrong. I smile. Destroy the fittings if you feel like it, dear. You've got reason enough.

The chicken isn't quite cooked through, and I park some pink still-muscley bits on the edge of my plate. This proves the last straw. Guilty as sin, and pleading the sudden return of my sickness, I apologise, but tell her I must go. Aidan might turn up if I stay much longer. I don't want to see him here. In fact, I would run back to the flat if necessary, but Stella insists on ordering me a cab and paying for it on their account. They have a cab firm on account? I refuse only once before accepting her generosity. What's a taxi fare compared to what I've robbed her of? Stella seems upset that I'm feeling ill, and behaves as though she has inflicted me with some terrible injustice. Two minutes later, as the car waits in the road, we say goodbye to each other and I apologise for, well, leaving in a hurry and abandoning such a delicious meal before the end, and – I mumble – 'everything else'. She has the last word, of course, saying she's a bit tired anyway and needs an early night and begging my forgiveness for forcing me to eat a large roast meal before I'm truly better and boring me with photos and tedious reminiscences when plainly I'm suffering.

Just before I slam the car door I hear her final good wishes: 'Take care now, Nancy, and just get better. Let us know if you're not well by Monday, yes?'

Oh please, no more. I collapse back into the seat. At

last. I'm out of there. Well, that was a king-size mistake. It obviously was to be a one-night stand. Sarah's sensible voice wriggles into my head: '*It's for the best really, and you know it, don't you?*' Of course I know it. Of course she's right. I've gambled and lost. I admit it. I'll ring Grace and go on holiday and drink lots and pick up a Greek man and get on with my life and then return to the job if they let me and work side by side with Stella and get over Aidan and be happy. And, if I lose the job, I lose the job. What does it matter? I'll get another. My career will survive. I'll live. I'm only nineteen. And, at the very least, I've bumped up the figure of Men I've Slept With to the glorious total of two. No, all things considered, I'm doing OK.

Resting my head on the window, I take in the view. London looks gorgeous, sandy brick walls casting long, long shadows under lowering biblical clouds and the evening sun, just about, still out.

CHAPTER THIRTEEN

✳

The phone rings. Two o'clock on Sunday afternoon, and life is starting afresh. I have, of course, been thinking about Aidan, but with the passing of every minute in which he doesn't call, the possibility of anything happening seems ridiculous, the recollection grows blunt and misted, and his face is lost. Dreams, eh? You always wake up.

'Nancy? It's Aidan.'

If a sofa had fallen through the roof I couldn't be more stunned. Speechlessness, as ever.

'Nancy? You remember me, don't you?'

I recover. 'Aidan? I don't know any Aidans.'

He laughs. I remember the sound.

'I don't really know what to say to you, Nancy.'

'How about "I am married to your boss"?'

'Yes. You're right. I'm sorry: I suppose that's all I can say.'

I get serious, wake up. 'I can't talk to you, Aidan, I've got nothing to say to you. What did you think you were doing? You do know, don't you, that Stella had me round for dinner? Why didn't you say you were married? Why? Why, you bastard?'

'I don't know, Nancy. I'm sorry.'

Is this all he's rung to say? Truly to pass like a ship in the night? Just calling to say goodbye? 'If you're just ringing to say that's it, sorry, but that's all there was to it, and it won't happen again, well, fine, because you're too right. I don't ever want to see you again.'

Don't go Aidan. Stay on the line.

'Nancy? Can we meet and talk about this? I can't do it on the phone.'

'What? So you can tell me in detail why you lied to me and why we have to finish it? Why bother?'

'Because, maybe we don't have to finish it?' He's asking me a question.

'No. What about Stella?'

'Nancy. I'll tell you about Stella. It's all right about Stella. Please? Can we meet?'

Can we meet? Can we? Is it to be up to me in the end? All I want and more since I first laid eyes on him: but why like this? I see their house, their cabbages, their bathroom. Theirs. Stella's. His wife. How can it be all right about Stella? No, we can't meet. I can't meet him. I shouldn't meet him. I mustn't meet him.

I could meet him. His warm body, his hands, his face. I think of me, I think of my only one life. Maybe I'll never find anyone like him again. Maybe we only get one shot at this. What do I want? Do I want to see him again? That's the question. And the answer? More than life itself. It's not so complicated. Do I want to spend the rest of my days never knowing what will happen if I refuse to see him? No. It's not fair. Their problems are not of my making. Why do I have to lose him? Let Stella lose him.

'Yes, all right. Where?' Primal relief.

'At the tube station, Gloucester Road? I can be there in an hour or so.'

'OK. Aidan?'

'Yes?'

'Get a move on.'

I put the phone down sharply so that he can't change his mind. My head reels and I have to sit on the floor. Time check: fifty-five minutes of calculation. I plot and prepare. How much time does he have? Are we talking a quick cup of coffee and a peck on the cheek at the ticket gates? I must not, I cannot hope for more. Will he have any more time? A walk in the park? Will he come back to the flat? I have to be prepared for every eventuality. Though in all likelihood we'll have a sober conversation, and then part, I have to cover every possibility. Sarah mustn't turn up. Where is she today? She was here yesterday and I convinced her, after confessing to having gone to dinner with Stella, that I was so sickened by everything that my infatuation has cured itself and I am well on the mend. She's out all today with Nick, I think. A bath? Do I smell? I had one last night. You never know, though. Maybe a quick dip to set my mind at rest. Not my hair, however; it'd be a bit uncool to have wet hair when I see him, and if I blasted it with Auntie's dryer it'd only do mysterious things.

After the bath I get dressed again, careful wardrobe inspection – what will I look most irresistible in? Teeth next, including flossing, and hurling a hairbrush at my head, then lying down on the sofa and trying not to move for ten whole minutes so as to slow my beating heart. At five to three I set off, normal respiration proving hard to maintain.

Outside it's sunny and warm. I start to run down the road, dodging people and running over the junctions without any care for safety, speeding with inches to spare in front of car bonnets and crossing the vast highway of the Cromwell Road without waiting for the light to go green. It's really dangerous, but I just kind of know that in this mood nothing can touch me. Then, when the distance to go is very small, I slow down. I don't want to get there before him. I don't want to look as keen as I really am. Anyway, you can't be exact about when someone will arrive on the tube. Maybe he'll be late. I want to stride in and catch sight of him before he sees me. Seated on a low wall outside the station, I compose myself. People mill about and move in all directions round me, to and from the station, up and down the road. An Arab woman, holding one shouting child by the hand and with another screaming in a pushchair, struggles in front of me. Her face is covered in black cloth, except for her eyes, and as she looks down at her baby, muttering something to make it quiet, I can see that she is crying. There is desperation in that small rectangle of human being and I think of Stella.

I don't have to meet him. I don't have to go into the station. I could walk back to the flat and then he would know what it feels like to be deserted, and catch his breath, and know he is doing the wrong thing, and save himself in time. The cold wind could blow for Aidan too. Yet I know I am allowing myself the luxury of pretending to think such responsible thoughts because I will never act upon them, that I am more likely to turn into a rabbit than walk away from Aidan. It's five past three. I get up and go to find my hot date, heart thumping under my ribcage, a sick feeling in my legs.

Nobody in the ticket hall. Damn, too early. Or maybe he's decided against it? Better in the long run. My nose itches, so I stick a finger up the nostril and give it a good scrape. No one's looking. As my nail hooks a satisfactory ledge of crust I am struck by a horrible thought: what if he is so eager to meet up now because he wants to make sure I don't tell Stella? What if he has been struck by fear and/or remorse and, now the thrill is over, is desperate to cover his tracks? Let's face it, that's far more likely than some soppy tragic reunion. Damn, that'll be it. Why did I bother to bathe? Life is shit after all.

'You dirty, dirty girl.'

Aidan's voice at my shoulder, falsely jovial. I turn and there he is, right by me. Aah! Of course! That's what he looks like. Sweet face; but I'm not going to humour him. I'm not going to be nice. He's not going to wriggle out of this scot-free; but then he smiles, so deliciously, like when you're playing that game where you're not allowed to move or wink or laugh, and your whole face fights against it, and the skin around your eye sockets tightens, and your lips stay shut, clamped in the middle and moving outwards to the edge of your face; but you can't win, and then you let it all go and explode and relax. I'm sorry, but the sight of him there is the best, best sight my eyes have ever rested on. This is a magic place now. Aidan, Aidan, Aidan, the stuff that dreams are made of! You're here again. He's wearing a green shirt, cuffs rolled a bit, but not with precision, and pale trousers, weekend chinos for playing in. It's a very odd moment, as though I'm meeting someone I love from another unearthly life, not this disappointing world. A familiar kind of total stranger.

'Hello, again.' He doesn't know what tone to take.

'Hello.'

I am embarrassed even to catch his eye; and I've had carnal knowledge of the man. What shall we do? My body is inflexibly tense: so he puts his face down on my shoulder and my cheek is brushed by the stubble on his jaw. Then, bending forward, he places his arms under mine, and closes them tightly; and thus, when he stands upright, my feet are lifted clear of the ground.

'Put me down! What do you think you're doing?'

'I don't know, Nancy, I don't know. You tell me, please.'

He sets me down, looking straight at me. I'm sulking.

'If only I knew what I was doing.' He looks away, then pulls himself together. 'Shall we go and sit down somewhere?'

I smile shakily. Exhausted. It's all been far too much recently. I mustn't cry. I mustn't cry; but I am. Damn, damn, damn. I can't help it.

'Nancy? What's wrong? Don't cry, Nancy. Oh, don't. Come here.'

Don't you be nice to me, Aidan. I go limp as a rag doll and start to sob on him. He takes my hand and leads me into the street and round the corner to a side road where he finds a bench for us to sit on, side by side. He passes me a handkerchief: it's a large, clean, crispy white one, ironed into a folded square. Pure quality. Reminds me of their house. Who ironed it? Him? Her? We are in the shade here, and I sob jerkily for a few minutes, trying to talk at the same time as I blow my nose.

'You – fucking – bastard.'

Don't go away this time, please. I sit there puffy-faced, and look sideways at him, hands in my lap stretching the handkerchief.

He seems genuinely troubled, I must admit, and speaks slowly: 'I know. I shouldn't have done it. I must explain things to you.'

'Aidan?' I sit up straight and wipe my eyes and haul some resolve into my voice. 'Let me first say one thing.' This is for Stella. I am being so responsible. 'If you want to get up now, and not say anything, and not explain at all, and walk away and never come back, then I would rather you did that, to tell you the truth. I won't tell anybody, either. Think about it.'

Then I stare in the other direction, because I cannot actually watch him take me up on the offer. The seconds tick. A warm breeze blows round the walls of the station building. What is Aidan doing? He's going to go, I know it, and I'll only ever see his back view again. So I'm going to look at his face, now, to memorise it. Oh, why do I have to have this sadness so soon?

'OK.' He's talking. 'Fair enough. I don't want to go anywhere. No, that's not true. I do. Could we, can we go back to your flat?'

'Aidan, you're married!'

'Nancy, that is not a problem! Trust me. We can't talk here. I'll explain in the flat. Can we go there?'

'Now?'

'Yes. If that's all right with you, Nancy?' The man's almost pitiful.

'All right. Yes. That's fine with me.'

I bolt the flat door, but Sarah doesn't turn up. We move slowly and calmly. Every ounce of anger and frustration steadily evaporates. The sun shines and we say little. Stella's face drifts away and is gone. With the curtains partially closed the day pours through the gaps in vast dusty beams of afternoon light and travels across the sofa and our bodies on it and gives us stripes. I suppose we take our time, really, in the unhurried daylight. I look at him and see a nice man who doesn't know what is the best thing to do. He looks at me and, well, I don't know what he sees, but I'm not hiding anything. Undiluted quality time.

We lie there. I am leaning on one elbow, staring at him. He is staring at the ceiling. Despite his earlier apparent need to explain about Stella, he has not yet done so, and I am in no hurry to bring up the subject. It can wait, I suppose caustically, since presumably she isn't going anywhere in a hurry.

'Nancy?'

'Yes?'

'I'm sorry you had to go round to our house.'

'I could have done without it. Why didn't you say you were married?'

He is still looking at the ceiling. I am confident being so hard on him: somehow, this time, I don't think he'll be giving me the slip.

'I didn't want to lose you Nancy. So soon after I found you. You'd have run a mile, wouldn't you?'

Oh, how sweet.

'Well, if I knew whose husband you were in particular, rather than just married in general, I probably would have done, yes.'

What a bare-faced lie. I know how low my standards are.

'No, the truth is, I just liked you. Liked being with you. Simple, really. Forgive me. I just couldn't face saying it that night. I mean, there you were, and you sort of asked me out, and no one has asked me out for years, Nancy, years, you know.'

Easy explanation for that, Aidan.

'And it was all going so well, and after a while of sitting there looking at you, I just couldn't wait to get my hands on you and get those clothes off. I didn't set out intending anything to happen, honestly. Also, I've not been that drunk for years.'

'Oh, right, so it's all my fault. I waylaid you. And I suppose, your wife doesn't understand you, Aidan, is that the case? I mean, chuck 'em all in, why don't you?'

I am playing such a hardened sampler of married men; but his expression changes so rapidly I don't have time to regret the comment.

'I don't think we understand each other, but that's my problem, I'm afraid.'

'Oh, right, I see.'

Of course I don't.

'Well, if you do, then you're a lot smarter than I am!' He rolls over and kisses me. 'But then I'm starting to suspect that anyway, believe it or not.'

I snigger, and tell him not to be silly, and remind him that he has the great weight of, oh, at least twenty more years of wisdom on his shoulders than I do, and he protests that he isn't that old yet, and I ask him why on earth I should believe anything which comes out of his lying mouth, and he says, 'Because it's true.'

Still, there's so much about him I don't know. Or, more accurately, so little that I do. I must rectify this.

'Aidan, what I don't understand is, why, if you're so important, with such an important job, and I suppose so many people to see, and things to do, and decisions to make . . .'

'Yes?'

'Well, I don't understand how come you had time to wander into Toolis TV in that week when I started?'

'Oh, that was my holiday actually. And last week. I'm back to work tomorrow. And I needed to see Lesley, I told you.'

Can I believe him?

'What about?'

'Are you jealous?'

'No!'

'You are. You think I'm after Lesley? That I'm some kind of tomcat? Do you think I cheat on my wife all the time?'

'No.'

'You do.'

'I don't. I really don't. I'm sorry, Aidan.'

'It's OK. No, Lesley's doing something for me. Working out a budget for a film I'm trying to get made.'

Poor old Lesley. She'll find work in the nuclear winter.

'Don't you have people to do that at your place?'

'Yes, but it's not going through that company. It's best to keep each of your eggs in different baskets in this game, if you know what I mean? And Lesley's the best production manager in the business. Why else do you think Heather employed her? She's the meanest woman in London. Overspend is not a word in her vocabulary.'

I've learnt that much for myself.

'So, Aidan, tell me, when did Stella start up the company with Toolis? I thought she was at the BBC when you met?'

'Nancy, can we not talk about Stella? Just for a little bit? Let's imagine there's you and me and no one else in the world at all. Please, for me? Can you say nothing at all for five whole minutes? I know, how about making us some coffee?'

My pleasure.

A bit later.

'Nancy? What are you doing on Wednesday?'

'Aidan, I think you're forgetting that I have a job to go to. Shall I remind you where I work? With whom? That sort of thing?'

'No, no, it's all coming back to me now. Well, I can understand, you'd rather hold down your career than me, yes, fair enough, it's not that I have any contacts in the business, couldn't be ever so slightly useful to you one day, maybe . . .'

'I suppose I could be struck by a sudden infectious disease.'

'Exactly. It's just that I have to drive to see this woman in Cambridge, and I thought we could have a kind of day in the country afterwards, but, you know, Miss Nancy, the choice, as they say, is yours.'

Yes! I've won the Lottery! So I put on a po-faced expression as if to say, well, I'll think about it.

'Of course, you'll probably be running around London with some muscled young suitor, far too busy to consider an old fossil like me.'

'Probably.'

'Where shall I pick you up then, Nancy?'

'I'm easy.'

'I've noticed.'

I dread telling Sarah. I know what she'll say: married men are *always* trouble. Maybe I shouldn't mention it at all? No, the situation is complicated enough. As it happens, I don't get much time in which to dwell on such a minor dilemma. In she marches, slamming the door, fifteen minutes after Aidan has left. I am sitting on the dishevelled sofa in jeans and a long T-shirt, unquestionably fresh-shagged. It must look pretty trashy. She's a bit pissed off already, though.

'Fuck, I've had an irritating day! My dad's said he won't give me an allowance any more this summer, but he'll pay for me to do a secretarial course so that I can earn my own way from now on. I don't know what's got into him. More like your father.'

Oh, I don't think so. Nothing like my father. He's nice, Sarah's dad. Both times we've met he offered me a cigar. Big, smiling, generous businessman. He's divorced from Sarah's mother, who married again and had a couple more children and lives in LA half the time. Both parents are rolling, and spoil Sarah with money and houses and holidays. So, since she hasn't needed to work, up till now, she's been spending most days sampling the delights of the capital and her boyfriend. Nick and she have been going out for ages and are the steadiest couple I know. Virtually married, they do everything together.

Now I think I agree with her too cheerfully: 'Your dad's cut off your allowance? The bastard!'

'Well, what have you been doing all day? Carrying on that sordid little affair?'

'Sarah!'

'Oh, sorry.'

'Well, actually, you're not far wrong.'

'He didn't ring you up? He hasn't been here?'

'I'm afraid so.'

'You've had sex, haven't you? You dirty tart!'

'Oh, and you would act so differently, I suppose, Miss Moral.'

'Of course. No married men for me.'

'It's going to be fine. I know it is. He'll sort himself out. It'll all be OK.'

'Oh, really? Like so many affairs with married men end happily for everyone, I suppose? And what about the wife?'

'Oh, don't go on about it now. I don't want to talk about it. Just let me wallow, please.' And picture Aidan with those warm boxer shorts off.

'Oh, OK, it's up to you.'

She goes to her room. Despite our bantering tone, I know Sarah genuinely disapproves. Even though her divorced parents now have what seems to be a remarkably amicable relationship, it wasn't always so. They split up when she was eight, and fought over her in court. I don't much like to probe, because she doesn't say much, but I think either or both of them had affairs, and other people were somehow involved, and nobody ended up happy. Whatever the details, it's clear she is still abnormally threatened by any hint of marital breakdown. The sensible agony-aunt tone in which she dispenses her ultra-reasonable advice actually masks real fear. The thing is, though, because she is so biased, you have to take what she says with a tiny pinch of salt. She has a dim view of *all* affairs with married men, no questions asked, whereas I reckon that, statistically speaking, they can't *all* lead to disaster. I don't want to upset Sarah; what I would like to do is show her a happy ending.

Phone rings. I'm convinced it's Aidan, maybe calling from the tube or something, and dive on it.

'Nancy? Hi, babe!'

Fuck. Grace. Fuck, fuck, fuck. Typical. I rang her yesterday – can you believe this? – to say full steam ahead for the holiday, and she wasn't there. Nobody was. The phone rang and rang. Twenty-four hours later, she rings here, and I've changed my mind again! Developments have occurred. Wild horses could not drag me from London now. I suppose I have to tell her.

'Grace. I rang you yesterday.' Get that in quick.

'Oh, sorry, babe, we were out. Rebecca's mum was here and we all went to Brighton. Swimming. It was bloody cold in the sea. I tell you, I can't wait for Greece.'

'That's what I called you about.'

'Excellent, because I've been checking round, and I think we should book as soon as possible now.'

'That's the thing. I don't think –'

'Well, we could leave it till a couple of days before, but I think it's a bit risky.'

'No, it's not that. I don't think –'

'What? What? Oh, no. Don't tell me you're not coming. Don't tell me that.'

'I'm not coming.'

Silence. Complete silence. Is she still there?

'Grace? Are you there? Listen, I'm really sorry, but this job, it's for all summer, and I don't think I can just walk out for two weeks, and also they've said I could keep it on permanently if I like, so it's too good an opportunity to miss, and I don't want to piss them off. You understand, don't you? Grace? Are you there?'

'I can hear you. But I don't believe this, Nancy.'

'I'm really sorry.'

'Well, what about just one week? Please? I have to have a holiday and I can't just go with Rebecca.'

How about a week? Seven days. It would fly by; but I said I was available all summer. I can't go away; no, all right, fair enough, I won't. I won't waste seven days that could have Aidan in them.

'No, I'm sorry, I just can't.'

'You could, but you won't.'

'I can't.'

'OK. I expect I'll see you sometime, then. If you ever condescend to come back.'

'I said I was sorry!'

She cuts me off. She's upset. Oh, no. I've really let her down. Maybe I should have explained about Aidan? Oh, why is this all so difficult? Damn her to make me feel bad like this! It's not my fault. A headache's coming on.

Phone rings again. Grace, to apologise?

'Nancy? It's Aidan.'

God, this is too much. Who'd have thought real life could be so dramatic? I swoon onto the cushions of the sofa while he talks about nothing at all really; there's lots of background noise because he's calling from a phone box, and I reflect on just how right was my decision to stay in London. Even after Aidan gets off the line I lie there clutching the receiver until that nasty off-the-hook tone goes and Sarah pulls it from my grip.

I can't wait till Wednesday. A whole day with Aidan. The gentle country winds ruffling his aged hair. Sheer pure double-cream chocolate-chip American cookie-mixture bliss. Sarah, having made her position clear, seems to have given up on me as a bad job. Humour is her way of keeping a distance, I suppose. Every time she sees me she says something like 'Put your tongue back in', or 'You can wipe that smug grin off your face', or, simply, her favourite: 'Tart'. I can't stop laughing in hysterical bursts. Hormones are no doubt coursing through my body, flooding aside every other pedestrian chemical. I inspect my face for spots. Look at yourself as others look at you, that's my maxim for self-improvement.

At work on Monday I eye Stella and reflect only that I know something she doesn't. I don't feel guilty. As far as she is concerned, I don't feel anything at all. This isn't personal.

On Tuesday evening I run round the entire perimeter of Hyde Park and Kensington Gardens, seriously doubting whether any of the bodies still flat on the grass could be half as happy as I am. I interrupt this exertion with spells of lying in the fading sun, so as to get a hint of healthy redness, and plot. I know it's immoral, but I can't help it. OK, I won't help it. I can but don't. By the next day my skin will have relaxed into an interesting golden. Stella the Glamorous will be crouched in that dark office, denied the sunshine, arms dry and flaky like the paper of a wasps' nest. At least I have youth on my side, if not beauty. Will Aidan and I get a chance for sex tomorrow? Oh, for Christ's sake, girl, you're craven, my conscience protests feebly, having retreated to somewhere near my ankles. I can see it all: a benevolently sunny day, light beaming through the bright green tree leaves, we lovebirds cradled in a nest of grass reaching high over our heads. Perfect. Rustic idyll. Nancy, how could you? rebukes my mother. It wasn't like that in my day. Girls like you deserve everything they get, admonishes my father.

Condoms will have to be taken. Mind you, Aidan might bring some. He's dealt with it twice now, in such a responsible way. How nice it would be to go without; but I don't want a baby, or diseases. Does Aidan have any germs? Who knows what lurks beneath that too-prepossessing foreskin?

Ambling home tired, face more reddened by exercise than by the sun, I range idly through a dreamy superstore near the flat. Up and down the aisles, pecking here and there, needing little, but ending up with a basket of things whose selection is wholly influenced by advertising: a beautiful blue glass tub of seaweed bubble bath; way overpriced hair conditioner, with free shower gel on offer, both in relentlessly pseudo-French-bio-clinic bottles; and soap that is part massage oil, enabling you to soften as you wash, thereby saving valuable minutes in which to waylay other people's husbands, and thus just what I need right now.

In the queue at the one-basket-only till the man before me, a red-faced smelly alcoholic who is putting a loaf of sliced white bread, a tall bottle of whisky, a short bottle of gin (and no tonic) into a crumpled reused carrier bag with another shop's name on it, lowers his gaze to the tight profile of my T-shirt, and remarks: 'I wouldn't say no to a nibble of them. What do you say?'

'Oh, I don't think so.'

'Well, if your boyfriend chucks you, you know where to come. Don't say I didn't offer. I'd be good to you.'

'I'm sure you would!'

I reply jauntily; a nice word for everyone. All's right with my world.

Wednesday morning, sun shining still. Great. No problem with the perennial dilemma, outfit all practised the night before: jeans, T-shirt and lace-up fawn desert boots of Sarah's. We are going to the country, after all. I do my teeth extra assiduously, including picking out pork shreds from the chow mein of last night's supper, and swirling with mouthwash so that my maw is swilled with disinfectant and my teeth squeaky white. *Tsing!* I leave the flat without waking Sarah and Nick, savouring every paving stone on my way to the tube and smiling at strangers and getting dazzled by the early morning sunshine and probably looking insane.

Cash from the hole-in-the-wall, I note the balance is getting dangerously low, determine to find out when I'll be paid, put the subject out of my mind, I'm going to get my own way today. Reflect on Aidan's body, wonder where he is now, realise he'll still be at home, or maybe just leaving, no, probably not left yet – mind you, what about the traffic at this time of day? He'll be gone by now, will have said goodbye to the wife, hopefully not kissed her, wondered what to do about the mess in his life, thought of me, been struck by the redemptive power of love even in the midst of an emotional maze like this, be dying to see me, heart beating like my own, the smile on his face, he'll be grinning at strangers, well, perhaps not from the car. What will he be driving? She's got a BMW. Will it be that? We can play that tape again. Or does he have his own? Mind you, he used the tube the other day. No, he must have his own car. A man in his position? Surely. Keep your eyes on the road, Aidan.

I buy a ticket at Gloucester Road station, approach the barrier, ticket sucked in, spat out, scooped up, gates released, move through, down the escalator to the Piccadilly line northwards, away from the heart of London, and on to the unknown. I'm going to meet him outside King's Cross station. Here the platform is packed and there'll be a battle getting aboard. Wonderful, a train. It's five past eight already. I am not going to be late. I push my way in, admittedly ahead of a quite old woman, and she loses her foothold to fall back, luckily, into the embrace of a City-suiter still on the platform. He gives me a dirty look and brays: 'For God's sake! Do you have to behave like an animal?'

Actually, yes. The doors clamp shut against a wall of backsides, leaving behind my victim and her saviour. I do feel slightly ashamed, but only because I got caught. Mainly, I'm elated to be on and moving. The carriage air is heavy with scent and aftershave. At South Kensington even more people fight their way in. Oh, go and see some museums, for Christ's sake, or are they not open yet? I know this route now. I'm so London-wise, not a tourist any more. Nothing happens at Knightsbridge, since they don't want to go to Harrods either; similar inertia at Hyde Park Corner, well, that's understandable, not much doing here; now Green Park, aah, a breath of air, yes, go on get out; a surprisingly small exodus at Piccadilly Circus, again at Leicester Square; next Covent Garden, and a few more step off, then whoosh – the rest all pour out at Holborn. Suits, men and women, shiny brogues, high heels, shaved chins, made-up faces, oh, you misguided fools, rather you than me. Tell me, how many of you lot are about to spend a day with the one you love?

King's Cross. I jump out. Conscious of my tingling arms and legs like you never normally are, I'm thinking he and I are so close to each other now, he is probably only a matter of yards away, he is here to meet me, to spend the day with me, not his wife, but me, me, me.

Stop.

He's married.

A married man. Time for a good talking to, Nancy. Come on, Sarah's right. This is insane. Stop and think.

I settle on a platform seat. Stragglers wander past. The train has gone. I'm trying to think, but thinking is as hard as concentrating on something boring, like a cardboard box, when you've got the giggles. You *want* the giggles. I *want* to be thoughtless about Aidan, I *want* to live on love and air and sex and have my feet swept off the ground.

No! No. No. I must be firm. This is all a terrible mistake. It will only lead to trouble. Eight thirty-five. I must not do this. I get up, and head for the exit. There's the sign to the Piccadilly line heading back south. I stop. I have to take it. I must go home, or go to work, or go anywhere, except to meet Aidan. All around people head to left, and right, and towards me, and away, and past, and behind. They all know exactly where they're going. I retreat back against the wall to avoid the human traffic. What shall I do? It's madness to go and meet him. A fresh surge in my direction. The entrance to the passage where I stand is now filled with people, all heading for the Piccadilly line going south. Oh no, a school trip: hefty girls in brown uniforms, a determined teacher shepherding them together and shouting, 'All of you straight ahead for South Kensington!'

The Natural History Museum. I am caught in her flock. They are going to wash me down south with them.

No, thank you. I break away and push unreasonably against the flow. They are furious, then their clatter is behind me and the way ahead clear.

Now I can breathe. OK. Fate has decided for me. I'll make sure that if Aidan wants to carry on with me that he also intends to finish with Stella, and, more importantly, nothing else must happen until he has. And that is that. Seriously. You can't say I'm being selfish now? That's fair enough, isn't it?

No?

Oh, I'm sick of scruples! Bugger Stella! Let her lose him.

CHAPTER FOURTEEN

※

Through all the gates and up all the stairs I say to myself, this is a perfectly normal day, and you've no reason to be excited, so, calm down and, again, think about dull, dull things. Dry sponge fingers. Diet crispbread. Sober up. Now I'm in front of the station by the newspaper stand, still in the shade of the building, but the day is sunny out there, the road full of cars and buses and noise.

I can't see Aidan. Standing by the railings as agreed, I haul myself up to sit on them so as to appear windswept and carefree like film heroines. It's a bit perilous, to be honest; the metal digs into my thighs and I can't keep steady. Swaying back and forth, holding on with one hand, I'm forced to use the other to shade my eyes from the sun. Inevitably, I teeter. Hurry up, Aidan, or I'll have to get down, and quite ruin the effect. Oh, I give up. It hurts too much, so I jump, and jar my feet on hitting the ground.

'Shit!'

'Nancy! Mind your language.'

There he is, me looking stupid as ever. In yet another suit; expensive and floppy and smooth and adorable and fit to be hugged. He traps me against the railings for a brief half-second, but I don't get the kiss I want.

'We better hurry, as I'm parked round the corner and I'll be booked in two minutes. Come on.' He grabs my hand and I follow his lead. 'It's up this street, not far.'

I run like it matters, like the law is after me.

'Here we are.'

We've reached a sparkling dark blue Range Rover parked by a warehouse in a seedy side street. Prostitute country? Aidan climbs into the driver's side and unlocks the passenger door. I step up sharpish and slam it after me. Seat belt. Door locked. Aah. Relax. Back together again. I sigh with the pleasure of having it all before me. We lean towards each other. Now the kiss.

'Nice to see you again, Nancy.'

I just smirk while he manoeuvres the vehicle. Hand on gearstick, ram it forward, check the mirror, drive ahead. He knows the way. I'm not going to say anything for a while.

'Do you like the car? I only got it yesterday.'

'Really? My God. It's wonderful.'

New? He bought it new? Boy, the thrill of naked cash. And I must say, it's another thrill to see him drive, hands in control on the wheel at quarter to two.

'What's so funny, Nancy?'

'Nothing, nothing. It's, er, it's nice to see you, anyway.'

He turns to me, grinning, and nods. A lump in my throat threatens respiration.

'Now let's have a nice day, Nancy, all right? And not think about any problems at all, and I'm going to get to know you, and you can get to know me if you can be bothered, and we're going to put everything else on hold, not for long, just for today. Would that be all right with you? It's not too escapist, is it?'

I forget my demands.

'No. That's fine.'

It's too soon, isn't it, to expect him to satisfy all my conditions for continuing to meet? Have a heart, Nancy. The man is married, for God's sake. You can't leave a marriage like you walk out of a pub. Oh God, is this whole business all crazy wishful thinking? Have I gone mad?

Aidan, smiling. Have I gone mad? No. I haven't. I'm

here, aren't I? With him? Trust him, Nancy, not some unproven theories. Marriages break up all the time and often it's a very good thing. So, calm down. Stop worrying and, for now, work on making sure he wants to walk away from her. Then he'll be able to. The logical direction of my reasoning pulls me up short. When Aidan and Stella split up, he'll be mine for the taking. Do I want him all for my own?

Stop. How can I think so far ahead yet? Don't rush it. And don't worry. For now, I have to be everything that Stella isn't: whatever that is. If things are going wrong at home, then I should make them better for him away from home. If Stella is a source of worry, then I shall be a fount of merriment and humour. Aidan is making me happy; so that's the least I can do for him.

'Nancy?' We're momentarily stuck in traffic. There's an odd careful tone in his voice.

'Yes?'

'Do you want to have children?'

What? What! And I thought I was being forward! Trying to remain calm: 'Er, well, I don't know. One day, I expect. I haven't thought about it much yet. Why?'

'Oh, just a theoretical question.'

I am stunned. What is he saying to me here? Already? Is *he* testing the water? Might this theoretical question be theoretically asking whether I want to have *your* children, Aidan?

'Oh, right. Well, yes, Aidan, I think I would. Theoretically.'

'Yes. I think . . .'

He's staring away from me, out the window, and then the traffic starts to move again, and he finishes his sentence at the same time as getting back in gear and moving ahead.

'. . . I think I would too. Yes. I think I would.'

Keep it going, keep this conversation going! But Aidan

seems to have said all he wants to, for now, and I am too excitedly confused and shy to press him further. The moment has passed; but what was it about? Think, Nancy, think. What was he saying there? Was he speaking to you in code? Could he, could he have been giving me the explanation I have asked him for? Could he have been telling me that he wants children, because Stella can't or won't have them? That that is what is wrong with their marriage? Can he not talk about it outright because he feels it would be too much of a betrayal? Surely it has *something* to do with the whole business? Is he, in this indirect way, asking for a serious relationship? I must say, I'm cautiously optimistic.

Better change the subject then. Hope I don't sound too cheerful. 'So, where are we going? Who's your meeting with? What's it about?'

'Can't tell you, I'm afraid. To be honest, Nancy, you'd do best to keep your eyes open and your mouth closed about this one.'

What is he on about? 'Seriously?'

'Seriously. I'm going to check out a woman who claims to have some dirt on a government minister. You know, aggrieved dumped mistress thing. You've always got to have your ears wide open in this business, Nancy. She might know something interesting that might connect up with something else. One of my researchers has spoken to her, but she needs a bit of persuading, maybe getting cold feet, I think. The minister set her up in a love nest but he's now chucked her out to move in her replacement. Apparently. She's sleeping in her mother's front room. It could all be made up, of course; but somehow, I don't think so. You know, these guys get voted in and they think they can do what they bloody like with people, tread on anyone, lie through their teeth, they don't care. And they're running the country, for Christ's sake!'

Bloody hell. He's taking me with him on a mission like

this? Screw Toolis Television, here is the real McCoy. Shame I won't be able to put it on the CV.

'And I'm afraid I won't be able to tell you any details, so don't ask me. Sorry. Is that OK? It's just that if you know nothing, you can't say anything.'

'Oh, sure. That's fine.'

A privilege in fact. Just being with you is enough. I keep quiet, for a bit. Partly in awe, partly to let it all sink in. A month ago – no, less – two and a half weeks ago, what was I doing? Sitting in the flat watching television. Picking my ears for light relief. Nothing but the end of the reading list to look forward to. Going out with Eric. Getting bored. Blimey. I was nothing. Now look. Here I am. With Aidan. Romancing. Planning a family. Out on a top-secret mission to root out corruption. In his big car on the open road. Bigger than the other cars. I'm sorry, but there's nothing like it. No, actually, I'm not sorry. I'm happy. I'm with him, here, now, and I'm happy.

Around nine forty-five I ask Aidan to stop at a motorway service station so I can call the office. Toolis answers and, though initially flustered, I manage to resurrect last week's excuse – a return of the summer flu. I don't think she believes me, but I don't care. So blasé. This is the life. I'm not a child any more. No one has control over me now.

We reach our destination after about an hour and a half of me gabbling away and Aidan not saying much. He drives into a council estate on the outskirts of Cambridge and stops in the car park outside a pub. There are no trees around and it's been raining lightly. A red sports car is already there; the driver's low door opens and a denim leg appears. Aidan lowers the window and puts out his head.

'Henry. You beat me.'

Henry? He knows this man? What's going on? I'm disappointed: I want Aidan all to myself today.

'Of course, Aidan. Size isn't everything.'

The rest of Henry is visible now, walking towards us. Tall, confident, striding, public school head-boy sort, that instantly recognisable breed. The kind of man Sarah hangs round with. There's a clique of them at college. I'd never get off with one, even though they're usually handsome enough from a distance. Henry is sporty and wholesome in his brogues and jeans and new leather jacket, but close up, I now see, he has a hard, mean-lipped face, and when I try to analyse what is actually attractive, he's only really got his height to recommend him. Dad would both love and hate me to bring this man home.

Aidan's different. Sure, he's as middle-class, Middle England as they come, despite the upbringing in Africa; he's got the right voice and haircut and all the suits and shirts and shoes and ties; and no doubt he and Stella, though I hate to say this, do understand each other; but there's more than this to Aidan. Aidan knows there's more to life. This boys-and-cars banter is only one of the many languages he speaks. I think he could charm even my father. As he greets Henry, who is exaggeratedly wiping showroom dust off the Range Rover bonnet, Aidan winks, covertly, at me.

'Hands off, Henry!'

'How's she running?'

'Like a dream. Now, Henry.' Aidan checks his macho watch. He's in charge. 'We'd better get over there.'

'Sure. I'll get my stuff.'

Henry turns back to his car. He's said nothing to me, and I've not caught his eye once. Aidan leans into the back seat and pulls a briefcase over. I unlock my door and prepare to get out. This is so, well, grown-up. Aidan grabs my arm, though, and pulls me back into the car.

'Look, Nancy, I'm sorry, but I'm going to have to ask you to stay here. It's the kind of meeting where you can't have any extra ears in, if you know what I mean? We don't want to scare this woman off.'

'Oh. I see. Sorry.'

I pull my door shut again and feel like a fool.

'No, I'm sorry. Normally it would be fine. It's just today . . .' He shrugs and looks repentant. 'I wish you were coming in. It would be a laugh.'

He checks what Henry is doing (backside sticking out of the car as he rummages head down in the seat), leans over, and kisses me full on the lips.

'Thanks for coming. You'll not get too bored, will you? We shouldn't be much more than an hour.'

'It's OK. I'm fine. But, Aidan?' I have to ask. I can't just have him disappear.

'Yes?'

'Aidan, you've not done this before, have you? You know, taken a girl out like this who you're, you know, erm, having a thing with? In fact, have you ever done anything like this before? I mean, while you're married?'

'No, I have not! Oh, Nancy, don't think that. Of course I haven't. Oh God. I suppose it's fair enough for you to think it, though. I don't blame you for being worried.'

He puts a hand through his hair, holds back his forelock, and is silent for a while. Then he looks directly into my eyes.

'To be honest with you, I genuinely don't really know what I'm doing now; except that I do know that, though I shouldn't, I do want you here with me. I need you. I know that sounds like so much of an excuse from a messed-up old man who finds that a beautiful and lustful young woman likes him, and I'm so sorry, but I'm not really sure what I should say. You're right to be worried. I shouldn't be doing this, it looks awful, it is awful, I should take you home –'

'Aidan! It's OK, it's all right. We'll sort it out, yes? We'll sort it out. Together. Don't worry. I believe you. You know that, don't you? I am having a wonderful time, and we'll fix it. OK? There's nothing so dreadful we can't mend, is there? Don't worry, Aidan, it's all right, I'm . . . it's –' just don't say you love him, Nancy, just do not, though it would be so easy – 'it's OK. Now pull yourself together.'

He manages this. Henry approaches.

'All right. If you're sure. OK. Here we go. But we'll have a great afternoon, yes? Just you and me?'

'You bet. You are going to make up for this outrage.'

He laughs, and sets off with Henry. I watch their backs. Henry is a head taller and has a crisp, firm, young outline. He strides keenly forward. Aidan, older and smarter, is more relaxed. He hangs back, taking his time. Then they turn a corner and are gone.

An ocean of strangeness floods my head. What the hell am I doing here? Sitting by myself in an empty car park? Waiting for Aidan, Stella's husband? It is unspeakably odd. I ought to be at work. I've not got a leg to stand on. Nowhere for me to go. Out of place doesn't begin to describe the sensation. Twenty-five to eleven. The pub is shut. No indication of shops in any direction. Very weird indeed.

Nothing to do, either. There's a road map book on the back seat, plus, oh, a couple of new paperbacks in a bag. Let's have a look: a life of Wittgenstein and some French poetry. In French. They look like they came with the car, everything's all so new. I'd better not finger them. God, how does Aidan find time to go browsing in bookshops? Talk about thinking woman's crumpet. It's all too much. I slump back into the front seat.

I could listen to some tapes, if he has some; but there aren't any. On with the radio then. Out rolls some not-too-old rolled gold. The eighties. Just about all right. At least it's not the seventies. Lying across both front seats I start to read the clean new Range Rover manual. It's very, very boring. I can see where the Cellophane on the seats must only just have been torn off. What do these things cost new? How much does Aidan earn? What is his and Stella's joint income? Did they have a prenuptial agreement? Because, poor sad messed-up pair, they're going to need one. Oh, don't be so nasty, of course they didn't. We're not in Hollywood.

Cool air on my head.

'Lunch time! Were you dreaming?'

I swing up to a sitting position. Aidan's back. A long strand of saliva spans from my mouth, across my shoulder, and attaches itself to the seat.

'That's attractive, Nancy.'

'Oh, shut up.'

'And you were snoring.'

He's looking at me. How nice, waking up to that face.

'What time is it?'

'Quarter to one. Henry wants a quick bite in the pub before he goes back to town.'

'Right.'

It's a dive of a place. The carpets are sticky. Aidan orders ploughman's, well, three ploughmen, and some lager, a half for each of them and a pint for me, and pays with a fifty-pound note. Landlord not pleased. Aidan asks for a receipt. Landlord even less pleased, and passes it to him dripping. Aidan shakes the paper and folds it into a leather wallet. I hate ploughman's. The acid from the pickled onion on the corner of your lips. The tombstone slab of far-too-strong Cheddar. Too little bread. Drying cucumber on the salad. I keep quiet, though, since I'm not really meant to be here. I must be invisible. Aidan's taking a risk having me with him at all.

'Where shall we sit?'

All the tables in the empty pub to choose from. Henry picks one by the window.

'We can check the motors aren't being shredded by the locals.'

'Good thinking. Oh, Henry, this is Nancy, by the way.

Stella's goddaughter. Staying at the moment. Thinking of working in TV.'

Oh, great. Thanks very much. Again, that disturbing thought. I can't help it. Has Aidan told me the truth? Has he introduced other young female relatives to his researchers? A horrible feeling. I meet Henry's eye, and nod, but say nothing. He'll think I'm fifteen and still anti-socially shy. For that matter, I feel like it.

'So, Henry, what a dog, eh?'

Who is Aidan talking about?

'I know. Can you believe it was going on for eight years?'

'Well, considering him, yes.'

'You're right. But what an old slapper. And the mother? That eye make-up? You can see where Miss X learnt her tricks from.'

I'm sure Henry winks at Aidan when he says 'Miss X'. I wish he'd hurry up and go.

'So do you think we've got everything now, Henry?'

'Well, a lot more than I managed. I knew she'd love you, though. The older gentleman.'

'Watch it, Henry. I pay your wages.'

'Oh, admit it, you charmed the pants off her. Honestly. "Talk about yourself. I like your hairstyle. Take your time. They're nice boots. Tell me everything." Who could resist?'

What a pair of jesters. I manage a bit of bread and cheese and some salad, but don't even attempt the onion. When my pint is half full I head for the Ladies. I get back to find the men have left the bar and the drinks and plates have been cleared. Outside, the sun has started to shine. Aidan is sitting on the sports car front and Henry seems to be taking orders from him. I keep clear and inspect the flower box by the pub door. Dead geraniums with a tangle of human hair caught in the brown leaves, eleven cigarette stubs, and a screwed-up orange crisp packet holding a mountain lake of rain. At last Henry goes.

'Sorry about all that, Nancy,' Aidan says, 'but, you

know, I couldn't avoid mixing work and play today.'

We're in the car, but haven't moved off yet. He's rolling a cigarette and I'm investigating the map book.

'That's OK. We all have to make our daily bread. Even though some of us are approaching retirement age.'

He explodes with laughter. I tweak out a grey hair from above his nearest ear.

'Ow!'

'Just how old are you, Aidan? No avoiding the issue, now.'

'Twenty-nine.'

'Bollocks.'

'Thirty-seven.'

Oh, that's not too old. I'd better double-check, though. 'The truth, please.'

'Thirty-nine.'

'Oh. Really?'

'Really. Honestly. I'm still a boy.'

Oh, well. Sixty at our son's twenty-first. If I give birth this year. God! I'm already going broody. I relax into a comforting fantasy where Aidan is wandering around the party bow-legged and dribbling in a cardigan. That'll be OK, I suppose; but we can't leave it much longer. I'll have to put my career on hold, and, as for Stella, she is going to need dispatching pretty damn pronto.

'Well, if you're a boy, then this is child abuse.'

'Oh, Nancy, please. I'm not sure I like the direction this conversation is going.'

'Nor me. I tell you what. From this minute on, let's not mention our age difference. After all, I do want you to see me as a woman, in the fullest sense of the word.'

He splurges tobacco off the tip of his tongue. 'Oh, but I do, Nancy! Believe it. You're all woman to me.'

Not a crisscrossed line of worry on his face. Aah, the power to make my man happy! Idle chatter with dreamy Aidan. This is definitely the life.

'So, where are we going? Up to you, Nancy. Your day now.'

Aside from my obvious desire for an untrammelled roll of passion in some cornfield, I quite fancy a quick step around Cambridge. History. Tradition. The spires of academe. The heady stench of learning. I had an interview to get in to a Cambridge college, in fact. Stayed there the night before, went out for a drink with another girl, got very drunk, woke with a hangover, talked a load of garbage, and didn't get in. I hope she didn't.

'Oh, I don't know. What do you want to do? A walk round Cambridge?'

'Oh God, no. I'm tired of cities. Tired of people. How about a romp in the country? All romantic like.'

'Excuse me. What kind of girl do you take me for?'

'Shut up. I know very well what kind of girl you are. Are there any nice places round here? Pass me the map. Right. The bypass goes there, then heads to Suffolk. Newmarket. Bury St Edmunds. Ipswich. The sea. Shall we just drive in that direction? See where it takes us?'

'Fine by me.'

This is all developing very nicely, I must say; and it's not long before we do end up in a cornfield in the middle of nowhere, grass under the hedge and willow trees on the banks of a slow reedy river and one pink cottage a good distance away. A great oak tree which was probably an acorn round the time of William the Conqueror. Hazy sunshine. The back of a cereal packet. Aidan's suit jacket hanging on the gatepost and his trousers laid carefully over the top bar. He's trying to get some sun on those ancient legs. Really, not a big man. Small, but perfectly formed. Fine by me. More than fine. We stopped at an off-licence and I am drinking beer, but Aidan is stuck with the soft drinks. Propping himself against the green verge which runs round the field's edge, he is making me a roll-up. I have pulled up his shirt and my head is on his stomach, though no filth has taken place yet. My face is pressed nose down into his navel. Not even a millimetre between us.

I sit up. Aidan passes me the cigarette.

'Are you happy, Nancy?'

'Yes. Of course. Are you?'

'Yes. I am. Come here. Let's pretend there's no one else on earth. Hold me.'

We have been together for centuries. Part of the landscape.

'You shouldn't smoke, you know, Nancy. It will kill you.'

'You can talk! Dictate to me after you've given up, Professor. I thought you hated hypocrites?'

'I know. The rot's inside us all. But don't do as I do, Nancy. Do as I say. I should give up. I don't want to corrupt you as well. Give up smoking, it will kill you. I don't want you to die. There are some rules in this life which you would do best to obey without question, and that's one of them.'

'Oh, do tell me some of the others, Old Man Rivers. Mind you, I know one already.'

'What's that?'

'Don't mess with married men.'

'I rest my case.'

I have decided not to mention Stella any more than necessary, as well as tacitly agreeing with Aidan not to. It would ruin the perfect day; I know that; but I am itching to get to the nitty-gritty. So I just casually slip her into our conversation. It can't do too much harm, surely?

'Aidan, why did you marry Stella?'

'Nancy, I asked you –'

'Oh, why can't we talk about it? You have no right to ask me, Aidan. You have no right to get defensive on this!'

'I have every right. She's my wife. It's my marriage. It's my life.'

'Well, if you want me in it you can damn well speak to me!'

'OK, Nancy. OK. Sh-sh. Calm down. It's OK. Don't worry about it. None of it. Can't you see, that's the best thing about you? You are nothing to do with Stella and me! Stay that way, all right? Keep it separate. Leave it all to me. Yes?'

Through teeth never more gritted: 'OK. Sorry.'

I suppose he's got a point. I mean, I only have to look at the woman all day. He has to look at her all night. That hurts. Do they still sleep together? Oh, leave it, Nancy.

Yet I can't quite give up. It's the counsellor in us all. 'Maybe just the wrong woman?'

He laughs a low laugh. 'Maybe that's it, Nancy. Maybe that's the answer. Just a big mistake. We all make them.'

Only Aidan knows the joke and only he is laughing. He obviously thinks it's nothing to do with me. I turn away. It's always the same. Always other people in relationships, always other people in love, always other people's problems are their own to share. Even when it all goes wrong you're not allowed in. All I am ever allowed to do is watch, and wish I hadn't seen. When do I get a life? Why does everything have to be the same now, with Aidan? As usual, I am blinking to stop my eyes from letting me down. Then Aidan's head is on my shoulder, his arms around me. I put my hands over his.

'It's no good, Aidan. Let's just call it off now. I'm having a lovely day, so we'll carry on today, all right, and then that'll be it until you know what you're doing.'

'Oh, Nancy, please. Oh dear. I don't know what to do. Maybe you're right. Maybe we should call it a day for now.'

'No! I didn't mean it. Don't leave me alone. Just tell me now. Are you ever going to leave Stella, or not? I have to know!'

My face is boiling hot and my temples throbbing. It's

extraordinary. I've known the man for less than three weeks and here I am, slamming down ultimatums like dust-filled doormats. The sun is still above us. Mid-afternoon. All shadows have retreated. I am getting another headache. If he says no, where will I go?

'Yes.'

His voice comes from behind me and blows straight into my ear. It's like a cool whistling wind. He hides his face on my shoulder and mutters the rest.

'Yes. I am. My marriage is over.'

Oh.

I didn't expect this. Part of me gasps with relief. It's utterly bizarre. My emotions are fluttering all over the place like mad moths. Now I can dance and sing and laugh and fool around and be cheerful about not having any money and go shopping anyway and reassure Sarah and ring Philip (I must ring Philip) and go and see my parents, especially my mother. And soon I can ring Grace and Rebecca and tell them the real reason I'm not coming to Greece. Well, yes, you understand, things were very difficult to start with, but everything's sorted now. They'll laugh and tell me I should have *said* and then all will be forgiven.

Another part of me, however, feels a kind of grief for Aidan and Stella. A marriage is a very serious thing. Strangely, as though I am not involved at all, an unwelcome voice asks, oh, no, do you really have to do this? Surely it is a terrible thing? Oh, Stella, what have I done to you? Maybe it feels like this if you're a head of state and have just ordered the troops to go to war. Here we go, it's real now. Lives are going to be changed.

'Oh, Aidan.'

I sit up and pull him to me. I've an urge to utter some tasteless statement like 'You won't regret this decision', as though he is buying a house, or 'You've done the right thing', or even, 'Congratulations!'; but manage to hold back.

'I don't know what to say, Aidan.'

'That's OK. There's nothing to say.'

A chilly sliver of caution. Does his choice commit me to stay with him now? No one has ever depended on me before. I banish the thought quickly, reassuring myself that we're not responsible for our less-than-honourable thoughts and that our brains are public thoroughfares open to all suggestions from the cesspits of our evil souls; but then another fear bubbles to the surface. When will he leave her?

'When?'

'What?'

'When will you tell her? Stella? About us? I think you should strike while the iron is hot. If you leave it till a good time, there won't be one. It'll only get worse. Why not tonight? When you get home? Tonight?'

He sighs. A whole body-sagging sigh.

'All right. I'll tell her tonight.'

I hug him. My brave boy. It'll all be OK, Aidan. And now, surely, we can attend to the physical side of things?

It appears not. Aidan, though keen at first, then worries that the corn might be too spiky and there's nettles in the grass and the people in the cottage might be Peeping Toms with binoculars, and farmers have a way of sprouting out of hedges. So I go off the idea too. He's right, I suppose: it's far too public. Anyway, I'm not desperate. I can wait. Soon I'll have him on tap.

Aidan snoozes. I chew on a grass and look to the future. Nearly four o'clock. The day is on the wane. We will have to leave each other soon, but needn't creep around like this for long. Aidan and me will be a couple. Aidan and I. Oh, hello, yes, have you met Aidan? Let me introduce you. The age difference won't be a problem. I may return to college, and commute back here, or I may just chuck in the degree; but that's too big a decision to make now. That, and work, and everything else: we'll sort it. Aidan'll have to move out of their house. We could get a place together. Whatever.

One more cigarette each before setting off. Aidan says the traffic will be getting bad. Oh, but won't the cars be heading out of London rather than back in? He assures me, however, that no, it'll be both ways, baby, and buries the stub of his roll-up in the earth with his heel. Hauling himself to his feet, he puts out a hand for me. We kiss: everything's all right. Back on the road we say little. I am to be dumped at King's Cross, Aidan will return to Stella. Every dreary suburban roadside detail in that hazy evening sunlight now appears beautiful to me through no quality of its own.

We arrive in London far too soon. The traffic's fine. Park in a glum side street. Off goes the engine. Aidan turns to me, right hand draped over the wheel, left one picking up mine.

'I'd better let you go then, Nancy.'

I give him a good look. I hope it's stern. He is going to tell her tonight.

'Call me, Aidan? Let me know what happens?'

'Of course I will. Come here.'

He hugs me in a clench made uncomfortable by the gearstick prodding my belly, and kisses me long and hard, then says, you know, he'd better go.

'Aidan?'

'Yes?'

'I've had the best day.'

'Yes. Me too. Bye, Nancy.'

'Bye. See you.'

The ground is dull and sudden. Aidan drives off. I cross the road and down the stairs into the belly of the ground and pick up that eternal Piccadilly line heading south.

CHAPTER FIFTEEN

✳

Back at the flat I realise it'll be far too risky to go into work tomorrow. Stella couldn't come in after Aidan's bombshell, but, still, it wouldn't feel safe. I'll be far better off lying low here and waiting for Aidan to update me. As it happens my decision turns out to be just as well because, after all that fresh air, I oversleep anyway. Another grossly bright day slams rudely into my eyes at nine thirty-five. Am I alone? There's evidence of a half-made breakfast in the kitchen and a black coffee on the sink. Sarah must have gone to get some milk, for nothing can persuade her to drink it black. She has curiously childish taste buds: there have to be spoons of sugar and sloshes of milk in her tea and coffee, and she cuts up her food into tiny pieces, and often has hot chocolate before going to bed.

I pick up the mug – it's still hot – and brace myself nervously for the phone call. I wonder if they'll pay me for all these days off sick? More to the point, what are they going to think in the office when they find out? When will I tell them? Will I have to tell them? Maybe I could just disappear, and write to Toolis. What is going to happen? When? Jesus, this is so embarrassing. Everything up in the air. I'll have to leave the job, though, at some point, since we can't very well ask Stella to go. Making myself scarce will be the least I can do. I can barely believe it: Aidan will have already told Stella. When will he put me in the picture? This morning? Tonight? I almost wish we could just fling along with nobody knowing, just for a bit longer. Still, ho-hum, here we go: another day of summer flu. I rest the phone on my knees. Toolis will probably answer, and give me an earful.

'Hello, Toolis TV.'

'Who's that?'

'Stella. Is that Nancy?'

Oh my God. Has she nerves of steel? Turning up at work? She's going to kill me. My forearms go cold. Am I up to this?

'Nancy? How are you? Any better?'

What? I'm not ill. Oh, I see. I get.

He hasn't told her. He's not told her. He hasn't. Fuck, fuck, fuck. He's said nothing. And here is sweet Stella asking me how I feel? I'd laugh, in another life. She must surely be regretting recommending me for the job, since I'm never there. Still, nothing like as much as she's going to.

Recovering, I stutter, 'Well, sort of. I mean, I don't feel like I did yesterday, but –'

I hear the door open and Sarah hauls in a bag of groceries. She sees I'm on the phone and unloads them in the kitchen. What do I say to Stella? Pinching my forehead, I remember that proximity to the truth always provides the best lies.

'– but now I feel even worse.' Sick as a parrot.

'Oh, Nancy, you poor thing. You do have bad luck, don't you?' (Hah! The pot calling the kettle black.) 'Of course, you must stay at home today, but don't worry, I'll tell Heather.'

Sure, fine, whatever; but why didn't Aidan tell her? Oh, I suppose there just wasn't a good moment. Was she chattering to him over dinner about my sickness record? He'd have smelt the pressure creeping up on him like smoke from under a door.

'I'm sorry, Stella, but I'll try and make it this afternoon. I'll see how I feel then.'

'Don't worry. Just get better.'

'OK. See you, Stella.' Fuck. Back to square one.

'So, Nan.' Sarah straightens my duvet on the sofa and reverses onto it. She holds a croissant mid-air on the way to her mouth and puts a new mug of near snow-white coffee on the floor. 'No work today? Is there anything I should know, about anything?'

I laugh hysterically to release the tension. 'I am going mad!'

'Yes, I know. Do you want to talk about it?'

Oh, till the cows come home.

'Till the cows come home.'

'I can spare half an hour.'

I fill her in.

'What do I do? Sarah, this is starting to fuck me up.'

'Well, Nancy. Since you have asked for my opinion . . .' She hardly ever calls me Nancy.

'Yes?'

'Don't tell me you don't realise what's going on here?'

'What do you mean?'

'I'm sorry. Let me give this to you straight. It is extremely unlikely that he's going to leave his wife. I don't care what he's told you. He's lying. Right?'

'Well, no.'

'OK. How shall I put this? You have slept with this man how many times? Two, three? Come on. How long since you met him? A couple of weeks?'

'More like a month.'

'Nancy! The truth, please.'

'Three weeks.' Almost.

'Well. Don't you see? He just wants sex, and if he can't have it without promising to leave his wife, then he'll promise. Don't you see? You're his bit on the side. One day out in the country, part of which you spend left deserted in the car like a dog, I may add, is hardly the most romantic occasion, is it? It's not exactly an offer of marriage.'

'Don't be so patronising! It wasn't like that! You don't know what it's like!'

'Yes, and you don't know your arse from your tit since you met this man, Nancy.' She got that saying from me. It sounds ridiculous. 'I realise I haven't met him, or his wife, and you may think you know them, and what their situation is, but, frankly, you've told me enough already, thank you very much.'

Bitch. The phone rings. Thank God.

'Hello?'

'Nancy?'

Aidan. Yes!

'Oh, hi.'

Sarah knows what that tone means. She scowls out, after pretending to look for something, and slams the bedroom door.

'How are you, sweetheart?'

He still loves me then.

'Ha-ha. Not so fine. I just spoke to Stella.'

'Why?'

'Oh, don't worry, it was just to say I'm not going in. You didn't tell her then?'

'Um, no. I'm sorry, it was just impossible last night. But don't worry. Actually, I can't really talk about that now. I have to be quick; I'm at work.'

'Oh God, is all this farce worth it?'

'Nancy, don't say that.'

'I wish you were here.'

'Well, I could be pretty quickly. What are you doing tonight, early evening?'

'Meeting you.'

'Correct.'

After a day's sunbathing in Holland Park I meet Aidan at six and we manage to steal an hour and fifty-one minutes on the sofa. He tells me he's waiting for a good time to tell Stella, perhaps the weekend. Soon, definitely. The main thing is, I am not to worry. As he dozes I take in the glory of his presence. Lying on his side, face resting on one arm and the other folded in front of him like a cat's paw, he's got his legs brought upwards and bent at the knees to protect that beautiful stomach from enemy fangs. I kiss his head. He's more than just handsome. That face. That laugh. I love him.

We get up and go for a walk, reaching Hyde Park Corner near eight thirty. Verbal diarrhoea from me, as usual, boring Aidan with my plans for world domination. We sit on a bench, and I hug my knees while he rolls a cigarette.

'So where will you live when you are Empress of Planet Earth, Miss Nancy?'

'Oh, er, there. Nice and central.' I nod towards the large house that sits bang on Hyde Park Corner.

'Apsley House? Number One London?'

'What?'

'Number One London. That's what it's called.'

'Really?'

'Really.'

'God, that is so cool! Imagine it. Nancy Miller. Number One, London. England. The World. Shall we live there? That could be our new address. What do you think?'

'Oh, I don't know. Bit close to the main road, if you ask me. One gets used to having a front garden.'

'Oh, shut up.'

I hit him. He pulls up his elbows and surrenders.

'I'm sorry. I'm sorry. We will. We'll live there. I'll call the estate agent in the morning. Number One London, please.'

I'm sulking. 'Well, good. You do that, Sunny Jim.'

'Oh, come here, Nancy. Come on. Come here.'

'I hate you.'

'I know. But you know what, Nancy?'

I can't see his face. He's got his left arm round my back and is putting the cigarette to his mouth with the other. Now I'm against his chest and looking at his knees. It's not very comfortable.

'What?'

'I'm beginning to think I love you, Nancy girl.'

Say no more. I am royally smug in the office on Friday morning. The thought of Stella doesn't bother me. I must be getting normalised to the situation now. In she walks at ten to ten, very early for her, and I don't bat an eyelid. No one else there yet.

'Morning, Stella.'

'Nancy. Good to see you. Feeling better?'

'Much better.'

'Sure?'

'Definitely. I feel fine.'

'Oh, I'm so pleased. I was sure I'd poisoned you last week. I do feel kind of responsible.'

Yes, I have noticed. I am your surrogate daughter. While other childless people spoon ice cream to the cat, Stella mothers the receptionist. Who, if only she knew it, is sleeping with her husband. All tickety-boo.

'Don't be silly. I can look after myself.'

'Of course you can. Sorry.'

'That's OK.'

Toolis rolls up soon enough with Lesley and some desperately thin girlie woman I've never seen before. Neglecting to introduce us, and clearly forgetting to enquire after my health, she says, oh, you're back, are you, and instructs me with today's special task. This is to phone 'The Sufferers', as Lesley calls all those sad fucks who shared their taboo complaints with me. I am to weed out the criminally insane, the incoherent, and the unacceptably dull, then pack the rest on ice. Which translates into bubbly-speak as, we can't send a researcher to see all of you yet, but don't feel abandoned. Please bear with us. You, yes you, are so important to Toolis Television. After this, I can tip the whole load of them onto Alastair's desk. He's already asked me to compile a list of the ones who sound like they're female, under thirty-five and with nothing too catching. Strangely enough, although I have long harboured a fearful dread of ever speaking to any of these people, I'm cool about it today. It doesn't depress me. Nothing can. I don't care if I go all shy and stutter and screw up. Aidan loves me. He'll tell the wife sooner or later. What's the rush?

By lunch time I gather that the new woman has been hired as the presenter for Toolis' new baby, the women's programme pilot. There is a general air of popularity already established. She seems to know everyone, except me. I suppose she's been here one day already, since she has a desk set up, but as she's still twirling around offering to make everyone's coffee, I wouldn't say it was two. Stella at last puts me out of my misery, and introduces her as a very old friend from the Beeb. They've known each other for years and Stella put her forward for this job. Apparently the new girl has done quite a bit of TV presenting already (can't say I've ever seen her) and is hoping to break into the big time. She proffers a limp hand.

'Hi-yee. Pleased to meet you. It's Jo-jo, second j little.'

Is it really? How pathetic. Oh, I'm sorry, but Jo-jo instantly annoys me. She speaks quickly, the barest trace of dribble evident at both corners of her mouth. A calculated baby face, whopping blue eyes and a bit too much fine blonde hair following the line of her jaw. Big head on a shrivelled neck. A-ha! Anorexic. Plainly this creature's hook into the nation's sensibility is to be her resemblance to a helpless infant. No doubt the programme will be one of those studio talk shows where some skinny big-mouth blonde nods sympathetically at dumb obese inner city dieters and agrees that society's pressures to conform are just way too harsh. Already I want to give her a sharp cuff round the head and tell her to cover up her emaciated body: she's wearing a pink, fluffy, short jumper which shows a deathly white and taut stomach above a satiny pale blue skirt. Bloodless tweezer-prong legs meet the floor in shiny silver trainers. It's impossible to guess her age, for no doubt self-starvation has made her prematurely haggard, but I suppose this club style puts her in the mid-twenties at the oldest. Petite, with short, indefinably-styled, peroxide yellow hair, a bit like an elf in a children's book that lives under a leaf and wears a hazelnut shell on its head, and she knows it, Jo-jo is plainly adored already by Toolis and Lesley. I expect Toolis sees pound signs in her every cute little word, and Lesley, so far, has smiled at everything Baby Woman has said, including a request for a hundred pounds petty cash. Should I shake her hand? Probably.

'Hello. I'm Nancy.'

'Lesley tells me to ask you if I need anything.'

I bet.

'Is that OK?'

'Sure.' I keep my answer brief. With any luck I won't have to have anything to do with her. Avoiding those glassy baby-doll eyes, I bow low over the phone and dial a slave to haemorrhoids.

'Nancy?'

Stella is writing a letter at her desk. I have just this second cajoled the photocopier to allow me a single page of some documents Toolis has asked me to copy, quick as you can, please. By and large, I'm pretty much mistress of the aged machine now; you just have to butter it up. Getting it to co-operate involves balancing patience with skill at knowing its moods. Cross that line, the blockage light flashes, and the old wreck sulks.

'Yes?'

'How do you spell' – (what sounds like) – 'Tem-ezy-pem?'

Honestly. How should I know? Does she think I do drugs?

'I'm not sure. Like it sounds, I guess.'

'Well, will you check this whole letter for me? Grammar and spelling? And could you bear to type it up? I have to get it biked over within the hour.'

Stella is sidling in my direction. Is this an order? Or a favour? I stare at her. She stops with a hangdog expression. The situation is ridiculous, but, somehow, it's curiously bearable at the same time. I am amused that she can't decide how to treat me: child, confidante, employee? Do I just have to obey her? Or can I do a deal?

'Of course. On one condition.'

'Yes?'

'Finish this copying?'

She has to accept. I anticipate the inevitable groan of defeat. Meanwhile, Toolis, Jo-jo with a little j and Lesley are having a meeting, an earnest little triangle pointing inward. Murmurings of crèches, flexitime and glass ceilings rise in bubbles. I am typing slowly and badly. Stella's letter is on two sides of A4 and, though I can gather she's trying to sell her smackhead idea, it makes little sense to me. The writing is huge but so looped it's barely legible, and I am getting up to ask her what something means when she shouts out, seriously loud: 'For God's sake! When are we getting a new photocopier? How many times do I have to say this?'

The chair legs of the repellent three swivel round in a finely orchestrated synchronised swimming manoeuvre. Their attention assured, Stella slams down the lid. Then she snatches up her handbag and exits the room in a furious hurry. Toolis turns back as though nothing has happened.

Lesley says, oh *dear*. Jo-jo looks embarrassed but mystified. Poor innocent, she doesn't know about our little dramas yet.

I don't get to see Aidan again till Sunday afternoon, when I am forced to ask Sarah to go out specially, a request she both visibly and audibly resents. There's nothing for it, though, we have to be alone, and near a bed-type article. Hey, he might have come clean with Stella. We might have that to celebrate.

He turns up with flowers, red roses no less, and I'm distinctly hopeful, but he begins by saying he's not told her.

'Now, sit down, baby.'

Holding my arms above the elbows he presses me back onto the sofa, then puts the roses on the coffee table. I make a sad face, even though I'm angry. Ten roses. Not a dozen.

'Now, and this isn't an excuse, but Stella's under a lot of pressure at the moment. It wouldn't be fair to say why.'

And, oh bugger, I suppose I daren't ask.

'Well, I'll tell you anyway, she's –' he looks at the floor – 'she's waiting for some hospital tests. They should come in about ten days, or a fortnight. I'm afraid I can't do this to her before we find out. I should have explained before, but I thought it was unfair on you. I'm so sorry, what with you both having to work together and everything.'

Awful chilly suspicion clamps onto my brain and before I can stop myself the words are out: 'Oh, she isn't pregnant, is she?'

Fuck. I've really entered no-go territory now; but he merely gives me a not-altogether-friendly look.

'No, she certainly is not. It's a blood test.'

Well, good. Oh, but I don't feel guilty! How typical! Waiting for test results! She would be! That would explain her temper in the office. Bloody victim woman! Draining his pity. God, I'm horrible. I say nothing, just rock my chin in a weak masquerade of sympathy.

'Oh, look, I'm sorry, Nancy.'

'No, I'm sorry. Aidan, would you rather I leave the job now? I don't mind, I mean, this is a bit tricky for all of us, don't you think?'

'Oh, no, I shouldn't do anything that drastic for the time being. We'll see how it all pans out.'

'Is it serious? Is Stella ill?'

'Well, she could be. That's all we know at this stage.'

I'm sorry, but I do resent this 'we' business. Terminal illness or not. And is he going to give any more details? Not that I really want to know. He's gone all coy. Must be gynaecological then, uterine cancer or something. Connected to the childlessness. Maybe she's going to die? Oh, really. This line of thinking is entirely negative, and since I only have a couple of hours on my hands here, I don't want to spend them talking about Stella. I snap us out of it.

'Don't worry. It'll be fine. These things always are. And don't worry about me. I'm fine too. Sure, we'll wait until you find out. Let's take this calmly. No rush. Yes?'

'Oh, Nancy. You deserve better. You must think I'm a love-rat.'

'And you must think I'm an unfeeling heartless monster.'

He laughs, nervous tension released. 'Dearie me. What a perfect pair.'

We proceed to make do.

Rebecca rings up that evening (I suppose Grace must be out) and fills me in on the holiday fiasco. I can hardly hear, she's talking so quietly, but I think I get the overall picture. They're still going to go to Greece, for two weeks, but guess who they're taking instead of me?

'Eric?'

'What? As if. Don't be sick, Nancy. Try again.'

'Oh, I know, the Italian man-eater?'

'Luisa? No way! Grace says she's too good-looking.'

'Oh, just say then. Who is it, your mother?'

'Yes! Well done. How did you guess? She's dead excited. She's not been away for years. She's even bought a new bikini.'

I have to stifle my laughter. Grace really will kill me now. 'Oh, that's excellent, Rebecca.'

'I know. I'm really pleased. I must confess, I couldn't quite face going with Grace on my own. She'd have wanted to go clubbing all the time. You know what I mean? But how's the job, anyway?'

'Oh. Great. Really interesting. I'm learning loads.'

'Well, you know, to be honest, Nancy, I think I'd have done the same in your position. I don't blame you for staying at all. Your career's worth the sacrifice. And Grace will come round, I'm sure of it.'

God, Rebecca's an angel; but I don't mention Aidan. Twenty minutes later the phone rings again and this time it's the aforementioned Luisa. Jesus, her English *has* come on; she wonders whether she could rent my room for an extra fortnight because she's never, how do you say it, strutted her stuff so much in all her life? I'm only too happy to oblige.

CHAPTER SIXTEEN

The next two weeks, though insane, are the most wonderful of my life; they're also the most nerve-racked and guilt-ridden. I'm in love with Aidan. This is it, the real thing, what everyone is always going on about. The agony and the ecstasy, it's all true. And it does hurt: I nearly have heart failure every time he rings on the flat buzzer, and before every time we meet, and it'll only be a matter of minutes before we are again face to face; then, of course, I suffer an acute sorrow when we say goodbye and he walks away. If he says he'll call, and I stay in to wait, and then for some trivial reason he doesn't, I go a little bit more mad every time, and then, when the phone does ring, I rejoice like a mutt at the sound of its master.

I must say, this whole phoning business is a nightmare. He can't ring my work, and he's asked me not to ring his because he can't speak there. Then in the evening it's hard because he's at home and can't ring me, and obviously I can't ring him at home in case Stella answers. All that's left is his mobile, which he usually calls me on, plus odd conversations here and there when the coast is clear. Far from perfect, but we manage.

I try not to think about Stella, or that she may be ill. Though I see her most days, it's in the context of Toolis TV and nothing to do with Aidan and me. It's easy to split things; and I wander around in a goofy daze, disguising it somewhat at work, but driving Sarah berserk at the flat. I'm paid for the first time, and a cheque for a whole month's wages is placed into my hot little hands. God, I'm so rich! I could get used to this; it's better than being a student. Maybe I should stick with Toolis TV for as long as possible, right till Stella is beating me out of the door with a broom handle? Man, home, job, money: I've got it all, and I start smiling at shop assistants, and giving coins to the homeless, and buying the *Big Issue*. I even ring up Philip to assure him everything's fine and of course I'm behaving myself. No point telling him otherwise; he hardly knows Stella, let's face it, and all his worst fears about me would be horribly confirmed. No need to worry him. After work I've taken to picking up an evening paper in Oxford Street, like all proper Londoners, and then going home by bus, daydreaming in the upstairs of a double-decker as we swing round Hyde Park Corner. There it is. Number One London. It still stands. Our dream home in a dream world. This isn't normal life. Reason has been superceded by something quite else. It's like being drunk or high on some mind-altering drug, but all the time, all day, never coming down. I am obsessed, I am addicted. Now I know what such terms mean. The sun shines and I'm not as cautious about life these days. On the contrary, I'm more committed to it. I even fancied it might actually be quite nice to have Aidan's baby now, while I'm young and supple. I'm serious – forget the degree, screw the career. And so the other evening I suggested to him he needn't bother with condoms any more. He always brings them. Quite rightly and responsibly, however, Aidan protected me from myself, refusing point-blank to humour any such whim.

'Nancy, don't even think of such a thing.'

'Oh, why not? You should be grateful. I thought men hated condoms. Anyway, if I got pregnant, I wouldn't make you marry me.'

'Thanks.'

'I thought you wanted a baby?'

'I do.' He looked at me weirdly.

242

'Stella can't have them, can she, Aidan?' There. I said it.

'No.'

Silence.

Then he carried on: 'I'd love to have a baby. I'm really curious about it. It'd be the last great experience for me, apart from death. That's the thing, though, isn't it? Once you've had a child, then there's only death left. It's all downhill.'

'Oh, cheer up, oldster. Once it was born, you'd love it. You might even feel young again. It would restore your faith in life.'

He laughed, and put an arm round me. 'I'm sure you're right. It must be a wonderful thing, when you first see your own baby, mustn't it? Completely out of this world, I suppose. But you'll have your kid, Nancy. There's no rush.'

I can't really describe how much I loved him at that moment.

'Well, we're going to have to get a move on, Aidan, if you don't want people to think you're the grandpa.'

'Oh, shut up.'

These are my days: happy, sunny, blessed. But then at night I bolt awake to terrible horrors in the small hours and ask myself what in hell's name am I doing? To think, I even played with getting pregnant! Thank God we didn't take the risk; but I must have gone mad, seriously mad. So has Aidan, I think; playing truant with me, he must dread the crunch as much as I do. He's scared, and I'm alone and afraid, really terrified of what will happen when he does tell Stella. I'm having an affair with a married man whose wife, worst-case scenario, might have some terrible disease. In daylight the bottom line is, I'm too happy to worry; the situation even amuses me. But when it's dark I cannot escape the seriousness of it all. It's never funny then.

I so want Stella to know about it. I want him, and I

want her to know that I want him; but most of all, I want her to know that he wants me. Even though I try to keep clear of her when I can, I have to chat to her sometimes, and be friendly, and even, almost, to lie.

'What did you fill your evening with, Nancy? What did you get up to over the weekend?'

'Oh, this and that, up and down, in and out, you know.'

Sometimes, because I have divided my brain in such a way as to make it all bearable, I nearly burst out with it and tell her the scandal of this wonderful married man I am having an affair with. Then I remember who he's married to, and stop short; but it would be so easy to let it slip. She's always nearby. She hangs around me, kind of desperate, like a stray cat winding round your leg. Maybe she wants to confide? Oh, please no.

Another complication that propels Stella in my direction is that Jo-jo, who is supposed to be her friend from way back, has picked up on the not-very-subtle body signals emanating from Toolis and Lesley and, no doubt because she has gathered on which side her bread is to be buttered here, seems to be trying to chill out Stella. Stella makes advances and Jo-jo subtly rebuffs them. The bitchy money-grubbing cow! Call yourself a friend? I almost feel sorry for old Stella. The net result, though, is that Stella is hurt and looks even more to me as her only ally. It's getting to be quite a problem, in fact. We're going to *have* to tell her soon.

When Aidan mentions Stella, usually the mundane details – no, especially them – I feel pain as though cut. Yet instead of screaming at him I have to be patient. This doesn't come naturally. It's horrible to imagine them in the same house, let alone bedroom, him feeling sorry for her. Reluctantly, because it will reveal me in all my insecure terror, I ask Aidan if they are having sex any more? He hugs me and replies in a surprised voice, that of course they aren't, would we be here if he was? They haven't done that for a while. Silly me; but Aidan's comments, though rare, for my sake, and casually made, give me no choice but to realise that, even so, they are still playing husband and wife, and living side by side, sleeping in the same bed, having breakfast together, passing each other the corn flakes, and seeing the same view of Canary Wharf from the same bathroom window. They are proof of a truth which I have never actually witnessed: that these two people, who, separately, are having so much effect on my life, influence each other even more.

Jo-jo came in the other morning with a selection of all the main women's magazines, and dumped them on my desk. She asked me to make a list of what all the major articles were about, so as to ensure her programme is as up to date as possible on women's issues. I set to the job straight away, first of all peeling off one sample of swimming-pool-blue eye-shadow, two slushy books and three shampoo sachets from the assorted covers. Should I keep the lot, or was Lesley watching? Feeling generous, I realised I'd better share them out.

'That's convenient. Six freebies for six people. Lesley, why don't you have the shampoo for distressed hair, Alistair can have flyaway, and I'll take the one with, let me see, "added nutrients for women who juggle their lives". Jo-jo, I think this eye-shadow is definitely you, and Heather and Stella can have a romantic novel each to take to bed.'

Expecting some sort of fall-out I was mildly disappointed when, after a fashion, they all laughed. Toolis even bobbed over like a Pacman ghost to check out the novels.

'I might find time to read them.'

She'd softened lately. Maybe I'd been emitting infectious happy waves?

'They are free, after all.'

Maybe not.

Once she'd sped off, I checked out the magazines' contents. Opening the very first one, my eye was immediately caught by the headline: 'Married Men – Are They Worth It?' Crunching open the heavy pages I was reading the article, and getting more and more irritated by its knowing pessimism (married men who are unfaithful to their wives are lower than scum, not to be touched with bargepoles, only one thing lower and that's the women who sleep with them, traitors to their sex, etc, etc), when who should I sense looking over my shoulder but Stella? God, did she have nothing better to do? I tried, ever so casually, to turn the page, fingers shaking, but it was too late.

'What are you reading? Oh, that looks interesting: "A survey has proved that men who are unfaithful to their wives are seldom able to conduct healthy monogamous relationships ever again." Isn't that fascinating? You know, I have to say, I think that women who sleep with married men really are the pits. I can forgive a lot, but not that. What do you think, Nancy?'

'Me? Oh, well, I don't know. Er, circumstances vary, I suppose. It's not always the woman's fault. Maybe?'

'Oh. Maybe.'

And with that she ambled off again, leaving me shivering in relief. Although her tone had been perfectly casual throughout, I was worried that she might know something – if not about me, at least that he was being unfaithful. Suffice it to say that since then I've been dreading more than ever when she finds out.

Monday, 19 August is different. Stella comes in at eleven thirty, in a definite state, ignoring me and heading straight to her desk. Something's wrong. She's had the results? They're not good? That must be it. What do I feel? Fear. Pity for Aidan. What will happen? Talk about a baptism of fire for our relationship. Why has she ignored me? Does she know? I am still warm from Aidan's embrace of yesterday. Did she catch him when he got home, dopey and careless? Or, did he tell her? They've had a fight? Oh my God, he must have told her. She can't look me in the face. A horrible winter cold pervades my whole trunk. She'll want to kill me, and him. Stab us in their cabbage patch with the complete set of Sabatier knives. Maybe she has killed him. What is it they say about a woman scorned? There is no anger like it? I retreat to the kitchen for a traumatised black coffee, then keep my head down till lunch time. At twelve forty-five I sidle up to Alastair.

'Alastair, can you cover the phone for an hour?'

If he says yes I can escape, temporarily. Oh, please say yes.

'Sure. Maybe Juliet will ring. I left a message on her machine asking her to the party.'

'She's never going to ring you, Alastair. Face it.'

Juliet is the woman he called on my first day. He's not spoken to her since then, but firmly believes she did like him really. I'm getting tired of telling him there's been no call.

'A boy can dream, Nancy.'

I make a face. He shakes a book at me.

'Go on then, run away before I change my mind.'

'Nancy?' Stella's put her head up and our eyes meet for the first time today.

'Ye-es?'

'Would you come out to lunch with me?'

Oh, my God. It's an order. She definitely knows about me. It's not the test results. She's going to rip me apart. What do I do? Refuse? I can't. What will she do to me?

Calm down, she can't do anything. It'll be better to get this over with. Yes? Yes. It has got to happen sometime, and it'll be such a release of tension. So what if she does make a scene, or hits me? Whatever. At last! She knows! Adrenaline rush, and I almost dance after her.

'Thanks for coming, Nancy. I hope it's not got in your way of doing anything?'

Eh? We are in the street now. The daylight dazzles after those dark stairs. Why's she not angry?

'And sorry, I almost commanded you to come out with me! I just thought Heather wouldn't make a fuss if I put on that tone.'

She doesn't know. There's nothing wrong. Oh, bloody hell! I manage to mutter weakly, 'That's OK.'

'Well, lunch is on me. I've just got to share my news with someone!'

News? The test results? Sounds like good news. She's OK. All is well. So Aidan can tell her now?

'What news?'

'I'll tell you when we're sitting down. There's this marvellous little Italian restaurant near here. It does a very good lunch for a bargain all-in price.'

Ma-arvellous. The rich don't get rich by being generous, that's for sure.

'Now, what street is it in? I've not been there for a while, as I usually go to the French place and put it on expenses, but it's a bit of a media meat-market in there. Oh, that's right, I remember.'

She leads the way confidently and I have a hideous foreboding where she is heading. I'm proved right. Within a few minutes we enter the restaurant where Aidan and I ate on our first date. Well, the irony is flowing thick and fast, and I wait for the grumpy waiter to hover by the table we have chosen. There he is, happy as Larry still. Over he comes. I inspect my nails.

'Signora, how are you?'

Does he mean me? The piranha teeth flash.

'Sergio, how are you? And your wife, and Antonio?'

'Oh, signora, we are so happy in our new house.'

Don't tell me: she knows the waiter, she's done him some benevolent deed, and he and all his descendants will love her name for ever. Who but the lowest form of life could ever hurt this gracious woman?

Stella beams and he goes off to get the drinks. I have ordered a large gin and tonic, and so has Stella.

'That man is so sweet, you know, Nancy. We got chatting once and he told us all about his family and moving house from a council flat into their own place.'

You patronising cow, Stella: but the drinks are here. I take a gulp. Right. Down to business.

'Tell me your news then.'

Stella is swallowing and shakes her head as if to say, one minute. I must wait a little longer to discover what I already know. The painful ridiculousness of the situation is such that I catapult caution to the winds and an injection of pure mischief floods my blood vessels. Life, after all, is a bitch. What am I doing here? Stella's telling me her good news. Stella, my friend. What a farce. What the hell?

'No, Stella, actually, let me guess. You've – oh, I don't know – had some test results back? The news is good. You're going to live after all?'

She's unfolding a large pink table napkin across her lap. Looks at me, bemused.

'No! You are a fool, Nancy. Try again.'

What? No reaction?

'Give up? I'll tell you. I've been offered a new job!'

Is that all? What about her health? I can't bear this. Here's me revving up to a big scene, and now we have to talk about her wretched career?

'Oh. That's nice.'

'It's a brilliant offer, Nancy. Lots more money, much bigger company, really respected documentary maker, amazing offices.'

Actually, maybe this conversation will be interesting. If she leaves, preferably soon, then it will facilitate everything. Come to think about it, it's heaven-sent!

'There's just one problem.'

Only one, Stella? 'Yes?'

'It's in Edinburgh. I'd have to move.'

'Ah.'

Scotland. Now wouldn't that be perfect? So far from London. And I note the detail: 'I'd have to move.' Not 'we'. So she's as good as saying that all is not right between them? Why is she telling *me*, though? And why did she apply for the job if she wasn't prepared to move there? Is she saying that she's leaving him? Fine, if so; but this is undoubtedly odd. She's a very odd woman. It's Aidan she's got to talk to. Don't they speak to each other at all? What is she really trying to say here? Does she want my advice? What do I say? I'm not supposed to know that they aren't happily married. I'm not supposed to have a clue. Maybe she wants to make me curious, make me ask if there's trouble at mill? Maybe; but I'm not even going to pretend to take the bait. It's definitely not mine to reason why; yet I can't forgo such a perfect opportunity to try to persuade her to take the job.

'It's not such a problem, Stella. It's only geography. What are you actually afraid of? You must want it if you applied for it. Do what you want to do. You could move up north. Why not think in terms of starting afresh? See change as a positive thing.'

Because you'll be needing to relocate your whole life soon. I am being so cryptic. I bet she's mystified.

'Why do you say that, Nancy? You're probably right. It's just, my thoughts are all over the place. I need an impartial opinion.'

Don't we all? Shall I tell her the truth? Why not the truth? I could tell her the truth. There won't be a better moment. Look at her. The interested expression on her face opposite. Listening. To me. Tell Stella the truth, Nancy. Do the right thing.

'Because, well – because . . .'

I cannot do it. I am dumb. I cannot tell the truth. The waiter is back.

'OK, what would you like to order?'

'Oh, right. You first, Nancy.'

And the moment passes, for now.

We've ordered: I just stabbed my finger at the first thing I saw. Stella's also asked for a bottle of wine. Thirty-five minutes of my lunch hour are gone already.

'So what were you saying, Nancy?'

'Oh, I've forgotten. When?'

'Just now. About the job in Scotland?'

I'd better ask her a question before she recalls that I failed to answer hers. Picking up a bread roll from the basket, I unwrap a butter square.

'Well, why did you apply for it, Stella, if you weren't prepared to move up there?'

She looks, very briefly, like a child caught out; cross and confused. I can see the battle between telling me the truth and chickening out being fought on her face. She chickens out.

'Well, I don't know, really. I – I don't know. Temporary madness, maybe?' Then, half-heartedly, she tries again. 'I don't know. Maybe part of me does want to get away?'

Oh, just spit it out, Stella. Come clean. You're wondering whether to leave your husband? Say it. I won't be shocked, I promise. Still, I must keep her confidence bolstered until she is on that train with her suitcase packed.

'I'm sure, Stella, I'm sure. I mean, you must be sick of London? So much pollution. They say Edinburgh's beautiful, really lovely.'

'Yes, it is, I know. But, Nancy –'

'Yes?'

'Aren't you wondering about Aidan's part in all of this?'

Shit. Aren't I just?

The weirdest moment in the weirdest lunch. She's asked me outright. What about Aidan? It's a second chance for me to tell her. I must have another go. Heart beating. Try again, Nancy. Tell her the truth. Tell her that Aidan is having an affair. Tell her that he plans to leave her anyway. Say the words.

I look round. There is a hard clean cloth on the table. A little slim-waisted glass vase, not too steady, with one red carnation in. Knives and forks and a wine glass by my gin and tonic. A couple of lovebirds holding hands at the next table – they wouldn't notice if a bomb sprayed nails in their faces. Nobody approaching. Stella is waiting. What about Aidan? He has had the chance to tell her. It's obviously too hard for him. I have far less to lose. He'll be relieved if I do it for him.

Your husband is having an affair. Say the words, Nancy. Say them. I grip the edges of the table. Will I be able to utter his name?

'Aidan? Am I wondering about him? No. Should I be? Wouldn't you both move to Scotland?'

Out of my mouth has issued the most innocent and casual sentence I think I have ever uttered. With one finger, in fact, I'm now rubbing an eye. Stella freezes, then relaxes, and smiles.

'Yes. Sorry, Nancy. Of course we would. If I accept it. We'll think about it. Sorry, I must be going a little mad. I don't know why I'm boring you with this. Forgive me?'

'Sure.'

I wipe my forehead, never more furious with myself, but so relieved. No wonder Aidan can't do it. Scaredy-cat Aidan. Scaredy-cat Stella. Scaredy-cat me.

The food arrives. We keep quiet while our plates are put down, huge white platters which, we are warned, are scorching hot. Stella has some tasteful pasta shells with wild mushrooms, but I am somewhat daunted by my choice. So this is what I ordered? It is, I suppose, an up-market version of chicken Kiev. Not unlike an asteroid that has crashed into the Gobi Desert, a huge golden-breadcrumbed boulder sits alone in the middle of my plate. Damn! No doubt it's stuffed with garlic. I'm meeting Aidan for an early evening drink tonight. He's not got time to come to the flat. Vegetables arrive in a separate dish and I reassure the waiter that I can manage to serve myself. I cast a glance at my watch: five to two. I'm going to be late. Toolis will bollock me. Bugger her. It's Stella's fault.

Loading on the vegetables, and then eating them first, slowly, takes up a nervous ten minutes. We talk shop a bit, I ask after her garden, and how's her mother, and then she enquires, obviously only out of politeness, if anything's happened in my love life lately that she should know about?

If you could stop the moment you would see me holding my fork directly above the chicken boulder. As she says the words (run the film slowly) and as I take them in, all control to my wrist departs. The fork descends too fast (don't speed up) and stabs the as-yet-unpunctured chicken parcel with such force that a yellow jet of hot butter spurts forth (both mine and Stella's eyes focus on it) and arcs high through the air until it hits the first resistant object. This happens to be the eye of the male lovebird at the next table. He screams (speed up now) loud enough to turn the heads of everyone in the room and bring the chef from the kitchen wiping both hands onto his apron.

Inevitable confusion and apologies follow. The couple were leaving anyway. Stella, who has kept a straight face throughout, watches their departure and then lets out such an attack of hysterical laughter that I can only join in.

'Nancy! You make me laugh so much!'

I know. Hilarious. Bolting the rest of our lunch, we finish the wine in a hurry and stumble back to the office at half-past two, full, flushed, drunk, and better friends than ever.

CHAPTER SEVENTEEN

✳

Stella swans off at five to three saying she's exhausted, but still laughing, and leaving me to battle an increasingly nasty headache and the onset of nausea. If I wasn't meeting Aidan I'd go straight home and collapse into bed, but I've got to tell him face to face about lunch time. We've got to plan what to do next. I swallow a couple of paracetamol and several coffees, endeavouring to spend as much of the afternoon as possible in the relative peace of the kitchen. I can't stay in there all the time, though, and Toolis asking what food we all think would be good for the party doesn't help. God, is that happening next week already? Doesn't time fly when you're enjoying yourself? Will Aidan come to it?

Jo-jo has lots of ideas, all hearty and stodgily sensible, shamelessly exhibiting that pretence of a healthy appetite with which anorexics think they fool the world. I'm not conned. I'm sure I've smelt sick in the ladies lately, and as for eating, I've only ever caught her scraping at an apple. Alastair helpfully mentions that he went to a party once where there was only fish and chips on offer, and Toolis laughs; Jo-jo grimaces, and then Lesley wonders, perhaps, if we could get away without serving anything at all?

'Because they'll all leave to get their dinner, anyway.'

'You've got a point. What do you think, Nancy?'

Hmm. What would be the most expensive option? 'How about getting caterers in? Fork buffet for seventy-five?'

'I don't think so.'

Around quarter to five I sick up my lunch and feel much better. Making up some excuse to go out, I whip to the chemists for toothpaste and a new brush, wondering why I don't already keep such vital bit-on-the-side tools in my bag anyway. Back at the office, Jo-jo catches me doing my teeth in the kitchen and is on my case in an instant.

'Hi, Nancy. What are you up to? Going out tonight?'

'No. Just doing my teeth.'

'Oh, come on. You can't fool me. You've got a date.'

She's leaning skinnily against the doorframe, battling to hold the door ajar with her foot. I hope the others can't hear. My face is going red. That's a dead giveaway; so I'd better play this down.

'Maybe. It's not a crime.'

'Ooh, you sound guilty! Is it with your boyfriend?'

'Yes.'

'Well, that's very nice. Nothing wrong with that. What does he do?'

Shit. Don't tell her a thing; but don't go all secretive either. What does he do? 'Er, he's a doctor. A cancer specialist.'

'Really? That's fascinating. How old?'

Oh God. What else will she ask? I realise with a sinking feeling that she's in her blood-from-a-stone research mode. I've heard her getting loads of poor suckers to share their deepest secrets.

'Well, he's in his forties actually.'

'Nancy! You shocker! An older man! Well, I never. Still waters run deep, eh? And where did you meet?'

I can't help grinning, much against my will. She's hard to resist, I have to say. I can almost see myself telling her everything; but mustn't. Jo-jo's an old friend of Stella's. It's far too dangerous. I whisper in reply.

'Well, it's a bit embarrassing, actually. Don't tell anyone. He's the father of a friend of mine.'

255

Those blue eyes bulge. 'Nancy! This is outrageous! I'd never have believed it!'

'Oh, don't go on. My life's a nightmare at the moment. My friend doesn't know. And, well, I'm afraid –'

'Yes?'

'He's still married to her mother.'

Jo-jo gasps theatrically and draws a melodramatic hand over her brow. 'Say no more, Nancy. Oh damn, I have to go. Just keep me informed, though, will you? I'll be watching this space.'

I promise. Lesley is calling her. Great, off the hook for now. I swill out my mouth and scarper from there in a sweaty fluster, but by the time I reach our rendezvous, a pub near King's Cross, I'm cooled down, and right as rain, and smelling like a flower garden once more.

Aidan's not arrived, so I get the drinks. Lager for me and a bitter for him. A good trick is to fix my gaze onto a picture on the wall, if there is one, so that Aidan won't catch me looking for him and also he'll get a good look at my fresh young face as he approaches. In here the scene is of Victorian children skating on a frozen pond, their hands demurely behind their backs, scarves streaming away in the icy wind. I memorise every detail to fill in the time: the kitten plodding along beside them, paws probably rigid with frostbite, a red ribbon blowing from its jet-black neck; the trees in the background bent over by the wind, leafless and darkened; the children's little coats and the galoshes on their shoes. No doubt they're all heading for the poorhouse.

Then Aidan's face is in front of me, immediately taking a gulp of his drink. Here again.

'How are you? Thanks for getting me this.'

'That's all right. I'm fine.'

He gets out tobacco and papers from his briefcase. I watch him intently.

'Nancy, can I ask you a personal question?'

By all means.

'Do you think you might be short-sighted? Sometimes I think you could be going blind, you look so stiffly at the wall.'

Damn, foiled again.

'Of course I'm not, I just stare at the wall so you won't think I'm watching the door to see you arrive.'

Why do I always tell him the truth?

'Oh. Right. So, what have you been up to today?'

'Well, funny you should ask. Your very lovely wife kindly took me out to lunch to a little Italian restaurant which you just possibly might have been to before, and we had a bit of a heart-to-heart.'

He stops mid-Rizla-lick.

'Really? What about?'

'She was in a bit of a state.'

'Go on.'

'Well, at first I thought she'd had bad news about those test results, but it wasn't that.'

'Oh, right, well, I was going to tell you. She got the results this morning. They were OK. So what did you talk about?'

Oh, excellent! Good news for all concerned. Aidan knits his eyebrows. I consider saying she's found a pair of my knickers in his suit pocket but, irritatingly, the truth comes out again.

'No, it was that job she's been offered in Scotland.'

'What job?'

Eh? Now I'm really confused. He doesn't know? She hasn't told him? Why not? She told me before him? Jesus, I can do without much more of this. And, now I think about it, why was she not more surprised at lunch when I guessed about the test results? If she got them back this morning? What is going on? I wonder if they live in the

257

same house at times. Oh, I don't know. It isn't any of my business. Their problems are not my concern. I proceed to tell him everything Stella said to me.

'I feel terrible, Aidan. I shouldn't have told you.'

'Bit late for that, Nancy.'

'You'll have to pretend you don't know.'

'Oh, don't worry. I expect she'll tell me.'

'It's horrible to even think it, but isn't the timing perfect?'

'You don't say. Maybe she's leaving me!'

'Maybe. But if she does decide to go, then it won't be so hard to tell her.' I rest my hand on his. 'I must confess, Aidan, I tried today, at lunch, but the words just wouldn't come out.'

'Oh God, Nancy, don't. Don't do that again. Please, this is not about you. I must do it.'

'But, Aidan, when? There's no reason not to, now the tests are OK.'

'I know. And I will. Leave it to me. OK? Promise?'

He gives me a puppy-dog expression, and, of course, I melt. I must stop hassling this poor man. He looks knackered. I change the subject, and fill him in on our lesser office dramas.

'Lesley lives for work. And will probably die from it, at the rate she's going. Toolis' commands are her wishes. So pathetic. Toolis despises her, but has a soft spot for Alastair. No other human being seems to affect her whatsoever. It's a mystery.'

'It wasn't always that way.'

'What do you mean?'

Aidan is slyly grinning as he stubs out his cigarette.

'Heather used to be married. Quite a while ago now. Her husband was a charming rogue whom she trusted completely until he embezzled the not inconsiderable profits of her advertising company she'd started from nothing. He'd married her for her money.'

'Really? How do you know?'

258

'Don't ask. Just trust me, Nancy. Remember, I'm in the information business. He was sent to prison and they got divorced. It was Stella's money that started off Toolis TV. Heather's a survivor, but she's never loved again.'

'God! I had no idea. I can't believe it. Poor Toolis.'

'It's true. Now, what else can I tell you about your workmates?'

'Oh, nothing, I shouldn't think. They're all pretty boring – a miserable lot, as you know. Alastair fancies Jo-jo. He always stares at her, and never makes any offensive comments when she's in the room. He doesn't want her to know he's a chauvinist pig. She doesn't notice because she's too screwed up about men, I think. I mean, she must be anorexic; she's got those slightly grey teeth and yellow fingernails from making herself vomit up stomach acid. In fact I think she's still at it: every time she eats anything at all she rushes to the loo and there's a lingering smell of sick in there now all the time. It's quite disgusting.'

'You sure it's not your alcoholic chucking?'

'No, it is not. I was only sick today because your wife got me drunk! It's definitely Jo-jo. Receptionists notice these things. She's such a fake, all sugary and cute and lovely to everybody, but she obviously hates herself. And I have never seen anyone thinner. Oh, I don't know, I have a thing about anorexics. It's dreadful to say it, but being that much of a victim is just repulsive, isn't it? Sorry, that sounds awful. And I mustn't be so nasty; she's a friend of Stella's, isn't she?'

'I think so. From a while back.'

'It was really funny, actually. She nearly forced the truth out of me earlier.'

'Who did? What?'

'Jo-jo. She asked me if I had a boyfriend, or something. She was so excited when I said I did, and he was married.'

'Nancy! What have you been saying?'

'Oh, don't panic. I made up all the other details. She doesn't know anything.'

'Oh, my God. I am ageing so fast these days.' Aidan's head is in his hands. Then he goes quiet and stares into his pint. These silences are on the increase.

We keep clear of dangerous topics until he has to go. As he says goodbye outside, a bus crashes past and I can't hear a thing. Most of our farewells so far have been shrouded in vehicle exhaust. Oh, for a place of our own; but I must be patient. Any day now such tawdry scenes will be a thing of the past.

'Everything will sort itself out, Nancy.'

'All right. I believe you. Thousands wouldn't.'

'Don't worry so much.'

I go home and worry.

We've arranged to see each other again on Friday, since Aidan is busy all week, and I have to bide my time till then in limbo. It goes very slowly. Stella flaps around in a kind of sub-menstrual tetch. Whether this indicates she has come to a decision about the job, or not, I cannot tell. I'm avoiding any more heart-to-hearts with her and she makes no further attempts to bend my ear. Maybe she's regretting taking me into her confidence – I don't know – but the only specific indication of our collaboration comes in the form of occasional panicked glances at me, which are as quickly switched off as on. Most of her frustration is addressed to the photocopier, and Toolis' poor neck must be stiff from turning in horror to witness another tantrum. Then, on Thursday afternoon – and she picks her moment carefully, when only Alastair is around, and he glued to the phone – Stella pulls such rank on me that you would imagine we have had no social connection whatsoever.

'Nancy. Could you please call this man on this number and ask him to come and see me?' She points to an entry in her address book. The prospect horrifies.

'Select-A-Pencil? Derek? I can't. Heather has forbidden me to have anything to do with him!'

'Really. Do you know why that is, Nancy?'

She is furious generally, but not with me. Blanket rage at her life, I suppose. I feel specifically guilty, nevertheless, and almost whisper my reply.

'No.'

'Because they once sold me a copier that actually worked! And you know what? They charged accordingly. Heather hyperventilated over the price, and had such a fit that I at last managed to get them to take it back and give us a refund. She actually threatened to resign, so I caved in. That was in the days when I cared about such things. Well, not any more. Nobody! Never again! I put my money into this company and if I want a new photocopier I will buy one! I am not having her puritan ways dictate to me! Right?'

'Right.'

Does this mean she's decided to stay? Would she invest in a place she was leaving? Oh, I don't know. To quote her own words, she is all over the place.

'So please ring him and . . .' Here her momentum sags. She's tired. 'Oh, all right, I needn't see him. But at least get him to send all their brochures or whatever. Now, I must go.'

Thank God for small mercies. I call Derek immediately while the coast is clear, and I think it's fair to say that no one has ever sounded more pleased to hear from me. Sales slather drips from the receiver. I manage to deter him from nipping by immediately, but he swears on his grand-mother's soul that those brochures will be with me first thing tomorrow. I'd better be in early so as to hide them from Toolis. Dear, oh dear. The stress is killing me.

That evening Aidan rings to say he thinks he may only have time for a drink again tomorrow, so we'll meet in the pub. Better than nothing, I suppose, though I'm pissed off.

Still, only twenty-four hours before I see him once more; and they pass.

When I arrive, Aidan's there already, waiting for me. He's never looked so adorable. The media suit, the floppy hair. Irresistible; the formal clout of the businessman allied with the crumpled cloth of conscience. An onrush of carnal urges surprises even me.

'Aidan, why can't we nip back to my flat for an hour on the sofa?'

He laughs, but I don't like the tone.

'Sorry, it's not possible.'

'Why not? What's the rush? You could still be at work, for all Stella knows. Don't forget, you're a busy man.'

'I just can't, OK?'

What's happened? And have they talked about her job? I know it's none of my business; but, no, fuck it, it is my business.

'Why not? What's going on? And what about her job? Have you talked about that? You must have. What's going on?'

'Nancy! For Christ's sake! Stella's having a dinner party, that's all. I have to be there.'

A dinner party! Fiddling while Rome burns!

'You are joking!' That stupid woman. I am furious. 'So, what's she making then?'

'What?'

'For dinner?'

'I don't know! Cold meat and salad, I think.'

'I hope you choke.'

'Thanks. I'll let you know.'

I look at Aidan, long and deep into the eyes. Innocuous statements like that last one have the power to launch me into a lonely orbit miles and miles and miles away from him, but even from there, I fight back.

'Oh, well, thank *you*, but don't rush, take your time, Nancy can wait, Nancy doesn't matter, don't bother to

262

tell her about anything, she's just an invisible part of the furniture, you sort her out once everything else is cleared up, she doesn't have feelings.'

I am staring grimly ahead now, each of my eyes a little twitching stirring whirlpool of grief, through which swirly lenses I can just make out the time on the clock above the door. Six fifty-seven. People in proper relationships probably don't make much of indifferent hours like this. Six fifty-seven: early evening drink. Three thirty-four: snatched weekend afternoons. Seven twenty-three: invariably the time I would kiss him goodbye on evenings such as this.

'God dammit, Nancy! What is it with you?'

'What do you fucking mean, what is it with *me*?'

'It's all about *you*, isn't it? You just don't think about anybody else, do you? You think you're the only person that matters. You think it's all so easy. God, you're so young! You know absolutely nothing. You think life is so simple, all black and white. Don't you? Sex. Love. Marriage. Divorce. Babies. Jobs. Everything. You do, don't you? Basically? Well, honey, it just isn't that easy. Do you want to know why I have to be back for dinner? Because I'm trying to get a commissioning editor's job, and there's some smarming to be done. It's not very nice, but that's how the world works. So grow up. Life isn't a fairy tale. Welcome to the real world.'

Gasp.

I can't believe he said that. So, he despises me? I am *so young*? He's going to leave me. He must be. Well, that's it. We are coldly silent for over a minute of hell, and since I don't know what to do, I do nothing. I can't look at him.

'Nancy?' Now Aidan is smiling, fast sugaring the pill. 'I'm sorry. I'm so sorry. I didn't mean that. Any of it. God. I'm sorry. Nancy?'

I must be silently crying.

'I'm sorry. Please, I'm sorry. Listen, I don't know what

Stella is doing about the job. But she seems anxious that I come to that party you're having.'

I shred my beer mat while he continues. He'll tell Stella. I'm to stop worrying. After the party, next weekend, so as to keep the prying noses of the office out of it all, thereby protecting me as much as anyone. I shred faster, in real fury. I don't want to be protected, I'm not some vulnerable child, I want the gory facts in all their deceitful lying detail to be smeared over that hypocritical place in a glorious sweep of revelation. Yes, me, Nancy! With him! Then we can swan off, hand in hand into that now rather clouded sunset. Welcome to the real world! Thanks very much. Show me the fucking real world, Aidan.

Damn you, Stella. Damn your home cooking. Damn those wholesome ingredients. What is going on? What is wrong with their marriage? How much in trouble is it really? Why is he continuing our risky affair if it all matters to him still? Does he love me? So what if he said he did? Did he mean it?

'Aidan? Are you sure you still want to?'

'What?' He's been staring into space.

'You know, erm . . .'

Leave Stella. Leave your wife. Dump that cow. Move in the new chick. Look years younger.

'Well, leave Stella?' Get the name in. Twist the knife.

Aidan stares at me then. He shakes his head like an exasperated teacher with a dense pupil. My heart beats faster. I've gone too far. He's had enough of me. He is going to chuck me. He is going to do it. He's going to finish it all. Oh God, please no. I'm sorry, I'll believe in you, anything, ask of me anything, just mend this, make this all right again, just don't take him away. If he walks out of here the pub will turn into a pub again. My life will turn into my past again. Not that. Please.

'Yes. God, yes. I do.'

I sigh.

He sighs.

I sigh again, and lean forward to kiss him. We'll meet again. See you Sunday, he says, when we part, and I head home, happy by a thread. He is going to leave her. We're still together.

CHAPTER EIGHTEEN

❋

Sunday afternoon, and Aidan has just rung to say he can't make it. I feel like death, knees hunched in front of me, whisky in hand. Something came up. Something to do with Stella. What, I wonder? A shopping trip? Garden party? Friends round? Why is she keeping up this façade? Fuck her! She must have been in the next room when he phoned; he was whispering, then ended the conversation suddenly.

'I've got to go. Bye.'

'Aidan, wait. When can I see you?'

'Oh, I can't think now. At the party?'

Great. Thanks a lot. We'll have a lovely time there. I'm not that much of a masochist.

'No, I mean properly. How about the weekend?'

By which time you should have told her.

'I can't, oh, I'm going away. But look, Nancy, I've *got* to go.'

Going away? So he'll tell her on Friday, I suppose. Then, too right, he'll need to scram.

'Where are you going?'

'Look, I can't talk.'

'Friday night then?' He's being so tricky I don't even suggest he comes here. 'A quick drink? Usual place? Six o'clock? Try and ring me before then?'

'OK. See you. Bye.'

Very, very unsatisfactory. Another five days. Still. This time next week, Stella will know all. And, we'd not have been able to do much today anyway, since Sarah has actu-

ally refused to leave the flat this time as a matter of prin-
ciple. She's in a sulk in her room, where no doubt she
intends to stay until Nick comes by for her later. Hoping
she'll have calmed down by now and be ready to sympath-
ise, I nudge open the door with my foot. Talking about
not seeing him is better than nothing at all.

'Don't worry. He can't make it.'

She is lying on her bed with her back to me, smoking
angrily and reading a magazine. Now she rolls over and
leans across to the full ashtray on the ornate bedside table.

'Surprise, surprise.'

'Sorry?'

She pulls herself up against the pillows. I allow one thigh
onto the end of the bed.

'Oh, sit down properly. I said, I am not surprised, Nancy.
That he is not coming.'

Oh, no. Is this going to be a *real* conversation?

'Why?'

'You know why. Because I don't think he's serious about
you. I think he's treating you like dirt, and he can do it
because you let him. And, I'm sorry, but I don't think he's
going to leave his wife.'

'Right. Anything else?'

'Yes. I think you should get out of it before things
become any worse. Then, if he's really interested, he'll be
over here pdq.'

'What do you mean?'

'How can you not see this, Nan? Drop him. Don't see
him. Stand him up a couple of times. Certainly don't ring
him. Leave the answer phone on, I don't mind. I mean,
how hard will that be? The phone line's not exactly hot
with his calls, is it?'

Wince. Catty!

'I'm sorry, Nan. But I'm sick of all this. I'm not going
to lie to you. He's certainly not going to leave his wife,
and a two-timer like him isn't worth it even if he does.

Why don't you understand that? You've got to end it.'

I bow my head and laugh to myself.

'I don't think you understand, Sarah. How can I describe this to you? I couldn't actually do it. It isn't physically possible. It's no more possible than – than – than I could fly.'

'What bullshit!'

'It is not! You don't understand. How do you feel like, well, now? You're going to see Nick tonight. Is your heart racing? Does the thought of seeing him make you feel sick? Are you watching the clock, counting the minutes before you see him again? Do you count the minutes when you are with him? Do you dread the time when he's not here? Of course you don't. I know you don't. If he called to cancel tonight, well, no big deal, you'll see him tomorrow. You'll catch up. You'll stay at his place for the rest of the week. You're going away together soon. You can phone him up whenever you like. Just think how it would be if all those things were taken away from you.'

'Oh, shut up, Nancy. Don't be so pompous. What you don't realise is that I can perfectly well imagine what that would be like. It's my idea of hell, actually. What I don't understand is what you get out of it, apart from God knows what quality of sex, once in a blue moon, when he dictates, plus endless hassle?'

Sarah is quivering with furious honesty. She may think she knows the score, but has she no concept of how complicated all this is for me? No idea that she is actually very fortunate to have such a straightforward relationship with Nick? They have been going out together since she was fifteen or something. They met at school, he was a couple of years above her, and then she applied to go to the same university. Now, if you ask me, she takes his reliability for granted. He's very nice and steady in a rugger-bugger way, and crazy about her. She assumes he'll be around for ever.

I don't think she has the first idea of what life is like for the rest of us on the outside.

'Leave my sex life out of this, Sarah. I may not have an ideal relationship, but at least I've got a life. At least adrenaline hits my blood stream occasionally. I'll tell you what I get out of it. It makes me alive. I feel like I can't get ill. That cars won't hit me. That I won't get old. That I'll never die. Try and understand that, Miss Middle-Aged.'

Jesus. She won't forgive me now. I'm not wrong.

'Fuck you, Nancy.'

'And fuck you too! You and your fucking boring convenient boyfriend! How dare you lecture me?'

She doesn't answer, just swings off the bed, flings the pack of cigarettes into her bag, and walks out.

She doesn't come back for two nights. Monday and Tuesday are hell. The office is driving me mad. Aidan doesn't ring. I don't have the guts to call Sarah at Nick's and there's not a squeak from her. What am I going to say? I mentally prepare for her return every minute since our fight. I have to apologise. I have to squirm. What if she doesn't forgive me? What if she chucks me out of the flat? If she does, I've had it. Not only is there no other place in London for me to go to, but she and Nick are flying to the Caribbean next Saturday, and will be gone for a fortnight. Thus, if all goes as planned, I'll have the place to myself to coincide with Aidan telling Stella about us and needing a place to run to. He can then get us another flat and I can leave the job. My future will be safe in his hands. God, I'm looking forward to it. Right now, it's Tuesday evening, and I'm so tired.

Those are her footsteps. Key in the lock. I switch off the telly and get down to the floor. Abased like a fawning cur, I stretch out my arms and bow my head. I hope she's not brought anyone with her.

Her laugh. Thank the Lord. 'Nancy! What are you doing?'

I flail my arms up and down. 'Sarah. Good, kind, wonderful, Sarah. Please forgive me. Oh, please, please, please forgive me. I am so unworthy.'

'Oh, all right then. You horrible cow.'

'I know I am. I know. I'm so sorry.' I flail faster. 'Forgive me, oh, please, please, please forgive me.'

'Stop, stop, stop. It's all right. I'm over it now.'

Rolling onto my side, I look at her. She's smiling, but I can tell we're not yet off that tricky knife edge.

'Really, I'm genuinely sorry, Sarah. I said some unforgivable things. I am so sorry. My only excuse is that I have gone mad at the moment, as you know. I didn't mean them.'

'Nor did I. I said things too. Please forgive me. Let's not talk about it any more, OK?'

'OK.' Thank God. I still have a roof above my two-faced head.

'Thanks, Nan. Now. I've brought this video – it's meant to be quite funny – and some wine. Let's get pissed.'

Wednesday turns into a very long day. Hot already when I leave the flat. The door's been wedged open at the office and I find Toolis by the photocopier.

'If it's not broken, don't fix it, eh, Nanette?'

Head level with the machine's mouth, she's watching it spew out copies. Shit. I gave Stella Derek's brochures and she wants to place an order for a new one today.

'I suppose not. But, then again, if something isn't right, why not chuck it out and start again?'

Her mouth yaps shut.

'Hmm.'

Jo-jo froths in wearing a sleeveless summer dress. Hi, everybody, hi, hi! Jesus, she's skeletal. Poor old thing: the woman looks a million, even though she's had her hair reperoxided, the pink of her scalp showing through. Who does she think that fools? Her car broke down at Staples

Corner and she had to get this adorable man to tow her to a garage and then she hired another car and then it took forty minutes to get a space near here to park that in, so that's why she's late. So sorry.

Unimpressed, I check my watch overtly. Only nine fifty. What is she on about? Showily making up for lost time, she opens a wide-paged notebook and, after scrabbling for a few seconds in her new patent leather bile-green bag, takes out a healthy diet bar. This she unwraps hungrily and starts to chew on six inches of a substance closely resembling gravel bound by road tar. The dribble begins to foam and I can't look any more.

Lesley, flustered, is very late. Toolis has already wondered out loud where can she have got to, and Alastair has reminded the room in general that he thought she had a hospital appointment. Oh, amputate the whole nose, I reflected, and my disgust must have been self-evident, because Alastair laughed.

'Try and have a kind thought for once, Nancy.'

I blushed, caught out. He'd read my mind. I was guilty as sin. Now Lesley apologises for her absence, out of breath.

'I'm so sorry, Heather. My appointment was at eight this morning, and I was early for it, I got there at seven just in case, but God knows why, the specialist wasn't even there till ten, and then he had to see I don't know how many other people before me, and then my appointment took a lot longer than either he or I expected.'

Lesley pauses here to leave us in no doubt that complications have arisen. No one asks for more details.

'So it wasn't until twelve that I was even out of there, and then I caught a cab to get here, and that got stuck in traffic, and then I realised I'd left the mobile at home so I couldn't even call –'

'Don't worry. Just fill in the hours another time.'

'Well, I do worry, Heather. It's not fair on you, or the

company. I don't have private medical insurance in order to wait so long to be seen. It's a disgrace.'

So that's what she spends her vast income on. I've seen one of Lesley's pay cheques: eight hundred pounds a week.

Stella doesn't turn up today. The rest of them all trail out around four, I think to film a piece about choosing the sex of your baby with some woman who has six daughters and is desperate for a son. Alastair found her through the oldest daughter, whom he chatted up in a bar. I'm left alone. Or so I think: but Jo-jo runs back five minutes later to pick up something from her desk.

'Oh, Nancy, I meant to ask. How's it all going?'

'What?'

'Your secret affair? With the married man?'

Double take. I'm wrong-footed for a second, and my jaw drops.

'You know, you told me the other day. The doctor? Your friend's dad?'

'Oh, right. As if I could forget! Well, it's carrying on. It's still a secret, though, and he goes back to the wife every night. I want to go public, and have him all to myself. I'm not sure what to do.' I finish with a nervous apologetic giggle.

'Oh, don't worry, Nancy. Although, and I'm sure you've heard this all before, you *do* want to be careful with married men. They very seldom leave their wives.'

Oh, thanks for the tip. Just go away. I raise my palms to her. Stop now.

'I know, I know, Jo-jo. Don't say anything.'

'Sometimes they do, though. It could all end happily. Listen, why don't you let me meet him? I'm an excellent judge of men, married or not.'

Oh, please no. Leave me alone. She's so keen to help, you'd think she gave a damn.

'No, no, I can't, I'm sorry. But listen, thanks.'

'Oh, go on, Nancy. I could suss him out in two minutes.'

'No. All right? No.'

She takes the hint this time and flies out again. I wipe the sweat from my brow.

Party tomorrow. I'll see Aidan, but won't be allowed to look. I've never witnessed Stella and him in the same room before. What will it be like? All useful research, of course. Body language should tell me a lot. They'll probably keep a certain distance from each other. Will I get to speak to him? Hardly. No, actually, Stella will probably introduce us; she's always going on about how he could give my career a leg-up. That'll be deliciously tricky. Dearie me. It's all been tricky. How long now since all this started? I calculate, wastefully scribbling on the back of a new envelope. Today's 28 August. God, they'll be back from Greece at the weekend. Since I started here, therefore, forty-four days. Since the Friday night, our first date, thirty-nine days. Since I met Stella, thirty-seven days. Since I realised the significance of who she was, thirty-five days. From start to finish, if Stella gets told all, say, by this Saturday, it'll be forty-seven days. Nearly seven weeks. Six weeks. Six tricky weeks.

Some film stock company rings up for Lesley. I say she's gone. Oh, you're joking? No, I never joke. Well, could you do me a favour, love, and have a snoop round her desk to see if she's got our order ready? Because we can't deliver the stuff by yesterday if we don't have a faxed order. All right. Hold on there. Yes, here it is. OK, I'll fax it pronto. What's your number? Where's a pen?

Nothing apparent on the surface of Lesley's desk, so in panic I pull open a drawer. Ah, here's an old pencil. OK, I've got that, bye. Phone down. I put the pencil back and am about to close the drawer, good as gold, I won't rifle through it, when I notice a half-opened matchbox revealing what looks like a collection of small pink pearly flakes. I lift it out carefully.

The phone rings.

'Good afternoon, Toolis Television, how may I help you?'

'Hi, Nancy. It's Stella. Sorry I never made it in today.'

Distracted, I'm not listening. Rather, I'm looking into the matchbox. I don't believe this! Pieces of prawn shell. It's unbelievable. Aidan was right. Lesley *is* the meanest woman in London. It makes me feel sad, almost. All those angry refund demands for her tainted sandwiches, and they were all planted! All fake! Nothing genuine!

'Nancy? Are you there?'

'What were you saying, Stella?'

'Oh, I was wondering if you could do something for me?'

'OK.'

'I had a look at those photocopier adverts you gave me, and I wonder if you could call that man and order the one on page 14? I think it's called the "Royal Wastie". And don't worry about Heather, I'll clear it with her. Is that OK? I'd have done it but other things came up.'

Thanks, Stella. What a bitch. She doesn't know that Toolis isn't close by, able to hear such an incriminating phone call.

'That's fine. Sure.'

'You're an angel, Nancy.'

Yes. I'm always being compared to one.

'I'd better go then. Meringues in the oven.'

'OK. See you tomorrow, Stella. At the party.'

'Oh. You may not.'

'Why not?'

'Well, we've been invited out to dinner, a bit last minute, only it's quite important, some people Aidan wants to get in with. So it's not the sort of thing you can turn down. Aidan was keen to fit in both, but I've put him off the idea. I don't think we can risk being late to dinner.'

'Oh.'

But, Stella, the whole thing was your idea! It's your company. I don't get. How can you not turn up to your own party? And Aidan and I need to see each other. He's not your possession! He wants to come. He's a busy man. We have to steal these moments whenever we can. They're not yours to take away from me!

'I know you wanted to meet him and have a chat about your future, but we'll do that some other time, OK? You don't want to be introduced in the office anyway, do you? Don't worry. Although, I mean, I could come alone, and be there at the start, only twenty minutes or so, and then slip out perhaps? I could get away with that if I was by myself. Maybe I should? Oh, sorry, I'm all over the place, as usual. Yes, maybe I'll do that. So, probably you will see me tomorrow.'

'OK. Fine. Bye.'

Damn you, Stella, he's not yours! You can't have him! You can't tell him what to do! He wants to come! I am so angry with you. I hate you. Why can't you just leave me alone? Get out of my life. And his. Leave us alone. I look round the room, and I hate everything I see. Dingy little room. Messy little desks. Compromise. Mediocrity. Deceit. Hypocrisy. I am so sick of it. It's ridiculous. Why am I still here? I have had it with this place.

Then and there, I make up my mind.

I've had enough. I don't like it, so I'm not going to put up with it. I can't wait till the weekend. I'll leave at the end of this week – no, sooner than that, actually. I won't come in on Friday. Tomorrow will be my last day. I have had enough. Time to come clean. I am going to tell her. I am going to tell Stella everything at the party.

Picking up the box of prawn shells I place it on a page of clean white paper and, taking off my shoe, hammer down with my heel until the cardboard is flattened and the contents ground to dust. Then I crunch the incriminating bundle into a ball and hurl it out the window. Screw you,

Lesley. What can I do now? Her order form is in front of me on the desk, so I add a nought to all her figures in the 'number of items' column, and fax it through pronto, as promised, then screw that paper up and throw it out the window too.

Now, Stella. Your turn. The mouse can roar, you know. I march to her desk and find the photocopier booklet. She has circled the top one on page 14, indeed the Royal Wastie. Cost: £6,000. It's a handy little machine. Ideal for the smaller office. Beneath the Royal Wastie, I see the Royal Watkins, wider capability, the more durable model, £15,000. My eye is drawn, however, to the bottom of the page. There the Royal Walmesley reigns supreme. It's massive. Big as a tank. The button panel, highlighted in close-up, sparkles like the controls of a Boeing 747. This machine does everything. Digital. Connects up to your computers. Goes far beyond mere photocopying. Cleans the office. Sorts out payroll. Audits the accounts. A bargain at £29,950.

Right. Sliding Stella's copy of the catalogue back where I found it, I return to my desk and open an unmarked copy. Then I dial Derek's number.

'Nancy! How are you? It's good to hear from you, it really is.'

'I'm fine, Derek. Honestly. I have never felt better.'

'That's excellent news. Now, what can I do you for?'

'I'd like to order one of your photocopiers. It's on page 14. Stella Fitzpatrick asked me to call you.'

'Well, that's wonderful. Hang on. OK, so that'll be the Wastie, I take it?'

'Let me see. No, it's the one at the bottom. The Royal Walmesley.'

'Really, Nancy? You sure about that?'

'Yes, that's what she said. Now, she wants it delivered as soon as possible. Could we have it on Monday?'

'Well, yes, of course. We do have a few in stock.'

'Great. Now, do we do this by phone, or do you need a signature or something?'

'I'll need a signed fax confirmation, but I can fill that out for you now, and if I sent it to you in a second, could you return it today? We'll need that, if we are to deliver on Monday?'

'Fine. I can get her to sign it right away.'

'Excellent. Now, I presume this is for a hire contract, Nancy. Not, erm, outright sale?'

I think about this. Toolis would want outright sale, wouldn't she? Won't they pay more in the long run if they hire?

'No, we'd like outright sale, Derek.'

'Right. That's, that's, that's . . . that's wonderful, Nancy. I'll do it for you now.'

'Could you, Derek? Because Stella wants to get off home?'

The fax machine issues forth his ready-filled order form in under two minutes. He is so efficient. I have a letter signed by Stella in front of me, so I practise her signature a few times on another new envelope before I write her name where he has marked a huge X. Oh, perfect. Easy-peasy. A life of crime and subterfuge for me. Then, after faxing it back to him, folding the order form, and putting it in my pocket, I call Derek again.

'You got that Derek? Yes? Great. Now, we don't want it before Monday, all right?'

'I swear, Nancy. On Grandma's soul. Whatever you like.'

Right. That's done. Ten past five now, and I feel great. What is there left to do? I'd better take all my stuff away tonight, so as to be ready for an easy exit tomorrow. Wrench open the drawers. Nothing of mine in them, but they're very untidy, disordered stationery everywhere. I sort it all out, arranging the pens in rows, and the ruler parallel with them, then lay out the remaining little bits and pieces neatly at the front. In the other drawer, I place the women's health book right at the back where I found it six weeks ago on day one. The day I first saw Aidan. Six weeks suspended between heaven and hell. I feel a century older. Older and wiser. Ready for the real world.

Sarah and Nick are there when I get home, and we all go to the pub around nine thirty. It's quite fun in an odd way, almost as though Sarah and I never fought. Aidan's not mentioned, though Nick knows everything and I'm sure Sarah has diagnosed that I'm skidding right off my rocker at the moment. So I do my best to act reasonable and controlled and they're both very sweet, in fact. Nick asks me about my job and I enquire about their holiday and we are all so civilised. I am chain-smoking, mind, but that's the only pointer to inner stress. The minute we get home I collapse on the sofa and fall fast asleep. At four forty-five in the morning I wake, feeling terrible. Full of lager with no food to soak it up. Swallowing, with difficulty, two paracetamol and a cup of water, I lie very still to keep the throbbing of my head to a minimum and wait for the pain to end. But it won't. Resigned, I draw back the curtains. A beautiful night out there. I am not angry any more, I'm lonely. Next door Sarah and Nick are no doubt spooned together. I want Aidan here, lying next to me. He's not slept with me overnight yet, apart from that first time. It's my dream to wake up and find him here, the warmth in the duvet not just my own.

Still, any day now.

I am going to tell Stella tomorrow. It isn't fair to ask Aidan to do it. Poor Aidan. Though he has said he will tell her at the weekend, I know he won't. He can't tell Stella about us. Not this weekend, probably not ever; yet someone has to be grown-up here. Neither of us asked for this complicated situation, but I am going to resolve it, once and for all. I'll do this for Aidan.

Beneath a full moon the roofs of London town are grandly visible. The serenity of the night imparts an elegance to my decision. Everything, at last, is clear.

CHAPTER NINETEEN

✳

Party day. Tell Stella the truth day. Mingle, circulate, corner my victim: then move like a shark attack in for the kill.

I have a spring in my step when I arrive at work, but Toolis hobbles that straight away.

'Nanette. You'll be down on main reception tonight. It's very important we screen all the guests.'

What? I have other plans.

'Is that for all evening? Won't you want me to serve the drinks?'

'No, no. I can't have people turning up off the street. Go and ask the little man downstairs to show you how the door works.'

Damn, damn, damn! When am I going to get the chance to tell Stella now? But who knows, this might even make things easier. Maybe I can nab her as she arrives, or, more likely, leaves. Could even be quite neat; but what if I miss the chance? Anything, or more likely everything, can go wrong. Oh, stop worrying, I grouch at myself, just make sure you do it. By hook or by crook. Stamping downstairs in a temper, I'm furious again. Which is just as well, as I need to stay angry all day. I have to tell Stella, and to do that, I have to hate her.

Mac is the grizzled receptionist for the whole building. I only ever spoke to him that once, on my first day. He proceeds to spend about an hour telling me very slowly how to open the door when the buzzer goes and what to do with the not-so-immense switchboard. Inside his booth he boils cups of tea and watches a tiny portable TV set. It stays on quietly all the time I am with him. Mac is gaunt and wears a white shirt and shoe-lace tie and cheapo black trousers. His fingers shake and he chain-smokes. The whole place smells of smoke, so I suppose I'll be able to have a cigarette tonight, at least. Small mercy though; they'll all be upstairs having a laugh while I'm down here biding my time. The wrong side of the reception desk. As ever; but not for much longer. As I head back up to the office I tantalise myself with the prospect of imminent revelation. What will they say? Aidan and Nancy? You, and Stella's husband? Don't be ridiculous. Is this a joke?

After lunch I get sent out to buy the party food. We're going for the ready-made option. Wonderful: it's a chance to be by myself for an hour or so without having to make conversation.

'Oh, wait, Nancy. I'll come with you. You'll need help carrying.'

Shit. Jo-jo has bounced to her feet, or at least as well as a stick can bounce. That taut midriff is still on display. Tsk; so liable to street grime.

'No, thanks, I'm OK. I'll be fine.'

'Nancy, I insist. You can spare me, Heather, can't you?'

Of course she can.

'Of course I can. Actually, Jo-jo, could you get me a new dress for tonight? Size 8. Something formal. Dark. No frills. And absolutely no linen – it creases too much. Hold on, here's some money.'

'Sure, Heather. Trust me.'

Jo-jo's been on the phone most of the morning. I really should take a leaf out of her book when it comes to getting what you want. She is, quite simply, Little Miss Insincere. Oozing, sliming, oiling to those from whom she can squeeze something, be it discount, interview or information, she stares glassily at the ceiling while she speaks, picking her teeth with a transparent-varnished thumbnail, and then makes some disparaging comment about them the second she puts down the phone. It's awesome.

Now that she's tagging along I have a sense of foreboding. I know why, too: she wants nothing less than a full low-down on my affair. And she just might get it, if she pushes hard enough. She's that nosy. I don't quite trust myself not to throw caution to the winds and tell her everything. It would be a relief, I must say; but, no way, I can't. I just *must not*.

We have been entrusted with fifty pounds' petty cash, which I almost had to wrench from Lesley's fist, and once in the shop we start to collect all the usual items you shove into your mouth at such events: celery sticks; carrot shards; cucumber spikes; plastic wheels of dip with a different flavoured glob suspended between each spoke; reddened and greasy chicken tikka limbs which are impossible to hold, let alone eat; cold prawns in batter, a circle of death round a well of tangy sauce, this hardly the fate their mothers dreamt for them. Jo-jo, whom I have no doubt will later watch others guzzle while she nips on a breadstick, now flits from aisle to aisle adding chicken satay skewers and salmon tubes rammed with sour cream and some sausage rolls for Alastair, stacking it all up until we have a K2 of finger food in the trolley. The bill, miraculously, comes to £49.97.

Up till this point I have managed to avoid much chat, since we were deafened by the crowds in the street and in here I've been steaming ahead with the trolley every time Jo-jo draws near. Now she remembers she has to get Toolis a dress, so I suggest that I wait here with the food while she hunts one down. Oddly enough, she agrees. Well, thank God for small mercies. Maybe we can get back to the office without mentioning *that* subject once. My fingers are crossed.

Twenty minutes later Jo-jo reappears.

'I've got her something perfect, Nancy. Look.'

She lifts a tiny dark garment out of a plastic bag. Its only feature is a white lapelled collar. Minimalist in the extreme, it's the epitome of discretion.

I laugh. 'Hah! She'll look like a pilgrim father!'

'Mother, surely?'

Oh, don't be pedantic, woman. I check the label to ensure there's not even a small percentage of linen involved, and then squint closer. After peeling back an inconveniently placed sticker, I notice the dress hailed originally from the children's range. Suggested age: 11–14. Laughing to myself, I press back the sticker and keep quiet. Toolis will think Jo-jo is making fun of her.

'Excellent. Let's get back, or this food'll go off.'

'Actually, Nancy, I thought we could go for a coffee, just a quick one. OK?'

No. Bloody not OK.

'I think I'd better get back, really. Heather will want me.'

'Oh, don't be silly. I need to sit down after all that shopping. I'll take the blame if Heather says anything. Come on.'

She picks up one of the four bags of food, so I trail her with the other three through a million shoppers and into a bar. At least she has the decency to pay for the coffees.

'Thanks.'

'That's OK. Now, Nancy, I've got you away from the office. The coast is clear. Tell me everything about your man.'

Shit. I knew it; but maybe I'll try to be bullish this time. Leaning backwards so the chair rests on two legs only, I fold my arms.

'Why do you care?'

'Oh, come on. Don't be defensive. I love stories about real people. Human interest. It's research for me. Remember, that's what I do for a living.'

'You're paid to be nosy?'

'Exactly. Jammy, isn't it? I'm fascinated. Oh, come on, Nancy. You can confide in me.'

Yeah, like I'd stroke the head of a cobra.

Jo-jo is stirring the foam into her cappuccino, not looking at me.

'What does it matter, anyway? It's not like I'm involved. Come on. You don't have to give me any names or details like that.'

True. What does it matter? Why am I being so precious? It might actually be quite nice to confess to a total stranger. All right, I'll tell her; but I'll keep Aidan as a doctor and – what was it? – the father of a friend.

'What do you want to know, then?'

'Oh well, let's see. How long's the affair been going on?'

The absolute truth? Five, six weeks.

'A couple of months, I think, or maybe three?'

'Right. That's quite respectable, but I expect you want him to come clean now?'

'Exactly.'

'And I presume this has been a fully, erm, sexual relationship? I mean, there's been –'

'Lots of shagging? Sure. Loads.'

We both laugh.

'The best, in fact.'

That's true.

'Sorry, Nancy. None of my business. But, let's see, well, are you very good friends with his daughter?'

Eh? Oh, right. Think fast.

'Yes. Very good. We're at college together. She introduced me.'

'Of course, she would have. So it's him or her, is it? Would she forgive you if she knew?'

'No. Never. She thinks her parents are very happy. And the mother's lovely, obviously.'

'Oh, this is excellent! Just like a problem page!'

Jo-jo is rubbing her hands with glee. I'm just a case study to her. Fucking woman! Right, I'm leaving, now.

'Oh, Nancy, I'm sorry.'

'I'd better go, Jo-jo.'

'No, no! Stay. I'm sorry if I offended you. I don't mean it. I know it's serious. Sit down, sit down.'

I give up, and crumple back in the seat with my head in my hands.

'Do you love him, then, Nancy?'

'He's the love of my life.'

There. You've got it out of me. The heart of the matter. I hope you're satisfied. I look at her. Silence. She's shut up at last.

'And he can't tell his wife and I don't know what to do because I can't live without him. So I'm being vile to everyone and going a bit mad.'

'Sure. Of course you are. Oh, poor Nancy.'

Stick Woman smiles at me. All right, she might be quite a nice person after all.

'What shall I do, Jo-jo?'

'Well. Let's see. Option One. You know what I'm going to say, don't you?'

'Walk away; but don't bother. I can't.'

'All right. Option Two. How about, you let me meet him?'

'You? Why?'

'Because, I'll tell you why, other people can see what you can't. I mean, have you introduced him to any of your family or other friends yet?'

'No.'

'Right. So you don't know what anyone else thinks of him. You see, what you need is an outside opinion. If I met him and thought he wasn't on the level, I could get talking and ask him incriminating questions and things. We'd soon see if he was messing you about.'

No, you wouldn't. Because he isn't. I laugh. Imagine

the scene! Jo-jo giving Aidan the third degree as to his intentions!

'And then, if he was genuine, it would be obvious. You see, an outsider can always tell if couples are really in love, or if it's just one-sided. People can't usually fake it well enough to fool a third party.'

'I don't know if that's a good idea.'

'Oh, please, Nancy! Please. I admit it, I'm completely intrigued now. Let me meet him, even very briefly.'

'I'm not sure.'

'Nancy, please.'

'No.'

'Ple-ease.'

'All right!'

Just get off my back and I'll promise you anything.

'When?'

Indeed. When? In the end I promise Jo-jo that I'll sort it for one evening next week. Stella will know the truth by then and all will be in the open and I'll be gone from the office anyway, so whatever we arrange now is irrelevant. This appears to satisfy her. She says she can't wait, and I'm not to worry. I ask if she's going out with anyone? – just to be fair – and she says she isn't. I didn't think so. The conversation stops dead and we head back to the office. Unreasonably, I fear I've told her far too much, like when you wake from a heavy night out and recall, oh shit, did I really say that? Still, what the hell, it doesn't matter. When we get back and Jo-jo shows Toolis the dress, the little woman immediately peels the sticker off the label and a twisted smile breaks on her face.

'Oh, thank you, Jo-jo. It's perfect. And, from the children's range!'

'My God, it's not? Oh, I am so *sorry*, Heather.'

'No, it's fine. Don't worry. Children's clothes are half the price!'

The afternoon passes. I start to hop with apprehension.

I'm going to tell Stella. My bowels loosen. When answering the phone, I keep forgetting who is calling for whom, especially when, around four o'clock, Aidan himself rings and asks to speak to Stella. This is all too much. My mantle of professionalism falls away and I cradle the phone woozily.

'How are you? Are you OK? It's lovely to hear you.'

'Shh, Nancy, I'm fine.' As if his whispering will make any difference this end. 'Can I speak to Stella?'

Bastard.

'No, you can't.'

'Nancy. Put me through.'

'I can't. She's not here.'

'Oh, right. Well, see you later.'

'Will you? Are you coming to the party after all? Stella said you weren't.'

'Yes, I think we can make it at the start.'

'Excellent! Bye then.'

Screw you, Stella. He's coming to the party. Back to plan one. Tell them both.

'I'll have it in here, boys.'

Boxes of drink are being lugged through the door by some clean-jawed young men from a nearby wine shop. Toolis tugs at their heels, growling.

I'm going to see Aidan tonight! The old heartbeat has quickened and from now on I'm in a fluster. Think, think. Maybe there will be an opportunity to come up here? What are the chances that I'll be able to catch them alone, conveniently waiting to hear the news that will finish their marriage? Not good. What if I do manage it, and Stella does something embarrassing like faint, or shriek, or froth at the mouth, and smash her glass on my head? It is a bit ridiculous, I can see that. I'll have to manipulate it all too much. Too messy, ugly.

Stop, stop, stop.

What *is* happening? I always thought of myself as an honest person, someone from whom you got it straight. Now I'm an awful scheming vixen. God: it's dreadful. Oh, well. Hardly my fault. All part of growing up.

No, it's too complicated to plan. I'll tell Stella the truth. Somehow. No doubt it will be simple in the end.

So I wait. At six fifteen I station myself at the general reception desk. Mac empties the ashtray, hands over his empire, and I am alone. An opened bottle of white wine and a plastic cup stand where I have hidden them on a shelf beneath the desk's surface. The guests are due to arrive at half-past. Toolis has made me buy a visitors' book for the occasion, which no guest is to pass without signing. I pour myself some wine.

They begin to arrive, first one by one, the sad lonely prompt ones, then in clusters, freeloaders hanging on to one invitation holder. Some I recognise by face – there's Ben, the accountant – and some by voice, but most not at all. Stella turns up at the same time as a group of others and, while they are signing the book, she rushes upstairs, dead smart in a black number with pearls. Aidan will be coming from his office. One down, one to go. Every time the door buzzer rings I lurch. It might be him this time. No, it isn't. After the initial influx, the hordes lessen. So does the wine in my bottle. Next to where I have parked it is a paperback, *Living with Lung Cancer*, a letter folded inside. This details a hospital appointment for an operation next Monday. Macdonald McKillick is to bring in everything he will need for a long stay after surgery. Jesus! Poor Mac. He might be dead next week. Bloody hell! Of course, I might be dead next week. We all might be dead next week. Treat every minute as though it will be your last. I have to tell Stella.

'Cheer up, Nancy.'

Alastair has brought down a paper plate of things to

eat. One or two prawns, not enough salmon things, several comatose sausage rolls, but I accept.

'Stella asked me to bring them, so it's her you should thank.'

You don't say.

'How's it going up there?'

'Oh, swimmingly!' He burps. 'Nancy, can I ask for a little bit of advice about women?'

Will wonders never cease? He puts his elbows on the desk.

'Do you, do you think that possibly Jo-jo likes me?'

'Jo-jo? You fancy her, don't you?'

'Well, what's wrong with that?'

The buzzer goes and I release the catch without asking who it is through the intercom.

'Nothing. But those bones would snap if you climbed on top of her.'

'Now then, bitch, bitch, bitch.'

Aidan! I turn to face him, incapable of hiding a smile. Smarter than usual: royal-blue shirt sharply ironed, under a freshly dry-cleaned suit, and new yellow tie with tiny navy fleurs-de-lis. My very own vision of manhood. Lurch. Heave of the gut. This is crucifying me.

'Aidan! Good to see you!'

'Alastair. What's this horrible girl been saying to you?'

'Oh, just a bit of woman trouble, you know.'

'Tell me about it. It adds years onto your life, trust me. Best avoided. Shall we go up?'

Oh, what a wit; and, no excuse to dawdle with me awhile. Such a pro. He's not even caught my eye.

I call after their backs: 'One minute! Could I have your name for the visitors' book, please, and where you work, so that we all know who and what you are?'

Alastair looks appalled. Don't I know who this is? Mr Big? You arse-licker, Alastair.

Aidan returns to oblige, muttering under his breath. 'Who am I, Nancy, and what company do I keep?'

Alastair can't hear.

'You're a villain, sweetheart, and what you do is nobody's business.'

'Thank you.'

They disappear into the lift. Quick, start plotting. How long will he and Stella stay? I'm clock-watching now, that's for sure. Give him, what, ten minutes to get the first drink sorted? Another ten to say hello to important people, ten more to consolidate a few conversations, five more minutes to get bored with them? Then look around, get a refill, wonder where your bit of fluff is? Wife by the side? Or not? Will she be circulating too? How long will they stay? Three-quarters of an hour? Oh, this is so stupid. How can I guess? I'll have to go up there. Jesus. I am truly terrified. I feel sick. I *have* to go up there. There won't be a chance to get them together again in a hurry. Can I leave my post? The guest supply certainly seems to have dried up. I'll just whip upstairs for a quick scan. Check out the lie of the land. No harm in that. The buzzer goes. Damn. Some young woman. Not sure she's got the right place.

'I was left a message by, er, Alastair? My name is Juliet.'

So. Everything does come to he who waits. Lucky Alastair. I release the door catch. Oh, a red-head. Juliet doesn't look too confident about finding the party alone, so I generously offer to accompany her upstairs. Hopefully we'll discover Alastair getting off with Jo-jo. Just before I lead the way into the office, though, an unavoidable rash of self-consciousness brings a blush to my face. That, plus the consumption of too much alcohol already, on top of the nerves of an empty stomach, and I feel my head boiling. I am too embarrassed to go in. What if Aidan smiles really obviously at me, or says something he shouldn't, and everything becomes clear? The subdued roar of party babble is leaking from under the door. Can I do this? Juliet is waiting politely. No time like the present. So, forward. I push the door inwards.

We are greeted by a wall of backs. There seems to be quite a crowd in our little office. The room has expanded to fit them and no longer do I see the two-bit shoe-box in which I spend my days. Its nature has been subtly changed. The electric lights are off, and the evening sun casts tall waving shadows on the wall opposite the windows. Dark forms do finger athletics with their cigarettes and bend forward to sip their wine and then back with their heads to laugh. I don't recognise these apparitions.

'There's Alastair. Thanks for showing me up here.'

Juliet bravely heads into the flesh-and-blood rabble. Swiftly, it eats her up. No one has noticed me yet. Edging to my right, I approach the bottles of wine laid out on my desk. Empty food plates are stacked there, plus a couple which still have some faded party fare on them.

'Nancy!'

Lesley's head, then body, and finally legs, are pushing their way out of the living mass. Once released she puts down an empty platter, gasps, and, digging into her pocket for her inhaler, shoves it into her mouth.

'I need to sit down. Mind out.'

She plops into my chair, which swirls her round on impact. Furious, she grabs the desk to steady herself. I watch dumbly. A few wheezes later, she points to one of the plates and speaks again.

'Hand them round, could you?'

Oh fuck this. Great. Hi, Aidan and Stella, I'm your waitress tonight.

'Go on. Don't just stand there. I've been doing it all evening. The smell of meat is making me ill.'

She's watching me. I can't refuse. Maybe, once out of her sight, I can hide them somewhere; and I suppose they do give me a passport into the centre of the crowd. I set off and pray Aidan doesn't see me like this.

'Nanette?'

Toolis? Where is she? I am forcing the nearest collection of reluctant strangers to have at least one thing to eat each.

'What are you doing up here? I thought I told you to stay downstairs?'

Her head is now level with my outstretched wrist.

'And where's Lesley? She's on serving duty.'

'She's having an asthma attack and asked me to help out.'

'Oh, for goodness' sake! Give that to me and get back downstairs. People could be waiting to come in!'

'Yes, Heather.'

Toolis takes the plate and the human ocean opens in front of her. Before leaving the room my gaze follows the channel she makes and I see that one group resists her advance. Just as I am going, a split-second vision, and though now the mob are reforming behind Toolis, I catch the backs of two heads in this group turn to look down upon her, laugh, and, a pause later, make way. The woman picks up something from the plate and puts it into the man's mouth. She laughs. It's Stella and Aidan. I flee with a bottle of red wine.

So that's what they're like together. Why? I don't understand. Why? I *hate* this. Jesus, her face, as she put that food in his mouth! God, he'll never dare tell her, and my latest effort was stillborn, like all the rest have been. I drain the second wine bottle. The party is supposed to last from six thirty till nine thirty. 'So that we're shot of them by eleven,' Toolis said. By eight thirty I'm hammered. My head is in pain. Battered prawns swirl with chewed sausage rolls in a lake of now-rosé wine in my stomach. My body temperature is racing up and I recognise the rumblings of nausea. Swiftly the sensation grows urgent. Where is the nearest loo? Second floor, I think. I shouldn't leave the desk, though. People have started to leave in dribs and

drabs and they have to have the door catch released. I
determine to hold on. This may go away. Passing faces
cheerfully say goodbye but I don't dare answer them, just
nod and buzz them out. Perhaps fresh air will help. Maybe
if I stand and hold the door open, then I can let people
out at the same time as curing myself? There seems to be
a lull, anyway.

I haul back the heavy door and step into the busy night.
People bustle past. The air is slightly cooler than inside,
but not much, and it's becoming clear I'll need an arctic
wind to force this dose of poison back down. Reeling somewhat as a surge rolls up from my stomach, I have to let
the door go. The muscles at the back of my throat are
relaxing revoltingly sweetly to prepare for imminent ejec-
tion. No time left to think. All discretion flees. I crouch
down and watch splurges of liquid shoot from my mouth
and onto the pavement, quite far out thankfully, but not
without splashing onto the peep-toe sandals of an unfortunate woman who walks by just then. Half a prawn lodges
under her strap. I daren't look up at her face. She swears,
and scarpers in disgust. I'm sick again, and again, and
again, passers-by making detours now, until a cool relief
springs through me and I'm better. After staying with my
head on my knees for a few minutes, I rise and push the
door, but it doesn't budge. It's slammed and locked. The
keys are indoors.

Shit.

Sick is spattered down my chin and front, and my legs
are hollow as I lean back on the closed door for support.

Oh, help!

It's opening inwards, and I'm falling backwards, dropping until my bottom hits the bristled doormat with a
spine-juddering thud. Putting out my hands to save my
head, I look up and see Stella's face. Oh, what now? I'm
in shock. Three guests, no doubt trying to depart, view the
proceedings with some surprise.

'Nancy? Whatever's happening down here? Are you all right?'

I lie back, carefully lowering my head onto the hard floor. Sleep, oh please, sleep. The three tread nervously round me like sheep at a hole in the road, then scud out sharpish while Stella holds the door.

'Don't slip on the sick!' Only fair to warn them.

'What sick? Oh, Nancy, you poor thing, are you all right? Was it that food I sent you down? A bad prawn?'

Oh, life's a bad prawn for me right now, Stella. And I'm not your dear, I'm your husband's lover, right? Not dear at all. Talking of which, well, thinking of which, are those Aidan's feet, standing by me now?

Yes. Such quality socks. What a perfect moment.

'Stella? Stella?' Now's my chance. Perfect! She kneels down near me.

'Yes?'

Drunk, painful, slow, word by truthful word: 'Stella – Stella, you won't believe this, but there's the most interesting, fascinating thing I should tell you, which would, you know, yes, yes – it would change your life for ever.'

Pulling myself back onto the elbows, I've got her attention. She's looking at me, level with my face, waiting for every word. Now this simple solution is so near. I will get it out, I will tell her. It seems like I have all the time in the world.

'It's hardly good news, but I really, really, really . . .' slur, '. . . do think you should be told.'

Aidan is listening too, I presume. He's behind me. My moment.

'How shall I, er, put it? Treachery. Yes. Someone, someone close to you, let's say, and as we speak, in fact, is –'

But then, Aidan's voice, somewhere above me, harsh and in a tone I've not heard before, interrupting: 'Stella! We really must go or we'll be late. There's no time to listen to this pissed kid all night. Let's get her a taxi home or something. I tell you what, you go and hail a cab and I'll get her up.'

He must be leaning down, I suppose, because his hands, cruel in my armpits, jerk me on to my feet. My head pitches from side to side. He's stopped me! From telling her. Why? Is he angry with me? *Pissed kid*? The cheek! Still, I'm in his arms again.

Aidan gets out his handkerchief, and I'm not too drunk to tell it isn't clean this time, and crispy bits scratch my face. It smells of his tobacco. He rubs my chin roughly, and my clothes, but not going as low as the legs. Where is Stella? Can't see her.

I lean forward to kiss Aidan, almost asleep now, but he shakes me back, jolting my neck, and hisses: 'Nancy! Not here!'

Next I am being pushed into the dark cavern of a black taxi by Aidan, and directions are being given by Stella, telling the driver to head for Knightsbridge. I think she then pushes her head through the open car door.

'Heather won't find out about this, don't worry. I'll go and give her some excuse now.'

Then Aidan: 'Right, off you go, bye-bye, come on, Stella.'

Engine revs. I really am almost fast asleep, half very loud noises, half can't hear a thing, but I muster enough strength to pull the door hard towards me, giving it my best drunken slam. It doesn't shut for some reason, something's caught, so I release it and slam again. Aah, this time it closes, and I sink back onto the seat.

We're moving forward. Before I sleep, head down on the leather, I remember my other ride home in a cab like this. How different that was. I was so happy. Now, what? Why did he talk to me like that? Oh, I know, it's understandable. I don't like it, but I do understand it. What a mess I've made of the evening. Was that really me? That pointless cryptic garble? Why didn't I say it outright when I had the chance? I am so angry. I hate myself. What a fucking embarrassing hopeless waste of time.

CHAPTER TWENTY

✳

I carry on being sick all night until every drip of liquid is expelled and we're down to the vile yellow acid. Even then I dry-retch for another hour or so, the state of my head punishing me for the outrage I have inflicted upon it. At last I fall asleep, deeply, profoundly, utterly, around six in the morning; breath beyond foul. What a waste of Toolis' wine budget.

The sound and smell of mushrooms frying. Sarah in the kitchen. I sit up, feeling hungry, and look at the clock. Two o'clock in the afternoon. Oh, no! What about work? Fall back on my cushion-pillow. Well, what about it? I was supposed to be calling in to resign today; but I don't feel so brave now. Oh, it'll have to wait till Monday. Is it a bit late to call in sick? What a mess; but it's too much like hard work to think at all. My battered brain refuses to oblige. I swing my legs to the floor and approach the kitchen.

'Can I have some, if there's enough?'

'Get away, Nan. Your breath's disgusting.'

I breathe on to my hand.

'Sorry.'

'You can if you tell me what happened last night. And clean your teeth. Oh, and your office rang. I said you were ill.'

'Thanks. I certainly am. You're an absolute poppet.'

Best not to mention that I'm never going back, not quite yet.

In front of the bathroom mirror I recall last night. The hideous truth. A ridiculous end to a ridiculous plan. Yet, yet, think how close I came to success! A few seconds more. If only I'd got to the point earlier. Damn. If it hadn't been for Aidan and his cold feet everything would have been perfect, with me too drunk to care about the consequences. Wasted, all wasted. Still, nothing actually lost, I suppose. And maybe Aidan will tell her tomorrow anyway. He said he would. Perhaps he already has? Maybe Stella did get my drift? Teeth now clean, I narrate most of the sorry tale to Sarah. She starts to laugh. In fact, she can't stop laughing. This cheers me up. I join in.

'Oh, Nan. Tell me you didn't.' She wipes her eyes with a faded Royal Wedding tea towel, leaving a strip of mushroom peel in her hair. 'Surely you can't take this situation seriously any more?'

'I certainly can. It changes nothing.'

Wheeling around theatrically, I take my plate to the sofa and switch on the TV. I dare not have an in-depth conversation with Sarah yet, despite her mood. I know what she really thinks.

I'm meeting Aidan tonight. At long bloody last. Oh, I'm so tired. He has to tell her now. This time next week we can be together, settle down. I've had enough of these mistress high jinx to last a lifetime. Breakfast, lunch, a walk in the park, supper, television, bath, bed. That'll do me. I rest my head and dream of such heaven. Is Aidan thinking of me right now? Will I get an apology for last night's behaviour? He's supposed to love me, not drag me off the floor and stuff me into a taxi. Funny way of showing love. Mind you, I wasn't supposed to be on the floor. The irony is, poor ignorant Stella was nicer to me than he was, though she'd have probably pushed me under the cab if I'd been allowed to finish my speech. Funny old world, I muse, over some toast.

Sarah goes out to do some shopping for her holiday and

I fall asleep again. The phone wakes me an hour later and it's guess who? Darling Stella.

'Nancy. How are you? I didn't wake you, did I?'

He's not told her yet.

'Yes.'

'Oh, I'm so sorry. I'll get off the line.'

'No, no, it's OK.'

Honestly, it's fine, Stella. Our caring conversations are second nature to me now. As water off a duck's back. I almost enjoy the sport. I'll almost miss it: but not quite.

'Oh, if you're sure. I do hope you're better. If you can remember last night, that is. I swept the sick off the step and told Heather you'd been struck by a terrible migraine all of a sudden, and had gone outside to get some air. I mean, the best lies always are those that stick closest to the truth, aren't they?'

I find. God, why is this woman so nice to me? Couldn't she just be horrible, for once?

'Mind you, Nancy, your little disaster was totally eclipsed by Lesley's, you'll be pleased to hear.'

'Oh. What happened to her?'

'Well, I have no idea how, but she managed to get a peanut stuck inside her asthma inhaler. You can guess the rest.'

'She inhaled it? You are joking?'

'No. It got lodged in her windpipe. She went blue. Could have died, but Heather saved her life. Stood on a chair and did the Heimlich manoeuvre, apparently. No one else was there by then. Alastair had disappeared with some woman, and we had long gone. Lesley told me this morning. She was clearing up.'

'God! Really? We could have lost our Lesley! And Heather saved the day!'

'Absolutely. It's awful to say it, but I really had to fight not to laugh.'

'Oh, go on Stella. Laugh.'

If you're not to cry.

'So how did your dinner go?'

'Oh, Nancy! My God! I've forgotten to tell you the most dramatic event of the evening.'

'What was that?'

'Do you remember when we put you in the taxi last night?'

'Not much.'

'I didn't expect so. Well, you pulled the cab door shut really hard, and I'm sorry to have to tell you this, but you shut Aidan's hand in it!'

'You're joking?'

'No. It was his right hand too. So he couldn't drive. You crushed and broke the last joint in all four fingers. I had to get him to casualty and we waited three hours for them to be set. I must say, he was in agony. So we missed our dinner.'

'Oh, no. That's awful! How embarrassing! Oh, I must apologise to him. And never drink again.'

Poor Aidan. Mind you, if he hadn't been forcing me *into* the cab . . .

'Oh, don't be silly, Nancy. It was just an accident. These things happen. Mind you, another thing, I was just wondering, and I know you probably can't remember this either, but were you trying to say something to me last night?'

Fingers at my throat.

'Sorry?'

'You were saying something to me, I thought, before we put you in the cab?'

'Was I? I'm sorry, Stella, but, you know, I have forgotten nearly everything about last night. Certainly after I was sick. Isn't that weird? Do you think there was something in the wine?'

'I don't know. How odd. What a bizarre evening.'

You're not wrong. Time to end this conversation. Bye, Stella. Must dash.

* * *

Five o'clock. Shaking off the fusty sickbed air of the flat, I let the big entrance door of the house slam behind me. Feeling better, I'm glad to see a comforting thundery look in the sky. Soon the rain will break and I will be in a dry pub watching it through the window with Aidan. Summertime's over. The end of August. Six weeks of sunshine. Six weeks' great adventure.

By the time I get out of the underground at King's Cross the day has grown darker. As I'm crossing the road, the lights change before I reach the other side and an aggressive driver tries to shave my heels off. I turn and swear with shock at the departing car. God! I've been having the greatest time this summer – exciting, exasperating, terrifying – but never dull. Now I am an addict to the highs and lows. I don't know or care what is right or wrong any more, I have learned to fight for myself with the values of a wild animal. Kill or be killed. I'm getting used to it.

I head for Clerkenwell. The rain is just beginning to drop down in single heavy splashes on the back of my neck when the pub comes into view. I speed up. Inside, I look around the darkened booths at the back before heading for the bar. The place is quiet. Aidan isn't here yet.

'Your man not here yet?'

The barman, a big ugly lump with a shaven head, leans up for two pint glasses. He's obviously got used to us.

'What? Er, no.'

Don't you laugh at me. I turn my back and carry the drinks to one of the tables that faces the open door. The rain is now pelting down. Funny waiting for Aidan, funny peculiar. It always is. There's the ordinariness of our meeting place, the dullness before he arrives, the oddness of my being there, the waiting for him, the stillness as I sit, how unremarkable that always is, until the door opens, and in he strides, and moves towards me, and is there, and it's as if then the sound begins, like in a musical, and the set, plain before, sprouts unfolding blossoms and swans and goblins and dancers. Stupid, I know, but there you are. This pub, the road I tread to reach it, the whole of King's Cross station and underground, the Piccadilly line between there and Gloucester Road, the way north out of London towards Cambridge, the roads we drove that day, every otherwise unrelated point and street have been transformed for ever into routes and crosses on a dreamtime map.

The pub is silent that night, few drinkers arriving. I am actually shaking, so concentrate on stilling my hands on the table in front of me. I can just manage this, with a determined contraction, but the minute I relax they start moving again, nails clicking on the wood. So, giving up on that, I attempt to steady myself mentally by picturing the future weeks and months.

OK; so he finally tells her this weekend. She hits the roof, and most likely kicks him out. You would. So, where will he go? Easy; to my flat. Sarah and Nick are off tomorrow. We have two weeks' grace. That takes us to mid-September. Right. When is Sarah's aunt returning? October sometime. We don't want to be there as a couple once Sarah gets back. Well, I suppose Aidan will get us a place, presumably. I'm not too worried on that score.

Right. What about the job, then? Aidan needn't tell Stella I'm the other woman, not quite yet. I've not actually burnt my boats there. Oh, actually, yes, I have. The photocopier. It's arriving on Monday, with Stella's faked signature on the form. Great. Well done me. So I definitely can't go back. That's OK, though; I'd rather Stella knows I'm with Aidan, and, if so, work would be completely unbearable anyway. OK; so I dump Toolis TV.

Then what? What about college? What about my degree? I could chuck in college. There's two more long years to go. Or would it be completely crazy to abandon it now? I really don't know. I mean, here I am already with a TV job, and no degree. I could walk into another of these reception jobs, and Aidan would help me. It's all contacts. There's probably something at his company. I have some experience now, after all. Maybe I should do a proper word-processing course, get so speedy my fingers become a mist on the keyboard. How much would that cost? Maybe Aidan will lend it to me, and I'll be able to pay him back in a few months. You obviously don't need a degree to get into TV; but, then again, you probably do to get on a proper TV reporters course. Hmm. Why haven't I checked? Oh, I will on Monday; and I'll talk to Aidan about this. If I stick it at college I could commute back up to London every weekend. It's less than two hours on the train. Nothing's impossible. See what he thinks. He should be here by now. Where is he? What time is it?

Six forty-five. I think I said six. Three-quarters of an hour late. The weak ale head on his pint is long gone now. He's obviously caught up at work or stuck in traffic. Anything is possible. Being an hour late in London is hardly unusual. Or, oh God, I forgot about it, maybe he's at home with his hand in pain? Would broken fingers hurt that much? He must be well pissed off with me. I stare into Aidan's beer and take a sip, to get near him somehow. It reminds me of a deep stagnant metallic pond, and tastes as bad, but I carry on. This gives me something to do, and anyway, to leave it undrunk will make my solitude more humiliating. The barman will notice. Although, buying two pints at once and drinking them alone doesn't say too much for my social life either.

How long shall I wait? He'll turn up. He has to. Till half-past seven? No, eight. Where is he? I am two-thirds through his pint. Maybe I should ring the flat and see if he called? No, I don't want to ask Sarah. I can't ring his office; he's asked me not to. I can't ring his home. Twenty past seven. The barman swaps with someone else and disappears out the back. Twenty-five to eight. An inch left. Quarter to. Empty. I so need to see him. Maybe he's waiting somewhere till the rain stops? Or struggling up the road even now? If he really couldn't make it or is stuck at home he would have got a message to me somehow. Shall I risk calling him on the mobile? Oh, what the hell? If someone else answers I'll hang up. Leaving the empties on the table, and hooking my bag over my shoulder, I get up and go to the doorway. The phone is just inside. I shove in 50p and dial. That's all I have. Please answer it, Aidan. Please.

Click. His voice, but only the recording, asking me to either speak clearly after the tone or wait to be diverted to his home number. Oh, I don't think so. The machine digests my 50p. Damn. I'm going. Pulling up my collar (I've borrowed Sarah's roomy executive raincoat) I leap into the downpour.

The rain attacks me at an angle. I forge my way to the edge of the pavement. Now I'm on the brow of the hill. It's at a crossroads from which all four directions are visible for a goodish distance. Searching long and hard down each one, I see only other cars, other people, other faces escaping from the rain. No Aidan. No Range Rover; but he won't be able to drive, will he? So is he on his way in a black cab? None in sight. There's a wall a few yards up, so I go and sit on it, indifferent to the weather. The coat, presumably only designed to guard against a light city drizzle, is not drenchproof. Fab. The rain seeps onto my skin, freezing me through. Right. He's not coming; and there's nothing I can do about it. It's mad to stay here any longer. I'll be picked up as a prostitute or a lunatic or homeless runaway at risk, and I'm not going back to the pub, because I can't afford another pint until I get to a cashpoint; so I dismount, scratching the inside of my wrists on the brick, and run back to King's Cross. He'll ring me later, if there's not a message waiting at the flat. The vast façade of St Pancras, no longer baking in yesterday's heat, threatens dark, cold, wet. I descend, shivering, into the underworld.

Incipient pneumonia back home. After the heat of the

tube almost steams my wet body dry, I get another soaking between the station and the flat. Reminding myself that to love is to suffer, I have a bath, put on fresh clothes and throw myself into an armchair. Sarah is watching television, deliberately pretending all is well, despite the fact that I have inflicted her with a heavy silence ever since ascertaining that there are no messages. I tried Aidan's mobile again, but still no answer.

'Can we turn over? I hate this programme.'

'Oh, spit it out, Nan. What's happened?'

'He didn't turn up.'

'Right.'

'But he'll call later, I expect. Probably stuck at work.'

'I'm sure.'

I can hardly speak all of a sudden.

'Hey? Don't worry, Nan. Please, he's not worth it.'

That last bit is a mistake. I think she realises immediately. I have started to cry. Raspy chokes of despair, again and again.

'Oh, don't, Nan, please stop, don't cry, please don't cry.'

Sarah moves over and hugs me to her buxom breast, patting my back while I sob on her shoulder, heaving with feverish exhaustion. When I've calmed down a bit, she props me against the back of the sofa and plonks a tartan coffin of paper tissues by my side. I dutifully wipe my eyes, racked.

'I'm sorry, Sarah.'

She kneels on the floor facing me, arms folded.

'It's OK, Nan. But what are you going to do? This can't go on. I'll help, if I can. Whatever you decide.'

Will she? An evil idea is forming in my head. I push one finger up a nostril. Aidan might be at home right now. About to tell Stella. What if he's telling her right now? What if he's told her? It's not really the best time to call, let's face it, but God, I want to speak to him. I need to speak to him. Just a few words.

'Sarah, you're right. I have to sort this out somehow once and for all.'

She nods optimistically like a relieved parent. I proceed to tell her what I know she wants to hear.

'I'm not as weak as you think I am, you know? I can't go on as it is. I suppose I must risk ending it with Aidan.'

As if. She sighs, the barest breath of hope.

'The thing is, I haven't had a proper conversation with him since last Friday. Tonight, he doesn't show up. Maybe caught up at work, maybe stuck at home. Oh, I forgot to tell you. I slammed his fingers in the cab door last night, when I was off my face, and broke some of his bones.'

'Oh, Nan, well done!'

'What did you say that for? It's not funny.'

'I'm sorry. I'm sorry.'

'Well. You see, he might be at home because his hand hurts, don't you think? Anyway, for whatever reason, it doesn't matter now, he missed our date. So, he's either at home with his wife, or he's at work, and I can't ring either of those places, or he's somewhere else completely. His mobile's off. Tomorrow he's going away, I don't know where. I can try the mobile then, but what if it's off all weekend? If, somehow, we called him tonight, then I could arrange to meet him as soon as possible, and sort it out for good. Put my mind at rest. Yes?'

'Nan, did you say "we" could call him tonight?'

'Look, don't panic, calm down. Yes, I did say that, but listen, what I mean is, well, obviously I can't ring his work or house, can I?'

'Well, the home number would be OK, surely? I mean, you do know the wife.'

'Yes, but if she answers, I can't ask for Aidan, can I? I won't even find out whether he's there or not, unless she happens to mention it. I admit it wouldn't be the end of the world, but it would be a waste of time. Time is what I haven't got, Sarah. I'm going mad now!'

'All right, all right. What about his office then? I can sound really official.'

'No. He's asked me not to. All his calls get screened. He never answers the phone himself. And his secretary would get suspicious. He really doesn't want any of this to leak out before he tells Stella. There's so much gossip in TV.'

'I could say I was some informant or something, who would only speak to him.'

'Oh, no, he'd hit the roof. No. But could you bear to try the home number? If he's there then that'll be the only one we need to do anyway.'

'*I* will need to do, Nan.'

'Please, Sarah.'

'Oh, all right.'

Angel. I may be talking to Aidan in a few minutes. 'If it's him, hand it straight to me. If it's her, ask for Aidan Rivers, and then, when he comes to the phone, put me on.'

'Actually, Nan, I don't know. I'm not sure I want to play a part in all this.'

'Sarah. Please. It's all for a good cause, isn't it? I mean, you're helping me do the right thing. Then there'll be no more lies, right?'

'What if Stella does answer? Who shall I say I am? What name if she asks?'

'Just say Sarah. It's so common.'

'Thanks.' She giggles, nervous, glad for the delay.

'I didn't mean that. Say you're, oh, anybody, a friend from work, whatever. Why should she mind?'

'I know, but it's just a bit nerve-racking. I mean, I feel guilty already.'

'Oh, you soon get over that. You might even find it quite exciting.'

'Dream on. I'm not as sick as you. But when shall we do it? I want to get this over with.'

'Now?'

Sarah nods. She'll do it. I fetch the phone. It's the least

I can do. Adrenaline puts every cell in my body on stand by. Ten to nine.

'Tell me the number and keep deadly quiet.'

I know it off by heart.

'Go, Sarah! Go! Go! Go!'

She laughs. Dials. I dare not breathe.

Urr-Urr. Urr-Urr. Urr-Urr. Sarah tilts her head and looks at the ceiling.

'Hello?' A little voice, far away down the line. A man's? He *is* at home? This is too much for me.

'Oh, hell-ow, is that Aidan Rivers, please?'

She's so relaxed; friendly, even. Brilliant. It's going to work. I lean nearer. This is easy. Sarah jerks a thumbs-up.

'Oh, great, well, Aidan, my name is Sarah and I live with Nancy, whom you know, and were supposed to meet tonight, and, well – I've got her here right now and she rather urgently needs to speak to you.'

Just as I am wishing she would get on with it, this last line is shot out in a torrent of information. She rams the receiver in my face.

'Aidan. It's me.'

Aidan's reply is very loud, receiver close to his mouth.

'I'm sorry, you've got the wrong number.'

And the line goes dead.

Talk about shock. Pebble, crushed by a mallet. I can't believe it. Sarah can't believe it. Such toil, tears and sweat for nothing. No, less than nothing – he didn't say a word to me.

'At least we know he's there, Nan.'

'At least you realised that subterfuge is something you're good at.'

I am so frustrated I could expire right this minute, lying back, sinking into the duvet and staring at the ceiling. A drowning soul's last glimpse of the sky.

'He'll ring you now, Nan. It's obvious you need to talk to him. Don't worry. She was probably standing right there and he couldn't think of anything else to say. Don't you think?'

Maybe. Or, he has just told her the bad news.

'Oh, yes, there's no problem with why he did it, it's just, it's just, oh, you know, I'm still stuck here going insane. Sarah, do you think it's best to get your first nervous break-down finished at a young age? Do you think it can be over and done with in a week? I think I'm about to have mine now.'

I'm not joking. She knows it, and walks to the drinks cabinet.

'Time to get smashed.'

Sarah crawls to her room at midnight. Aidan hasn't rung, but I'm sure he will later. I stay awake. Several cups of strong coffee keep me bolt upright. Also, I'm still digesting the Chinese takeaway we had at eleven, so my stomach's not ready for bed yet. Waves of hysteria come and go. What's happening there? Has he told her? Somebody just tell me what's going on!

The phone doesn't ring. I put a video that Nick left here in the machine and prop myself in front of it, a cops-and-cocaine number set in LA, which I stick with until the credits roll. Two in the morning and I am full of energy. Maybe Aidan will call in the small hours, or on the way to wherever he's going tomorrow, early. It would make sense. I'll set the alarm clock and try to get some sleep now. For two hours under the duvet I roll around, thinking, talking to myself, throwing off the cover, hugging it back on to me, lying on my spine, curling on my side, turning, squashing my arm across my front, removing it, getting up, putting on the CD player right close to my ears, wanting to turn up the volume, not daring to, well, just a little bit, singing along, all those sad eternal songs, the ones that thrill and swirl to a thundering crescendo and tell us there's a great heroic meaning to our lives, we will triumph through it all, tears and rain mixed in the wind – playing them all again, one more, another, another, another. Wide awake, I abandon the idea of sleep and pace the room, open the curtains, windy and cold and still wet out there, the jet-black night, rain on the panes.

Pulling up the window, I allow the outside to rush in, throwing chilly drops on to my T-shirt, wind up my bare legs. Kneeling on the floorboards beyond the edge of the carpet I push my face into the night, getting it all over my hair and skin until I am so cold I can't feel much at all, and wonder what position Aidan's beautiful body is in now, his eyes shut with his wrist by his nose maybe, all hot in bed and crunched up sweatily, naked? Or awake? Head raised from the pillow, hand rubbing his foggy eyes?

Wake up, Aidan, I miss you. I need to talk to you. I need to tell you I love you. I need to be one inch from your face.

Dawn. Saturday morning. The weekend. I've not slept, merely retreated to the armchair, watched another video, sound on low, and then stared at the slow advent of daylight. Window still open, so rain has soaked the floor, but I didn't want to be locked in, or to shut the world out. At six o'clock the alarm goes off. Thinking it's the phone, my heart quickens; disappointment, and I smash my palm down on the button. I'll run a bath. Taking the phone with me, trailing its obliging flex round the delicate legs of Auntie's furniture, I lay it on the bath mat. You, I tell it, bear all the responsibility for saving me from the abyss. You, I point a finger, are a good servant, but a bad master.

Bathing uses up an hour. Breakfast next. It's so strange; I'm not yet tired. Still frisky. Surely exhaustion will strike soon? Right now my brain seems sharp enough. No call from Aidan. Still in bed, probably. Sarah comes into the room around eight. She looks shocking.

'Sarah, you look shocking.'

'Speak for yourself. You look as though you didn't get a wink of sleep all night.'

'I didn't.'

'Oh. Why?' She doesn't wait for the answer, though, and drifts into the kitchen.

'Aidan ring, then?'

'No.'

'Oh, I'm sorry.'

'We all are.'

'Is that the royal "we"?'

'Shut up.'

'What are you doing today, Nan? Do you want to come to Nick's with me? I'm going to take my holiday stuff round, then we're going to have lunch and maybe a film. We can lie around here until about twelve and then go?'

'When's your flight?'

'Eleven tonight. Oh, come on. I'm not going to see you for a fortnight.'

She doesn't trust me by myself.

'Maybe. Can I think about it?'

'Of course. It's just an idea.'

A postcard arrives, from Rebecca, and the guilt resurfaces. It's of a naked man, orange muscles rippling. Out-of-focus sun and sea sparkle in the background and 'With love from Greece!' is branded bang across his knackers. On the back all she has written is: 'A *truly* excellent time being had by all!' Oh. Beneath this her mother has added: 'Thanks for giving me the chance to see this beautiful place. I never want to come home. Regards, Anthea.' Next, and taking up a good inch, I'm very relieved to see, is a message from Grace: 'Hi, babe! I admit it, I am not worthy! Sorry, sorry, sorry. Of course you had to stick at the job. Meanwhile, we're having a brilliant time! *Really*. Will ring as soon as we return to fill you in with *all* that has occurred on this island of romance – no more details now. Speak very soon, loads and loads of love, Grace – xxxxx!!!!!'

Thank God. They're happy. They don't wish I was there. And Grace *will* speak to me again. Very good news: but what can the cryptic postcard be hinting at? Unless – don't tell me – that'll be it: they've all met the men of their dreams in the Mediterranean sunshine.

Rain not stopping. I watch TV all morning, fuelled by coffee. Sarah's offer of lunch and a film is quite tempting, even though I can't go anywhere until Aidan rings. I know she knows I'm thinking that. The possibility of speaking to him still shines dimly like sun through fog, but, by midday, no call.

I must do something. Sarah's gone out to buy milk. Grabbing the phone, I dart through a ring to Aidan's mobile. Aidan, please, please answer me. The recording. I don't leave a message. Fuck! Damn. Everything is going wrong. I sat up *all* night. Sarah returns and I spring out of the chair to meet her.

'I think I will come out with you this afternoon, if that's OK?'

'Sure! Of course. Excellent.'

We have pizza for lunch and then go up to Leicester Square to take in a double bill. I sit back clutching a pop-corn carton as big as a breeze block, with Coke to match. It's the perfect place for a snooze, but still I remain awake for the whole four hours. We stumble out into the murky early evening at half-past six. Still raining. Sarah and Nick are heading back to his place, thank God. I've had more than enough of them and their relentless couplehood.

'What are you going to do, Nan?'

'Oh, head home probably, and go to bed. Maybe I'll have a walk round here first.'

'OK, then. Well. See you in two weeks.'

We faff around saying goodbye for a bit, then they walk away. As she turns she directs back a look of some concern, plus a loaded smile. Then they have disappeared, already lost among the gangs of desperate entertainment seekers.

What to do? Could head straight home, but it will be to a silent flat. Or, go and sit in a bar, and have a drink on my own, and be hideously unutterably tragic? That would keep me dry. Fine. I set off and inspect a few Soho wine bars, but they are too frightening, so I compromise my original intention and settle for a humble café, and sit down, and order a cappuccino. This, when it arrives, is as weak as water, with only about an inch of coffee under the froth. It takes less than nine minutes to drink. I am timing it.

On the seventh minute a dosser sneaks into the bar before the staff notice and wedges himself into the bench beside me, no respecter of personal space. I can smell him. His face is covered by random beard and moustache and he looks at me and mutters things, as though I should be answering; but I ignore him and turn away, feeling like shit and all of a sudden so unhappy I don't know what to do. I don't want to stay here now, that's for sure. Standing up, I catch the man's eyes, saying move, mate, in body language, which he does, still muttering, and taking his time; and now I can decipher his words, or at least some of them, and I definitely hear 'Little cunt!' as I head for the door.

I keep walking, no particular destination in mind, and head northeast from Soho towards Bloomsbury. Maybe you can walk away stress. I pass a pair of phone boxes, both the card and the cash sides empty. Their glass walls are drizzled with rain. I turn round back to the cash booth. The stubborn door closes heavily upon me and I dial Aidan's mobile. No answer, but a different message. A voice telling me it has been switched off. Please try later, it advises. Please, we really don't want you to give up.

I reverse out and carry on, not sure where I'm going, except that it is, if anything, towards Hackney rather than away from it. Stella is probably at home now, spending the weekend on her own. Maybe Aidan's told her already?

Where has he gone? Oh, I bet he's not told her. I bet they're still married, so to speak. How's their garden, I wonder. Have they mowed that lawn yet, and eaten all the cabbages? Are leaves falling, rendering Canary Wharf more visible through the trees? Oh, for goodness' sake! I remind myself it isn't even September, though I am already sunk in autumn depression.

At Holborn tube I continue heading northeast. Where am I? I need an A-Z, mine is left at the flat, so I search for an open newsagent. Most of the shops are shut round here now, and there aren't many people about. What *am* I doing, wandering round the big smoke, alone in the twilight rain? I need to walk myself home, if anywhere. To sleep. Home is not in this direction.

No, I know where I'm going.

I just want to see Aidan's house again. It's part of him. It's the closest I can get right now. If there are no lights on, if Stella isn't there, I could walk round the garden, maybe? There is a ghastly thrill to the prospect.

If Stella isn't there. And if Stella *is* there, at home in her house as she has every right to be? Do I just flee?

Maybe not.

Maybe I shouldn't avoid her. Maybe I shouldn't run away. Might this be another chance to tell her? Just in case Aidan hasn't done so already? No. I can't. Just walk in there and say it? Hey, Stella, do you want to know what I was trying to tell you the other night? Of course I can't. Could I? No, no; but the idea, now born, will not die. I *could* do it. Maybe I should confront her? Why not? Without Aidan there, how can it fail? Maybe. Oh, my God.

Yes.

Maybe it *is* time to visit Stella. Time to tell her face to face, time to make everything all right for when Aidan comes home.

On Theobalds Road one shop has its light on, a typical façade of glass misted by the rain and cold outside, full of little posters and for sale adverts and a huge gold cigarette packet suspended over the door. It's hot and stuffy inside, and an Asian man and woman are sitting behind a counter only sparsely laid out with chocolate bars. They sell some of the smallest type of A-Zs, so I buy one, plus a slab of pure chocolate, no compromising wafer, and take a look in my new guide under the strip lighting in the shop. Quite a long way to Hackney on foot. Good, that'll give me time to prepare what to say. Or to change my mind. It's five past eight. I aim for Old Street.

Darkness has begun to fall, or maybe it's just the gloomy grey weather, but I'm not in the slightest bit scared. I have a purpose. Muggers can tell when you know where you're going, and leave you alone. After forty-five minutes' trudging head down against the rain, I reach Old Street tube. It's beneath a massive roundabout, sinister and threatening, with darkened tower blocks looming and cars roaring by on the wet road. To the right, signs to the City. To the left, King's Cross. I open the book under a streetlamp. It instructs me to go straight over the huge roundabout, as there is to be more of Old Street. Soon I am at another junction. Again I consult the book. Getting near now. Hackney Road. Time: nine fifteen. Energy: getting lower. Legs: harder to put one in front of the other. The wind is whipping about, sending the rain in all directions and soaking my shoes and legs. I'm wearing Sarah's raincoat again, she won't need it where she's going, and again I am forced to reflect that it's completely useless. My very bones are wet. Hair glued to my head. I'm so cold. I must keep going.

Twenty minutes later and my destination is getting dangerously near. Now I need to find a pub for some Dutch courage. The first one I see is so full I can't face forcing my way to the bar. The second is empty but so well lit, with cream walls, that it has no pub atmosphere at all. The third is perfect: dark as hell, a few people in the corners, and an indifferent-looking barlady who seems not to mind that I am bringing in a puddle with me. I pay for a whisky and take off the coat before sitting down at a little round table. The first sip delivers a torpedo hit to my throat: slam; then spreads outwards. Right. Good. Now, what am I going to say? If Stella is there? If I am still going to do this? She mightn't be in. I mustn't get all revved up, only to find she's out. Better wait till I know, either way. I don't have to decide anything until I get to the house, anyway.

But, if she is there, it's a pretty simple message I have to give: *Hello, Stella. I'm in love with your husband. And he loves me. Yes, me.*

That's all I have to say. Then it'll be over, sorted. That easy. More whisky. Finish it. Check the A-Z. Go to the loo. Don't sit here long enough to find out how tired you are.

Outside, I shiver with cold. Dragon Park Gardens. Where are you? Very near. Aidan, where are you? Very far, no doubt. I could ring the mobile again, but, somehow, I am past talking to Aidan now. I am taking action instead. It feels good. Parts of these streets are distantly familiar from that evening when I had dinner with Stella, and it isn't long before that's their road in front of me, down a slight slope, and beginning to curve at the bottom. The house is round that corner. Lights illuminate the wet tar. Have I gone completely mad?

I feel sick. I don't have to do this. Turn round *now*, then; but my feet keep going. I just want a look, at the very least. As I walk down the road, slowly, feet scraping the pavement, I know she'll be there. I don't know how. I just feel I've been denied success so often that no fate can be cruel enough to deny me again. Crossing the road to their side, I am so scared, but carry on. The road bends. I can still turn away; but, somehow, no. Walk on a little. Oh, help me. Here is the gate.

Shut.

It was open last time. Oh, no! Has Stella gone away for the weekend too? I read my momentary dismay as a sign that telling her the truth is the right thing to do. Maybe I'll go and have a look, just to make sure. No harm in that. Checking behind me, and all around, and seeing no one in the streetlights, I climb up over the gate. Stepping down with care onto the potentially noisy gravel drive, I side-step to the grass to tread in silence. I shouldn't be here. Poacher. Trespasser. They still haven't mowed the lawn, which is as shaggy and soaked as I am. Down the slope to where the house appears dark and empty. Ah; her car is parked out of sight of the front gate. Now I am opposite the windows. She has to be in; I *need* to tell her.

There's a fuzzy light in the living-room window. I creep right up to it. It's coming from under the door, from the kitchen. She must be in there. I knew she was here! Ah, me, ever the onlooker. Not for much longer. Shall I invite myself in? I head round to the back door, then stop. Why not the front door? Go for the jugular.

Standing an inch from it now, I'm sheltered by the porch, and wipe the rain and sweat from my brow. I can still walk away. I should walk away. I should not be here. I do not belong here. I press the bell.

Oh, *why* did I do that?

Now there is no escape. Terror grasps me by the neck and stops me from running. What on earth am I doing? The river of no return, dark, whirling, treacherous. I cannot move. Petrified; but nothing happens.

Maybe she is out, and has left the light on to deter burglars? I lean on the bell again, for a long time. Maybe she thinks I'm a burglar? Would a burglar ring the bell? Maybe she is too scared to answer. Where is Aidan when I need him? Is that footsteps? Oh, help me. Fight or flight? Fight. Fight, Nancy, fight.

A weak light, its beam almost lost in a mesh of rose

leaves, attempts to illuminate the porch. The door opens inwards, drawn back slowly over a resistant doormat, and a voice speaks.

'Hello?'

It's Aidan.

CHAPTER TWENTY-ONE

✳

Aidan?

He's at home? What a result! Of course it's him, squinting out of the doorway while I stand here in the dark, unable to stop grinning. Relief, relief, yet more relief: and my fears all vanish. Could this be happy ending time?

'Nancy?'

'Of course it's me! Oh, I'm really sorry about the fingers. Stella told me.'

His right arm's hidden in a cream-coloured sling, hand in sticking plaster and strapped up tight by his left shoulder. It contrasts rather well with his dark green shirt: he resembles a soldier returned from the war. My wounded hero.

'Will you ever forgive me, Aidan? Do they hurt a lot?'

Aidan seems stunned, mouth hanging slightly open. Then he focuses: 'What do you bloody think? Of course they hurt!'

Eh? Is he angry? No, stupid me: he's whispering. Stella must be home.

'Oh, I said I was sorry, Aidan. Honestly, I feel terrible.'

'Why are you here, Nancy? What do you want?'

He *is* angry.

'What?'

'What do you want? I'm busy. I'll call you.'

'No!'

Why is he being like this?

'Don't go, Aidan. I came to tell Stella about us. Let's sort this out together, right now.'

'No. No, you don't. No way. Stop this right now. I'm on my way out, so I'll – call – you – Nancy. OK?'

'No! Aidan, why are you being like this? We have to tell her! Come on, you know we do. It'll be OK in the end. Don't worry so much. Oh, it's lovely to see you. Come here.'

I step up towards my true love, one arm round his waist and pulling him towards me. Back together again, at last: but his left hand jams suddenly against my shoulder and I have to jump backwards onto the noisy gravel to keep my balance.

'What do you think you're doing, Nancy?'

'Ow! Aidan! What are *you* doing?'

'Shh! Be quiet and listen to me!'

I stare. He comes forward out of the house, carefully drawing the door behind him so that it's within a couple of inches of shutting. Doesn't click it, though, keeping everything quiet. As he passes me, we brush each other's chests and, wary of him in this bad mood, I am forced to turn right round and retreat onto the step to face him. Now my back is to their door.

'Come here, Nancy. Over here, away from the house.'

He treads cautiously onto the silent lawn, with a feeble hook of his left arm, but I stay put.

'No.'

It's funny, but I'm not entirely sure why I'm resisting. Half of me is saying, go and talk to him, what more do you want? The other half, however – and I suppose I listen to it – is ordering me not to. It's insisting I have to stick to my ground this time.

'No. We have to do this, Aidan. Come on. It's the right thing to do. Everything will be fine. I promise.'

'Come here, Nancy!'

'No!'

'Yes!'

'No, Aidan!'

'All right! That's it! Have it your way.'

Aidan tramps off the shadowed grass onto the gravel, forgetting for a second to stay quiet, and approaches to within breath-smelling distance; he's eaten garlic recently. Stella must have rustled up a little something earlier, or else he can't do his teeth without his right hand. That must be it. Then he stops, stands there pinching his forehead with the good fingers, and I can see my man brace himself to face the music. Relaxing with relief, I give him a satisfied smile. I knew he had it in him.

'OK, Nancy. Fuck off!'

What?

'Just fuck off. Now! Get the fuck out of here and stop trying to ruin my life. Do you hear me?'

No. I don't.

'We had a couple of weeks' fun, but now it's over. It was never serious and you knew that. I'm married, for Christ's sake! We both talked a lot of crap. Do you get that? It's over. I am not going to say this again, and you are not going to ring me up again, or tell your friends to ring me up, or tell Stella, or anyone else, anything. Is that clear?' Hissing, between his teeth.

This must be a joke?

'No! No! What are you talking about? Aidan, I love you!'

'Well, I don't love you. And I never did. For God's sake, what *were* you thinking? Grow up! What do you think proper relationships are like? I'm married and I value my marriage. You just walk away now and don't hurt Stella any more. Do it for Stella.'

For Stella? Me, walk away? Aidan's face is contorted into a horrible grimace. He's close to choking with the effort of keeping down the volume. I'm gawping: his words don't really sink in. What *does* he mean? Is he *not* going to tell Stella? He *isn't* going to leave her?

'Everything – stops – now, Nancy. Right?'

No! Not right! Who *is* this impostor? I have never met the man. Turned to stone, I can only watch as his face swoops in and away from me, tense savage mouth spitting showers of spray. Particles are visible in the light from the porch lamp, descending gracefully, but all else here is fast becoming ugly.

'Right, Nancy? It all stops now.'

No. No. It can't! I will not let it. He can't do this. I have come so far. I have never, ever seen anyone in such a storm of maddened fury, and I am shaking, but I am not going to be intimidated. I'm not going to walk away. This is not right. This is wrong.

'No, Aidan. No.'

'Don't whine at me, you pathetic little tart! Fuck right off! You mean nothing to me now and you never did!'

Tart! Nothing! Never! Weird sensation, and I can't quite hear any more; sick, and dizzy, the air is draining from my head and out of my fingers, all buzzy. Thawing from my rock-like state, I melt in a rush, I can move now, and my arms reach out for support, to him, to the doorframe, to anything, and yes, there is something, but no, I cannot grip it, my fingers slide off, I am so weak, I have no strength at all, and I'm falling to the floor, again, I've done this recently, I seem to remember, but now it's different, oh, this is much worse, it's frightening, oh help me, I can't stop it, oh God, this is blackout – this is darkness – this is death.

Berserk fevered muttering. 'I don't bloody believe this! Oh, get up, you little bitch, get up, you are not going to do this to me, quickly, get up! Quickly, there's nothing wrong with you! Ow, damn you, my hand!'

Aidan? Someone else? I can't quite decipher yet. Did I pass out? I must have. God, I've never fainted before. Very odd. Right, yes, here I am; on the hard floor of their gloomy hallway, but the fall didn't hurt at all. It was really smooth.

Aidan *is* beside me, crouched all tense. Ow! What's that? My arm! A burning tight pain. Have I broken something? Dislocated my shoulder? And *what* has he just been saying to me?

'Get up! Bloody get up now! Nancy! Wake up! Quick! And there'd better not be anything wrong with you!'

'Aidan! Get off me!'

Now I understand why my arm is in pain. He's twisting round the skin in a concentrated spiteful pinch.

'Not until you're out of here. Get up. Come on. Hurry. Oh, no, I don't believe this, oh, bloody hell –'

'Aidan! What was that noise? What *are* you doing? Who *is* that? *Nancy*?'

Timing to die for: enter Stella.

Aidan lets go of me, awkwardly manoeuvring himself into a standing position, panting, 'She was at the door. Didn't say anything, just keeled straight over. Poor kid, I've been trying to revive her.'

And this simple lie brings the bad news home at last. I was wrong, all along. I'm on my own. He isn't going to help me. He isn't on my side. He doesn't love me. Aidan is my *enemy*. Horror, worse than any film, and a shiver I cannot control.

'My God, how dreadful, Aidan! Poor Nancy! We must get her up, take her into the kitchen. Nancy? Nancy? Can you hear me? Can you speak? Are you hurt badly?'

No answer. I want to die.

'Let's have a look.'

Drink on her breath, Stella crouches down and checks me out. She's dressed in Levis and an old jumper, and her hair's in a bit of a mess. I've never seen her like this.

'Good, no blood. Head feel all right? Can you stand? Yes? OK, up you get. Oh, Aidan, get out of the way. Pick up those things.'

She nods at the floor where a couple of umbrellas and a selection of unmuddied country walking sticks have been ejected from their brass urn holder. This lies toppled beside them. No doubt I pulled it over with me and she was alerted by the clattering.

'Come on. Put your head down and walk with me. That's right. Good girl. Come on.'

Stella escorts me into the bright light of their kitchen and I'm dazzled. She stops beside the big old wooden chair I remember her sitting in when I came to dinner, years and years ago, and steers me into it. I'm dimly conscious of Aidan following us into the room, a dark vague shape, threatening and silent like the shadow of cancer on a lung. He chooses the chair furthest from me. I'm back in the bosom of their happy home. God, who could have predicted this?

'Here we are. Sit here. That's right. Head down, go on, in between your knees. Well done. Stay there for a few minutes. Don't talk.'

I have to get out.

My head is throbbing. God, this floor is clean. I suppose that's the advantage of stone. Not a speck of dirt. Nothing. Head down low. Shut my eyes.

It's all over.

Aidan doesn't love me. Say it to yourself, Nancy. He-doesn't-love-you. It's-over. It's never going to happen. He has told you it's finished and he is not going to tell Stella and you have fainted and are now being revived in his kindly wife's kitchen. Right? Right. Well done me. I've really hit the jackpot this time. Just the best, best place to be.

Please, let me weep. The blood returning to my head goes *bang!* – *pump* – *bang!* – *pump* – he doesn't love me – *bang!* – *pump* – it's over – yes, really – *pump* – over – *pump* – finished. It's over. My world is exploded, the dynamite of Aidan's unspeakable tirade hurling the bricks of Number One London in all directions.

Nothing is as I thought.

Aidan doesn't love me. That's all I need to know. I do want to die. I don't want to work anything out for now. I just have to be alone, and burst into tears by myself, but I can't. I don't even have the right to any such refuge. I'm in the wrong place at the wrong time, again; trodden on my own booby trap. The ultimate trespass. Forbidden ground beneath my feet. A big cold shudder. I can't get warm. Fight or flight? No contest: I *must* get out of here. How do I escape?

I look up. What a delightful tableau: man and wife sitting down and speaking quietly to each other. I want to cry. Cups of coffee by them: they must have been already poured out. I'm parked alone at one end of their honest oak table while Stella is to my right, leaning towards Aidan. He's at the opposite end. That's what a *proper* relationship looks like. Heart to heart.

'Stella, don't you think we should send her to casualty? Anything could be wrong. We know nothing about her. I mean –' Aidan whispering very quietly now – 'what is she doing here? Really, we should. Stick her in a cab.'

'By herself? No, one of us would have to go. And she'd be made to wait for hours. It's not exactly an emergency. No, I don't think so.'

Could I ask to leave? I raise my head. 'Don't worry, I'm fine. Feel much better. I'll get a checkup on Monday.'

'Oh, Nancy, sorry to be talking about you. We are very worried, though.'

Stella has the decency to appear embarrassed, but Aidan looks down and scratches his head and doesn't acknowledge me at all. He doesn't see me. So that's what it means to be cut dead? Oh, please be nice Aidan again. Or has that person gone for good?

Oh, this is horrible. Crazy and horrible – I don't know which is worse. I didn't know anything could hurt like this. Pain that feels like I have been cut open, or a limb crudely hacked off. I must go. Less than nothing for me here.

Stella gets to her feet and moves over. 'You're soaked, Nancy. Let's get that coat off and I'll get you a sweater.'

No! I've borrowed enough of your stuff to last a lifetime. Don't touch me!

'It's all right, honestly. I'm OK.'

'Sure? Well, I'll turn on the radiator then, and dry your coat – give it here, that's right – and get you a coffee. Actually, a whisky would fire up your belly. How about both?'

'No, it's OK. Neither. I'm fine. I'm so sorry. I have to go.'

Please let me go. Let me out. You don't understand!

'Don't be silly! As if I'd pack you off in this state. You must have a hot drink and warm up and tell us exactly what's happened. I *absolutely* insist. You can't shrug this off, Nancy. In fact, it might be a good idea for you to stay the night.'

'Stella, let her do what she wants! We can send her home in a cab. Come on. Before it gets any later.'

She. Her. I don't exist in his eyes. Stella is unhooking a mug from the dresser.

'Aidan! Please. I'm sorry, Nancy, but have you ever been properly introduced to my husband?'

She pours me coffee from a hot glass jug by the oven and then takes a tumbler off the draining rack by the sink.

'Do forgive his lack of manners. He's a bit tetchy at the moment because he's not smoking. He can't make roll-ups with one hand. So it's you who's to blame, Nancy, but we won't mention it! That's why you're stressed out, isn't it, Aidan?'

'Oh, give it a rest, Stella.'

I agree. Even his bitterness is preferable to her ga-ga chat. I can't do small talk now, doesn't she understand?

'Aidan! Sorry, Nancy. Here, drink this before the coffee.'

Now there's a flask of whisky in her hands and she's sloshing some into the tumbler. I pull my chair in towards the table and take it from her. One sip electrifies the inside of my mouth. Then Stella turns her back for a moment and Aidan, staring aggressively at me, uses the opportunity to jab his thumb at the door and mouth a swift warning. 'Fuck off!' is as clear as if he'd written it down.

Bastard. I can't look at him. My head spins and, with the intake of alcohol, the beginnings of a sense of outrage. He really does hate me.

Can it be the same Aidan? Aidan who told me I made him happy? How can you tell lies like that? Aidan who said he loved me? Asking me to walk away and never come back? Leave now and never breathe a word? Never see or talk to him again? After all that has happened? It's not logical. How can such a thing be possible? How am I supposed to be able to jump straight from love to indifference in so short a time?

God, straight from love to embarrassment, more like: I mean, what am I doing here, in their kitchen? So wrong. Also, from love to humiliation: did he mentally dump me two weeks ago, once I got too clingy? Pity he forgot to mention it. And, worst of all, love to shame: I've been making plans. I'm in too deep. I've invested too much. I've ignored my family. I've screwed up my job. I've abused my friends. I've completely deceived Stella. Perfectly nice Stella. I've lied for England. I've lost my mind, given away my body, and sold my soul. I've descended to his level.

God.

Let it sink in.

Aidan has robbed me of *everything*.

How did he do it? How does he have the nerve to command me to walk away? Off you go, Nancy. Just put it all down to experience. Fresh entry, bold type, into the CV of life?

No chance! The arrogance of the man! The arch hypocrite! When I think of all the things he said to me! Mr Pursuit of the goddamn Truth! I fell for it *all*! Hook, line *and* fucking sinker. How dare he! How *dare* he?

God, I've been used: but I'm not walking anywhere. I'm going to get him.

Oh, yeah? How? Revenge, eh? Sure. Nice idea. What can *I* do to Aidan? Here? Now? *Me*? The hair is plastered to my head. Wet T-shirt clinging inappropriately. Jeans damp from waist to ankle. The sandy suede of my boots, I mean Sarah's, has gone a wet khaki all over. I've conked out on their doorstep and now I'm getting the mad baby invalid treatment, as usual, from Stella. Sure, I can get my own back on Aidan. Ha-ha.

I'm a nothing and he knows it. I never had much but he's thieved even that. All I want to do is take from him a mere fraction of what he has stolen from me; my dream, my future, my hope. I thought this love was a reality, not a lie! Make it hurt, like it now hurts me. On purpose. But what can I do to him? What weapon do I have? All I know is I loved him. 'Loved.' Huh. Am I already saying that?

Hold on a minute. I know we had an affair.

Think.

Twenty minutes ago, only twenty minutes ago, I came here intending to tell Stella everything. Twenty minutes ago I thought her husband and I had a future. I told Aidan that was the purpose of my visit, and that is when he turned on me. Stopped me from doing it. Walk away, he said. Fuck right off, he said. He values his marriage. He cares about Stella. Don't hurt Stella. Do it for Stella. Stella, Stella, Stella.

Tell Stella anyway. God, could I?

I *could* destroy his marriage. Right now. I do have a weapon. I *can* get to him. Tell Stella anyway. The prospect is terrifying, but might make me feel better.

No. Bad idea. What exactly would I tell her? Hey Stella, your husband just finished with me. Thought I'd tell you we *were* an item. That would really look good, I don't think. Before, maybe: there would have been a point to telling her then. I had Aidan to gain. Now, I'd look worse than a selfish vengeful child with a tantrum, breaking the toy it cannot have. Telling Stella is tempting, but it's not the answer. Besides, I don't want to hurt Stella. It's not her fault. I want to hurt *him*. There must be another way.

She pushes me the coffee.

'There you go. Say if it's too dark. More milk? Sugar?'

'It's fine, thanks.'

She sits herself down on the nearest chair to me, and moves in protectively close. Aidan, meanwhile, is banging his left index finger, hard, on the table's edge. Go away, Nancy. Out, out, out. God, this is awful. I can sense that Stella's interrogation is imminent, and brace myself. She folds her arms and sits back. Here we go, surely?

'God, Nancy, you do make me laugh! Sitting there all bedraggled like a kitten dredged from a pond! I must say, I've never had such a shock in my life when I saw you out cold in the hall! I don't know how, but you always manage to do the last thing I ever expect! *Such* a crazy mixed-up kid! What *are* we going to do with you?'

Bedraggled? She's laughing at me? Thanks very much. I know what Aidan thinks of me, but is that all I am to her? A stupid little kid? Right. That's it.

I know what to do now. Cut the scruples! Thanks, Stella, you've sorted me out. I may resemble a poor little washed-out victim, fucked, chucked and now sneered at; but looks can deceive. Let me tell you exactly how crazy I am! Who needs to mention that the affair is over? And anyway, maybe I won't even get that far before she turns on him. I am going to scuttle their scummy marriage and enjoy doing it. Let the roof cave in; I don't care. I'm not scared any more. Screw the pair of you!

'Seriously, though, Nancy, how are you feeling? You do look better.'

Putting down my coffee I lean backwards and clasp my hands behind my neck, thus stretching the maximum glory of my chest in Aidan's direction. Big smile for him. He glares at me momentarily, then looks at the time. That ridiculous all-action watch dwarfs his wrist.

'Well, Stella. I feel a lot better. Thanks very much.'

'So, fill us in. Why do you think you fainted? Any particular reason? You have been eating properly, haven't you? And why come here? No offence, but were you just passing or did you have something particular in mind to see me about?'

Crash! Aidan's coffee cup hits the floor.

'Shit!'

'Oh, Aidan! Mop it up.'

Stella's quite cross with him. Aidan rises to get the mop and begins to prod weakly at the pool on the floor. What with only one hand he's doing a pathetically bad job of it, but she doesn't move to help him. She's annoyed that he interrupted my answer. I, however, am more than pleased that he did. She was looking at me when it happened, but I saw him quite deliberately swipe his cup onto the floor with the back of his left hand, genuine panic on his face, real fear that I am about to shoot my mouth off. In that tiny instant he revealed to me just how worried he is. But did he really think a splash of coffee on the floor would shut me up? Dear, oh dear. His bowels must be loosening. Excellent! I'll say my piece and then go. They won't want me around for long. Sweet, sweet revenge. Screw the pair of them!

Here it comes.

'Oh, leave it, Aidan. Sit down. Now, Nancy, what were you going to say? Did you come here for a particular reason or something?'

Oh, or something. Definitely.

'Yes. I did.'

Long stare at Aidan. Must get my money's worth. He's

seated again, but fidgety, and picking, and probably wondering if he could pretend to drop dead. No cup to play with now. Hah! I hope he's crapping himself. Stella is nodding encouragingly. She's going to hit the roof. Who would ever have thought it would end like this? My heart is in my mouth, blocking my breath.

'Yes. I thought it was time to tell you this. Aidan –'

Her eyes ask me, yes? His swear, don't you *dare*.

'Aidan and I –'

His once-beautiful face carved in a granite scowl. Stella transfixed. God, this kitchen is so unnaturally tidy! A heap of clean cloths folded, all food cleared away, everything in place. As it should be. At last. Here is the heart of the matter: and I may wet myself with fear if I don't hurry up.

'– we, I mean he and I, are seeing each other.'

No reaction. Did I really say it? And where on earth did that 'seeing each other' come from?

My gracious hosts look like they've been shot with an immobilising ray gun. Aidan has been frozen in action like some craftsman at Pompeii, scraping a hole in the table with his thumbnail. Stella, her arms folded, has her eyes focused on me.

Nothing moves.

Oh, come on! Somebody. I'm blushing now, not that Aidan is. God, his face! Sheer loathing. Unspeakable man!

Then, from him, an exasperated sigh, and the volume's back up, but just a couple of seconds too late: 'Stella! Who *is* this girl? Because she sure has got one hell of a problem!'

Ha-ha. Stella ignores him, and movement returns. She stands up, pushing back her chair as though the meal is over. Total control. Same frozen expression. Looking at me all the time. What is she going to do? Her hand is in very easy reach of that Le Creuset frying pan. I shrink my body for safety, short breaths, ready to run, but never taking my eyes off her.

'Nancy.'

She now has the chair in front of her. It's small and polished dark with a kind of inlaid cushion on the seat, and she's gripping the curve of its back with both hands, leaning forward now slightly, and pausing, like you might before giving a speech. Ignoring Aidan, she turns to me. My stomach contents liquefy. Oh, help.

'Nancy. Is this true?'

What the fuck? Is she *smiling*? Does she not believe me? She has to!

'Yes, it is, Stella! Don't believe him! I'm telling the truth!'

'Nancy, Nancy –' a calming hand, but she looks excited – 'calm down.'

She *is* smirking. Why? What's going on? Why isn't she furious? I have never seen Stella so in command. That alien opposite may not be the Aidan I knew but this, for sure, is not the old Stella.

'Calm down, and tell me, are you saying what I think you are saying? What, exactly, do you mean by "seeing each other"? Please define the euphemism for me, if you would be so good?'

'Well –'

Aidan whines: 'Stella –'

'Shut up, Aidan. You were saying, Nancy?'

'Well, we're, you know, going out together? And, erm, he wants to leave you –'

'Nancy. "Going out." Explain what you actually mean.'

What do I say? Her voice is distant, impersonal, like she's taking a police statement. Does she want the dates and times when *full* intercourse took place?

I must look like a child about to cry, because then she starts to explain, painstakingly, gruesomely kindly: 'What I mean to say is – oh, look. Just say "yes" or "no". Are you and my husband having – sex?'

'Yes! We are! I promise you! I'm telling the truth!'

'Excellent. Thank you. Aidan and you are having sex and

he has expressed a wish to leave me? Is that the substance of it?'

'Yes.'

'Oh, this is excellent!'

She clenches her fists and raises her eyes to the ceiling as if to praise God.

'Of course you are! And there was I thinking you really were sick so often! Oh, thank God for you, Nancy. Talk about a dark horse! Thank you. Very much indeed.'

I don't get.

Long pause.

Then Stella, head down like a professor, patrolling the room with hands clenched behind her. Aidan leaning on his left elbow, sighing as he massages his temples in despairing strained impotence. She's not finished.

'How *extremely* interesting. Thank you so much for telling me, Nancy. And I hope you are both *very* happy. Seriously, thank you very much.'

She smiles, and it *seems* genuine.

'I just thought it was better that you knew.'

'Oh, it is, Nancy. It is. Believe me. A great deal better. Worlds better.'

Switching her gaze to Aidan: 'So. Aren't you going to tell me she's lying?'

He looks up at her. 'Of course she's bloody lying! I told you to send her home.'

'I think it's becoming clear why now, isn't it?'

Aidan blushes, visibly, deeply, embarrassed. Attack is futile, but he has a go. 'Well, if you don't believe it –'

Me, trying to stand up: 'I'd better be off.' But my legs are weak as string all of a sudden.

Stella is behind me and pushes down my shoulders. I'm back on the chair and going nowhere.

'Nancy, no! Sit down. Have another drink. Please stay a little. Please. For me? There. Stay there. That's right. Now, let me just fill you in on a couple of things you might need to know about your future together. The night is still young, after all.'

Aidan, gesticulating: 'Stella! This is insane! It's time she left!'

'Save your breath, Aidan. Now then, Nancy.'

She's looking at her watch, then glances pointedly at him. He looks at his. She smiles, and begins to speak extremely slowly and carefully as though English isn't my first language.

'So. Where do I start? Isn't this *exciting*? You two a couple! Nancy and Aidan! Doesn't that sound good together? You'll get married, of course. Will you take his name, Nancy? Nancy Rivers. Oh, yes. I think so.'

This is really scary. Anger would have been preferable. I'm trapped. Walked head first into the night from beyond the grave.

Stella starts to pace round the room again, head in the air and arms waving this time. Then, clapping her hands: 'Oh, Nancy. I am so delighted! And I would *so* love to help. Give you a few tips, you know, to help things along?'

I cast a panicked glance at Aidan, but nothing doing there. He stands and, angrily pitching his chair aside, goes to stare out of the window. Stella leans momentarily against the doorframe into the hall, then moves again. Physically, she's all over the place, the agitation of her body at odds with the assurance in her words.

'Nancy, let's just run quickly through what you actually know about Aidan. His likes and dislikes, that sort of thing. OK?'

No comment. Nothing but sick dread. Stella with her hands on the back of the chair again, questioning me, darting into close-up.

'I'll run through the check list. Now, let's see, you'll know, I presume, that you're not the first?'

Eh?

'Stella!' Aidan's head whips round. 'Shut up!'

'No, I won't.'

She's turning from him to me, back and forth. Playing with both of us. 'What I mean is, you're not his first affair, Nancy. He didn't tell you?'

What?

'Oh dear, Aidan, you are naughty! Ha! You never tell them, do you? No, Aidan's attitude to monogamy has always been distinctly elastic, I'm afraid. But I expect you're happy with that? You're OK about it? You won't mind all the other women? If so, get out now, because, trust me, there'll be a few.'

No!

No. No. He's had affairs before? Several? I'm chilled, and not from the cold. He sleeps around? Fear; and Aidan petulantly checks the time again.

'Stella, I'm not staying to listen to this!'

'Yes, you are. You know you are. And sit down, unless you want me to tell her *everything*?'

Everything?

He reverses onto his seat, glowering. Crossing his legs and avoiding my eye, he takes up where he left off with stabbing the table. Stella ignores him and turns back to me.

'Right. Where was I? Other women. The problem of. Yes. It's a tricky one. You know, even I don't know how many there have been.'

Don't tell me this. Stop now. Leave me alone. Help me, Aidan?

'Stella, get off your high horse. You can talk. I bet, Nancy –' he deigns to speak to me! – 'that in all your cosy little two-faced chats with my wife she never mentioned that she had an affair with me?'

I don't know how I'm able to answer him, but I do, numb. 'What do you mean? She's married to you.'

'She wasn't always. Were you? She was married to some-

335

one else once. Stella forgets her morals haven't always been up to scratch.'

Aidan, a disgusting sick expression of triumph. My gob definitely smacked. Stella remains unruffled, though.

'I don't, actually. I have never for a minute forgotten it. I confess. Oh, I'm going to confess it all tonight! This is such fun! To think, I can help our young Nancy here! Introduce her to the ways of the world. Yes, I was married before. Sorry, Nancy. Should have said. I suppose I *have* sort of deceived you, a little. By omission. Easily done though, isn't it?'

Blush, but I cannot leave now. Not before I know *everything*.

'Yes, I was married before. I was only a slip of a thing, a bit like you now! Isn't that a coincidence? Although we've a lot in common, I suppose. And, do you know what? My first husband was a friend of Aidan's. A good friend, then. But, as you have probably gathered by now, Aidan never strays too far for his entertainment.'

He slaps the table. 'Damn it, Stella! Not this again. You seemed to enjoy the drama at the time, as I recall. Course, it got you out of the house, didn't it? Quite some distance, if we're both honest. Bit bored of that marriage, weren't you? She walked out one day, Nancy, and never went back. Literally.'

Aidan's looking at me, vile half-smile, as if to say: there, bet that shocked you?

'You left him, Stella?'

'Well, Nancy, I don't see him here, do you? Sorry, it's no joke; but yes, I did walk out. For handsome little Aidan here. Oh, I was love-struck all right; but I'm sure you'll understand the appeal. That silver tongue, eh?'

I could die.

'Dear, oh dear. No, Nancy, I don't think marriage and me are meant for one another.'

'Not the only thing you weren't meant for, Stella! Hey,

336

Nancy, I bet Stella didn't tell you what else she isn't cut out for?'

Oh, leave me alone! I refuse to answer.

'Try, *motherhood*.'

'Motherhood?' I don't understand.

Aidan fills me in. 'Stella, I am shocked. Who did you say you were to this poor kid? Mother bloody Teresa? What fairy tale have you described? Muddies the water a bit, doesn't it, when you walk out on your own baby?'

'Stella! You had a *baby*?'

He answers for her, pulling himself up but slumping straight down again because of the sling.

'You bet. Walked out one day and never came back. Mother of the Year, I don't think.'

'But, Aidan, you said –' Even as I say it I realise he'll have lied. Stella's been watching my confused face with barely a flicker.

'Oh, Nancy, tell me, what *did* Aidan say? That I'm infertile? Barren? That I've denied him the joys of fatherhood? Oh, I like this. It gets better and better. Been discussing the state of my faulty ovaries, have you? Well, for your information, they're fine, and yes, I am the mother of a twelve-year-old girl. She lives with her father.'

Jesus! Whatever else am I going to hear tonight?

'Stella sends her a Christmas card, when she remembers, with vouchers to pay for the child psychiatrist.' Aidan, dead pleased with himself, but she returns a look of neat scorn.

'Oh, ha, ha, ha. You're such a wit. Let me pinch myself to see if those kind of comments hurt any more. No, not a thing. Can't feel it. It's no good, you can't get to me now. All that guilt, it's flown out the window after tonight's fascinating revelation from our young friend here. And to think what knots I've tied myself in over you. What a joke! Wouldn't it be amazing if I was over it? My God, what a waste of a life.'

She turns to me. 'There I was, Nancy, all those years ago.

I'd had enough of my marriage. I didn't tell anyone, just packed my case and walked out, and went straight round to Aidan's, my knight in shining armour, and guess what? He had a woman there, in what you might call an advanced state of undress. That was a great feeling, I can really recommend that one! Didn't expect me to turn up, did you, Aidan? Didn't think I'd actually leave him, did you? Women aren't so attractive when they're available, are they?'

'Oh, leave it, Stella. No one asked you to fly off the handle. Do you know what she did then, Nancy?'

It's my name but he isn't looking at me. He's fixed on her. I hate him.

'No? She only went mad. Only ran screaming into the road, straight across four lanes of traffic. Had to be arrested and detained, for her own safety, in a mental hospital. Only had a nervous breakdown. And from then it's victim, victim, victim.'

'Not any more.'

Aidan ignores her. 'All that poor-little-me act. It worked in those days. I only had to rescue her. Pick up the pieces. I only had to bloody marry her!'

'He promised he loved me, promised he'd be faithful, promised I was the only one from then on. And yes, I swallowed it. Hook, line *and* sinker. We moved in together and my divorce went ahead, in fact, yes, *that's* where I met Heather, at the lawyer's; but, anyway, when it came through –'

'Too much hassle to try for custody.'

'– we got married. Oh it was a lovely day, Nancy, but you've seen the photos, haven't you? Beautiful. Oh, yes. Paradise. Guess how soon I discovered he was having an affair? Already? A month after our honeymoon. One month. Of course, I suppose I was lucky. It could have been a week. Could have been a day. Could have been a bridesmaid. Probably was.'

Stella flicks out an indifferent hand, and Aidan sniffs,

though perhaps not taking quite the required level of offence.

Then Stella turns a full circle, arms folded, and asks: 'Guess how I felt, Nancy? I'll tell you. Guilty, of course. Guilty that I'd dragged all those guests up the garden path for the second time. And my poor mother. Huh. She'd barely forgiven me for walking out on one marriage and depriving her of her only grandchild. She'd loved my first husband, thought I treated him scandalously, warned me that Aidan was a bad bet –'

'The voice of experience, of course. You know how Stella's beloved daddy died, Nancy? Heart attack on top of his mistress. Who just happened to be Stella's godmother . . . Oh, you worshipped him, didn't you? Poor spoilt little girl whose papa had the selfishness to drop down dead and leave you with nasty old bitchy mama who never wanted you in the first place! No wonder you got your claws into the first dumb sucker who came along! No wonder you had a baby instead of sort it out! No wonder you abandoned her when she cramped your style! Reproduce the bloody problem! Why not? It was all Daddy and Mummy's fault! God!'

He forces himself up, crosses the room, and slaps the spotless surface by the oven, hard. There's acres of it to choose from, a dark grey fake stone substance. Then, gripping its edge with his one good hand, he tries to glare her out. To no avail.

'Oh, calm down Aidan. You can't rile me. I'm beyond hysterics. But remind me, do I faintly recall you occasionally mentioning the negative influence of your father? Or don't you drone on about him to all your little protégés? Tell us again, where did you learn your bad habits, eh? From whom did you pick up your loose morals? Your continental sexual values? Tell Nancy, because, to be honest, you've bored me for long enough.'

Aidan passes on this one, laughing the empty laugh of

a loser. I want to kill him. Stella sits down, her manoeuvre indicating that if he's standing up she'll do the opposite, and continues her tirade.

'No? Well, let me have a go. How, try as you may, you can't quite erase that image of your father, can you, the craggy cold judge, creeping out to prostitutes in Manchester? And only a few miles from the family home in the heart of the countryside. Shame, shame. Great role model for the children. Poor little Aidan. The baby of the family. Isn't ignorance bliss? Bet he never told you about his happy childhood, Nancy? You should meet Aidan's father, he's a darling. Made me feel welcome, I don't think. Oh, they've got a great marriage. Wife barely conscious most of the time . . .'

Doctors in Africa? Working for an aid agency? Their only child, a blissful growing-up on the open plains? Goddammit! I know *nothing* about this man! I don't think he is even *capable* of telling the truth! Prawn shells in *every* desk!

'Come off it, Stella! Leave my mother out of this! You've got a nerve. When you're permanently doped up and awash with every type of booze on the market! You know the two don't mix! When were you last sober, Stella? When did you last have toast for breakfast instead of Prozac? When did you last attempt to deal with your life instead of paying a fortune to a shrink to complain why I'm ruining it? God! Bloody victims! I hate people like you!'

'Really, Aidan? I hadn't noticed.'

He's smacking his hand back against the surface with every accusation.

'You know it, Stella! Bullies and victims! People like me can do nothing without people like you! And you!'

Apoplectic finger in my direction.

'Leave her alone, Aidan.'

'At least one of us is doing something! At least one of us is taking some action round here!'

'We'll see about that.'

'At least one of us can get out! I've had enough of this. I'm going.'

'Oh no, you're not, Aidan. We both know you're not. And we both know why. Sit down.'

'Fuck you!'

Aidan crashes back into his chair and thumps the table uselessly hard. Why *is* he sticking around?

Stella rises to her feet, laughs, and continues to taunt him. 'Oh, temper, temper. Goodness, is that the time? Dear, oh dear. How about another drink, Aidan? No? Well I will, and I'm sure Nancy will join me. She's fond of a drop. So, Nancy, where were we? You don't remember? Let me see. Well, I suppose it was the general subject of other women, wasn't it? Aidan Rivers and his inability to keep his hands off. That was the rough area, wasn't it? Surely. Well. Da, de-da. Tick, tock, tick, tock. If it moves, he sleeps with it. Has sex, I mean. I don't expect much sleep is involved, is it, Nancy? Between you and my husband? Stay the night often, does he? No? I didn't think so. Oh, but Nancy, you're such a classic! So perfect, sitting there in the office. So handy. So available. You might as well have had the words branded on your forehead: "Asking for it".'

'She did.'

Aidan exhales a shitty little laugh. How I wish I'd never met him! God, that that day had never dawned! I'm choked with nausea as I realise I *was* asking for it, sitting there all coy at the desk answering the phone. Begging for it.

Oh God, no. Sitting there all coy answering the phone - like who else? Of course. Billie. My predecessor. Just a few weeks or days before me, maybe. Oh, cut the maybe. Of course. No wonder she left the country in a hurry. Begging for it! Like God knows how many others?

Weakening all over, I think of the taboo complaints people. The hidden suffering of our daily lives. Shit, I

should go to a clap clinic, and get checked out. I bet I'm
one of them now. I bet I've picked up something from him.
He went right round the world when he was a foreign
reporter. Thank God we always used condoms; but no,
let's not forget. Oh, no, no, please: but dread rolls over
me. I can't stop it. Juices *were* swapped. I've sucked the
fuckwit's dick. I cannot avoid the truth. I have played with
death.

Help me.

Stunned, sweating with fear. This is the worst night of
my life. I didn't know they came so bad. I just didn't know
the world could be this horrible. If only I had never met
him: if only I had listened to all that good advice; but I
cannot turn back the clock. Such a naïve little fool: I am
corrupted now.

I want to go home. Real home, my family, not the flat.
That's all I ask.

But Stella's still speaking to me. Quietly: 'I should have
warned you, Nancy. Oh, I've let you down. I should have
guessed. But I suppose I naïvely thought my husband was
at least monogamously promiscuous. Or maybe I didn't
want to know? Maybe I didn't care about the details? What
did I ever want with names? Until, shall we say, one was
imposed upon me?'

I don't have time to work this out before Aidan attacks.
'Stella! No! This isn't funny!'

'Stop me then, Aidan. What are you going to do? Gag
me? Hit me? The one-armed bandit? In front of our witness? Come on then. Come on. Over here.'

I watch their performance as she beckons at him, daring
him towards the doorway. Aidan, so livid I expect to see
steam come out of his ears, pushes back his chair violently.
It shrieks loud on the tiles.

'Right, Stella. This stops now.'

He's moving towards her. Is he going to hit Stella with
his one good hand? Oh, please, don't hit her! Don't hit

her! I don't want to see this! Now he's by her side, and, oh, thank God, puts out his left hand against the wall to support himself. Then all he can do is eyeball his wife, jaw jutting forwards with lips pursed in frustrated fury. Thank God I broke his fingers!

Yet Stella isn't scared at all. She leans round away from Aidan, and catches my eye, but makes no real effort to avoid him. He follows the movement but she dodges again.

'Where was I, Nancy? Oh, yes. Not long ago, maybe a couple of months, yes, nearly, seven weeks –'

'Stella, you dare!'

'– there was a knock on the door one evening, much like tonight when you came here, Nancy, though clearly the entrance lacked your inimitable style, and this person –'

'STELLA!'

'– who shall remain nameless, came in to tell me *exactly* the same thing that you just have. Isn't that incredible?'

What?

'Can you believe it? Just the same. They'd been having this secret affair for six months or so, they were madly in love, this was the real thing, he wanted to leave me, you name it. It was a shame Aidan couldn't make it that night to tell me as well, but there you go. He's here now. But what did I do that time? What was my reaction? Can you imagine? No? I went mad. With anger. I was furious. But why? Why did I care? Hadn't he played around enough before? Why was this different?'

Aidan grabs her arm with his good hand, starting to squeeze it viciously, his fingers digging in. She barely notices.

'Let me tell you. It was different because I'd never seen them in the flesh before, Nancy. It had never come to this before. He was never going to leave before. Now, if he left, I was going to have to face it. That I'd failed. Admit it. Ten years, Nancy, ten years of pretending everything was fine. Ten years of pretending I had no regrets. You bet I was furious with her, after all the work I had put into fooling the world! She was going to make me come clean. Confess that it wasn't true love, that I'd abandoned my child for nothing. No, less than nothing. For this seedy little villain! That was why I hit the roof.'

Despite what she is saying, Stella's the queen of ice-cool. Aidan, however, is molten. Pulling her towards him, their heads are right close.

'Not another word, Stella. That – is – enough.'

'Don't threaten me, Aidan. There's nothing you can do. You can't touch me now.'

'Not one more bloody word!'

'So he left me, Nancy. Walked out. The circle was complete. I wept. I pleaded. I begged him to stay. I'd have had him back. Make it all look good. That was all that mattered. Until tonight. But he went anyway. To her place. He's not slept here since then. Comes round to get his things. Picks up a bit more stuff every time.'

'No! It can't be true! Aidan, tell me it's not true!'

He's *already* left her? *Another* other woman? I thought I'd heard the worst. Tears in my eyes: but Aidan, busy shaking Stella, is beyond noticing me. Pushing her back and forwards, he has limited effect, and she doesn't bother to stop him.

'Sorry, Nancy. You're too late in the day. I don't have a husband now. I don't have a marriage. The horse has bolted. I'm not your rival. I never was. *She* is.'

'*Who* is? Who are you talking about! And why didn't you say? How come nobody knows this? If Aidan has already left you? *Why* pretend everything is all right? What's going on! I don't understand!'

I'm twisted round to look at them with jaw hanging and palms lifted in surrender.

'Then guess, Nancy. Guess who it is. And guess why I never said? Rather, why *we* never said? Oh, a few weeks' silence was in all our best interests. We all had reasons to

344

keep the status quo for a bit longer. Maintain a happily married front while decisions were made. Damage limitation. So, we all acted very civilised. All good friends. Nobody knew except we three. Wait and see, that was the policy. Part of me still hoped it might blow over and he'd come back, you know, get bored?'

'No! I *don't* know! What *are* you talking about? Who *is* she?'

'Guess, Nancy. Remember, Aidan never strays far. Guess.'

'Shut the fuck up, Stella!'

Aidan pushes her, trying to slam her back against the wall. This time though, she does retaliate, and, because he isn't expecting it, easily pulls away from his grip. She rams at his breast bone with both hands so that he loses his footing and starts to fall, unable to save himself. His body weight lands on the bandaged right hand and Aidan treats us to a scream of real pain.

Then the doorbell rings. I have never seen anyone look so happy as Stella does now.

'Oh, Aidan, saved by the bell.'

Beaming at her husband as he groans, battered, on the floor, she pats her hair and walks calmly to the door. A welcoming 'Come on in' can be heard, and whoever has arrived precedes her into the kitchen.

'Hi-ee!'

It's a filthy night but under that leather jacket the midriff is still on show. Jo-jo.

Jo-jo?

Her? No? Please, no! But Stella's nodding with gusto as she comes through from the hall, and I understand.

The women's programme. Stella's company. Aidan's promotion. Ambition. Money. Profit, profit, profit. Of course they kept it all quiet. All in each other's pockets. Far too close to home. They made a deal. Deadened, I picture the awful conspiracy of compromise. It's the way the world really works, but don't tell the children. Keep it quiet. That's how grown-ups behave.

From now on I can only observe.

'Jo-jo's come to take Aidan back to her place, Nancy. She's his chauffeur at the moment, amongst other things. Drove him here tonight, but didn't come in. Just a courtesy, you understand, but she wanted to keep clear for a while in case there were *too* many hysterics.'

Stella looks at me, then at Jo-jo helping Aidan up. She's waiting for their full attention.

'Because, Nancy, they've got some good news! Aidan told me this detail *literally* the minute before you came by. He came round specially to tell me. *So* sweet. They forgot to mention it last night, but I suppose they *were* very busy ferrying away his last few possessions, and then, so inconveniently, I had to go and get a bit weepy. Seeing them here together, you know? But I'm calm now, and I think you could say I've taken it rather well. Not that I was much surprised, of course. It is about time. I mean you're not as young as you were, are you, Jo-jo? Forty, is it? Yes? So, guess what, Nancy?'

Jo-jo looks panicky, thinking Stella's finally lost it. Aidan, pulling his ear, is shiftier than shifty. Me, I'm past caring. They're getting married? They want my blessing? Whatever.

'They're having a baby!'

Oh, of course they are. My soul is tired.

'Isn't it wonderful that they decided to have it, Nancy? I bet you're as pleased as I am! And I'm so glad to have someone to tell! But I expect Jo-jo's wondering what you're doing here? Don't you want to explain? Tell her what you came to tell me?'

Jesus. Now I *really* get. This is the trap. This is what we've *really* been leading up to, the showdown Stella has been itching for ever since I told her about our affair. This sick little introduction is Stella's revenge, and I am to be

346

her tool. Break up the happy family, Nancy. Do it for me, you know you owe me. Be my personal assistant and wipe that smug reproductive glow off Jo-jo's face!

My victim stares at me. She's puzzled now: half-smiling, but afraid. Her blue eyes have never looked bigger. Oh, it's perfect! Wipe the slate. Give Jo-jo the real picture. Tell her Aidan's already screwing around. Tell her who with. Introduce her to my married man. Give her time for a rethink. Will she want his child then? My choice. Walk away? Or kill the baby?

So, I can make a difference. It is up to me in the end. Right.

Don't let's hang about. I smile back at Jo-jo – she's mystified – and get my warm coat from off the radiator. I should be able to find a cab on the main road.

One quick glance at Aidan. My hero the weevil. He's looking shrivelled and cut-price and titchy. What's that Shakespeare play where the guy runs round with a donkey's head on, and then the spell wears off?

Hah! I bark out a laugh at Stella which I hope says it all. Her eyes sparkle at me.

'Right then, Stella. I must be off. But, oh, yes. The reason I came here, Jo-jo –'

I'm putting my arms into the coat, and Stella holds it out for me like my mother used to. Aidan, watching every move, has gone green.

'– was to hand in my notice. I've got to catch up on college work. Reassess my future. That's all, isn't it, Stella?'

We're face to face, but she doesn't reply. None of them speak, in fact, nor offer to show me the door. Honestly! Have these people got no manners?

I let myself out and leave the house behind me, starting to run once I'm through the gate. The rain has stopped, the street is empty and I flee up the hill without stopping for breath until I reach the top. That's better. I look at my watch. Ten past midnight. So, morning has broken. 1 September. Ha-Ha! I feel different: not the old Nancy any more. She didn't make it through to adulthood. Died in the attempt; and I start to laugh. When, about ten minutes later, I take a last look at Dragon Park Gardens from a minicab window, I know for sure I will never, ever travel down that road again.